Scott's main character, Brownie, cruises the highways, city streets and back alleys, as well as the deep forests and lofty peaks of Oregon in search of the true meaning of his own life, as well as that of multiple creatures, cultures and nuances thereof. A week in one man's life, all colored and haphazardly layered as he sees fit in a comedy of event and circumstance disturbingly believable; Comparing and critiquing mercilessly those he meets, and in whatever manner he chooses, while perhaps selfishly cranking and drilling on his own persona in the process with even less mercy. The story is a fast romp; laced with wisdom and fraught with angst. Brownie's existence unrolls like a forgotten gym towel… in the dim light of a laundromat. Quarters and dimes are the coin of his realm and can't be found fast enough. Somebody open a window or turn on the fan.

—◇—

Brownie

Kenneth M. Scott

Proof Copy

About Time Publishing Company

541-954-6724

www.abouttimepublishing.com

To order copies of this book, contact:

Ken Scott,
541-896-3774
quilpower@gmail.com

ISBN 978-9847928-1-8

—*Thank You*—

—◇—

I would like to offer my sincere and heartfelt thanks to Janice Keuter... who, with timing and insight will always be the woman of the hour... it was she who convinced me to publish this book, and it was she who taught me with heart-waking example, the definition of constance. Janice, you have made life much more meaningful and are without doubt deserving of more than thanks. Your dedication, knowledge and love of poetry and literature should be shared with the entire world. You are a complete person.

—◇—

A special thanks to Michael Faris (About Time Publishing) who came alongside with sincere generosity and precious hours of help in the last moments of putting this in paper format and a first printing.

—◇—

And thank you in advance to a very limited number of friends and associates who will read this copy-proof with the goal of enlightenment for the author.

—Ken Scott

This story takes place in one particular valley amongst hundreds of others, each with similar hot springs, country stores, canning factories and logging mills. Towns, hamlets and whistle-stops, with a history of loggers, hippies, and just regular folks interacting and avoiding one another while life comes and goes like a bullet train; yet most live as though things will always be as they are. Theirs is a world not unlike yours or mine–given the luxury of such beauty and the choices of life dealt all around. Their eyes smart with the smoke of tragedy and their lips smile at the comedy of human circumstance all around. The waters flowing out of the Cascade range are clear and clean. Towering fir trees reach for the upper atmosphere with atomic force just as they do in the next valley over... and the next, and the next. The words of this story capture that beauty and the comical attempts of one man to understand and reconcile himself to his own portion of life. Choosing to no longer disregard or take for granted what is precious, he finds himself controlled by the same forces that make up the majesty of his surroundings... unable to overcome the gravity that takes the waters to the ocean-blue, or to stop the winds from fanning the boughs of giant trees without number on the mountainsides. A man interceding for what may, in the context of human circumstance, be his own end, or his salvation...

Except for Joe Halbert and Jacob, there are no replicas of persons met or personally known. Certain characters are modeled from real people... with or without their permission... but speak and behave in absolutely fictitious ways. Still others are fabrications or inventions of convenience as befits the story. The places described herein are reminiscent of the particular locale I have known as home for these forty years. Even though this is a work of fiction the people are not strangers... they are real and standing right beside us.

Let us love one another.

—Ken Scott

—*Prologue*—

Brownie appeared on the workbench... Constructed with parts gleaned from the boneyard of life's experiences, and with fresh materials developing unexpectedly from the zones of creativity. Other elements were pulled from electronic storage... some written and stored for decades: Essays, anecdotes, musings and meanderings, all lovingly preserved on a Macintosh... including the very first 128k...

I have been a sculptor of metals since 1971. Initially the results were crude, but satisfying. It was grueling, discouraging, barbaric in nature, and suited my temperament to a T... I had found a medium interesting enough to bring me back again and again... often enough to see improvement, and satisfying enough to overcome excuses and obstacles that might've otherwise won-out in life.

Writing has been similar, although I have enjoyed it without the pressures of deadlines and dollars, the satisfaction is the same or greater. The gradual improvements in style and content resulted from being there (showing up), being serious, and independent... as well as teachable (if such a combination is possible). The single most driving force in writing has been the realization that words, once written are "official." The courage to put one's thoughts and convictions on paper and sharing them is the perfect vehicle for developing self-confidence, and is the highest form of creativity.

Because I've spent a lifetime immersed in creative thinking... making a living as an artist... it's very easy to associate sculpting with writing: None of my works in metal are ever truly finished, but there comes a time to call it good and move on... to "next". I'm often asked what might be a favorite work and I can honestly say, the project at hand.

Inspiration gets us started–deadlines make us finish. How long a project will take to complete is not as important as how soon can we get started? Clients come and go, and stories will too, but Brownie will never be finished, nor will I.

Brownie is the expression of an idea that came about over a long period of time. Even I believe he exists. He is an entity. And when I visit or pass by physical places referred to in the book they are filled with memories of his story, as though it actually happened. My sculptures number in the thousands and are of a material that could last for centuries and centuries, depending on how they are received. Brownie's influence has been released too, but he is not made of steel, nor is he a man of paper, he is a man of words. His impact upon the world will have a certain relevance and be subject to that one thing in particular... the use of words.

Rather than musings and thoughts gathering like clouds expanding with water, just waiting for the time and place to pour, what has come forth to my surprise and delight is more like an artesian well... at this particular time and this exact location. Brownie's story is based upon eternal truths and will never end... the well has sprung forth. Even though I'm grateful for all the years it was but a trickle, the idea of abundance-to-overflowing threatens to erase such memories.

The odds of realizing certain aspects of a meaningful life decline as the years increase... and no doubt life's circumstances beyond our control will prevail... but in my case (considering the past, and acknowledging the present) I am blessed beyond what I could ever have imagined or deserved...

May you be blessed, in the reading of... Brownie

—Ken Scott

Brownie

by

Kenneth M. Scott

– Part One –

Brownie

by

Kenneth M. Scott

- Chapter One -

W.M. Brown, ticketing agent for Concept Airlines, slid the luggage of Mister Whoever... traveling to wherever... onto the conveyor belt. Adios, and good riddance–boredom can only be endured so long. Tired, and with the day's shift about over, he'd simply been on automatic; detaching little by little, knowing he'd soon be on his way home with a three-day weekend at hand. He stood and stretched.

Two lanes over, yet another traveler shoved an array of belongings onto the scale. A duffle bag, two cardboard boxes and one tubular something or other... At times it was as though he could predict how a person looked just by their baggage (and vice versa), but just by looking at a person could he point out their luggage? Well... maybe someday he would give that a shot. He sighed, *So what? Either way, it's baggage. Just people's stuff. And with name tags and little wheels on the bottom, it's easier than ever to bring an entire trainload of crap through the passageways and compartments of life.*

"Excuse me, are you available..." his gloomy thoughts were interrupted by a vivacious young woman glowing with life and optimism.

"Sure, wha'cha got?"

A thin sheaf of papers fluttered across the counter top

with the grace of a bird. A twinge of guilt fluttered by when his big hand thumped onto it.

Miss "Cuteness," one hand still on the counter top, leaned to one side, and then with the slightest grimace, straightened back up... an elegant leather bag slid onto the scale... all in the same movement... apparently unaware that every square inch of fabric on her body floated back into place. The scale read a scant thirty-eight pounds.

Instead of the usual flourish from ink pad to paper, the agent found himself rolling the validation stamp onto her ticket as quietly as possible. Then, though barely able to gaze into her eyes, he handed her the travel document and managed a professional voice; "Gate B-6. Thank you for flying with Concept, and have a great time in Dallas."

"Thank you." The two words hung sweetly in the air. A gentle breeze took her away. A small leather purse draped across her shoulder... the total of her carry-on luggage.

That sums it up, he thought, *she comes from a stable home, been sheltered all her life, gives of herself innocently to everyone and couldn't carry anyone else's luggage even if she wanted to. And who would load that precious thing down with anything to carry?*

His eyes clouded with the knowledge that lots of people would... *will... that's the pain of it. She's just getting started.* He turned around to place the bag onto the conveyor. Luggage rolled through endlessly toward flights to all parts of the world.

Nestling the soft leather bag onto the belt, the name tag read: DIANE J. HALSEY. "You're in for a longgg, rough ride, sweetheart," he whispered. All the other tags rolling by transfixed him for a moment. He read them silently, thinking; *Yeah... you're all in for a rough ride... The cargo-*

hold of the world is gonna swallow you up. You'll be tossed and jostled 'til you won't believe it. And for gosh sakes! Just pick one bag large enough to hold the stuff and strong enough to make the journey! All that time spent nitpicking about color and shape just to be squished and smudged out by asphalt and rubber from here to Kalamazoo anyway.

The names no more tell what's inside the bags than a person's name tells what's inside their heads. And even though the quality of the bag might be a hint about the contents, it ain't gonna be long before wear and tear will cause the outside to take on an identity all it's own.

Heading in the general direction of the employee's locker room, he walked alongside the conveyor belt reading aloud the name tags on the bags: "Donald Humphrey, John Kendall, Harold Wilson III... Hmmm, like, the third time's the charm?"

The never-ending gaggle of gliding paraphernalia jostled along life's highway without a sound, *So. Just what is a 'Walter Raleigh' without the 'Sir,' or a 'Robert E. Lee' without the 'General'?*

Shoving through a door neatly labeled employees, he was abruptly face to face with his own reflection. Mirrors above a row of sinks underscored his gloom. On his shirt, the black, plastic name tag with, W. M. Brown, Agent, Concept Airlines, in white letters and a colorful logo summarized the whole thing; "What is a W.M. Brown without the Agent?" he asked aloud.

The hollow tones of his question resonated from the many porcelain fixtures in the room and the answer seemed just out of reach behind the cold surface of the mirrors... leaning closer, his face glared back... what you see is what you get.

His name tag flip-flopped onto the counter and slid

into one of the sinks... *It's a wonder the labels don't just get ripped off and blown away in the wind... yet somehow we all manage to hang onto them until the very end. And if not preserved by fame or disgrace in the history books, those words are transferred onto a piece of bronze, or chiseled into granite... and that's all she wrote.*

W. M. Brown, slid onto one of the changing benches (in front of the appropriately labeled locker, *I've never forgiven my well-meaning mother for picking my name from the Myron and Frank's Jewelers sign in downtown Atlanta, Georgia. Gee, thanks for the name, Ma... and thanks also for the endless honeyed distortions drawled, slurped and slathered from the day I was born: Maron, Myrn... and you guessed it... Moron. I can't wait for the day I stand proudly with my children in front of that sign and say; 'Yep, kids, there it is... This is where your Dad got the name, Myron. Ain't it beautiful?'*

His eyes glazed over and narrowed slightly as obsessive thoughts continued; *After forty-five years, a person should know or at least relate to the name they go by. For sure, the American Indians had it right, earning their name through some heroic deed or significant encounter.* Lacing up his shoes, with example after example running through his mind like wild Indians, he began to affectionately list a few of his favorites when a fellow agent emerged from one of the stalls; "Whada'ya say, Willie?" washed his hands and sauntered out without waiting for an answer.

Willie!? Bill, Billy, Will and Willie, debuted and flopped within ten seconds on the third-grade playground! He would have preferred just plain Ol' William Brown on the Concept Air name tag, but no dice... company policy. Customers had no choice but to call him Mister Brown, or Sir. Neither of these seemed appropriate.

His older brother, at age seventeen, had joined the United States Army and returned with "Brownie" tattooed on his shoulder. It was a decisive move; a colorful statement with stars encircling the name and proudly displayed; "Call me, Brownie. It means something. I'm somebody."

Myron, aged fourteen, had gone immediately to a tattoo parlor next to the greyhound bus station. His parents hit the ceiling. He couldn't blame them... he'd forgotten the stars and had to agree; his wasn't nearly as pretty as his brother's.

A few years later, in his late teens, living in less than wholesome neighborhoods, he changed up to the name, Rocky. Perfect. Gladly brawling with anyone who dared challenge his right to the name–or the look on his face. So, there ya go... the new label more accurately described what was in the bag.

Rocky was just fine, but he was called other things too. Insulting things referring to one's sex life, or heritage... and even stupid things with dirty words attached... ugly... and he wasn't about to let them stick. Every blow given or received meant one less label to carry on into adulthood. Yes. Crude but effective... lessons were learned and things were settled at the primary level... things like respect, accountability, an awareness of human nature... adding up to a basic and foundational look at one's self. Beneficial at any level of society. From there, life deals the cards. Hopefully other, more civilized opportunities would come along, even in the school of hard knocks if someone were teachable. Although proper thanks and appreciation was due to the many who reached out to the "underprivileged" (including himself), what he'd learned on the streets was indispensable.

And then one day in his mid-twenties Rocky went away... there was the young Brownie with three stars across the top of his old tattoo. "Hi, I'm 'Brownie," he'd say, and then add, "W.M. Brown."

Most of the time no one asked what the initials stood for. But when they did, he would say, "William." If pressed for the 'M' he would say, "As in Money." The joke was obvious.

Yet he could dream. Even as a child, without questioning the actual source of his own interests in books, music, nature, and humanity in general, the dreams had never gone away (self-actualization was a term he was actually familiar with), and circumstances permitting, he'd pursued them from time to time. Faithfully shouldering his personal carry-on bag, though rearranging and sorting again and again (gradually downsizing as he'd seen life go by), the secret M for Money compartment was the last to go.

Facing the locker, he dialed his combination; *I guess people have at least two kinds of baggage... some they would like to fill, and some that are over-filled. But there's another kind of baggage; at least I'm not one of those guys sitting in prison... tired of waiting for empty bags to fill up. Gives new meaning to the phrase, "Grab bag."*

With yet another look at his name on the gray, metal, locker-door, he squeaked it open, Hmmm, this label must be wrong. There's no W.M. Brown in here. Looks like this could be his dirty laundry though.

Then his eyes moved up to the locker's single shelf to a variety of toiletries and other containers. *There's something objectionable about being called, bud, pal, dude, or hey you... just another boring label... like aspirin, or deodorant; at least BAYER ASPIRIN says something more specific and might even create expectations.*

Not many people with the name Ripper would have the nerve to name their child Jack. Every good Jack has to carry the weight of every bad Jack. A person's name should be entirely unique, for them and them alone. Too bad we don't know how our kids are gonna turn out... but if we labeled them right, at lease they'd know what should go in the container, and maybe even be proud enough to fill it with honorable and decent things.

Agent W.M. Brown removed and hung his uniform in the locker; put on his sweats, and Nike Man headed for the exercise room. Thirty minutes later he was Naked Brownie (with three stars) under two of six shower heads, alternating between cold and hot. Standing under one of the other sprays an anonymous employee whistled and lathered. Neither man spoke to the other. Anonymous finished quickly and on his way out paused to read what was written on William's shoulder.

Naked Brownie, continued showering, the needles of water on his head of kinky-curly hair pinged away as he imagined what would have happened had he yielded to an impulse to punch the guy.

"Sir, could you tell us what the man looked like?"

"Well, he was naked; looked pretty much like all other naked guys... except for one thing..."

"What was that?"

"Had the word 'Brownie' tattooed on his left shoulder."

"Must've been his name then?"

"You're the detective, but I guess if it was commenting on the color of his skin, it would've said 'Speckled Brownie'... never seen so many freckles!"

"Hmmm... could you recognize the man if you saw him again?"

"Oh yeah. But especially if he was naked, otherwise the tattoo wouldn't show."

"What do you think was his reason for punching you?"

"I can't imagine; maybe he didn't like the way I whistle."

"You were whistling?"

"I always whistle in the shower."

"Do you remember what you were whistling?"

"Yeah, The Star Speckled Brownie."

With a turn of the dial on the combination lock, Agent W.M. Brown was gone, Nike Man was gone, Star Speckled Brownie was gone, and Citizen Car-Pooler now sat in a Ford Taurus with three others: John, Kelly, and the driver, Charlie... who could really be Sparky, since that's what the personalized license plate read... or maybe that was his wife's name. William had never asked, but today he wanted to know, "Who's Sparky?"

"Oh, that's our dog's name. She owns the car... or thinks she does anyway."

The rest of the commute was about dogs and pets in general. The last syllables of "See ya tomorrow..." were muffled behind the closed car door as the backside of William's right hand went up in the usual wave. Sparky disappeared down a narrow street lined on both sides with apartment buildings.

—◇—

Mrs. Brown met him at the door with a peck on the cheek and an open hand for his paycheck. The same gesture she'd used for years. He preferred it that way. Less embarrassing than putting it on the table where the paltry amount stared up accusingly at him. Although the fact that it was not enough would inevitably come out (one way or another) before the evening was over.

He couldn't argue with that. Neither of them would. Facts were facts. After twenty-five years, a daughter, and a grandchild, what was the point? There was a bright spot up ahead though... a small one: According to rumor, a promotion was in the works for one of the agents to become supervisor, and it could very well be him. His own shift-supervisor liked him, and lately had even mentioned the fact that he was an excellent agent. Things could be looking up.

No. Maggie wasn't bitter about the money; besides, she loved Brown. She'd met him in the Brownie era, but from the day they'd met, she'd called him Brown. At first he thought it was cute. Such a petite thing, acting like an army sergeant. He let it ride, and as they grew closer, he was intrigued because of her contrasting affection and the obvious distance such an address implied. As the years went by he realized that it was because of her matter-of-fact personality. What the hell? Couldn't she read the label? Maybe that was it. The first time she saw him with his shirt off, she'd asked (matter-of-factly); "What are the stars for, Brown?" He'd had no answer. Nowadays he usually wore loose fitting shirts to help hide his paunch. Brownie was hidin' out too.

She was introduced to him as, Margie; Maggie was his idea. Most of the time he used endearing terms such as Sweetheart, Honey, and even Baby Doll did the job. Syrup came easy for Southerners.

He learned from the outset to never call her, Marge. "Uh-unh-unh... too frumpy..." she'd said, wagging her finger at him. And she never failed to correct him or anyone else, even strangers, who made that mistake. But (as a matter of fact) Marjorie was her name. She let him try that one on her for a while, but something about the way it was said (or he said it) turned her off. *If she is so set on being called what she likes, why won't she call me what I like?* he'd wondered again and again. And if they were going on matters of fact, it seemed that she took it for a fact that she was a sweetheart, and every other superlative he chose to lavish upon her; "Can't argue with what's inside the bag, even if you can argue with the label," he'd decided.

Funny about life… You never seem to get to the bottom of the bag. There's always some little surprise waiting for you. Then again, like in a marriage for instance, you can dig around forever and not find what you might have thought was in there.

Lately he was starving for familiarity. If only somebody would call him sweetheart… He couldn't reasonably ask Maggie to do it. He'd blown it too many times. Proven beyond a doubt that he was not, whereas Maggie really was, a sweetheart… but… just a little too damned matter of fact is all.

Okay, so he'd left Myron with his mother, Billy on the playground, Rocky on the streets, Agent Brown in the locker, and Brownie was hidin' under his T-shirt. So who was sitting in front of the tube on a Friday night waiting for the dinner bell? Brown? Hmmm… that one didn't sound right either.

He felt a familiar gentle hand on his shoulder; "Would you like me to bring it in here?" Maggie asked.

"No thanks, Doll, I'll sit with you in the kitchen."

Two chili dogs smothered in onions, sweet pickle chips, oven-fried potatoes, and iced tea. Small talk about work, her day at home, and before long? Dinner was in the bag.

"Thanks for dinner, Hon."

"Wanna go for a walk, Brown?"

"Sure..." Then with a sincere smile, he added; "I'd walk with you through fire, Baby." "How about just around the Mall?" she responded.

"Okay..."

- Chapter Two -

Brown was quite aware that a walk in the mall usually led to the same place: Shoe stores. He liked shoes... and had given them lots of thought.

Shoes are like people. They have soles. They have purpose. They can be run-down, spiffed-up, pretentious, cute, superfluous, lonely, single (as in lost along the highway), and married (since most have mates).

Looking across a well-stocked shoe store was like looking at humanity in all of its variety. Just sitting there... all types... being what they're supposed to be: Practical, no-nonsense Birkenstocks; lazy loafers; wishy-washy flip-flops; and straightforward wing-tips... all orderly and uncomplicated. Defined. Categorized. They, too, were waiting for their destinies: To be filled; to be tossed into corners; to be lost along the road; to be cared for; or to be tried on for comfort, over and over again... too snug, too loose, wrong color.

It was obvious. Shoes were either male or female: Sweet, prim, curvaceous, elegant, sophisticated, or rugged, suave, efficient, debonair, sporty.

And they definitely had personalities: They could be cheery, carefree, jaunty, buoyant, sprightly... sexy... and some were just happy little shoes.

Empty shoes suggested hollow thoughts about those who owned them. Lying abandoned on the floor in various awkward positions? Why, he could almost see the missing legs straining upward painfully, offering ghost-like stories, compelling him to animate and hear the voices of the owners.

Frankly, he'd just as soon they did become animated; *Forget filling them up with folks who don't need them, he thought. And why not? This could be the very reason I often find myself standing in shoe stores, just staring at display shelves and discount bins.* Brownie longed to see those babies spring to life: *Let those cowboy boots out of the chute; get those bunny-toed slippers to hopping; waltz those pumps all over the floor; let's see those patent-leather cha-cha-chas, and those stiletto-heeled tangos; all tripping and slipping up and down the aisles amongst the bare-footed, undeserving shoppers. Propel them forth into usefulness. Don't consign them to the dark corner of a closet! Walls bulging out with the empty, unfulfilled promises and dreams of the owners.*

The shopping malls made it difficult for people with a problem like his. He didn't enjoy shopping in the first place; the benches were always more inviting than the stores. And why were there no doors leading into the different stores? Like being on a huge lake, drifting in and out of bays and coves; any little canoe could float right in without even thinking about it and suddenly find itself surrounded with a product of a particular kind... and a salesperson.

He'd realized his shoe problem a few years ago. And tonight, like most people with chronic, annoying habits, he was in denial. Just cruising slowly... looking at the weird stuff on display and the weird people who were looking at the weird people looking at the weird stuff... and ever watchful for the perfect bench to plop onto.

He and Maggie had become separated. She'd most likely gotten hung up browsing through the knickknack shelves (he hated knickknack). Suddenly, like a sleepwalker discovering himself in the same place over and over again, he looked around in amazement... and dang! There he was again... a shoe store... staring at the ankle straps on a pair of duck-footed Birkenstocks (the worlds ugliest shoes), trying to imagine himself in them and the revolting stereotypical image he had about the people who do wear them... The Track and Trail shoe clerk offered his opener; "Hello there... need some help?"

Shoot... now he had to make the best of it; "This is a rather handsome shoe," he said, picking up a lady's tennis shoe; "How much is it?"

"Let's see... the price tag says forty dollars a pair."

"I don't want the pair, just one."

"That is the price for one, we throw the other one in for free."

Brownie, thinking, *Watch it boy, this guy is on the ball,* countered; "You have only one here on display,"

"Can't do it. Can't split a pair... nope... but as I said, you get a right and a left for the same low price. A perennial two for one sale."

Brown responded just as quickly; "What you're saying is that if I am one of those people with two left feet I have to buy four shoes to get two?"

"That's correct...." the clerk shifted his weight and crossed his arms, eyes narrowing.

Brown took another tact, "Look... I want to level with you, this is for my wife, who is just too embarrassed to come shopping for shoes herself.

"Why's that?"

"She has only one leg..."

The clerk's lips formed a little "Ohhhhhooo, " let go a silent whistle, then stepped back, thinking this over.

Brown continued, aware the salesman was feeling sorry for him and that he finally had his attention; "There are lots of one legged people out there who could use the other one... hundreds of 'em," he added, hoping to shore up his case. Saying this, they both looked out across the mall. Brown half expected to see the majority of the shoppers hobbling along on crutches with one trouser leg pinned up. He didn't.

The astute salesman craned his head closer and said dryly; "Look bud, these things are like geese; they're mated for life. We can't split 'em up."

About then, Maggie walked up, wearing a summer skirt and blouse. Brown slid one arm around her, "This is my wife."

The clerk looked at her legs; at her face; Brown's face; Maggie's legs.

"Do you like this shoe enough to try it on, honey?" he asked, holding one up (Maggie always tried on the left shoe).

"I guess so," she said in characteristic sweetness; "Do you have the left one in a size five?" Yes. He had him!

"No, Ma'am, we sold it just this morning. We have a whole rack of rights today though..."

Darn! Maybe not.

Maggie, gullible-Maggie, bit the Clerk's bait immediately. "Oh, gosh..." her brown eyes swept the racks compassionately.

But, Brown knew when to quit, "Never mind honey..." turned her around, nudging her toward the stream of shoppers; "...lets go look at the prosthetics. You're walking great today." The mystified expression on her face was for him... and him only.

As he walked along the mall, arm around Maggie's waist, he was proud of the salesman all the same; *We need people like him. Protecting the sanctity of matched pairs is a service to humanity, in spite of the fact that we're careless and undeserving. There's nothing more useless, accusing, and forlorn than a single shoe, lying along the highway with its tongue flopped out and wagging in the wind, moaning; "stupid, stupid, stupid." On the other hand, a pair of character-filled hand-me-downs on an occasional hobo... feet peeking out from under a newspaper, or dangling out the door of a railway car? That's a declaration of rugged endurance, and perhaps even motivates an observant or more fortunate person toward a useful and productive life.*

He scanned the mall carefully... almost every shopper was wearing tennis shoes... his eyes glazed over; *But hobos don't wear character very much these days, and neither do most of us. We can thank tennis shoes for that.*

If shoes are like people, then tennies are symbolic of the duped masses who've lost their identity in a sea of sameness. We put on a pair and announce to the world: I'm a walker today; a runner, a basketball guy, a biker. But that's too limiting, and too often a facade. Why not announce what we really are? Establish an identity for ourselves?

I sit. All the time. That's what I like to do; I'm a sitter and these are my sitting tennies. I'm also an eater, so, these are my eating tennies; I'm a fat-bellied, beer drinking, testosterone ridden, Monster-Truck-driving redneck; a frail little widow who's got to get to the corner before the bus comes; or; I'm simply a beautiful piece of humanity which explains why I'm wearing my platinum-soled, gold-woven, work-of-art tennies.

Three teen-aged boys bounced by on state-of-the-art rubber soles and neoprene. His thoughts wandered on; *Even though the Tennie manufacturers have been adding colors, bumps, ridges, Velcro this-Velcro that, and zig-zaggy patterns... top to bottom... they haven't dented the surface of their potential market. But they have altered our way of life and put an end to an era.*

Let's call a spade a spade, and tennis shoes for what they really are: To have absconded with an entire era, they're not just sneakers... they're thieves!

He remembered a song he'd written years ago, and started singing it under his breath along the dimly lighted streets as he and Maggie strolled home:

He's the shoeshine man, who works down the street,
What interest's him's what's on your feet.
He can tell a lot about you from the shoes you wear...
About where you work, about what you care.
He can tell by looking if you're feeling rough,
When not only your shoes, but your soul is scuffed.
Buffing and waxing is what he'll do ...
N' he can take care of what's wrong with you.
He's the shoeshine man.
So climb on up, set yourself down,
Shoeshine man'll take away that frown!
When you leave, you'll leave with a smile.
Looking down at your feet, you'll smile for a while.
He's the shoeshine man. Just listen to me,
The shoeshine's cheap, the philosophy's free.
When he gets hold of his snapping rag
He's on those shoes, baby, that's his bag!
Just bring those shiners with their buttons and bows,
He'll polish 'em up from the heel to the toes.
Snappity, snappity, snappity pop!
When he gets started he can hardly stop!
When he's through you'll see your face there...
Smile n' leave your care... with the shoeshine man.

That night, listening to Maggie's familiar sleep-sounds, he wondered; *What would the shoeshine man of old say if he was around today? He sounds more patient than I am... probably draw me a cool drink from his well of wisdom,*

*and unselfishly urge me to overlook the people that appear
garish, cheeky and defiant in shoes that were never intended
to be on their feet. He would say they're just victims of fast
changing, complicated times. In his day there were no signs
that said: no shoes, no service" What that would've meant, back
then, is you can only go as far as your shoes will take you... in
this world anyway. Brownie's last thought was; And if I happen
to see a beautiful woman in a stunning shoe, or a bearded man
in a suede walking shoe, I should be thankful and encouraged...
there are occasionally perfect matches, and still lots of reasons
to admire shoes... if not people. I may be impatient, but I don't
hate anyone... in particular.*

—◇—

- *Chapter Three* -

Saturday was an ordinary day; Brown and Maggie shared the newspaper over coffee with the usual accusations of; "Yes I did," and "Nooo... you did *not* put it back the way it was, Brown." Breakfast ended with the news they were to baby-sit grandson Cooper while daughter Julie went for an unexpected job interview, one hundred miles distant.

The idea of Julie moving away was sad, clouding the first few minutes of Brown's day, but being with his creative grandson was always a kick. He never let up. Bouncing and laughter non-stop; what a kid... After dinner they'd all watched TV for a while; once Coop was asleep, Brown said good night to Maggie and headed for his own bed, where he preferred to sleep.

He drove slowly through the familiar town... the good areas and the bad ones... in the poorer sections he identified with financial problems, in the commercial districts he was dumbfounded at the things people had for sale... in the nicer, residential sections, he wondered how to get his piece of the cake...

In a certain area of the city, he simply had to pull over. This wasn't the first time he'd cruised this street hoping for nothing more than a glimpse. Ahhhh... but this time... Beautiful! He was actually on the sidewalk within mere inches of fulfilling what had long been a desire. This... Now, *this* was the last word in class. A masterwork. Never had he seen a woman look so perfect. His mind filled with the thought of sweet and tart raspberries floating on air. Such creamy, vanilla skin browned to perfection. Obviously firm, yet soft and inviting. Here was substance.

Depth. *And* on a pedestal... of course!

She stood out beautifully amongst an ethnic variety of colors... white, yellow, red, brown, and even black. And though all were inspirational he'd made his choice and held steadfast. This was a fashion show of sorts. Each would go with someone at the right time, but his choice stood out like royalty among peasants. Before handing over the money, he thought it over... hesitating. *The price is high, but it's only money, and morals suspended in a moment of time. She's fabulous... how can I resist?* The deal was made, and in seconds he'd escorted her across the sidewalk and into the shabby and aging van he'd driven for twenty years. She was obviously way out of his league, he felt like apologizing, but realized it would be useless. She would never in a million years speak of such things. Her job was to be tempting and tasty, and this she did with poise and perfection. Just to sit there in the quiet interior was almost more than he could endure... Wow! He fired the ignition. The noise of the engine vied for his common sense... He stayed at the curb wrestling with his thoughts for a moment longer; *Maggie's gone for the night. Sure. I feel a certain guilt, but I'm tired of feeling so alone. Saying, no, to every temptation that comes my way.* The entire vehicle, the entire universe, swelled with fragrance and promise. Aggressively, he pulled out into traffic, and sped off down the street. *To hell with self-control.*

The apartment was just a few miles away, but before getting there he had to pass through an even seedier part of town. Here, prostitutes walked brazenly in the glow of streetlights and neon signs. Pimps and drug dealers lurked in the shadows, and when a certain familiar neon sign held his attention far longer than was appropriate (considering what was in the passengers seat) he had to admit; *I feel a certain fascination for this place too. Not because I want cheap thrills, but because I can easily see parallels with what they're selling and what I've just picked up. There are choices here too. A wide assortment for the offing and not nearly as expensive. Cheap in fact. A person could have a carload just by pulling up to the curb... any time–day or night... there for the choosing.*

He was neither an elitist, nor was he a pretender. Of course he would've enjoyed one or two... and had on occasion. *Is that so wrong?* he wondered. But at least tonight he drove on past, focusing on what he was about to do. *Yeah, this is a special kind of abandonment for me. Way beyond Dunkin' Donuts. A treat. You get what you pay for.*

The little recipe next to him originated in New *York, New Yorkers are cosmopolitan. Cultured. Most of them know who they are... maybe a bit straightforward; but honey, I'm in the mood for straightforward!*

The gas gauge indicated low on fuel, yet he boldly passed the last service station rather than spoiling the moment. Didn't want to talk. What could he say to make this any more special, or more obvious?

The apartment was a welcome sight... very dark, and no one seemed to be about. Good. He was sure that although this wasn't necessarily an affluent neighborhood, all around were normal happy families. Basically orderly and secure citizens making it through life. Very few would understand what he was about to do... just this one time... succumb to the fantasy. He negotiated the sidewalks with speed and agility keeping her close, just in case someone happened along or glanced out a window. With the one free hand trembling he managed the locked door and purposely avoided the mirror in the hallway... too ashamed of what he would see. There was little time wasted with preparation...

no words were spoken and not one moment was lost... ecstasy beyond his dreams, and then it was over.

Sitting on the side of the bed, head in his hands, he wondered; *what have I done? I'm out of control.* From the corner of his eye he saw a piece of paper propped up on the dresser. In front of it was a Bavarian chocolate, cream-filled donut, and these words from Maggie: "Brown, I know how you love these... and me. I look forward to my return. Enjoy your treat."

The lights were out and he was alone, tossing and turning on the bed, aware that he'd chosen his destiny. All he could see for the rest of the night was that donut on the dresser and three slices of New York cheesecake, slopping around in his stomach in a sour pool of melted raspberry topping.

On Sunday morning, after a lousy night's sleep, all evidence of gluttony (two thirds of a cheesecake) was thrown into a dumpster on the way over to get Maggie. He felt a little better. People turned to food for consolation all the time, didn't they?

But he was also feeling better because of a certain purchase. He loved electronic gadgets: computers, VCRs, cameras, whatever... but telephones in particular. These he really admired. He stared at his first-ever car phone, a technology that was long overdue and would surely change the world. With something akin to reverence, he punched up Julie's number. Maggie answered; "Guess who?" he blurted excitedly.

"Why should that be so hard to do?"

"Guess where I am..."

"Sounds like the bathtub."

"I'm in the Van. We've got a car phone!"

"That's great, Brown; when do you need a car phone?"

"All the time. I can check in with you when I'm on the road..." and then he added; "like right now."

There was silence on Maggie's end while she gathered her thoughts, knowing that it was useless to logically discuss anything he was this excited about; "Well, so what are you checking-in about?"

"I'm going over to the Optometrist's... they're open on Sunday! I made an appointment. I'm tired of all these drugstore, reading glasses everywhere... all over the place... I might need bifocals, ya know? I'll check in with you later... is Julie back?"

"Well, she should be back before long. She might be..."

Brown cut her off with; "Hey, this is costing money. I better get off for now..." and the line went dead.

Maggie calmly went back to what she'd been doing before the phone rang.

—◇—

- Chapter Four -

Conveniently and wisely located in a large discount department store, Doctor Jack's office was open seven days a week. Mr. Brown arrived a little late, but enthusiastic. Before going in, he rummaged under the seats and throughout the van for every pair of junk glasses he could find. There were several; all of which were war-torn and scarred, including a couple pairs of sunglasses. Hanging all of them in a row from the neck opening of his shirt, arranged like a gaudy necklace of brass, glass and turtle shell, he sauntered in.

The receptionist was tepid. If she noticed anything different about him she didn't let on. And that's okay. The coffee-caddy blinked at him from beyond several glass shelves loaded with hardware for bad eyes. Ten thousand pairs of blank stares followed him over to the tray of cups, cream and sugar.

Great. There was a telephone sitting right beside one of the waiting area chairs; the car phone was too big and bulky to carry around. He should get back to Maggie... probably hung up too quick last time. The eyes were still watching... he faced away toward the wall, trying to focus on the wallpaper's tiny print. Some of the patterns on the wall looked like tiny hearing aids. Fighting an unreasonable suspicion that these vision centers had a direct link to hearing clinics, he dialed, consciously held his voice down when connected; "Maggie... I'm in the Optometrist's office now."

"What? Are you calling from the car phone?"

"No, I'm in the waiting room..."

"Then why does your voice sound so far away?"

He ignored the question, glanced over his shoulder, and was embarrassed to find himself in a staring contest with a pretty little lady who, for some reason, had a mean frown on her face. "I gotta' go..." and once again Maggie was left with a dead line.

The "little lady" with very chic glasses, and a folder labeled, W. M. Brown, glared at him as though by using the telephone he'd just sinned. Hanging the phone up guiltily, his offered smile failed to disarm her. With eyebrows up questioningly, he pointed at himself, and then to her, then back to himself; She nodded with a curt affirmative.

"I'm with you," he assured her, and stood in immediate surrender.

By the time he'd refilled his coffee she'd disappeared around the corner. There were several doors down the way. Holding his hands out mimicking someone with a serious vision problem, he groped and weaved along, feeling the air as though expecting to bump into a wall any second; purposely passed the room she'd entered... continued on down the hallway squinting into at least three wrong rooms... finally turned back and felt his way into her little cubicle.

Behind a row of machines stretched the length of one long table, she stood erect, hands on her hips. The cold look on her face was perfectly matched with the icy harness he obediently placed his chin and forehead into; "Are you going to poke me in the eye?" he asked. But even this rolled without meaning across the frozen tundra of her efficient and bored little soul.

A technical explanation of what she intended to do rambled on until she finished with; "...performing a few tests, one of which will be the introduction of a small puff of air into your eyes..."

I knew it!

"...then, we'll go on over for Doctor Jack's exam."

The way she'd said this, Brown was certain Doctor Jack was standing directly behind... but he faced straight ahead moving only his eyes in wide circles like a helpless calf about to be branded.

"Stare at the red cross," she commanded; then with an evil hiss; "... tell me when the green dot is exactly in the center."

I can do that.

"Now tell me when the two lines become one."

No problem.

"Now..." she said with a guttural growl (rolling another machine front and center) "...for the airrrrr." *God... I'm sitting here with my head in the noose and this lady has not warmed up in the least. Can a mean person be trusted to blow puffs of air into one's eyes?*

Just before he jumped up to say; "Stare at my fist, and tell me when you see stars sweetheart!" A harmless little piff went into his right eye. Then, Piff in the left! *That was easy. That's all? That's all you've got, honey? I'm truly disappointed. No wonder you're mad. Who wouldn't be?*

Moments later, like a paper-trained puppy, he followed his chart down the passageway. He'd met Doctor Jack before. What a nice guy! So kind he wouldn't hurt bacteria. But of course, he wasn't in the room yet.

"Grumpy" pointed to the black leather examination-chair surrounded with more gadgets. He recognized the sitting part and plopped down... cranked up another smile and with both hands proudly reached up and flared his necklace; "How's that?" he asked.

With her lips compressed and pushed to one side in a half smile, "Hummpf," wheezed out of one nostril, and with a final; "Pffft..." she was out the door.

That should be considered a win; He wiggled one finger through a missing lens; "See ya..."

Great. The rhino was gone; *Rhinos, wart hogs, wild pigs, and hippos are dangerous.... In a continual defensive mode because they have to be; they can't see very well. Any strange noise or moving object is enough to cause their little tails to shoot straight up in the air. I'm sure if you were to put glasses on them, they would be happy to find they'd been uptight for no reason—most of the time. But still... there's nothing they can do about the warts.*

His reverie was interrupted by the sound of the phone ringing in the outer office. There was an extension across the room. Good. While waiting for Dr. Jack, he could call Maggie; See if Julie's back yet. He changed chairs. A black stool with wheels scooted nicely across the room to the desk. An enormous eyeball poster censured him for exceeding the speed limit in a confined area. But before dialing he paused... wisely deciding that Maggie had heard enough... plus, in the rack next to the exam chair, a Sports Illustrated magazine'd caught his attention. Swimsuit Issue! He raced back past Mr. Eyeball, now confident there were no graphics with little arrows pointing to ->Lust<- of the Eye.

Oops! Squeaky-clean Doctor Jack was early. The magazine would have to wait. Amidst smiles and handshakes he surrendered the stool without being told, and climbed back into the exam chair.

"How can I help you today?" asked the Doctor.

Brownie pointed to his necklace with all ten fingers splayed out; "None of these are doing the job."

Instead of finding humor in the necklace the doctor became very serious; "Well, let's see if I can help." He jumped right in, measuring distance, alignment, distortion...

Although Brown had no idea how Doctor Jack acted with friends and associates, his office manner was that of a well established, modern-day Hindu holy man: Impersonally sweet; words trailing off, coaxingly; "And now, look to my leffffttt. Tell me, is this better or was number one better? A little betttterrrrr? Goooooooood."

The letters rose up cryptically, like Scrabble... especially the hand held ones. Silently trying to pronounce an entire line, "favgztn! sqwitzo, ditneb?" Brown found himself apologizing over, and over; "I'm sorry, say that again?"

"Reeaaddd the liiinnnne that seems the clearessssttt."

Oooh! thought William; *I hate it when he's so patient. And that black, flattened eye cover... spoon-thingey... sets me off; seems like its best use would be as a paddle board, right on his balding head. Break him out of that Hindu mold; Come baaaacccck Dr. Jack! Plop... flap, flappity-flap! Ooooohhhh, I hate it when he's so impersonal.*

"Now, can you focus on these lettttterrrrrs?"

Yeah, if that Sports Illustrated were up there, you bet I could. And just because I keep turning my head slightly toward the magazine rack is no excuse for you to look at me like that. He tried to justify his wandering eye by holding up a pair of glasses with one lens missing: "This one offended me, so I plucked it out."

The half-hearted chuckle Doctor Jack managed to provide meant the Hindu thing was still on track; "Which one do you like bettterrrrr; this one or this one?"

"I really like the one in the aqua, Lycra do-dad."

Either ignoring the wise crack or prompted by it, the Doc picked up a pointed tool with a tiny light on the end. "Let's see what it looks like in here for a minute."

Uh, oooh. He's onto me. He wants to confirm what I could've told him if he'd only asked: If ever a guy needed a pair of rose-colored glasses it's me: A guy who doesn't even know his own name; and that lust of the eye thing... not to mention, a certain jaded look, with occasional glints of deceit.

The Doctor leaned over, shielding his own (no doubt perfect) eye with the black instrument, and peered into the eye of the storm. Swirling around in there were things beyond prescription... if not description. But he was too kind; "Looks verrry gooood..."

The assemblage of instruments was swung out of the way so that W.M. could get up. Doctor Jack stood... blocking view of the magazines. They were done.

In the fitting department, ten thousand blank stares, and one other, truly exceptional stare waited for him; a pair of perky, green eyes, sporting, Shirley. A beautiful, warm, borderline optical illusion with auburn hair.

She laughed convincingly at his necklace, and like an expert pickpocket, had it off before he knew it... soothingly guided him through a tangle of tinted, hi-tech, scratch-resistant, non-glare choices and he floated out the door in a colorful balloon of customer satisfaction.

He got into the van. Great, there was the phone.

"Maggie, is Julie back yet?"

"No."

"I'm goin' over to Carlos's house."

—◇—

- Chapter Five -

Carlos was the only one who knew him as Brownie. The original plan had been for both of them to take an old, dilapidated utility-trailer, mounded and overflowing with metals of all kinds: pipes, gas cook-stove, a rusted out barbecue grill, an old Mercury fender, a wheelless Red Flyer wagon, and any metal not connected to something useful, to the salvage yard. But now there was a change of plans; "C'Mon Brownie, I can hook up the trailer and you'll be able to dump it in plenty of time."

Brownie wasn't so sure. "That's a big load there, Carlos. This trailer is a monument to "Sanford and Son."

Even though he had the same skin color as Sanford and Son, Carlos was not insulted. He and Brownie were good enough friends that remarks unintended to be racial slurs were not on a hot plate before they had time to thaw out. Carlos was Brownie's name for Carl; a reflection of both men's humor, since Carl was not a Mexican.

Leaning against the trailer (and possibly strategically placed there by Carlos) was a fifty's bicycle with balloon tires; Brownie took a step back, eyeballing the potentials; "Hey that looks like a pretty good bike there; you throwin' that away too?"

"That is, in fact, a good bike. I thought about tossin' it out too, but maybe not. Seems a shame for the Ol' Trailmas'r to go out in such disgrace."

Brownie took note of the word, Trailmaster, emblazoned across the frame; "I might give it a home for a while."

"Really? D'you want it? Why don't you take it then? Nobody rides it no more..." Carlos looked self-consciously at his waistline... Brownie, ignoring his own bulge, would guess that his friend weighed at least 240 pounds.

"All right we can put it in the van..."

But Carlos put his hand possessively on the handlebars and looked him in the eyes, smiling.

Brownie pulled on the bike. Carlos held on, pulled slightly back on the bike.

"What? Okay, okay; I'll make the dump run."

"By ya'self... I gots to practice wid' the band." This was a good excuse... Carlos played mean blues, on his tenor saxophone. Brownie played the blues harp. They played together often, though Brownie had never played any gigs. They'd put music to several of his songs, and the few times they played them (jamming with the band) were some of the best times of his life. Even so, this chore seemed a little demeaning.

"Carlos, I don't want to get all dirty, unloading this stuff!"

"You serious...? All you have to do is drive up under the magnet... and zip! They sucks it out. You can drop the trailer off on your way back from Julie's."

"Here..." from a box in the garage, Carlos pulled a wadded up shop coat, greasy and full of holes, and obviously no longer a fit; "...you can wear this."

Brownie threw it in the back of the van too, and slammed the door.

Driving away, he thought about Carlos. They'd been friends for a long time. Both had lived in San Diego until Brownie had moved up to Oregon. When Carlos followed, years later, Brownie was glad. But somehow, up until today, he had never noticed how much they looked like each other. Brownie had acres of freckles on square inches of skin... big brown ones floating on a background of thousands of smaller ones... Carlos was a big, brown man; in fact, it was Carlos who'd asked him twenty-two years ago if the freckles were why he called himself Brownie. That was when the Brownie tattoo... started hidin' out. You can't fix stupid but why advertise? Now, looking in the rearview mirror for the ten millionth time, his very curly hair and large lips added to the appearance of his being (possibly) part Negro. He had never even considered it, even when growing up no one had ever said it, although he had been called Freckle-face often enough.

Had Carlos just been kind all this time? Because for Brown, it was very easy to identify with the black culture. He loved their sense of rhythm, their soulful music. He liked strutting around, imitating the hip, black-stride... had done it often with his kids. And even his black friends. Now it occurred to him (looking in the rearview mirror) that he could easily pass for a black man with a trailer load of junk.

Rain, a familiar event in Oregon, began hitting the van's cracked windshield... he called Maggie.

"What is it Brown, I don't think I like this car phone. I'm a prisoner to it already. Why don't you just come on over to Julie's? We're gettin' hungry."

"I got this little errand I need to run first..." he paused; looked at his watch; "...why not meet me at the Taco Stand in one hour; that's only five-thirty, can you handle that?"

"Okay. Don't keep us waiting, Brown, or we'll eat without you." This time Brownie was left with a dead line. The rain was coming down harder.

—◇—

An older, faded-white Chevy van pulled into the

metal salvage yard with its unsightly trailer attached. The sounds of heavy metal-crunching machinery penetrated the closed environment of the cab. Rain had turned the area into a mud hole. Workmen walked around with mud-spattered clothing and cutting torches... lugging pieces of metal from pile to pile. Forklifts and battered dump trucks sloshed around in the goop with no concern whatever.

The sign said: Loaded trucks stop here to be weighed. Turning his radio down; "I can do this, no problem," said the driver to no one, hanging head and arm out the window in eighteen wheel truck driver mode. "I just pull up here... to get both..." ...van and trailer... onto the... scale!" he pronounced with finality and a tone of self congratulations.

A raucous, buzzer sounded; "Which means: This man just got weighed," he said very cleverly, smiling to himself while acknowledging the rough looking man in the scale house window, who impatiently motioned for him to move his insignificant load (compared to the towering piles of metal all around).

A huge magnet hung from the arm of an aged, yellow crane. One of the workers waved at Brownie to back into the first of several unloading bays. He peered through the wet windshield at the giant, steel Moon Pie swinging above him; "That thing's looks to be about the size of this trailer... Carlos," he muttered with concerned ridicule for his friend, vaguely recalling the words; "sucks it out."

The rain continued. He watched the yard-workers with appreciation. Real tough to be out there in this kind of weather. Sparks flew from their torches. Huge chunks of junk metal were tossed all around with zeal. Determined to continue his demonstration of backing skills, he shoved the gear lever into drive and eased into position for the backing-up part. From there to the sound of mud and goop squishing from his tires, he actually did a very nice job … "All right! I did good; I look good! Looking… Goood!" None of the "boys" even so much as looked his way.

In his euphoria he carelessly opened the door and bounded onto the ground. Oops! His latest leather loafers instantly looked like what the "boys" were wearing; jumped back inside the van and immediately felt foolish. "Damn!" The damage had already been done. He sneaked a peek to see if anyone was watching. Nope.

Again he opened the door and looked down at three inches of goop everywhere. Closing the door about two seconds late, a passing forklift gleefully splash-painted the entire left side of his van a caramel brown, complete with metal-fleck. Mud ran down his face and shirt. Unfortunately, the inside of the van was now tastefully decorated with opaque brown streaks too.

Suddenly the van shook violently from the rear. He looked around to see the trailer, junk and all, being lifted off the ground. The rear of the van began to lift too… dangling by the little ball-hitch of the trailer. When the magnet snapped the junk out of the trailer, both trailer and van bounced and shuddered in the mud. To anyone outside the van, the word he shouted may have sounded like, "Sucker!"

Now the boys were looking at him greedily… all of them… as if hoping they would now get to use their torches on his van (obviously ripe for demolishing). But then, with a couple of tobacco-spitting dismissals, they turned away.

Realizing that two short, squeaky beeps from the crane whistle probably meant "leave…" he pulled out from

"Tin-pan Alley" feeling vulnerable and unacceptable to these highly intelligent, metal-salvage savages.

Pulling the van and trailer back onto the somehow mudless weigh-in scale, he got out and looked inside the trailer... What? Still half full! He looked up to the man in the window, held both hands out, palms-up and shook his head. When he mouthed the words; "What's the deal?" a blank expression was all he got in return. He can't hear me, was Brownie's natural thought. He pointed to the junk in the trailer with an exaggerated shrug of the shoulders and a twisted frown.

Scale man's head disappeared from the window; poked his head around the door and yelled; "The magnet won't fit inside the trailer. You'll have to unload the rest by hand."

Brownie's eyes opened wide; "I didn't bring any rubber boots..." and then added weakly; "...it's pretty muddy out here."

"Scaley" with a twisted, devil-may-care grin looked down at his own feet and said; "I don't have any either and I go out there all the time." By this time Brownie had climbed the stairs leading up to the scale house. Peeking around the door at Scaley's feet, he saw no rubber boots or shoes of any kind. What should have been legs, pants, and shoes were more like mud-pillars... it was impossible to tell where the pants ended, and the shoes began. Brownie started to see the picture; "He's suggesting that I wade in that stuff?!" Before he could ask this point-blank, Scaley said, "Okay, okay, go back over there. I'll send somebody to help you."

"I can't do that!" Brownie whined helplessly.

Scale man's huge eyebrows heaved upwards in silent response. Brownie continued: "They're mad at my van...

that's why... They don't like..." he paused, pointed at the van which was now camouflaged all over in brown... his words trailed off.

"Look, Hershey Bar, I can't do this without your help, either take it over there, or take it home!"

What? Now it dawned on him; *Oh, now I am insulted! He's leaning on me because I'm black. Can he call me that?* But the haven of his van being preferred over jail (were he to properly defend his black friends) he reluctantly climbed back in, negotiated the U-turn toward the crane, but bungled the backing (jack-knifing at least twice) before finally turning the engine off. He turned up the radio, and tried not to look out, while two "Demolition Technicians" were unloading the rest.

But then: What's this? Why's this man looking at me like that? Just outside the mud-spattered windshield, he could barely see the gruff, unshaven face of an older man in a railroad engineer's hat, scowling at him. Now what? I'm getting tired of this! Rolling the window down... slightly... he poked his ample lips through the crack; "Are you mad at me for this?"

The man still scowled, shifted closer to the window, craned his head even closer to the narrow opening and said; "I want to set my magnet down about right here (waving his hand over the top of the van) so bad I can't stand it! We don't do this (pointing to the trailer being unloaded) except for cripples and grandmas, Willie... I can't stand lazy people!"

Brownie missed the racial epithet, since that was his name at times anyway; "Hey man, you need to broaden your horizons a little bit, I didn't wear the right shoes for this..."

"Well, no shit! You guys love shoes, but I still think

you're lazy," he called out, walking back toward his crane, "And why don't you talk like all the other niggers... you act just like 'em."

"Why don't you get a real job?" Brownie hollered back, through an even tinier crack while cranking his window back up; "Instead of playing railroad all day. You might learn something from all those grandmas!" he added (knowing no one was listening or cared) and started up the van again. The "boys" unloading the trailer jumped out and slammed the tailgate.

Brown jammed his foot onto the accelerator. Mud rooster-tailed into the air, but the truck didn't move... I'm stuck... he pressed the accelerator to the floor; watched with a mixture of satisfaction (and a little fear) from his side-view mirror as mud went everywhere... onto the Metal Maggots, and onto the high-stepping, Crane Man, running for his magnet... apparently determined to get it onto the van after all, before it could get away. The (now wonderful) rusty sludge came down from the sky like lava from an erupting volcano.

The van's tires began to take hold, throwing the trailer into a sweeping, fishtailing effect. Once to the right and then to the left, violently smashing into Crane Man's two-story-tall pile of metal, who, simultaneously in the process of making it even higher, gleefully dropped his magnet (with current load of junk) onto the pile as well, and with great effect. Metal crashed down, bouncing off the van and trailer. Brownie (eyes wide as hubcaps) catapulted out into the main drive just as the entire mound tumbled and filled the alley in a glorious metallic landslide. And, as an added bonus topped the trailer off with a fresh load of junk. "The boys," none of which had been crazy enough to stick around when they saw what was happening, stood at a safe distance, spitting and laughing.

Without stopping at the scale house, Hershey Bar Willie squiggled across the scale, out of the yard and onto the highway, leaving a trail of mud behind like an immense slug.

Looking through the rearview mirror he could see one large, rusted, round chunk of metal spinning around slowly on the scale. It had fallen from the trailer... now with more junk in it than when he'd arrived at the Junk yard. "Weigh that, you creep!" he shouted to the top of his voice. The window was still up.

—◇—

The rain stopped. The evening sun sliced through the breaking cloud-cover in lemon colored shafts. But Brownie fumed and puckered... too sour... he did not feel like making lemonade.

Only a few blocks away from the salvage yard, the trailer started to wobble and whip around erratically. This was an unfamiliar part of town with older, once beautiful, single-family houses. Stately maple trees arched and canopied the wet streets. He pulled over to the curb.

A rusty spike of metal protruded from the sidewall of the van's right, rear tire. A slight breeze shook the leaves overhead. It was mid august but he sensed the approach of fall. Chilled, he put on the tattered shop coat, grabbed the spare, only to find it flat. Frustration! Maggie and Julie would be at The Taco Stand soon.

The car phone! Maggie first: no answer. Carlos wasn't home. A service station was the only option; it was time he looked for one. The Trailmaster! Why not ride to the service station and over to the taco stand?! It couldn't be more than two or three miles away.

A freckle faced, middle-aged man, coated in mud (but bathed in the yellow glow of the sun), wearing a ragged, short-sleeved, and gray shop-coat, pedaled a bicycle along a quiet street; the unbuttoned coat billowing behind. Two boys in their early teens rode up beside him on state-of-the-art mountain bikes: Alloy frames, Shimano derailleurs, awesome neon-iridescent paint jobs, and all the accessories. They rode along beside him for a while, looking at his bike and checking him out in general. No one spoke. The man was puzzled; why don't they just go on by? Ultimately after trying to ignore them, he says; "Hey guys! How ya' doin'?" He flashed his best, bright, white-toothed smile.

One of the boys responded; "Hey! Pretty good, Muddy Man, where'd ya' git that bike?"

"Why?"

"It sure is cool..." they laughed scornfully, and sped up, leaving him behind.

The man's muddy face colored a brownish, rusty red; but trying to make the best of it... he shouted good-naturedly at the disappearing boys, "Wha'chu talkin' 'bout, man! Ain't you never seen no Trailmas'r?" and pedaled doggedly on ahead into the cooling breeze.

The sun continued to set. Yellow rays of light reflecting on the wet streets gradually changed into streaked, rainbow trout pink. But Brownie, feeling more like a sucker; tired and hungry, finally lost it and shouted; "Carlosss! I could kill you right now..."

The loud outburst caused two fine lookin' women who had just pulled up to a stop sign in a red convertible to look directly at him. Normally he would not have taken notice other than the usual: A casual, male appreciation of these two and the sassy car; but tonight was an exception; he was totally embarrassed, and since already in the intersection, he couldn't possibly stop. How could he? He chose to ignore them completely and rode on past. Somehow, one of them read something in his expression, or plight, and related it to the other; laughter from both women pierced his pathetic heart.

His retort; "This's a Trailmas'r bike... you honky bitches!" went fallow at the rear of the car as it turned right, and sped away, but it felt so good to let the Black Man out... he was beginning to feel better.

Further on down the street, another person, a very old person, dressed in khaki cutoffs, and a low-necked, sweaty, white T-shirt, shuffled along the sidewalk. He wore brown wing-tip shoes with no socks, emphasizing all the more his fish-white, spindly, hairless legs. And almost as hairless, a wheezing brown dog strained while his master jerked absently upon the leash. Brownie, still lost in thought, turned the corner and swerved, narrowly missing the two and came to a stop. The startled old man struggled to untangle the dog, which had darted between his legs, and muttered; "What in the hell was that?"

"Dat was a Trailmas'r bicycle," Brownie said with some cheer in his voice, but still a little too harshly for the old man. He immediately saw how pathetic the old man appeared and was ashamed of himself. Even more so when the old guy said softly, "Looks like that tire's almost flat."

Somewhat flabbergasted and confused by such undeserved kindness, Brownie saw that the bikes rear tire was indeed very low. He apologized, asked how far to a service station and rode on in a standing position, hunched slightly forward to keep some of the weight off the rear tire. Fifteen minutes later, calves on fire, he rode into the service station. He knew his family would've started eating without him and had no time to deal with the van's tire thing, so, without speaking to the attendant who merely glanced up and kept on pumping gas, he coasted on over to an air and water self-serve machine. Then, when he attached the air-hose thingey, instead of air going in like it should, the remaining air fizzed out of the ancient tire. Taking a closer look at the air machine he read: air: twenty-five cents. "Coin operated air? " he shouted. "How is that possible? Air is everywhere! What planet is this!?" Feeling defeated, enraged and pressed for time, he shoved the Trailmaster into the bushes, then jogged off along the sidewalk. The yard-lights of the taco stand could be seen less than a block away.

Shortly, he sat in one of the booths out of breath, staring at the sign of a fat Mexican, dressed in a colorful serape, a taco in each hand, grinning across at him. I hate that sign... He scanned the rest of the room... a lot of stares coming his way. He turned and looked out the window. There was yet another stare: A Negro wino looking at him through the plate-glass window... He slumped into the Naugahyde even further, too discouraged to fight back: the wino went down with him. Oh my god... What he'd seen in the window was none other than... a reflection of himself. The clock on the wall said: seven o'clock.

He dropped his head onto his palms. It's been a mighty long day. Maggie probably had Julie drive her home... why not call and have her come pick me up? Nahhhh, although she should've waited for me, he argued unreasonably.

The decision to eat, right then, in that place, was a supreme act of the will for a man who, when pushed to his limits in the hunger department, could go from one fast food place to another ordering and canceling for hours. When he was that hungry, somehow it just had to be right. He just couldn't help it: A relentless waterfall of hamburgers, tacos, fried chicken, spaghetti, pickles, ice cream, and french-fries... would spill through his mind. Even the slightest indication that the preparation was below standard (perfectly browned bun, crisp fries, juicy tomatoes... whatever!) would cause him to short-circuit. "This is all wrong," he would think; "I must be in the wrong place; I'll be disappointed here," and off he would go. And don't ever, ever, be rude if you are the person taking his order.

With this haunting him, he waited in line for several minutes; ordered burritos and noted the efficiency of the assembly line... oops... one of the food-handlers skimped on the onions, and half of what she threw at the two masterpieces (he was personally escorting with his eyes), went through the grating below. Resisting the impulse to say something to the food handler, he waited 'til the order was being bagged, "Excuse me, could you have the lady put a few more onions on those?"

The cashier (surely not the owner) said in a loud and freezing tone; "Extra onions cost ten cents."

Embarrassed, leaning over and speaking below his normal range; "Fine... I don't care... I just wanna be able to taste the onions..."

Both burritos were flopped back onto the assembly line like two fish about to be gutted. Cashier lady had her nose up as though these same fish had been dead for days. With utter contempt she grabbed a monstrous handful of onions and slopped them onto one burrito, then repeated the same gesture for the next; carelessly re-rolled, and papered them; walked over and smacked them onto the counter, then smiled with sick self-satisfaction. Big mistake...

And shesh! Smugly standing there in front of her open cash drawer motioning him to move aside with a curt wave of her hand... only added to the list of errors! The next moment, before even realizing what he was doing, Brownie had slammed a burrito onto the change portion of the cash drawer... refried beans flew up to the ceiling and oozed into the register... mixing with quarters, nickels and dimes; "What's a burrito without onions, lady?"

The proud look on the woman's face turned to fiery hatred instantly. Brownie was inflamed even more. She could not believe it! And staring in open mouthed amazement she almost fainted when the other burrito smashed into the bills section, followed by: "You can keep the change, and the beans honey!" A statement that was probably lost amidst pinto beans and green chili sauce on her hat, hair, and shoulders.

The enraged man turned and walked away, with just a hint of the classic black-stride, toward the door. Another man, just entering, coincidentally black and looking almost as shabby, stuck out his hand for a high-five; "Way to go, Blood. Mmmmmm, mmmmm! That was fine. Way... to... go!" The high-five turned into a pulling gesture, such that Brownie found himself sitting in the same booth with the down-and-out, "Blood."

A glass of water (apparently untouched) on Brownie's side of the table was a welcome sight... either way he drank deeply. Feeling taco lady's eyes bearing down on him and realizing that he may have just broken some law or something... this was no time for a chat... he stood up and said; "Excuse me," and went outside, inhaling deeply.

The derelict followed him out the door; "Say, brotha', could you buy me sonthin'? We gots to stick togetha...

Whitey ain't gone give you thangs, even if you be axin' fo dem."

"I'm not your brother," he replied flatly.

The other man looked into his face, real close, white eyes wide open; "You sho' looks like a brotha'."

Brownie stepped back a little and dug into his pants pocket; dropped some change into the guy's hand, turned and left him standing at the door. The derelict shouted out; "You's still my Blood!"

In the taco stand's rest room behind the building, Brown, understandably shabby and unkempt, was determined to tough it out: He hung the shop coat on a hook; peered at a red faced, freckled idiot in what was left of a small mirror; repeatedly splashed water over his face and hair, successfully dislodging clumps of mud and thin layers of junk yard slime. But, too appalled with the surroundings to finish, he left disgusted and returned to the service station where he used the last of his change to air the bike up.

A vending machine labeled snacks, reminded him of his hunger: Insert Quarter Here: He reached around for his wallet, and... What? No wallet? After frisking himself several times he at last remembered the shop coat was still in the john at the taco stand. The trip back took only seconds on the Trailmaster, but too late... the wallet was gone, and so was the shop coat. Oblivious to Taco Lady, he rode around by the front plate-glass window in full view, waved, made a stupid face, and pedaled furiously back to the van punishing himself all the way for being so... so stupid and stubborn. How could things get any worse? He called Julie and Maggie: still no answer. Then, seconds before committing suicide, the gloom lifted... a Visa card! Tossed there after gassing up earlier in the day... just lying in the ashtray. Suddenly, he felt like a person again.

Hauling the van's spare tire back to the station (on the handlebars) was hard work. "Eight bucks," said the attendant when the job was done. But when Brownie pulled the Visa from his shirt pocket, the attendant took it and said; "Could I see some identification? Something to verify the signature?"

In the right circumstance a brown face can go white, and Brownie's did. With great control he tried to explain his situation. Station Man ultimately gave up and allowed the "derelict" to sign the slip, knowing that he would sleep better without the guilt of having turned the needy away from his door, and reasoning that if the man had a tire he surely had a car to put it on. The clock on the wall said, ten-thirty.

At twelve-twenty, Brownie pulled up to Carlos's house; unhitched the trailer at the curb, and drove off. Junk is junk... even if it's not the same junk, he reasoned with some satisfaction of revenge.

After pigging-out at a late night, fast food joint (without any complaints, or imposed standards of any kind whatsoever... from either side), he belched and waddled across the parking lot to the van. Grateful that whoever had his wallet had only about twenty bucks, some photos and his driver's license. Maggie wouldn't have to be told. The clock said; one-fifteen.

Maggie!

He tried phoning her one more time.

To his surprise she answered, "Well, where have you been Mister Carphone?"

"Where have I been?" was what he said, but what was

in his heart was; "Why don't you just ask me if I'm okay?" Maggie was not one to turn to for sympathy. She was the child who had walked into a neighbor's house one day and said calmly; "There's a kid fell out of the tree. I think he's dead... and I think he's yours."

With that in mind, he blurted; "I've called you and Julie all night."

"We thought Cooper swallowed the nipple off his bippy. We've been at the hospital for a stomach pumping half the night. We left a note on the door..."

"Sheeesh... is he alright?"

"Yeah... Julie just called. She found the nipple... behind the couch."

There was still one day left of his three-day weekend. To go home was not really necessary, was it? "I'll be home in a few minutes."

Out of consideration for Maggie he washed the remaining mud off in the kitchen instead of using the shower next to their bedroom; slipped as silently as possible into bed (resisting a strong desire to spoon with her) and within seconds was snoring like a chain saw.

—◇—

- Chapter Six -

The next morning (later than usual) Brown walked into the kitchen in just his undershirt, feeling a bit frisky; Maggie was not impressed; "Carlos called, wants you to call him."

Coffee cup in hand he dialed him up; "Carlos; Brownie."

"Man you've got some 'splainin' to do. Why would you trade my junk for all that other junk? And why is the Trailmas'r settin' up there like a cherry on top?"

"I wouldn't know, I left that trailer empty except for the Trailmaster; it must be spawning, Carlos."

Carlos gave that some thought. "Those ain't the kinda' eggs the Trailmaster would lay, man."

Brownie smiled. He had to play this out; "What kind would it lay?"

"Shit! I don't know... Bbs... or ball-bearin's..."

"Well maybe it's just making a nest, keep your eyes peeled, she could start shootin' em out any minute."

Both men laughed.

"Wanna tell me what really happened?"

"Not really, maybe later. It's a longer story than I care to get into... if you don't mind. I'll tell you at the Barbecue. In the meantime you're settin' at net zero. Nothing lost, nothing gained."

—◇—

The hot shower felt so good. He watched himself shave in the mirror, rubbing the steam off the mirror occasionally. He could see Maggie too. She was making up the bed. He called out to her; "Maggie do I look a little darker today?"

"Why? Did ya get some sun yesterday?"

"Probably... a little bit; it's hard to say."

"You're pretty brown anyway," she said, and moved on.

Brown looked again; *definitely darker.*

He had awakened that morning, determined to visit his mother in the country. "Sure you don't wanna go?" he asked; "Pretty day... it'd be a nice drive."

Once the van was on the road (complete with wash-job and spare tire), he was glad Maggie'd refused. He'd wanted to be alone, but then, just before leaving the more developed part of town, where sidewalks gave way to dirt paths and ditches, he spotted a teen hitchhiker. Maybe what prompted him to pull over was the skate-board the kid was carrying; plus, the sidewalks were long-gone and at least this kid was trying to get somewhere on his own.

He shuffled magazines, coffee cup, and the McDonald's breakfast sandwich bags off the front seat and into the back of the van. The kid hurried up to the door. Without even a hesitation, packed himself in, dropping the skateboard between his legs and shrugging a small backpack off one shoulder onto his lap. Instantly William got hit with a mixed smell of patchouli oil, and a twinge of regret. Their eyes met. He saw short, pageboy hair, a pretty smile, pierced nose... with a studded blue stone... and? Heck! This wasn't a boy, but a girl and not as young as he'd thought; *About eighteen years old*, he guessed

They rode in silence for a few minutes. "Where ya headed?"

"Bear Mountain hot-springs, I've got a camp up there."

Which seemed unlikely to William, since for one thing she was female, and likely to be accosted by all the drunks and filth up there; "It's really just a place in the woods," she clarified, "but I call it my camp. I go up there to clear my head whenever I can."

William visualized the girl sitting on a log smoking something that definitely wouldn't clear her head, but said; "I'm not going that far, but I'll get you part of the way,"

"Okay, thanks." A simple answer.

"What's your name?"

"Feather... " she said proudly.

William's face warmed; truly embarrassed for the girl. Her name was trite; to the extreme, like Twinkle, Ace, or Candy. He wasn't sure he'd even be able to use it. *Hold on a second, he thought; I can see it. Light and easy; freely blown around by any wind... soft, fluffy, vulnerable...* but he said; "How did you get that label?"

"It's not a label. It's the name I use... for now. But it'll change someday. Why do you say label?"

"Too long a story... What's with the skate board?"

"It helps me get rides. Is that smart, dumb... what?"

"Pretty smart for a feather," then, realizing what an effect the skateboard had on him, he added; "It worked this time."

And then she volunteered: "D'you like the Saturday market," and without waiting for his answer; "It's cool. So many spiritual people there."

The misty look that came into her eyes did not go unnoticed.

"Mind if I ask you a question? Why would a punker be hangin' out with hippies? You dress like a skater-punker type, but hang out where the hippies do. I didn't know there was an overlap with those two groups."

"Well, skater and hippy really *are* labels... " Her lips compressed momentarily, and then; "Don't forget mall rat; I used to be one of them too... "

"Yeah?"

"Sure. I've been living on the street since I was fourteen. I'm going to school at Lake Community now," her voice trailed off with each sentence into almost a pained whisper. William had to lean over toward her to catch the end of each statement. He softened each time she spoke, and found himself sincerely interested in this child; thought of his own daughter for a second, and was struck with the importance of having one's own children in this world in order to relate to others.

The highway continued its winding course up a gradual incline into the mountains.

"Tell me why you use, Feather, for your name,"

"For spiritual reasons," she responded with enthusiasm.

"Yeah?"

"Un huh," she sat up straighter and leaned forward in her seat. Something about her facial expression indicated that she was losing touch with the scenery passing by: "I'm on a ride for the stars... to infinity. The heavy stays on the bottom, the lighter floats to the top. My objective is to be light, which, is not easy," she paused to let this sink in, then; "Our own standards, like honesty and such? Determine whether or not we get to drop the weight," her voice had become much stronger. "But you can only go so far with your own standards, 'cause the added weight is screwed on under the skin, embedded in the heart and mind. Everybody is on a path, but most of 'em don't realize that. It's vertical to the earth and funnel shaped; and the closer to the top the brighter the light... brighter and brighter; refinement and more refinement; up that cone... honesty gets you a long way; humility takes you from there. You know... being willing to learn."

Hands stretching out wide in front of her, she continued; "The surrounding space is wide and the choices are many at first, but less and less as you progress... upward and upward; 'cause the cone is narrowing see? You've got free will, but there's just fewer choices where perfection is concerned. Perfection is perfection–facts are facts."

Looking out at the beauty of several tall, rugged fir trees leaning out across the blue river paralleling the highway, William had to agree, yet was having a little trouble keeping up, ran his hand across his forehead and scalp; *I thought all these kids were earth worshippers. Where is she going with all this God stuff? Is she talking about a particular God?* Then, as if she knew his thoughts, she said: "And it really doesn't matter what you call God at this point. Why should we know his name, when we don't even know our own... yet." William's hands tightened visibly on the steering wheel. She had his attention again.

She looked over at him for emphasis and continued with hardly a pause: "In this cone there are currents of ego to ride around in forever; swirling, and whirling with dizzying revelations... all about yourself. But we can't afford to get hung up; that's a trap. You may want to visualize infinity rather than the cone, but try to wait; infinity is beyond the cone, and since you are finite, first things first." She took a deep breath, eyes narrowed and looked at him full in the face as if to say, "Are you gettin' all this?" William smiled at her, leaving no doubt that he was, but also figured she must be parroting something she'd heard somewhere else.

She took up where they'd left off: "So, forget infinity, stay in the cone. At the top is that tiny, tiniest pinpoint of an opening, where light, brighter than any laser, is blasting through–frying anything that is not made up of light also. And when you go through that speck of an opening you won't have to visualize anything! Some people tend to visualize a sphere, but spheres are for going round and round, like in circles," she laughed... twirled her index finger; made a moronic face... "Getting nowhere."

"The cone exists whether we like it or not. It's real; it's there, declaring a destination... and a process. A process where we get sifted, and strained 'til we are small enough, and bright enough, to fit through that opening. Maybe, instead of a cone, it would help to picture a dunce cap... for now."

This, she hadn't intended to be funny or cynical in any way, but William cracked up. She caught his meaning and laughed with him; "I didn't mean... like that..."

The laughter trailed off. "I know you didn't..." and, for a moment while both enjoyed a glimpse of majestic snow-capped mountains off in the distance, William reflected. He had never entertained these matters in this light before, especially with such graphic models. The words were different, but the message was almost the same as that his mother might have used, except his mom would've said there was one little piece missing, "What about love?" he asked, breaking the silence.

The simplicity of her answer stunned him; "Love is the only thing with power over gravity. With love you can float right off..." she moved her hand up and out, like a feather drifting away.

William noticed with regret that his destination was not far up ahead; "Well, Feather this has been a good talk..."

"Sure... I loved it," she astutely read his body language and began gathering up her gear; rummaged around in her back-pack and dug out a piece of paper. "Here ya go..." she held it out to him.

"What's this?"

"It's a little poem... you can read it later."

The lane to his mother's house loomed up ahead. He tossed the paper onto the dashboard; "Well, it's still a long way, but at least I got you part of the way. I wish I could take you all the way..." he added, very tempted to do just that.

But was relieved when she said; "No, that's okay, I don't mind. I've got all week-end."

She tumbled out of the van and walked up past a row of mailboxes; striking pretty much the same hitch-hiking pose, first seen many miles back. She yelled something as he started to drive off. He stopped, hung his head out the window; "What was that?"

"I wish I could take you all the way too..."

He pondered the hidden meaning of her words, dodging familiar potholes in the graveled lane leading down to his mother's house. The urge to go back, to find out how he could get in touch another time, was simply too powerful even though his mother stood in her yard with her hands up.

"Myron," she exclaimed lovingly, "You came. Praise God!"

He wheeled into the driveway and backed out, telling his mother over his shoulder; "I'll be right back..." and was gone without further explanation.

When he reached the highway, the girl was walking slowly along the shoulder, contentedly. The smell of spruce, hemlock and sweet-cedar filled the van. The sun sparkled in dappled patterns all around. He honked the horn gently. Feather looked back at him.

—◇—

Blueberry fields and filbert orchards, flourishing in fertile deposits of river loam were now replaced by enormous boulders and craggy outcroppings as the valley narrowed. Comfortable silence absorbed them both, apparently in their own thought worlds, allowing a love for trees, rocks and rushing streams to wash through them.

Somewhere along the way, Feather had asked his name; he had replied; "Myron," without thinking, which, in turn, caused him to think about his mother; *Dumb move to leave her standing in the yard like that. No signal this deep in the hills for the car-phone either.* He knew that...

In the back of his mind he also knew that one of the reasons he wanted to visit his mother (other than the usual obligatory visit) was to ask her about his skin. She'd had a colorful life, that was no secret, and the thought of her having had intercourse with a black man wasn't particularly disturbing... but in the Deep South? Forty-five years ago? Not likely.

A very rough life, would better describe the life his mother had had, including several marriages and a severe long-term bout with alcohol. However, for the last fifteen years or so, her life had been very peaceful. She was a widow now, and religious.

The turn-off sign for Bear Mountain Reservoir flashed by. There was no sign for the hot springs, probably because it was not a state park, but had been upgraded by the Forest Service with port-a-potties, and a trail developed enough to get emergency equipment in and out. A sizable thermal spring emerging out of the ground supplied three pools; each one twenty-five feet or so in diameter; terracing down the hill in a beautiful setting of ancient fir and cedar trees; probably hand-dug over eons, by Indians, mountain-men, loggers, and hippies.

"Come see my camp," Feather invited, when they pulled off onto the crude, graveled parking area.

Such a beautiful day, how could he resist? A few yards along the main trail to the springs, she veered off into the deep woods. Large ferns, vine maples, rhododendrons, and a mossy carpet made up most of the undergrowth beneath the branches of stately trees. There were many rotting, moss-laden logs to crawl over, and when needed, some of the logs angling up the hillside fifty feet or more were used like balance beams as part of the "secret trail" up the mountain. Feather walked at a slow pace so that her guest (who carried a skateboard) could keep up... she paused at times, beaming like a proud homeowner at a house warming.

It was tacitly understood that they should be quiet, in order not to give away the "camp's" location. That was just fine with Myron, who enjoyed listening to the sounds of the forest. A raven's guttural caw could be heard occasionally, a woodpecker tapped a tree somewhere, and he even saw the ugly face of a large Pileated Woodpecker just as it glided silently off a nearby tree trunk.

Fifteen minutes of hiking up the steep mountainside

and they were on a knoll in the middle of a small clearing. Feather turned around with both hands out like an airplane. "This is it..." she sighed and sat down with a thump... cross-legged.

"Beautiful... " Brownie said between gulps of air... looking for a log to sit on.

"I don't come up here in the winter very much, the rain is pretty yucky, but in the fall the fires are great. I should do a cold-camp, but the fires are part of why I come, ya know?" After saying this, she stood up, tossed her backpack aside, and heading for some bushes said, "Excuse me..."

"Potty time," Myron thought. His breath was coming back. He looked around: Other than a fire-pit, and a few sticks roped to a tree in lean-to fashion, there wasn't much of a camp. Still, it was beautiful. Everywhere he looked there was something worth seeing. Innocent little lady-slippers grew close to the ground pushing through decaying Vine Maple leaves: mushrooms peeked from under damp logs; Huckleberry bushes with delicate light green leaves, grew out of old stumps, their small, pink-red berries provided an unnecessary elegance.

Scanning the forest gradually, taken in by each vignette of natural wonder, Myron was suddenly shocked! The scene before him was such a blow that he almost shouted out! Earth's ultimate beauty with all its terror ran through his hungry soul. His eyes had collided with nature's ultimate. His blood raced, and his skin tingled. A young woman with a voluptuous body stood on a log just across from him, entirely naked: Feather!

Here was beauty. Waiting. Not sultry and steaming, but cool and tranquil. Not necessarily innocent, cunning, or mysterious, but open... a creature on display, inviting interpretation. Brownie struggled to ease his mind into acceptance. She was revealing her body without fear. Was she offering an opportunity for exploration and discovery of a world he fantasized all too often about? How could she look upon raging fire with such coolness? The flame of course was his own, and certainly not disguised. He held in check the urge to rush into this world she reigned, or loitered unconcerned in, as an offspring of royalty who as yet didn't know the extent of her fortune... and the inherent power that came with it!

He stood still, with veiled eyes trying not to reveal his thoughts. How could he believe that this delicate statue was approachable? He was there before her, yet she was not detached or reserved in the least... she smiled. She could tell...

Slender legs transferred precious weight from one foot to the other, communicating grace. Such fragile arms, yet strong enough to throw him down the mountain; so weak that he could have pinned both arms to the ground with one hand; yet she had the power. Controlled him utterly.

She continued standing while his eyes roamed her body freely: perfect breasts crowned with pink; a stomach shaped with rolling gentle muscles; hips transitioning from girlish to full-blown woman. But he couldn't look fully at other areas. Not yet.

She simply stood there, wordless and he would prefer that she not speak... for years... not until he could prepare himself to hear what would surely be words tainted by her own life's experiences. But wait... had she not already spoken? He'd heard the lilt of overconfidence, the detectable false enthusiasm attempting to disguise her disappointments in life. The woman standing before him was the same little girl whose voice trembled and faded in the van, yet he couldn't let go of the desire to hear that same instrument play a tune just for him.

But was he really prepared to hear that? No. But wasn't it okay to bathe in the essence of womankind? No... certainly not... because the spell had collapsed like a house of cards with a breath of air.. His thoughts about her nakedness, and perhaps certain impressions not entirely defined, had flashed through in the space of time it had taken her to stand onto the log, shift her weight once and say; "Let's go to the springs, Myron."

Had he been a poet, he may have been more in touch with what coursed through his soul. He might've said: "Immerse me forever in what I know to be more than a dream. My soul roars out; this creation of me cries out for me; for my affectionate attention and mine alone. This cool exterior demands that I kindle a passionate fire fanned by the wind of my words through a flute of fine gold into a flame of purest oranges and reds... until tears of recognition that I have made her pour freely from her eyes." But Myron was no poet; he was the son of a loose woman and an unknown black man in Georgia... unbound on the planet without a name... and he could not even express that.

And Feather was just a child-woman. He turned his eyes away and said; "No thanks, I should get on back..."

"Oh, Come on, it's just down there;" she said, pointing down the mountainside in a different direction than the one they had just come from.

"Can't do it. I need to go..." (He hadn't told her about leaving his mother standing in the yard. Nor had he told her that to be naked in front of strangers... especially her... would be totally embarrassing) he added; "It's been great though."

"Well, you can at least walk out by the spring trail."

He agreed to that without saying so when he stood from the log he'd been on for about a year. Feather led the way. Her buttocks bouncing like delightful water-balloons. There were of course tiny imperfections; somehow comforting to Brownie, knowing he had not missed heaven after all. And strangely enough, he now felt nothing sexual... not in the least. *Clothing creates a mystery and a mood*, he decided.

When Feather first invited him he imagined the scene would be pretty much the same as it had been twenty years previous, but the place had matured even more and was lovelier than ever. Certainly hadn't deteriorated or worsened in any way. There were differences in the bathers, though subtle ones... a different overall mood, or lacking in a certain spirit of authenticity... he couldn't quite formulate what he was feeling. Maybe he was merely experiencing a form of culture shock. After all, back in those days he had been a much younger man.

Perhaps the difference was in himself, a rigidity that had set in with the responsibilities of life. Even so, at this point his take was that these were pseudo-hippies without an idea of the mores and goals of the hippy world he had dabbled in. This was no longer a movement, it was something else... a catch-all, or a holding basin for the overflow of his own generation's failures... Which would explain the undercurrent of sadness he felt. And his feeling of slight disdain might actually be frustration, knowing that stagnation was eminent. Certainly they were not aptly named.

The smell of patchouli oil reeked everywhere. In one section of the pool it appeared (he wasn't sure) that a certain couple were being just a little too "affectionate." But if so, no one seemed to care. He began to think of words: *lawless, primitive, immoral... pagan*. Then, out of the blue, *fatherless children.*

Feather was already in the springs. She'd told him the waters were healing. A shared belief apparently, by the way some of the bathers reverently splashed and poured it onto their heads, faces and breasts. A handmade sign tacked onto a tree trunk admonished all: This Is Not A Bathtub.

Further on down, past the final pool, was a different story. There, people were slathering grayish mud or clay they'd dug from the side of the hill onto their bodies and faces; some were apparently in the rinsing stage... other's were just sitting along the edge of the creek, lined up like so many tar-babies, allowing the stuff to dry.

Myron took it all in. Everyone here used the roads, the stores, and the forests; enjoyed the security of the nation's military; paid no taxes; by and large just riding on the efforts of others... He stepped over closer to the pool and said in a soft, sad voice; "Feather, I'm leaving. Bye."

"Thanks again for the ride, Myron."

He walked quickly down the trail, trying not to imagine his own daughter in that world.

An older couple pulled in beside him just as he was about to get in the van; "Been up to the hot-springs, ain't ya?"

Brownie answered in the affirmative.

"You don't look like you belong there..." said the woman on the passenger side.

Brownie looked down at his shorts and blue golf shirt... "Are you kidding?" tossed a thumb over his shoulder and scoffed; "You wouldn't catch me dead in that place."

The man leaned over from the steering wheel, and said, "Why not? We're no better'n they are. We're all psychos."

"Oh shut up, Stan...." Said the woman, who was apparently his wife.

But Stan ignored her; "Life's a big put-on, or should I say a big take-off? Everybody wants to get nekked, or have someone else get 'em there..."

The wife pushed her husband back to his side, irritated, and said; "Aww hell! Stan, even the simple minded know to wear clothes."

Stan raised up from his somewhat cowered position to respond but was way-laid when she continued; "Oh sure, occasionally some Looney-tune will be running down the street naked as a jay-bird, but it's known by all, that the guy's gone bonkers. He'd get hauled away with the big net soon enough."

"All's I'm sayin' is, if we were honest, most of us would admit it... we'd like to be nekked... if it wuz allowed."

"And I guess you would like to do your loggin' naked..."

Brownie felt the homey acceptance of these simple folks. They probably would've discussed this, or anything else, with anyone who cared to listen.

The old man answered; "I never thought about it... I might even try it... I work out in the woods, who'd give a shit?"

"You'd be crazy..." his wife barely inserted as Stan went on without a break; "Not those businessmen wearing their three piece suits. Maybe they ought'a break outta the mold a little. Oh, there ain't no insanity there... far from it," he quipped in a singsong voice and ended with a sniff and a wag of his head.

(Brownie was all ears and Stan knew it) "No suits, no confusion... just nekked guys and ties. What's so good about wearin' a different tie ever day? Three button coat this year, two button next year." He finished with a spit out the window; "Very boring."

A true logger; thought Brownie, who, by then had squatted down with both hands in the passenger window.

"You jest want'a see the women naked..." said the stalwart wife who, Brownie surmised, was really in great shape for the shape she was in.

Stan went on; "Hells-bells, Trudy, I don't give a damn about seein' 'em nekked, in fact it's more fun seein' em with their clothes on."

Brownie added that he agreed with that... but then maybe not...

Stan looked pleased to have an ally and said; "I just wish they'd come clean with it. It's the man's got the problems... like the thing called a cleavage; ain't a cleavage just inviting a man to get a little crazy? Who do women think they are? What if a man wants to stay sane for a few minutes longer, should some little cutie be allowed to make him want to get nekked?" Brownie detected that Stan's pause meant he was actually hoping for an answer to this one...

But, Trudy wasn't in the mood; "Whyn't you just go on and shoot your mouth off, you won't let nobody git a word in edgewise."

So, he turned to Brownie again: "Then there's the mirrors. How many times a day do you look into one for a reality check?" Brownie knew about the mirror thing pretty well, but knew he didn't need to respond...

especially since he couldn't anyway. "Do you go; 'Hello, am I zipped up, nekked, or whut?' Heck no, but women do. They use their rear-view mirrors, or those tiny, compact ones that show little more than their eyes, or lips, because they don't wanna see what elst they've done, (or are about to do) to the male population. No mam! Men don't enjoy undressing women with their eyes; it gets very tiring after eight or ten hours. Keep your clothes on... or give us a break... and come out nekked to start with!"

Brownie could see Stan had given this plenty of thought. But when Trudy responded he was surprised that she had too; "People ain't supposed to get naked in public. Even in our sleep we're told by our dreams it ain't right: Like when you discover you're naked in public with no place to hide, and you're scared? That's the fear of people finding out that you're really nuts for bein' naked in the first place."

Brownie was quite sure she'd misinterpreted that, but he and Stan waited quietly while she finished up.

"I tell you there's plenty of times you'd better hope a naked person gets locked up: First and foremost, anyone who's naked and carrying a gun... or a knife... or a weapon of any kind, and (she raised a gnarly finger) I would add; blunt instruments!" Brownie laughed, but when she looked questioningly at him, was fairly certain she'd not meant blunt instrument in the way he'd taken it.

She looked at him as if to say, "Now don't you start..." and continued; "If you saw a farmer plowing a field with only tennis shoes and a T-shirt, at least you'd notify his wife... that is, if you didn't call the sheriff." Her eyes studied the old car's faded headliner for a second and then held one hand up... starting with the pinky... counted one finger at a time: "A gardener cutting blackberries wearing only leather gloves is definitely gonna snag something" (this time she looked slyly at Brownie, completely upsetting his previous theory); "A hunter with just a red hat's probably likely to shoot something other than a live animal; A naked mill-worker in steel-toed shoes should've used the steel in his hard-hat some time back; A cook in a apron only... Awwww shoot! I don't know about you, but it's pretty obvious to me when someone's out of it..." and she was out of fingers.

A light went on in Brownie's head and he slapped the door; "And that's the naked truth!" All three laughed. Stan put the still idling car in gear and rolled off. Brownie went to see his mother.

—◇—

- Chapter Seven -

Myron pulled into the driveway and exhaled a sigh, his mother was pretty easy going these days, probably no big deal; he'd only been gone a few hours.

As expected, she was glad to see him and curious about what was up. He tried to explain, but some things you just don't talk to your mother about; "I had to take her all the way," he said in conclusion.

They sat on the porch in silence for a few minutes, with barely a separation between two old-fashioned wooden chairs. Myron observed the rust-eaten, yellow steel and aluminum awning overhead. "Are you comfortable here in this trailer, Mother?" (He'd always called her that).

"I'm comfortable. This is where Edward left me, and I guess this is where I'll stay. I wouldn't want to live in town even if I had the money. I don't mind looking out at people but it grieves me to see too much foolishness. I may be poor, but I'd rather stay here than put up with that.

The trailer was roomy and the property was adjacent to neighboring houses. "I wish I could do more for you..." he confessed, knowing that he would have been more concerned if she didn't have her friends and her church-life. Yeah, she was as content as the chickens that were pecking and scratching around in her yard.

"What can you give me that I need, but your love, Son?"

He looked around and had to agree. Apple trees, vegetable garden, what else could she want? A bowl of apples was on a small stand beside her. She picked one up and produced a paring knife; "I'm making a pie for you to take home to Maggie. Good... her hands were busy... she'd always had busy hands.

He'd seen her peel apples lots of times; "How'd you learn to peel an apple like that? I've never been able to do it."

"It's passed on through the generations, guess you missed the boat." She tilted the straw-bottomed chair against the wall. The peeling got longer and longer until, without even looking up, she plopped the chair forward with a solid thump, tossed the coil over the railing to a big Rhode Island Red hen who ran over and grabbed it, held its head up high to keep the springing thing off the ground, and ran away spraddle-legged to keep from steppin' on it, while two others took out after her. Her big thighs reminded Myron of Sunday dinner.

Aware that he was watching every move, she took another apple and leaned the chair back again; "You know if Cooper was here, I wouldn't have done that."

"Why not?"

"I'd give the peeling to him. I've given a lot of thought to apples, and the way I see it, apples are a lot like people. No apple anywhere on earth should be called apple unless it can live up to the name. The word itself creates an imagery..." she held up the next specimen and continued; "...cool, crisp and juicy. I visualize a red one, but there's lots of colors. They've all got skins; some tough ones, some not so, but the skin is for protecting something inside. It's needed."

Myron could just imagine little Cooper watching his great-grandma...

"Seems like the skin is a big deal. Hospital nurseries remind me of a produce-stand with row after row of fresh, shiny apples. 'Cept those are babies, so rubbery and silky smooth you just can't keep your hands off 'em. I guess that's why they keep them behind the glass. Beauty may be only skin-deep, but pretty skin is always an invitation. In the case of babies, beauty goes a lot deeper than the skin. They have a fresh little soul... That's only fair too... everybody starting out with pretty skin and with something pretty to protect inside."

"Here." She tossed him an apple, "Eat," and sort of grunted with tiredness as she started to peel again.

"This chair has me, not because the work is done, but because I can't go no more, not like I used to. You kids are long gone, and now your kids're shooting up around your legs like weeds in a turnip patch. Not one of them would sit five minutes in this chair. They got things to do. I hope so, but if you'd bring the little things up here I might get to peel them an apple or two."

This was not an unfamiliar diatribe. She usually managed to get this in, one way or another, every time he visited. She was right; "Hard to get everybody to stand still long enough... to catch 'em, Mother," was his lame reply.

"How else can I teach them about seeds being the future of all apples? About the sweetness of life surrounding those seeds; how blessed they are to have strength in their flesh; how there'll come a time when the seeds are more important than a smooth complexion. Never mind the shriveled up skin..."

Myron rolled his eyes. "Man! She should've been a preacher."

"Why... look at you, Myron! I'm not getting senile! It's a fact of life that apples grow on trees. Funny... we know apples grow on trees, but the apples don't.

"At their age all they can do is take what comes with

their side of the tree. Some will get the sunny side, some won't. If they're not picked, they'll fall off anyway. There's good apples and bad apples. Bad apples don't make it to market. And some of the good ones that do make it? Turn out bad from getting pinched and tossed around too much. You'll have to make up your own mind whether that's luck or providence."

She snorted in what he hoped was the conclusion. But this was the Baptist philosopher in full swing. She plopped another peeling out across the yard; grabbed another apple (by now he knew the drill), and fixed him with her gaze in accusation; "Whether they like it or not, at some point it'll be time to stop being an apple and start being a tree... those seeds will start doing a waltz in slow motion on a dirt dance floor to a tune heard by every living thing; moisture and soil will break their shells down so little shoots can emerge; gravity will tug at their roots... and that hot sun *will* pull at their branches."

Myron was getting fidgety.

"I know wild trees make for sour apples; poor soil makes for stunted trees; even in the best of weather. And apples, like the souls of men, can grow wild surrounded by thorns and weeds."

More fidgeting. She tossed him another apple; "Eat." A coiled peeling dangled in his face, she watched his eyes go up and down with the springing, and then she said; "So, it's important where you're planted, but even so, you just gotta' make do. That dance has to go on. Those leaves are gonna' have to wave and shimmer in the wind... n' be strong n' do good in spite of what may come."

Whew!

"Now..." squinting up into the sky, her face changing to wrinkled soft, she paused for a moment, "...looking into innocent eyes, it's easy to see beautiful pink blossoms giving off a promise, a fragrance for whoever... or nobody... eyes so full of spirit, they're saying to heck with the 'if onlys'. If only the sun shines; if only the rains come; if only the farmer prunes... Nope. I Just see a sweet promise wafting up to the heavens. There's no controlling of circumstance or the forces of nature. But I wouldn't tell them about that... not yet"

Then her face hardened a little. Myron couldn't help himself, grabbed another apple and so did his mother; "...instead, this would be the time for me to cheer on that spark in those perky eyes... of strength and determination... help fan it into a flame.

"Just like a bee on a blossom, I'm drawn to the eyes of these little ones. I can tell without peeling, which ones have integrity right down to the seeds... which ones will remember those times by their granny's chair."

She stood up with the last apple-coil and ripped it across the yard; barely missed the rooster; "Take that you ol' rascal!" She turned to face him, holding out her hands; "These gnarly roots I call hands will release their winding, twisting grip from the dirt and from those little apples before too long. I wish I had known it lots sooner..."

Myron stood up too, reached out and gave the old lady a hug. Picked up the bowl of peeled apples and opened the screen door for her; "Can I ask you a question Mother?"

"When have you ever stopped asking questions," she said, with good-humored cynicism.

"Why did you ever call me Myron?!"

"Because it was pretty."

"That's it?"

"Yep."

And that's where they left it.

They sat around the trailer for another couple of hours joking and making small talk. Then, with pie in hand, William (M., for Pretty) Brownie-Brown, said good night to Mrs. Florence Elaine Beardsley-Brown-Conklin-Carson-Wheaton, and drove down the mountain in the last light of a late summer day. For some reason he felt a little lighter, if not in skin, at least in heart. His mother, up in the foothills, sat on her porch, watching the evening star to come over the trees. Brownie thought of apples.

—◇—

Maggie met Brown at the door; "The police are looking for you."

No, "Hello, how are you?" No, "Kiss my rear!" Nothing but the facts.

But after a statement like that, facts are just what he wanted: Questions popped out in rapid succession followed by Maggie's answers: Two detectives had just left, twenty-five or thirty minutes ago; She had been gone from the house most of the day too. They were very hush-hush, asking her questions but answering none of hers. She was worried to death.

The only thing she knew for sure was that they wanted to know where Brown was, and if she knew Carl Benson. She'd given them Carl's phone number and address; Brown's mom had told them he'd left, "just a little bit ago;" The detectives decided to go over to Carl's instead of waiting for Brown... but he should stay put if he returned before they came back.

Brown started to call Carlos, but Maggie had already

done so and found that Carlos was not home but had spoken with his wife; he was fishing up on the Alice River. Oh my God... had he drowned? Brownie tried to make sense of it all but couldn't and said, "I think I'd better leave."

Maggie looked at him in disbelief.

Brownie rolled his eyes, "I can find out all I need to know about Carlos without help from the cops, and there are ways of finding out what they want without turning myself in..."

"That's stupid Brown. You haven't done anything... or have you?!" This question of Maggie's arose from twenty-five years worth of close calls and near misses, all connected with Brown's personality and character traits. Some people cringed when they saw him coming, others loved him.

Brown ignored the question; rushed around the house, changing clothes, gathering up a few toiletries, underwear, and... sure! He could sleep in the van! So, a sleeping bag; an alarm clock; a flash-light; "Maggie don't we have a Coleman lantern around here somewhere?"

Maggie stood in the kitchen doorway... earplugs in the palm of one hand, clutching his favorite pillow with the other, pushed them toward him, and with a wry smile on her lips, said; "What about something to read?"

The doorbell rang.

He was arrested on suspicion of murder. Carl was dead? No answer. He had a right to know, didn't he??? Yeah, but so far they hadn't identified the body for sure... they were pretty certain Brownie had murdered someone though, because they had a warrant for suspicion of murder with his name on it. Oh, and he had other rights... the right to remain silent, get a lawyer; Yeah-yeah-yeah... he knew the drill. Maggie stood in silence as they handcuffed him, and just before they hauled him away she said; "Do you want me to come see you, Brown?"

Now, why did she have to ask? Once when he had almost electrocuted himself trying to make a home repair, the medics were putting him into an ambulance with oxygen mask, machines, and tubes hanging all over him, and she'd said; "The kids and I may be down to see you later." Like he was going away to camp or something. This time he had nothing covering his mouth; "Hell, woman, I'm going to jail for murder! Cook me a cake with a file in it or something."

—◇—

William M. Brown was booked into Hotel Hell. The photograph with his name and number underneath meant that he might become a permanent resident... and just a number.

Ultimately he sat in his cell reflecting on all that had happened: The police had found his wallet beside a homicide victim... discovered that afternoon behind the Taco Stand. The body had been behind a haul box under random pieces of tar paper, tossed from the roof of the building by an early morning roofing crew. One of the workers had found it while recovering a hammer he'd accidentally dropped there. The dumpster was gone now... but could be found if needed... without certain contents.

The victim, stabbed to death, was a black man clutching a shop coat with Carl Benson embroidered over the pocket. W.M. Brown's wallet was in one of the coat's pockets. It was entirely reasonable to suspect that Mister Brown had struggled with the man, stabbed him, panicked, and fled the scene.

After going to Brownie's, they had gone over to Carl's, who wasn't home but his wife was. Violet thought Carl was up on the Alice River... fishing. Of course she panicked anyway. Could she come identify the body? She went with the police. Recognized the shop-coat as Carl's– more tears–but was relieved when the body was not her husband's. Carlos was still being sought for questioning.

In the interrogation room with his lawyer (a public defender), Brownie had answered all the questions as truthfully as possible. Part of his story sounded plausible. Even so, he seemed extremely unstable. The detectives were checking his story. He had not been allowed to post bail.

Their initial questions to the Taco Lady had been part of their reason to charge Brownie in the first place; "He beaned me."

"Hit you?"

"No, no... he beaned my cash drawer."

"Hit it, then."

"No! He smashed the drawer with a fully-loaded bean burrito!"

"Was he trying to rob you?"

"What, with a burrito? He was just insane; I don't know why he did it... You should have seen the hate in his eyes! You can't keep 'em out neither, not if they've got the money to buy somethin'."

Yes, he had paid her... from a tattered wallet. "This wallet...?" Not sure. Maybe

"Before or after he beaned you?"

"Before... I always make 'em pay before."

"What else?"

He had been one of the dirtiest, worst dressed bums she'd ever had in there. She remembered the dead man as the very one he had been with, and argued with, outside the door. Yes sir! She had watched them very closely. He went around to the alley and the other man followed within seconds afterwards. The clincher for the Taco Lady was when the Mean One came back around the corner on a bike and waved at her. She just knew he was up to something. And... Oh yeah... she'd heard the other one shout; "You'd spill my blood?" while they were still out front. And then, just think... he'd had the nerve to make an ugly face at her after killing that man!

Then, looking as though she was the smartest person ever to run a Taco Stand, she produced her masterpiece... proof! She had saved the water glass Brownie had used, foolishly reasoning at the time that the police would call-out the FBI to track down the man who had dared trash her cash.

To Taco Lady's smug satisfaction, the detectives had carefully placed the water glass in a bag. There would be no reason to save it though. Brownie had already admitted he'd been there.

The station attendant remembered that all Brownie had for money was a Visa and no identification. But he had sensed a lot of tension there, and against his better judgment had given in and accepted the card... What had the Bicycle Man done?

Later that night, Brownie was brought back to Interrogation, given one more chance to confess, and then, since he was still unable to prove his whereabouts at the time of the death (which was at approximately ten P.M.), he was held for further questioning. They were still uncertain as to the motive, probably an argument over money and for some unknown reason the suspect had been forced to leave suddenly... without his wallet... on a bicycle.

Brownie sat on the barren mattress until late in the night thinking; *Carlos this is all your fault.* Outside it was foggy and drizzling rain. The damp cold penetrated his clothes.

The next morning a small article appeared in the newspaper. Nobody read it.

William M. Brown was held in county jail (and missed work the following day). Maggie visited him. Carlos confirmed the story about the coat, which let Brownie off for now, but that didn't change the fact that the deceased had his wallet.

However, thanks to a suggestion from the public defender, a search was made at the dump site where yet another dead man was found, under even more layers of roofing material, and most importantly, with the murder weapon in his pocket. This one died either from Dump Trauma (run over by a bulldozer) or from other causes; one possibility being that the lid of the dumpster had fallen unexpectedly, knocking out or killing him during or after the stabbing. His victim either exited or was tossed from the dumpster seconds before the perp received his just reward on the head... and subsequently buried under roofing materials...

"Still Dump Trauma," insisted the detective, who'd freshly coined the term and could hardly wait to be quoted in the newspaper. But, alas (sloppy police work notwithstanding), the case was solved. File number 89-7653-46 was closed... suspect released. Maggie read the police report in its entirety. Unbelievable!

She seemed to be a bit out of sorts that evening. Brownie had expected that. He was also smart enough to know that since she would be even shorter with him than usual, intimacy was out of the question (as a matter of fact). And he was just a little short of acknowledging (to himself) that the vision of Feather's breasts, jiggling now and then in the back of his mind, had something to do with his own sexual motivation. He went to bed pouting.

The next morning, while each of them gulped down a quick breakfast, she asked; "Did you intend to tell me about losing your wallet?"

"Why should I? It was no big deal. All I lost was the wallet and a few dollars... a couple of pictures."

Pausing in the doorway, her hand on the doorknob, she left him with this lovely parting gift: "I want you to see a doctor. A psychiatrist."

—◇—

Maggie rode the bus to her job at the cannery. It was just a seasonal thing she could do to help ends meet. She thought about Brown. What was she going to do with that man? There was good reason to suspect that he'd slipped over the edge. This last incident was frightening. He could have been convicted of that crime! It happened to lots of people: wrong place at the wrong time kind'a thing. Why he couldn't just behave himself, mystified her. Just two weeks ago they'd had a great time... like normal people. Her thoughts drifted back:

They had walked through a bean field down to a favorite swimming hole: Brown, Maggie, Julie, son-in-law Tim (now ex); Tim's younger brother, Gregg; and Gregg's girlfriend. The narrow dirt lane was lined on both sides with tall bean vines. The poles were up and the green beans hung down in fat abundance. Streams of irrigation water spurted intermittently from large sprinkler heads in comforting summer sounds. The spray drifted across the road in a cool mist, refreshing them from the hot sun and delighting all with beautiful rainbows. Puddles of water warmed on the heated lane. Tim made sure he jumped into each and every one. Soon, Gregg joined in. Not long after that the whole crowd was jumping and splashing (even Julie and little Cooper). When Maggie slipped onto her butt with a plop! Everyone roared with laughter... except Maggie. When Brown (who had laughed the loudest) bent to pick her up she plastered him with mud.

What happened from there was predictable, but... if only they owned a video recorder! Tim chased Gregg down the road until Gregg slipped and slid about ten feet. That was all it took: Like a family of happy river otters they slipped and slathered for over an hour on their butts, bellies, sides and even on top of one another. The guys had "distance-trials," with running starts and belly flops. Maggie and Julie laughed 'til it hurt. When Julie, was completely covered in mud and transformed into a cute little black woman, Brown made fun of her, strutting around doing his black imitation; Maggie had a shot at it too... and was very convincing... according to her. Such a happy, abandoned time. They continued on down to the river for a swim and to wash the mud off. That night on the way home they'd stopped for burgers and shakes. A normal family.

She remembered other happy times when the kids were younger: Trips back to Georgia, to Brown's distant relatives, to Disneyland, Julie's high-school graduation (not quite four years ago).... How could Brown be so great at times and so screwed-up at others?

In traffic for instance. As though the cars in front of him were there for no other reason than as obstacles for him to get around or criticize. The ones who cut him off did so at their own peril. He saw them all as the same guy doing the same inconsiderate thing, over and over. No turn signal? "You idiot!" Following too close? "Stupid Ass! Bonehead! Meathead!" These were mild terms, compared to what must be just below the surface. Why did it matter if some guy flipped him off? They were just showing their own low-class mentalities. And... sheesh... they were quite obviously not the same person all the time (sigh), yet all that anger came out for the current offending car and driver. At times he acted as if he were an angry, caged gorilla... and at other times calculating and sly.

She had seen him play his favorite trick on "freeway idiots" more than once. He had a way of drying the inside of his upper lip so that it stuck to his gums when he folded it under, this caused his face to look as though he had either lost the lip in a fire, or it had been cut off with a knife. His big white teeth looked like a snarling German shepherd. Positively scary. The person who might be passing him in anger or revenge (for something Brown had just done) would look over at him and instantly turn white as a ghost, then turn their eyes straight ahead, all the fight apparently gone out of them. Brown truly looked as though he could eat them alive and spit them out in little pieces. But he would only do it when engaged with the "idiots," and loved the effect.

He had objections and charges that could never be cleared up: Why do the fat women always stuff it into little cars and then go slow in the fast lanes, purposely preventing him from getting around them? And why did the skinny ones drive around him in pickups and suburbans like a house a'fire looking at him as though he had just broken something sacred? Truckers, bikers, the list was endless. These days Brown was unhappier than she'd ever seen him. Yep... it would be good if he got some help.

Her stop was just up ahead. She could see the cannery off to the right. Diesel farm trucks were lined up waiting to unload the early morning picking. Mountains of green beans bulged up above the high, wooden sides of the truck-beds. It occurred to her that these could very well be from the same bean fields they had walked through that day by the river...

Maggie saw Brown's white teeth and eyes laughing and happy through a mud-plastered face. She saw herself running to keep him from grabbing her; him shouting; "Git yo'sef back here, Sapphire, I'se gwine to take-you-down." His happiness was contagious. Why did she get sexually turned-on at the wrong times? But... that night they had been very good together.

—◇—

Brownie's commute to the airline terminal was predictably boring... and particularly meaningless. Maggie had covered his missed day of work with; "William Brown has business that prevents him from being at work today." She was a stickler for truth.

But W.M. Brown wasn't a stickler for work. If he were, he would be somewhere other than in a car named Sparky with other men (who were practically strangers) headed for the air terminal... again. Why had William M. Brown never quite landed on his feet? What could he have done differently? The same eight to ten hours a day could be spent doing something he enjoyed, could it not? Just so much meat on the block, at so much a pound... that's how he felt. He had sold himself into slavery at a ridiculously low price. No wage, no matter how high, was sufficient... absent interest or pleasure... or both. Walking across the parking lot toward the terminal, he blurted aloud; "Hey guys! This might be idealistic, but some people actually enjoy their work; lots of them."

He may as well have been talking to himself... not one of the guys even looked his way. He noted however, that the driver kept talking about his car, Sparky, with fawning, stupid admiration.

Once inside and at the check-in counters, the shift supervisor, Clarence, greeted him cheerfully; "Personnel wants to see you at eleven, William; I'll take your counter 'til you get back." For a moment, a familiar slave mentality set his thoughts into motion; A reprimand! Maybe it was the absence... But then, the twinkle Clarence had in his eyes calmed him down. *Hmmm, this could be good news... maybe the promotion?*

Five years ago he had gone to work for Concept through a job-recovery program. Thanks to the environmental wackos, the logging company he'd worked with had shutdown. So had many others. All over the northwest, the economy was in the toilet and frankly he was at a loss as to what to do. So, accepting (reluctantly) the government handout, he'd learned minimal typing and computer skills over a period of eight months, and to his satisfaction had done very well in the classes. A lack of formal education did not mean that he was dumb... or uneducated for that matter. He had always been an avid reader. Yet, even with such a wide range of interests, still couldn't focus on any one thing that he could stay with long enough to become sufficiently adept. He had compromised and followed the rest of the sheep right on into the chute of governmental solutions!

Eleven o'clock found him sitting in a chair in the personnel manager's office, dumbfounded at the words coming from Ms. Wanda Fisher's mouth; "We have an opening coming up... We are required by law to fill it with a person from a minority race... here in the Northwest that's not all that easy to do... not a particularly colorful place... what with such a relatively smaller segment of the population being of the minority races... such as yourself."

"How do you mean that?"

"You are an African American; is that not so?"

The negative shake of his head turned into an affirmative nod when he realized her facial expression was encouraging him to go along with this.

"As you know, overseeing those under you is a position of responsibility, and a risk for the Airlines."

He nodded again.

"Well, as such, we require that a psychological evaluation take place for each and every supervisory position. The position starts officially in three weeks. Are you prepared to take it on?" She asked with a knowing smile.

"Of course," William replied.

"Good. This is a step up the ladder, Mister Brown. An even higher one is coming around the first of next year... (She seemed to be saying, "Play ball with us, and you won't regret it").

"We noticed a portion, a certain box, on your initial job-application was not checked. Would you take care of that, and get it back to me personally?" She handed him a manila envelope labeled, W. M. Brown.

William started to open it.

"No. Take it home. There are preliminary forms to fill out for the psych-evaluation in there too. Bring the completed employee application back next week... after the, uh... evaluation."

She then put her glasses on and turned to other paperwork, but glanced upward with a friendly smile; "Think about it."

Walking slowly down the hall, returning to his counter, Mister Brown did just that. Maybe he did like his job after all... but wait. *Was Maggie somehow behind this? No? Well, whatever or whomever... thank you!*

He waited until dinner that night to tell her the news. She was pleased. He didn't mention the unchecked boxes... the ones beside Caucasian, Hispanic, Black, American Indian and so on, but he did tell her about the psych-evaluation requirement; "That won't hurt..." she'd said calmly (but the somewhat masked pleasure in her voice was duly noted). They celebrated with a rented video, hot buttered popcorn, and make-up sex. Maggie listened to him snore for awhile before going out herself; He was trying, wasn't he?

—◇—

Chapter eight

The rest of the week went without incident. But early Thursday evening, Brown was just settling-in when Carlos called with; "Hey man, what's up with you? You still hidin' out from the law?"

Brownie wasn't sure he wanted to talk. He waited for Carlos to continue.

"You still coming for the 'cue?"

"Planning to..."

"It's Saturday ya know."

"Yep..."

"I got a problem."

Ah hah! He knew it; "What would that be?" he asked hesitantly.

"That, my man, would be hornets!"

He waited.

Carlos filled in the gaps. "They's in my tree in the back... jus' hangin' there; a nest the size of a basketball. Whooo wee! You never seen nuthin' like it."

"Well, like you said, you got a problem," he waited while the wheels were turning, remembered the junk yard experience, then added; "But I can fix it."

Carlos was glad to hear it. The relief could be heard in his voice; "How's 'at?"

"A vacuum cleaner is all you need. Can you reach the nest?"

"Yeah, with a ladder."

"Well, just go out there and put the nozzle over the hole while they're sleeping... sucks 'em right out. Your troubles are over."

"Why didn't I think of that?"

"You got other things on your mind son, like ribs, and potato salad, and beer, and music, and..."

"Yeah..." the hornets had Carlos stuck in another zone; "...talk t'you later."

Brownie had to see this for himself. He got dressed quickly, kissed Maggie, and left in happy anticipation.

Peeking through the crack of a weathered gray, cedar fence, Brownie could see Carlos was hard at work. A frayed piece of rope held a spindly ladder against the trunk of a dogwood tree. Nearby, an old torpedo shaped vacuum was connected to a very tangled orange extension cord squirming from beneath the garage door. A single glaring light bulb on the back-porch, plus the light spilling through one garage window, was sufficient. The sound of rattling and thumping caused Brownie to shuffle to a different crack, which brought Carlos into view again, dragging a vacuum hose and several lengths of chrome tubing from his seldom used garden shed. He connected as many lengths as possible, flipped the vacuum switch, and to the whirring sound, climbed up the shaky ladder, which immediately began swaying under his weight. Several black .357 magnum bullets whizzed out of an ominous, gray, paper nest the size of a soccer ball.

Brownie watched with mixed feelings. Inside that thing was enough revenge for any man, but just how many stings might satisfy justice wasn't quite clear. Don't mess with Brownie... was the name of the lesson.

Carlos fearlessly (mindlessly, was the word Brownie

used) and adroitly placed the chrome tube over the opening, which protruded out from the bulbous gray nest at a right angle, resembling the puckered mouth of some dreadful insect. His good friend was in a front-row-seat less than twenty feet away. Watching with delicious expectation. The low hum of the vacuum wasn't enough to drown out the sound the bee's bodies made rattling down the tube into the vacuum; fft...fft... ffft...fft... ff fffascinating. Carlos could hear them too, and was actually smiling. When he changed hands, a few more bullets whizzed passed his head but he seemed not to notice.

The maneuver went just fine, with only one or two close calls (when he would change his position on the ladder, or wiggle the vacuum tube). Then the smile would turn into a childish expression of fearful anxiety, but quickly revert into adult confidence when the danger was over.

"Damn! It worked!" Brownie said, with a derisive thump on the steering wheel as he whipped the old van out of the alley and cursed the car which had barely missed him.

Carlos stored his bee rousting equipment including the old, junky, canister-type vacuum in his garden shed, then walked quickly to the shop area of his single-car garage. He had lots of work to do. The 'cue was set for Saturday. The sparks flew 'til late that night.

—<>—

Saturday afternoon, Brownie and Maggie drove along the street in the black neighborhood. This was a small part of town, only one or two blocks long and two blocks wide, where the majority of African Americans in Lake City chose to dwell. The street was lined with cars, and people were milling about in the yards, but concentrated in greater numbers around Carlos's house.

Brownie's first observation was that the junk trailer was gone. Maggie was scanning the faces in the crowd to see if she knew anyone there. Crowds were not her thing. She was enthralled with the difference in cultures though, and found it hard not to be excited. This was the first time they had ever been invited to a black get-together of this size.

When Violet met them on the porch with a mammoth hug, Maggie was enveloped into folds of flesh; the quintessential counterpart of Carlos; "Why look at yo'sef honey, we's got to git you right out to dat bahbecue;" she laughed resoundingly, and still holding onto Maggie, reached out with the other arm and pulled Brownie along with them, back down the steps.

Carlos came out from behind the house, along the driveway, glowing; "My main man..." he exclaimed, sliding his hand out in a low, stealth, gimme five position. "Wait. Hold it right there... Violet, you didn't say nuthin' did you?"

Violet admitted she had... hoped that it was okay to say hello to their guests?

"I meant about my thang... my dealey."

"Naww, honey, I didn't, they's all yours," this she said while backing away and steering them to Carl.

"Close your eyes..." Carl insisted, pushing them gently from behind, toward the backyard.

Brownie and Maggie cooperated. Violet chuckled and rumbled softly in the background. They slid their feet along the concrete drive to the corner of the yellow clapboard house. The smell of smoke blended with the expected delicious barbecue smell. Neither had peeked; "Open 'em."

They could not believe what rose up into the sky before them... An iron tower, twenty-five or thirty feet high, with smoke wafting up and through it; "Dis is my new bahbecue," Carl said with great pride.

Brownie's mouth hung open. Maggie was speechless, mystified, and a bit intimidated by the strange apparatus before her. On the first rusty plateau of the tower was a grating, piled with ribs and chicken. In several strangely shaped cubbies or compartments, sitting on hubcaps, were aluminum pots and pans, either boiling with food in them, or soon to be.

Several old, porcelainized, iron stove doors placed at odd angles indicated that this level was for warming, or keeping food warmed. Rusted railroad spikes and valve springs, welded in a design along the outer perimeter and leading upwards, carried the eye toward the topmost pinnacle. The array of junk metal, projecting and cantilevering was nightmarish, yet somehow enchanting. Brownie gasped! Sitting at the very top of the steel pinnacle, resembling an avant-garde weather vane was none other than... the Trailmaster.

Carlos beamed brightly; "She nested, Brownie," and then pointed to a flat piece of steel which extended downward from the underside of the bike, descending through the center of the tower like a frozen swirling ribbon, almost touching the barbecue grating. Brownie interpreted the artist's intentions instantly: Welded all over the steel ribbon were hundreds of ball bearings... of all sizes. Smoke traveled up mystically amongst them and out and around the bike. The Trailmaster had indeed spawned!

Brownie had to admit it was stupendous. A masterstroke for Carlos. When he told him so, Carlos couldn't thank him enough for all the new junk he had left that other night. So much for net-Zero.

The crowd grew while the tower continued gaining appropriate respect.

Before long, plates piled high with delicious food were circulated. Great racks of charred baby-back ribs; chicken (crisp and tangy); local, sweet, boiled corn; yummy green beans; potato salad (as only Violet could make it); and all with such tantalizing flavors that everyone was compelled to overeat.

Carlos started the anxiously awaited music with a resounding sax-solo that set the mood instantly. Trumpets, guitars, snare drums and the like, appeared in willing hands. Brownie pulled his sack of blues harps out of the van. The party was underway. The street became a dance floor for the band, situated in Carlos's front yard. Maggie was delighted. The music went on rather haphazardly for half an hour or so, blending from one lively tune to the next without a noticeable ending or beginning for any tune.

As obviously planned, a microphone and sound system had gradually been set up. Carlos indicated that everyone should now pay attention: Violet could be seen just off stage. The brushes of the snare drum began to shuffle and shift in a sifting sound. Violet waltzed out onto the stage with an old-fashioned flour sifter.

Carlos picked the mike off the stand; *"Listen now, cain't you hear...?"*

Violet began to move in a rhythmic sway, sifting a full canister of flour around the stage (really just their front yard, which always looked as though there had never been a blade of grass on it). The white powder floated down to the bare ground. Carlos sang:

"Ssssift it.... Sssssift it...
Sift it, sift it sift it, sift it, sift it,
My baby's making biscuits.
She gets a cup of flour; she sifts it in the bowl,
Adds the milk, and the butter, and baby's on a roll.
Oh, I love my baby's biscuits,
I'm her biscuit loving man!
Such a piece of work the way she lays those biscuits In her pan!
I said sift it, sift it, sift it,
I love my baby's biscuits.
I'm her biscuit loving man!
With her little yellow dress and flour on her face,
Just a wiggle and a shake, n' she's queen o' dis place."

At this point, for all practical purposes, Violet, did indeed have on a yellow dress, and though a very hefty woman, appeared to weigh only about ninety pounds. And she did wiggle ... and she did move... with such grace. Carlos watched proudly in utmost fascination while he continued the tune:

"Nothing tastes better than a slice of ham,
Red eye gravy and her biscuits. Yes ma'am!
When she goes to the oven, n' pulls 'em out,
They's so pretty I wants to shout!
Oh baby, I love yo' biscuits!
I'm yo biscuit loving man.
Such a piece of work the way you lays 'em in yo pan.
Just a sifting, sifting, sifting."

Violet had by now created a snowstorm. The floured-yard had a wondrous dark pattern of barefoot tracks on a blanket of white. And, complete with a head of white hair, white cheekbones, and chin, Carlos too, had been dusted.

"They come outta that oven so nice and brown,
Crisp on the bottom and the tops are round.
The look on her face when she hands 'em to me,
That's a look the whole world should see.
With a kiss on my cheek and coffee in my cup,
She smells like heaven when she serves 'em up.
I'm her biscuit loving man!
Oh, baby, I loves yo biscuits!
Such a piece of work the way you hold 'em in yo hand.
Just a sifting, sifting, sifting.

(The beautiful, black, round biscuit-lady sifted off the stage).

"...Just a sifting, sifting, sifting..."

Enchanted with the scene unfolding before her, Maggie, who had been "seated" in a folding lawn chair by one of Carlos's daughters, applauded in delight,

She could just barely see Brownie who'd found a bar stool and was having the time of his life. *His blues harp fit's in so nicely... in fact, he looks pretty natural up there...* she mused.

When the applause faded away. Carlos handed the mike to Mike, a tall and skinny, jet-black man, who began to slap and rub his hands together. Gradually (Mike-to-mike) he began to slither and slump around the stage like a strap of leather... or a loose piece of bacon. He shook his hands out in front of his shimmying body, simultaneously rising up and down erratically, from knees to tiptoes. He started the song. The saxophone joined him with a bluesy snake-charming riff: Quiet and slow at first:

"When you cooks my bacon just cook it slow,
Cookin' too fast burns it up, you know.
If you cooks with 'lectrics or ya cooks with gas,
Jus' cook it real slow, don't you cook it too fast.
When you first throws it in, I know it's real loose,"

The microphone flew up into the air, Mike jumped too, did a three-sixty in mid-air, then caught the microphone and started trembling from head to toe;

"But pretty soon it's simmering in its own good juice.
Don't you heat that grease 'til it starts to pop...
Keep it down to a slow, slow sizzle; baby, don't you stop.
That slow, sloow, sizzle makes my bacon real crisp,
When you keeps the heat down, ain't no way you can miss!"

Pained facial expressions convinced everyone that the bacon was indeed, heating up. The musicians stepped up the tempo:

"But when you cooks it too fast, it's a flopping around.
Then the ends curl up, 'n it don't come out brown,"

Mike hit the dirt and rolled up into a ball, still clutching the microphone;
"...I say, baby, keep it down to a sloooow sizzle..."

His voice trailed off softly;

"Yeah... Keep that heat real steady, but keep it down low
If you burns my bacon, it's off you go...."

Louder now;

"Makes me feel so special when you do it just right
Looking forward to my brea'fast all thru the night.
I love the sound of that slow, slow sizzle... "

The music faded off with a crisp, sizzling sound
from the guitar and saxophone. Mike was still on the
ground. Floured white as a ghost and rigid as a board.
Two brothers hauled him off. More applause.

Carlos came back to the microphone; "And now
brothas 'n sistahs, we have a tune from our brotha,
Brownie..."

Brownie looked up–surprised; Carlos worked his
way back to him. Took his arm, and coaxed him forward;
"Ladies and gennemens... 'Booty, Booty,' by Brownie
Brown... written and composed by none other..."

Before he knew what was happening, Brownie was
standing front-and-center with the microphone in one
hand, a blues-harp in the other. He had never used a
speaker system with a harp before, but cupped his hand
around it and the mike (as he had seen the pros do); the
sound was awesome! Thankfully the key just happened to
be his favorite for the tune; a low, caramel-coated, orally
sweet tone oozed out across the neighborhood. He was
spellbound. This was his moment. The sound of his steam
locomotive, slow and laboring, cast everyone under its spell.

Carl sang the lyrics:

"I'm crossing the country on the B & O
No doubt about it baby, das' as far as we go...

I said, Chug, chug, chug, up the hills you know.
And then it's Whoosh, whoosh, whoosh...
Down the other side we go!"

Carl bent his knees almost to the ground with his hands gliding outward toward the imaginary train tracks... Brownie, swaying back and forth like a rocking boxcar, was in perfect, unrehearsed synchrony.

"I said a clickity, clickity, and clickitty-clack,
Ain't no better feeling than bein' on track.
I says a'choo choo, momma, we're on the mainline,
This locomotive motion is feelin' so fine."

A mournful train whistle, expertly crafted (two longs, one short, and one long), approaching an imaginary crossing was unmistakable.

"Don't you dare say, booty booty, or po'k chop to me.
I'm jes' happy go lucky and I gots to be free.
Don't you try to say that I'm wastin' my time.
I'm just a'windin', and a'twistin', but I'm... on the right line.
Black hole in the mountain, it swallows d' train...
N'it's outta sight.
Punching through the tunnel, it's as dark as night;
Seems like I'm never gonna make it out
To... the other side,
But when you take the locomotive honey...
That... comes with the ride."

The audience was caught up with the rhythm, and a nostalgic feeling for an era that was long since gone, but somehow lived in their hearts. The urge to be on that train, free and rolling to the next wherever, welled up courageously in every-heart. While Brownie's heart was on his tongue, rolling across the reed openings of the harp... and for a change what came from his mouth was a blessing to those who heard.

"Silver rails a shining, smoke stack's a'billowin' black,
We got a full head of steam and it's clickity-clak...
clickity-clak.
I said a clickity, clickity, clickitty, clack-clack-clack...
Ain't no better feeling than a'bein on track!
This is a freight train of love that ya bringing to me
Just bring it on home, sugar-mamma... special de-liv-
er-eee,
Chug-a- lug, chug-a-lug baby, choo, choo choo
There ain't no better feelin' than ridin' with you."

If the audience had found a groove, the musicians were in the slot. Eight black men sparkled at each other from behind or over brass, strings, and wood, in a connection known only to them. Bound as one in a timeless experience... And Brownie was included...

"Shoveling this coal's a lotta' hard work, the boiler's glowing red-hot
I'm a'sweatin' and a'strainin', givin'–givin' all that I got.
Sooner or later this ride's a'gonna'' come to an end.
Chug-a-lug, chug-a-lug mamma, could be just 'round the... chug, chug, chug... very next bend.
Whooooowee, whooweee, clikity, clickity, clickity-clack.
Chug-a-lug, chug-a-lug, honey, choo-choo, choo-choo, choo choo chooooooooo..."

Brownie's train disappeared around the bend in a gradual descending volume.

By the time every one of the musicians had "taken their turn" in the limelight (some more than once) the tune had taken more than fifteen minutes. But who was counting? Carl wrapped one of his sweaty arms around Brownie and held him close to his side; "Brownie Brown, ladies and gennemens!!" Brownie was breathless. The thrill of the moment swelled his heart bigger than a watermelon. He had made the transition. Brownie Brown and was one of the brothers.

In that moment, Maggie could see that it might be true. And perhaps this confirmed what she had long suspected: Her marriage was indeed a biracial one. She looked at the other women around her in an entirely different perspective. This was not a separate, foreign culture, but one that she might have a vested interest in... whether she liked it or not... but what was not to like!?

Carl addressed the crowd again; "We gon' slow it down for a bit... heah's a slow one... " His words and the music simply became background noise to Maggie who was lost in thought, trying to sort it out... into clear, black and white facts.

Hearing Carl's Master of Ceremonies voice again announcing; "Another Brownie Brown tune... " brought her attention back to the stage.

She watched her "Brown" shuffle his feet a little, looking very nervous, and then his eyes met hers across the curly heads of black hair between them. His Big hands cupped the tiny harmonica to the mike and a sweet rhythmic sound opened another door of his world to her. The oral satisfaction he felt was obvious. His own unique harmonica riffs interspersed with his words; He sang in a peculiar "Black-dialect." The whole thing smacked of a slow thirties-blues-rap mixture.

I'm like an old potato... a little fat and kind'a brown,
You can dig me later... or you can leave me in the ground.
You can use the whole potato, inside and out, even the
skin...
You can slice me thick, or you can slice me thin.
I think I'd better warn you, my best ain't when I'm raw,
There's lots of ways to warm me, and I hope you try them
all.
My best flavor is really when I'm hot...
But it don't matter to me if you like potatoes or not.
If you try to peel me I'll be slick in your hand,
And if you don't oil me I'll stick to your pan.
Maybe you'd rather mash me, but that would make me boil...
I'd rather be rubbed with your butter, than baked in
your tin-foil.
Cut me into super thin slices, turn me into chips...
Then you'll see just what nice is... when you smack me on
your lips.
You don't have to hurry, cause this old spud won't mind...
'Cause one nice thing about a potato... it keeps a long, long
time."

Brownie ended his song with a few bold harmonica
flourishes and had even danced a little jig. Carlos and
the band accompanied him with comedic, spontaneous,
toots and riffs. The audience rolled with laughter, while
Brownie had taken on the exaggerated role of a black
man, if not a potato... it was just fine if "one of their
own" poked a little fun.

Carlos gently took the microphone; "I know dat song's
gon' remind ever'body that they's still a little hongry,
so come on back. I know y'all know's how to eat..." The
music was not over, but it was time for a break.

Brownie came over to Maggie, a little embarrassed,

but radiant. She gave him the hugs and compliments she knew he wanted, and deserved. No doubt she was very proud of him. They walked arm in arm around to the Barbecue Tower. Brownie steered her over to the garden shed and around the back of it. No surprise to Maggie. He was up to his usual physical celebration when he felt good about himself. She welcomed the embrace. They had no words, just feelings. Each felt that something had changed in the last hour.

"There's Carlos's old barbecue," said Brownie, pointing to a rusting, fifty-five gallon barrel cut in half, with the two halves hinged together like a clam shell. Four angle-iron legs were welded on unevenly and haphazardly.

The sky looked dark, a slight breeze blew out of the west, which usually meant rain... again. It had been a fairly wet summer. Too bad. Brownie seemed to remember long, dry summers, his first years in Oregon. But that was then... He walked over to the barrel. There had been some good barbecues on this, as simple as it was. He knew he should not lose this moment with Maggie, but not only had this barrel caught his eye, so had the wooden one under a gutter by the corner of the shed. It was full of water, moss circled the top, and algae had turned the water green; the sediment and crud on the bottom was probably inches thick. He looked up at the sky. Definitely rain coming; felt a few drops. The wind picked up in the tall poplars out by the alley, sending a silver texture rippling through the trees as the underside of the leaves were revealed. Heck. Now the party would be ruined. Maybe it was just a shower. Often that was the case, clearing up just in time for a spectacular sunset.

He put his arm around Maggie's waist, nuzzled her neck, pulled her gently back around the shed, where they stood under the little overhanging roof watching the crowd by the tower. Carl built the fire up. The raindrops increased in size. They could hear them sizzling on the hot, iron tower thirty feet away. The crowd thinned, as the drops became a steady downpour. It was getting a little chilly. He tried the door of the shed with his free hand, it gave easily. He reached back pulling Maggie inside. She resisted at first but the warmth of the shed was inviting. There were two windows; one faced the house and the other faced the alley. The sound of the rain on the roof was cozy. Maggie was a bit surprised that Brown didn't make a move on her, instead he gazed out the window at the barrel. The water slopped over the side and seeped into the earth to who knew (or cared) where. It's just rain, he thought. Maggie moved over to the other window watching the guests scatter.

The barrel. He had an unreasonable urge to run out and kick it over. Carlos didn't need the rain. And even though it may have been there for the purpose of catching water at one time or other, it was simply wasting and rotting now. Hadn't been emptied in years. Hanging on a hook nearby was a dipper. Hah! No thanks. If he'd had to take a drink… say, in hot weather… you can bet he'd dip as close to the top as possible. But a proper drink would be from as deep as a dipper would go… to the cooler stuff. He looked up at the sky. The rain came down in sheets.

He turned and sidled over to Maggie's window. Not a soul was by the tower now. They could see people and lights in the house and out in the garage. He pressed up next to Maggie, put his chin down on her shoulder; watched the rain with her, still thinking: *I've kicked over lots of barrels… ever since I was a kid. Maybe it is a good idea to drain them once in a while, but I just liked to watch the water go splashing out across the ground in small tidal waves.*

Yeah! That swishing sound is satisfying somehow. Shoot fire! An empty rain barrel always helps the falling rain make sense; then the day has meaning. And maybe when I pass that barrel on just another rotten, rainy day, what's inside would interest me. I'd see purpose. A reason... and a promise for some future, hot day, when those wooden sides would be bulging out, offerin' cool satisfaction. He moved up behind Maggie, put his hand's around her waist, onto her still (for her age) firm tummy. Both had closed their eyes listening to the rain pelting down onto the roof and washing over the eaves.

A barrel looks full even when it's empty... he sensed he was beginning to sound like his mother but continued with his thought... *sittin' up fat and bulgy. What a nice shape.* He squeezed Maggie's waist, and allowed his hands to run down luxuriously over her hips, still hung up on barrels... *just a simple form, with a function. Just lookin' from a distance it would be easy to assume that it was full...* Both he and Maggie had been aware of the obvious camaraderie visible in the kitchen windows of the house. Such a happy people.

He spun Maggie around gently and kissed her full on the lips. "About time," she whispered, with a nibble on his ear. He chuckled and pulled her over toward an old recliner; bumped Carlos's old vacuum onto the floor; "Come here, little momma..." he said in the appropriate dialect.

Maggie slid into his lap; "Don't get too big an idea here Brown," she cautioned, surprised at her own desire.

Suddenly Brown let out a yelp, which startled Maggie right off his lap.

A jolt that felt like a bolt of electricity had hit his leg. Instantly he knew what had happened; "Hornets!" he shouted. Up until then Carl's vacuum-hose had been kinked, keeping an angry arsenal imprisoned, but now, Brown had unkinked it by dropping it onto the floor. A first instinct was to protect Maggie; He bounded out of the chair and shoved her violently out the door.

"Run!" Maggie needed no encouragement to do so, she was on her way. Shaking and flipping her long, black hair over and over, emitting high pitched squeals, she made a beeline for the kitchen door. Brown ran for the garage. The rain was still pouring.

Even hornets know not to go out in the rain. They stayed in the shed. Brown ran around the tower and collided with iron... a cantilevered hunk of junk took him out. He hit the ground... out cold. No one saw him. He lay face up, the rain making little puddles out of his eye sockets.

The moment Maggie entered the kitchen where most of the women were gathered, they rallied immediately around their sister, shaking her hair as well as their own. The universal fear of all women, of something, anything, getting entangled in their hair, engulfed them all in a collective yelping, self-head-slapping, hair-rubbing-fest, lasting for a few minutes and tapering off into only occasional squeals and enticing shakes (to the men watching) to rid themselves of the sensation of creepy-crawly things in there. Everyone calmed down. Then of course, Maggie ran over to the garage where the men were gathered, and with her encouragement the search for Brownie began. The rain had eased up to a faint drizzle.

Although he had only been stung a few times, and the danger was over, his subconscious was still in battle... still running... through an empty city lot scattered with big, rusted, steel barrels, grass and weeds growing knee-deep around them; some lying on their sides, some stacked. He jumped over one, accidentally knocking the lid off with his foot. Aha! A ready-made fortress. Crawling inside, pulling the lid onto the barrel he could hear the bees pinging off the metal sides. Safe. Dark.

A chemical smell surrounded him. "This is an empty barrel," he heard himself say aloud, his voice sounding ghostly and hollow. "What good is it?" He moaned. Frustrated, almost to the point of tears, he struggled to push the top off, but couldn't. The darkness remained. "It's fit for nothing... empty," he bellowed, still able to hear the bees pinging off the metal sides... maybe it did have value, after all. The sound of his own voice seemed to be a comfort. But wait, this wasn't his voice he was hearing; it was from outside the barrel.

The lid popped off, and there above him was an entire orchestra of black and brown faces. He vaguely recognized some of them in spite of rain spattered eyeballs. Someone shoved a bottle of ammonia under his nose. He felt nauseous; rolled over onto his side and moaned, feeling a knot on his forehead the size of a baseball. Maggie was there beside him asking questions, holding up fingers for him to count and showing much concern.

Due to his delirious muttering nonsense about barrels, it was unanimously decided that he should go to the hospital with what could easily be a brain-concussion. Maggie soothed him in the back seat of Carl's Lincoln while he rambled on; "...were created for, and have, a use. They're there! Waiting for a world that takes them for granted..." Insisting that virtually everybody could use a barrel: "...a rain barrel, a barrel of fun, a barrel of money, pickles, apples, monkeys, or for taking a ride over Alice falls. They have a use!"

Carl looked over his shoulder and shook his head

sadly; "Poor Ol' Brown."

And Brown raved on "...until they're needed, and then nothing else will do..." thank goodness they soon arrived at the hospital. The potato, a little fat and kind'a brown, was escorted in with Carl and Maggie on each side. He passed out again at the emergency desk.

—<>—

Peeking out of two tiny holes the size of pinpricks (way too small for a bee to get through) W.M. "Brownie" Brown saw fifteen or so black cattle standing in a circle. They were stiff and unmoving. Carlos stood nearby motioning and walking toward them, waving his arms. With dazed expressions, they moved together, and pressed into a tight circle... their heads facing Carlos, who walked over with a long metal strap. He threw it around them like a lasso, and laid it on the ground. Did the same with another strap and draped it loosely around their haunches. Did it yet again, and placed this one up around their horns and foreheads. He then took two enormous blowtorches, with roaring flames, and circled around the herd over and over again, pointing the flame at them. He circled closer and closer until the flame was actually on them. Now, the cattle had transformed into iron pickets... or... wait! They were barrel staves! And there were no cattle features left, except perhaps faint, very faint, individual resemblances etched into the iron. The three metal straps Carlos wrapped around them had gradually tightened with the transformation and were holding the loose shape of a barrel. He then took a ball-peen hammer from a holster on his hip and with tongs snagged individual, red-hot rivets from a small metal pouch; gradually making his way around assembling rings and staves with rivets and hammer. Alas, though he had improved it greatly, it was obvious that the barrel still needed work.

Brownie could read despair on Carlos's face and wanted to help, but was unable to move and completely immobilized. Struggling in darkness to free himself from what he assumed was another barrel, he realized that he *was* the barrel... had been all along. He looked through the two tiny pinpricks again to discover that a virtual cloudburst–of barbecue sauce–complete with thunder and lightning, poured out of the sky. Within seconds, thick sauce was sloshing over the side of the giant, steel barrel lined with brown cowhide. He was full. The rings were tight, and the barrel had become even stronger because of the unmistakable pressure inside his head.

Two days later Brownie regained consciousness. The first thing he saw was curtains of reddish orange, speckled with red and green vegetables... peppers, tomatoes, sprouting green onions... all brightly illuminated by the sunshine beaming through the curtains of the hospital window. Maggie was right by his side; "You've had a concussion Brown, and a major hematoma. In other words, a bump that had to be lanced..." her eyebrows went up; "you know... to relieve the pressure?"

Brown nodded and twisted one corner of his mouth up in disgust, reached his hand up to feel the bandage wrapped around his skull.

Maggie could see he was going to be fine; "You look like a giant Q-tip," she said factually... and cheerfully.

The room was awash with flowers from friends. The nurse walked in; pretended to be confused; "Is this a ward or a private room?" she asked, lifting tags and reading them off: "These are for W.M. Brown; This one's for Brownie; one's for William; another for Myron; Boody

Boody Man; Potato man; and here's one for The Brown Hornet!"

Carlos came to see him that evening; "You don't have to worry none 'bout them hornets, man."

Brownie wanted to know more.

"I done took care of 'em... I gassed 'em."

"What? You didn't burn the shed down?"

"No man, I backed the Lincoln up to it and run a hose from my tail-pipe in there." Brownie could picture it... the blue smoke from that thing would kill a horse. Carlos continued; "And then for good measure, I stuck the vacuum cleanah's hose up to de tail-pipe for ten mo' minutes... they ain't gon' bother us agin."

"Now, let me see yo' lips. You didn't ruin that harmonica sound none, did'ya?"

Brownie pooched his lips out.

"Mmmmm-hmmmm, Dat's Good, the fellas want you to do our next gig with us."

The pooched lips widened into a painful grin.

—◇—

- Chapter Nine -

Through the French doors in the hallway, Brown watched Maggie cleaning the small squares of glass. The doctor said she was to stay home from the cannery for a couple of days to "keep an eye on him." Holes in the knees of her jeans revealed brown skin, tanned from an occasional hour or two on their little patio in the sun.

Nestled onto the old couch they'd had for years, Brown was comforted and delighted by the capable strength in her legs and buttocks. Her efforts are consciously given to him... he's convinced of that. A thin waist and well-proportioned body, emanate another kind of strength... despite her scant one hundred-five pounds. He wants her to consciously offer that strength as a gift to him too.

His first awareness of her determination to "get that dirt" was when they were dating... she came over and went through the place like a hurricane... Afterwards the apartment was fresh and spotless, causing him to feel oddly stronger because of her gift. If somehow that gift could pass right on through to their physical affections... she could be so much fun! If only she could break out of her reserved disposition.

Yet another direct reflection of her tendency toward the mundane was dark and drab clothing. *Lighten up woman! Life is passing us by! Wear some high-heels, put on something red; if I don't get my loving from you where will I get it? If you don't tell me the things I want to hear, who will?* Maggie could see his reflection in the windowpane of the slightly opened door.

Her thoughts rambled on too... Poor Brown. She
wished he were happier... that she could help get him
out of his slump. Nothing she did made him happy for
long. They were so different. He was surface, nothing
hidden, letting it all hang out. Emotional, and sappy.
Face like a billboard, ready for anybody to read... *And
so spontaneous! He lives in the physical world.* She, on the
other hand, had an internal, meditative, self-controlled
temperament... learned to hide her feelings as a child.
Her mother, who never gushed with love to anyone, not
even her dad, was probably the reason. Both parents
were full-blooded Pennsylvania Dutch... not exactly
a warm heritage. But regardless of heritage, she had
sincerity. A simple "hand-holding" was big. She always
held Brown's broad, freckled hand when they sat
together. It meant a lot to her, but he seemed to take
it as insignificant. His temperament didn't bother her,
certainly not a deal-breaker, but she could see that it
was beginning to bother him... What he once absorbed
by youthful energy and stamina was no longer a walk in
the park... He had to learn to live with himself; with the
limitations that had to come; *He'd better settle down.* She
pushed the other door closed and polished the panes
enthusiastically; *I can't possibly become a scampering,
frolicking, Playboy Babe to please him... even if I wanted to...
so how can I expect him to be any different?"*

Brown, interpreting the look on her face to be the old
familiar "get that dirt" expression, sighed and turned
on the television.

As he reclined there on the couch, just from his
body language and facial expression, Maggie could
almost read his mind... *the big baby!* How ridiculous
that he expected such a fantasy. They'd both seen each
other at their weakest... physically and mentally. She

could recall a thousand examples of his weak moments without difficulty at all. What about the time they had gone to the lake a few summers back?

For most of the day Julie and her new boyfriend had watched the Ski-Doo aquatic motorcycles with fascination. She'd watched Brown wrestle with the desire to treat the kids to a ride... The rental was by the half hour, which seemed insufficient time, for the money. Periodically he would get up, suck in his paunch, dust the sand off his gaudy bathing suit and saunter over to the rental stand, attempting to schmooze the Rental guy. After a bit he would come back, plop back down on the towel beside her and mimic the Hispanic in disgust "Chou don't play... Chou don't have to pay, amigo..."

But when the heat of the day had passed, and the money crowd had thinned to nothing, Rental-guy gave in with a two-for-one at the regular price. Not a bad deal. He came back over to the family all excited, only to find that daughter Julie was too chicken to go out on her own. When Jeff, her boyfriend, offered to take her on the two-seater, it hadn't occurred to Brown for one second to just let the kids go out on the one Ski-Doo and call it good. No... the deal, he had worked so hard for was a two-for-one... He insisted on using the other machine in spite of the fact that Maggie had warned him; "Give it up Brown, you hate things that twirl and jolt a person's body around for no reason at all... why risk it?"

And it certainly hadn't helped matters when Julie had jumped in with; "Come on, Mom, he wants to ride it, Dad's no chicken..."

What choice did he have? He had backed himself into a corner and the only way out was on a Ski-Doo. Maggie's final protest was to point out the fact that the lake had become rough and choppy. But that was useless. She sat at the water's edge hugging her knees and watched the show.

"This is a walk in the park, don't worry Mag, these things are like motorcycles. Didn't I do my stuff on them in my day?" He'd called back to her while wading out into the muddy water. A statement, which she knew was more of an effort to build his own confidence than to comfort her.

Jeff and Julie had already mounted by the time he got out there. The rental guy took the kids through the particulars: Go-stop, on-off... blah blah... Brownie'd heard it all day. After making sure he had his life vest on securely, Rental Man took him through the orientation in spite of his impatience; "I got it. I got it..."

"Chou don't have to worry, see? 'Cause wheen 'chou fall off, the eengine stops. The key comes out because it 'ees attached to your wrest..."

"I know... I know... who's gonna' fall off?"

Brownie looked over his shoulder. On the beach were Maggie and an audience of thousands watching with the anticipation of rodeo spectators... waiting for the bull-chute to open. Jeff, and Julie zipped out across the lake on their two-seater.

Brownie started his, and nosed it around to face open water. On take-off the G-force from the powerful acceleration practically caused his feet and legs to flap behind in the breeze. And Maggie, having ridden on a motorcycle with him (too many times), knew he had no intention of slowing down. That would be nothing less than cowardly. He shot across the water like a rocket. Uh, oh, she'd thought; *that man is in deep yogurt, and on a machine more powerful than anything he's ever been on in his life!* Within seconds he was beside Jeff and Julie. They all waved at Maggie; then, the two Js took off in a series of donuts and swirls. Brownie gunned it... in hot pursuit. Jeff expertly swerved and darted back and forth causing waves that forced the pursuer to ski-jump in rapid succession... at full speed. Maggie watched with dread; the fool, he's convinced that everyone is watching. His only goal is to keep it from throwing him. She'd been right of course, he had confessed later (in private), that this was exactly what he had repeated to himself, over and over the entire time. *"They're watching..."*

Giving up on the chase thing, and a little frightened of him, the kids went about their business of having fun on the, admittedly, much slower machine. Julie even tried her hand at driving.

Brownie, meanwhile, rocketed back and forth, paralleling the shoreline at top speed. At the end of each run he would do a few circles and shoot off like a crazed caballero. *After all, everyone was watching.* The faster he went the more he'd churned up the water; the entire area was choppy with waves of his own making. *This thing is not going to throw me.* He locked his legs tighter onto the padded seat and hung on for dear life... gunned it to top speed. He kept watching the shore for Rental Guy, who told them he would wave when their time was up; "Pipfteen meenetts... por dos ees like thirty for uno, amigo..." but Brownie had negotiated it up to thirty minutes. Cool, huh? Where was Rental Guy? Oh well... he hammered down! Back and forth. His calves and thighs were beginning to tremble from having to hold on with his legs. Finally, Rental Guy was waving them in (thank goodness!).

Maggie could see the great relief and true manly

pride on the face of the bull-rider/rodeo-clown when he coasted back in. The thing had not thrown him. He stood up and waved proudly (*everyone was watching*). He saw Jeff and Julie come in behind him, then do a graceful three-sixty, and cruise right back out onto the lake. What?! Rental Guy was waving them back out with a big smile; "Chou can play and no pay Mon! Ko 'head."

"Why so generous now, you bone-head?" Brownie muttered, as he gyrated the Ski-Doo around and lurched back for the open water. Maggie watched him muttering and knew the gist of what he was saying, if not word for word. She had her own words... "Out of a swirling whirlpool, ladies and gentlemen... he's still in the saddle; more of the same, and more and more–too much–more."

After about six years were up, the kids glided in, just ahead of him; dismounted in the waist-deep water and walked up onto the beach; stood waiting. Brownie rolled off, surrendering his beast to Rental Guy. Maggie handed them towels and watched Brownie with her head cocked to one side; lips compressed.

When he tried to walk up out of the water his legs were like rubber. Literally. There was no strength. Maggie stared at him with a crooked smile, and nodding knowingly, raised her eyebrows and held a towel out toward him, as if to say, "Well?"

But the poor man was whipped. Breathlessly, he surrendered to gravity; floated onto his back and pretended to be enjoying the water. He smiled at Jeff and Julie who were aglow from the ride; "Go ahead I'm just coolin' down." Maggie slipped one arm around each of the happy children and escorted them back to their spot on the beach, leaving her man to suffer in private. A few times he made an effort to stand up and knew that he wouldn't make it. Thank God the life vest was enough to hold him up as he dog-paddled around a bit. Maggie watched from a distance; Who did he think he was fooling?

After ten minutes or so, he gathered up his courage and forced himself onto the beach. The only way he could stand, or feet or so, but had to walk across a concrete boat-launch ramp to get to the family, who were twenty feet beyond that.

Going up onto the ramp was not too bad, but when he tried to step down, there was no way; not even on crutches, not even on a raging bull, and especially not on his feet... buckled knees, spraddled him out onto the sand; first onto all fours, and then onto his stomach.

This time everyone was watching. Rental Man laughed knowingly. The kids thought he was pulling one of his jokes, and Maggie watched mortified; knew she had better not blow his cover. The bull-rider had become a beached, speckled-brown seal in a white T-shirt, flapping its arms at its side and scooting across the sand on its belly toward them. The barking noises were a good way to vent his pain... and his wretchedness. Who did he think he was fooling?

By now, Maggie, still spraying and wiping furiously had worked her way to the top of the second French door and finished the last window pane. Grabbed up her cleaning stuff. The glass gleamed like crystal; *So where's the glamour? For three days after that episode the man had not been able to walk down a set of stairs or even a curb without rolling his eyes in pain. Men!*

Brown is still ten years old... she reflected ruefully. And that was the problem. First, she's supposed to be his mommy and then he wants her to be some fantasy chick. Well? What about her, when did she get to be a little girl? Where was ten-year-old Maggie?

Brown changed the channel, catching Maggie out of the corner of his eye, as she sat on the side of their bed.

She could barely remember what it was like to be a child. To be carefree, loose, and happy. Brown was right; she was ho-hum, and matter-of-fact. Her Dutch heritage may have had somewhat to do with her reserved manner but there must be more to it than that. She was so dull, and colorless! When she tried to see herself, all she could see was bits and pieces. Odd shapes that were way too transparent, overlaid onto so many other bits and pieces of her life that it was impossible to separate them... just a muddy picture... Oh, how she wished she could see the whole. Get one complete layer out in front of her. Surely then she'd have a revelation!

As in most of life, first it happens and then we think it through... wasn't she having a revelation of sorts at this very moment?

Hmmmm... maybe that was it... she'd had 'em, but chose long ago not to billow over with excitement when the lights came on... Maybe she experienced the excitement of life as much as the rest of them... just more quietly than most.

And she was gullible. Always had been. Willing to believe anything, hopefully not because she was stupid, but because she was trusting. Innocent. Her only defense was to withdraw from a world where distortions, teasing and nonsense were the norm. At the same time she was a very serious person. Wanting something to believe in, something to count on. Black-and-white. No nonsense.

So, as a young girl (at about age ten in fact), unwilling any longer to risk embarrassment and disappointment...

she withdrew... into her own realm of yes and no. There, in the smallest of worlds, she was safe.

Maybe Brown had at first attempted to provide a "yard" for her to play in, to throw tantrums in, a place where she could scream with delight over nothing in particular, or plot harmless, childish revenge on those who teased her. But sadly, ten-year old Maggie was unable to come out and play... set in her ways... instead she'd learned forgiveness and patience. And though it was simply not in her nature to scream with delight, or be spontaneous, what she had brought to the table was self control, and hence, the ability to keep anger unexpressed from becoming disappointment and depression... *Doesn't that count for something? Nobody's perfect.*

As an inside person she was comfortable with a secure fortress, overlooking a yard. Her weakness was gullibility. Until she knew for sure nobody was putting her on, why bother exposing herself?

Not that she hadn't risked herself in life. She did, but in small ways. She was drawn to conspiracy theories, health food claims, and Brown, who was no threat, because she could see right through him. He made her laugh. Yes, she had risked herself with him. Now that she looked back she hated to think just how much that ability to make her laugh had influenced her decision to marry him. He was such a goofball.

He'd thrived on her acceptance. Grown up in many ways under her protection. Motherhood was easy to come by for her... probably the easiest, most fulfilling part of life. But her inability to play wholeheartedly and with abandonment... that part of her life was bypassed, and even if all life is not pretend, a lot of it is. Happy people played! Forty-five year old Maggie was long overdue.

And, Damn it! Brown had always known how to play. Which was fine for a good, long while... *heck, for twenty-five years of marriage. Then, one fine day, Brown finds himself wishing for a playmate,* no longer needing her to be rigidly mature, nurturing, or to put it bluntly, his Mommy... wishing instead for a companion, someone to have adventures with.

Maggie could see it. No. Really... he was getting ready to leave the yard! And maybe he already had. Mommy could either stay in the house and climb the walls, or she just might have to conjure up ten-year-old Maggie... then after a bit of mid-life therapy in the yard... say, some desensitization training... she could jump that fence too.

So, look out, Brown... There's more than one way to cope with life. Some people want to feel as though they have a handle on existence, so they pretend (or try) to believe things. Other people don't give a damn. It is what it is... and it probably ain't all that much.

—◇—

After two days in the hospital and four days at home, Brownie might have gone quietly insane, or perhaps it was simply a decision he'd made. A simple surrendering to the inevitable. It was an easy transition; the drugs helped, and so had the Psychological Questionnaire... Those were the thoughts he entertained anyway. When you're on the edge, stepping over the line is a short trip. Who would know when a person had moved half an inch? Not even the person... right? Maybe he really was nuts, but somehow imagining that he was insane helped him feel better than he had in a long time.

Maggie had gladly gone back to work after just one

day at home with him. But babying her sick little boy with bandages and pain pills before leavin' and after returning from the cannery was tolerable, at times even enjoyable. She attributed his calm spirit partly to the pain pills, and in her opinion, it was also highly likely that his injury was like a good spanking; recalling that for several days after the electrical shock episode, she'd actually had to nag him to drive the van over forty miles an hour in a fifty-five zone... he would just slump down in the seat and poke along, happy as a clam. But within a week he was his bad-old-self again, shouting at the idiots, and passing everything in sight.

But now they were dealing with pharmaceuticals. Pain pills. When those ran out, depression would surely come oozing out of his socks... for days. What goes up must come down... sigh... she could only hope for the best.

But he dodged that bullet. Instead, he seemed even happier. During this time, Brown puttered around the apartment, kept it cleaned-up (after a fashion) and even cooked a few meals. So, the swelling went down, the stitches were removed, and the doctor said he could go back to work whenever he felt like it. Maggie was glad to hear it; assumed he had gone back the very next day. They needed the money.

When she'd left for the bus that morning, he'd gotten up with her, made breakfast, kissed her goodbye, and pinched her on the butt as she went out the door. He sat back down at the breakfast table with another cup of coffee; added a little sugar, and then a little cream; stirring gently until the perfect tint of brown answered in the white cup. The grin on his face was automatic, coming easily when he was alone. Tapping out a little jingle with his spoon on the red and white checkered, oil-table-cloth (head spinning just a little):

> *"Where is Mister Coffee? Let me tell you for a fact!*
> *He's in my cup a steamin'; don't put nothin' in him, keep him black!*
> *Take that cool, clear water; bring it to a boil,*
> *Never mind the steaming, it'll soon be black as oil.*
> *Open up that container close your eyes... inhale...*
> *That tempting earthy fragrance... your heart begins to swell.*
> *Then take out a perfect measure, throw it into the pot.*
> *Stand back, anticipate your pleasure, black gold is what you've got.*
> *Coffee greets me every morning, strong and very black.*
> *I am the slave he is the master, and honey, that's a fact.*
> *Such satisfying flavor, I am chained and Mister Coffee has the key.*
> *Escape would be disaster... he... is what's come over me.*
> *With a deep rich accent from a distant foreign land,*
> *He cracks the whip and I come filing, cup held in my hand.*
> *Before his blackened presence, I bow on bended knee;*
> *I'll do him any favor, I like it black... he is my destiny."*

He felt great. *So? What's so complicated? Feather was right, the closer you get to the top of the cone the fewer choices you have. Black, white, or Brown... clear as a bell... three choices... yeah.* He drained the cup with a satisfying; "Ahhhhh." Went into the bedroom, put on a tank-top, jeans and leather loafers; looked in the mirror, admiring his still quite muscular arms, and sucked in his paunch, three-star Brownie twinkled on his shoulder.

The next day would mark a full week of sick-leave since the accident. The manila envelope from Personnel was lying on the dresser; The forms were filled out, but he still felt an aversion for them. The physical health questions were easy enough, but some of the things they asked in the psychological section were weird: Have you ever been insane? Do you have tendencies toward violence? Are you sexually aroused by inanimate objects? Goodness! How could any sane person get through it? And why would an insane person admit to any of these things? Crazy people don't care if they tell lies! He was mystified but had filled them out the best he could. He ignored any decisions about "previously unchecked boxes" on the employment application though... also ignoring the fact that the "corrected" form should be mailed back, or hand-delivered to Ms. Fisher very soon... and he still hadn't said anything about *that part* to Maggie.

He turned and headed for the front door... From the way he felt this morning, he wasn't even sure he'd ever go back to the airline. But after the last cup of coffee, he was wired to the gills and the natural tendency to associate a good day with doing something productive urged him on to the psychologist thing (get it over with... just in case). He finagled the psychiatric questionnaire from the manila envelope, found the phone number and called for an appointment. An opening at 11 a.m. *Bingo!*

—◇—

He parked the van behind a dingy building which served as an annex for various state and federal agencies (those with the glitz and the funding to rate better facilities were in the newer high-rise down the street). A group of people in their early adult years stood outside in the small parking lot smoking cigarettes and looking pretty much in need of whatever jobs the government might be able to hand out. Compelled to lock the doors of the van, he then walked over to read the directory posted beside the exterior elevator (retrofitted to the building): Doctor Marshal, Employer-Employee Counseling, room five-twenty-one... *Yeah, sure...* A small, very impersonal, stainless steel cubicle (space enough to hold about two people) responded grudgingly and wheezed up the outside wall when he pressed: Fifth Floor.

The "shrink's" waiting room consisted of two uncomfortable chairs, upholstered in a dirty, cream-colored burlap. William tried them both; sat right across from a sign he couldn't stop reading, over and over: PLEASE BE SEATED, THE DOCTOR WILL BE WITH YOU IN A MOMENT. *I did, I'm seated... I'm seated.. I'm seated...*

On a tiny, oak coffee table were several issues of National Geographic... all out of date. William lunged for one and then another and then another, desperately thumbing through all of them, trying to overlook the crying and crashing sounds behind the closed door on his left. After a while Doctor Marshal stood in the doorway. Apparently his last client had gone out by a different door.

Psychologist, Doctor L. Marshal, had bulging eyes that instantly intensified the feeling that one was about to be scrutinized. He smiled, introduced himself and invited William into the inner-office. He quickly glanced over what were apparently the same forms William had shoved into the designated slot (QUESTIONNAIRES) while in the waiting room... the only other slot said: Comments/Suggestions. For this one, William had an urge to take notes, confident there would be lots of input before this was over.

The "doctor" ran his fingers down the checked boxes

on the questionnaire, then with pencil and yellow legal-pad, looked up, smiled pathetically, and said in a non-threatening, high pitched voice; "Well, William, let's get started."

William was ready... forced a smile and settled into the chair; "You bet."

"Try to imagine me as a friend. Let's talk about the workplace. Do you enjoy the work? The people there?

I know what you're doing. You're trying to trap me into admitting I don't like the job; thought William, who said, out loud; "What are you looking for?"

"I'm not looking for anything... should I be? How about you telling me about yourself. Let's just do that: Start with your work; do you get along with everyone there?"

"Sure."

"You're light skinned... except for the freckles... however, your questionnaire reads that you are black."

"I am..."

"Full?"

"How full can a black be? I'm stuffed... is that full enough?

"We can move along faster if you try not to be hostile... or funny."

"Who's hostile? If you're reading the questionnaire... I checked "NO" for 'feelings of hostility'."

The doctor, not at all surprised at what he was uncovering, wrote on the margin of his legal pad: Combative, controlling behavior? A defensive William? Ashamed of being black?" And then he continued; "How about your childhood? Did you grow up in poverty?"

William had his guard up, and rightly so; "Look, Doc, have you ever examined a Negro? Watch the stereotypes."

"Well, I'm sure you are comfortable with your racial standing," he said, not at all convincingly. "There's no doubt whatever, that black is a definitive of white, and white is a definitive of black, and here in the Northwest, where there is a decidedly sparse population of blacks, I would suspect that someone of color may find it difficult to stay on track with his identity; without references so to speak... just a theory... don't make a big deal of it. Let's go on."

"Yeah why is that?" William asked... meaning, why so few blacks in the Northwest? But Doctor Marshal thought he had responded to his theory about black and white.

"You see, William, life is made up of paradoxes."

William had an urge to put his hands over his ears. Had somewhat looked forward to this time, hoping that he might actually get some answers, but now "hostile" seemed to be a viable option. He tried to give it his best though, shoving aside his current thoughts about who was supposed to do the talking? This man or him?

"Shall we do a little exercise to demonstrate?" and without waiting for an answer, the doc continued; "I'm going to say something and you tell me what would be the opposite: For instance; if I say, up, your answer might be, down."

"But never sideways?" W.M. Brown leaned back in his chair and crossed his arms defensively. *Borrring!*

Doctor Marshall, knowing as well as anyone else that he was not a doctor–didn't even have a P.H.D.–read his patient's body language and said; "Come on now, take this seriously."

William gave in; "Oh brother, here we go. All right. Shoot..."

Encouraged, questions rattled out of the doc's shrill little windpipe: "Heaven?"

"Hell."

"Evil?"

"Satan... I mean... God. "

"Work?"

"Play."

Get to the point a'ready; William wanted to say, but instead he said; "Doctor, this is very boring, ask me a hard one."

"Well fine... " he replied stiffly; "Negro."

Finally! "Male or female?"

The doc rolled his eyes; "Male."

William said; "Negro female. "

"Hmmmm... Ghetto."

"Which one? Harlem, Watts? I believe Brooklyn would be opposite of Harlem, and Compton would..."

The doctor interrupted; "I see, well... opposite to... not of..."

"Disneyland is the opposite to ghetto, then. Say, what is this supposed to tell you about me anyway?"

The Doc thought he would never ask; "You see William, in order to have a positive thought, you must have a negative one to define it with... a paradox; a reversal; a transference."

"I see..."

"No... no... Let me explain: Everything we think about, discuss, or endeavor to accomplish, is transposed against an opposite: The political struggles of a society; the have's and the have-not's; the liberals versus the conservatives; winners and losers. The black versus the white..."

"Now I see where you're going with this, why don't you just ask me directly what you want to know."

"Well, I want to know... are you comfortable being black?"

" Why? Are you gonna fix it so that I am?"

"I may be able to assist... By helping you understand the psychology of man; all men, black or white. It's simply an exercise in logic..."

Brownie, really not interested in the intellectual mumbo-jumbo this entire facade was wrapped in; certain this guy could go on forever, and hoping to save himself some time, cut to the chase; "But we both know that I'm really here to qualify for a position at the airlines, based on affirmative action and the quota system, huh?"

"Aha! Well now, this is exactly what I'm concerned about... you appear to be mulatto, and that might possibly cause mixed alliances, confused thinking, and who knows what else."

"I would think it would cause neutrality and fairness to both white and black. An ability to see from the middle rather than from the right or the left."

"Hmmm, do your mother and father live together?"

"Nope, they divorced when I was a baby."

"Is your mother black, or your father?"

"Father..."

"Do you see them regularly?"

"Only my mother; my dad lives in the southern United States... Just how black does an African American have to be, to be declared legally black... or a minority? Because I understand that only one-sixteenth Native American blood is necessary to qualify for Indian money from the government."

"I'm sure it's written somewhere but, as far as I know, there's a lineage thing done to establish a bona fide, traceable tribe. Politically speaking however, the racial thing simply boils down to which ethnic group you identify with... one way or the other... given the color of a person's skin. I can't imagine anyone arguing with them about their heritage. Nevertheless, William, our goal here is strictly based on leadership. Nothing at all to do with affirmative action."

Yeah, sure... like Brownie was gonna believe that...

The Doc continued, explaining (eyes somewhat glazed over) that certain questions must be asked: Questions about how many of his friends were black; how often he gathered with members of his immediate family, and on, and on, until Brownie had had enough, and asked; "What is the point of all this? I really don't get it."

"Well, as I said earlier, my job is to determine if you are comfortable as a black in a mostly white environment... are you angry, are you depressed, are you... ashamed... comfortable?

"Write down, comfortable and happy, Doc, and we're done. 'Cause that's what I am; content in both worlds, though I never really thought much about it 'til a few weeks ago. I may have had a subconscious need to know before then, but I'm sure I could be happy in either world… and maybe, as long as you're writing, you could put down that I consider myself to be a human being, and neither black nor white. In fact I insist that you write it down." He stood up, surprised at his anger and his own eloquence.

The Doctor was writing furiously, looked up and nodded, wrote some more, and then said; "Please sit down, William. See? I wrote it. Just what you said. I think we are making wonderful progress, I wish you would stay just a little longer."

William sat down.

"You seem to be quite comfortable with yourself, and that worries me a little… It is possible that you are blocking… living in a denial of sorts… too comfortable in your own, uh… skin… circumstances." Brownie couldn't believe his ears. This guy was in denial himself, obviously unable to accept that anyone but whites could be content in life.

He decided to play the game a little; after all, he was insane, wasn't he?

"Well, I do have weird dreams…"

"Mmmm Hmmm… Well, William! Tell me about them."

He told him the one about Carlos branding the blackened herd of cattle. The doctor sat on the edge of his chair, shaking his head up and down, lifting his eyebrows over and over again, encouraging every word, as Brownie exaggerated the dream beyond, way beyond what he had actually dreamed, including broad sweeping descriptions and gesticulations about the barbecue tower too.

Completely taken in; "Fascinating..." concluded the not-really-a-doctor man...

Brownie slouched back into his chair and studied the effect he'd had...

The doctor made a few entries on his pad and then smiled, "You know, William, I can help you with this..."

With what? William wondered, but kept quiet and looked compassionately at the doctor, in silent assent for him to go ahead... while the word, *help*, skittered about in his own mind.

"It's the paradox again, this dream confirms it even more clearly than I could've. In the simplest of terms we are faced everyday with the life and death of cultures, species, planets and people. And even in non-life, material substance, and right on down to the atoms... their protons and neutrons; there is a positive and a negative... What I'm trying to say is that you, we, are energy. Cattle are energy... we eat them for their energy. They live and die for us... life and death.

Some would think that as such, in his present form, man is juxtaposed between the forces of good and evil, and that he tries to control those forces (represented in your dream by the hardened iron surfaces of flesh against the whip). And those same people would say that the struggles man faces in his everyday life are due to that battle between those forces... the prize, of course being the souls of men... our souls." He waved that one off with a snort, and went on without a breath; "But this is simply an explanation designed to help those weak enough to need it, and desperate enough to believe it. An invention of man unfortunately flawed, because it also conveniently plugs into the all pervasive negative and positive.

"A more intellectual explanation should somehow transcend the mundane by offering something far higher. A tower of sorts leading to the stars and the eventual release and transcendence of our captive identities. A way to make sense of our behavior, our thought life, and our motives... instead of the bottled-up (and as in the dream, barreled-up) restrictive ideas of our own limited identities." The doctor paused, the smug look on his face was unmistakable; looking as though he had touched the very hem of the Creator of all identities (if one believed in such things).

William was impressed with the doc's recall and the interpretation of his dream, but had played poker face the whole time, and... *Just to keep him guessing...* let out a snort of his own.

But, still caught up in the heavenlies, the doc continued; "On the other hand, to deny that these forces do have a significance beyond the physical (for there may actually be something spiritual out there) would be tantamount to foolishness. Because... well... who can know?"

Good question.

"When we come back to the physical, as when you woke from your dream, we are invaded with the confusing stimuli and a mushy sauce called "daily living." The red sauce needs to be put in the barrels too, William. When the unconscious takes over (deep-sleep dreaming is one way) we are freed from the polarization of our thoughts as well as our bodies.

"Simply put; if a person is conscious, and insists that there is no right and wrong, they deny these forces, and are actually ignorant and weak themselves as they attempt to structure buildings with sand, in a world where gravity is obviously at work." He stopped waving his hands around and held them out toward William, palms-up, while imaginary sand filtered through his wiggling fingers.

William, listened with knitted brow, wondering just how much of that sand might be in the doctor's head.

The doctor was on a roll: "These people pride themselves at being free, fluid... and... and flowing," he added with a slightly musical inflection. "And perhaps they are, for the present... believing that it's all good and denying the obvious opposite."

The only people William knew that might "flow" with this description were the pseudo-hippies who seemed to live free from all social conformity. He braced himself, because obviously the doctor was becoming more and more agitated...

"They, however, exist in a world of their own making. Disconnected; totally open; vulnerable to... uh... whatever, and they go insane, or at the very least erratic and completely unstable... thanks to that very freedom! Provided (by the way) by the people who *are* holding on to reality... by that, I mean the sane ones William... who *do* believe in right and wrong. They know they have to hang on... they dare not allow themselves the luxury of freedom... not of that sort.

"What I'm saying here is that we must strike a balance; position ourselves with both positive and negative energy in order to have consistency and coexistence." His voice was hitting a higher note; "So, now you see, to say that you are in the exact middle, is like saying there is no right and wrong, no black and white... that too is unrealistic. Yes! I am worried about that kind of thinking."

William stood up and the doctor stood up with him, still talking; "Of course, we will always need the defining contrast of the negative; until we go on to the "next world," where the negative has no further pull on the positive."

William positively would've liked to pull on the guy's nose; edged himself over toward the door he had come through. The doctor slid ahead of him and shook his head, still talking, shaking his finger; "It is hard to imagine purposeful existence without these forces stretching us to the point of insanity, and which, actually and eventually do destroy our bodies. For a lifetime we fight the inevitable, and call it purpose. Who can blame man for going over the edge sometimes?"

My thoughts exactly, William agreed silently, edging toward the other door, hoping for better luck and suspecting that the previous victim escaped that way. The doctor had by now pulled his hair into a vertical position, moved over to the window and was looking out over the skyline, sagging, resigned to let William go... sigh... if he must.

William paused... worried... wondering if he might witness a suicide at any moment. The doc's reflection in the window revealed an expression that had suddenly changed to anger, and very possibly deranged; his voice began to hit even higher notes and to lose all sense of modulation... in somewhat of an erratic shrieking; "Existential...ists–make-me...sickkkkk! Swimming, in a sea–of magnetic attractions... (gulp)... and repulsions!!!! at the expense...of...of... those who follow-the-path-laid-out by the steadfast demands of God!" He stopped and looked utterly shocked at himself; "There! Oh, my... oh, my... Fiddle-de-dee! I've said it. You've heard it... can't blame me... really. There has to be a God! The positive *is* God... Ummm.... Uhhhhh... Can we believe that?!!?"

William sneaked a look at the clock, then at the doc, then for his escape route. Somebody had to leave the room, whether himself or the doc, neither could last much longer. Now, it was clear what had gone on with the previous appointment; such a commotion! This weirdo did this all day long? *Sheeesh!* "My time is up doc, can I go now?" he pleaded.

"What? What was that? Wait. No. Please; we're almost finished." He took a towel from a hook on the wall... wiped his face furiously. A brass plaque just above it read: CRYING TOWEL. William had read it as a joke, but now was not so sure.

Burbling and snuffling in the towel, the words that came out might have been, "Insanity (as defined by some): mmmbuumn knooo bulblicth... sets in when a belief is rock-solidly stood upon... but mmmmiddg abligh acbliblet... a sane person spends a good part of their lives trying to find out who they are; contrasting this-with-that... while an insane person is convinced without further discussion that they really *are* Napoleon. Flexibility is the only way to stay sane, William. Acknowledge the negative, but seek the positive. Don't be ashamed of your skin color... You must not deny your blackness, it will be to your good. You are a good man. The negative will become positive... did I tell you two negatives become a positive? To dwell upon the obvious..."

Further words (if any) were completely wasted on poor William, who'd walked out to breathe more appealing odors of cracked, plastered walls and dirty, hallway carpets. The *definitely-not-really-a-doctor-man* didn't even notice he was gone.

—<>—

Chapter Ten

Leaving the kooky psychologist behind was freedom itself... like escaping from an actual nut-ward. The fate of the employment questionnaire was left behind too, the doc could do whatever he wanted with it... *good luck with that.*

Traveling due east toward the hot springs, the morning air blowing through the van windows felt Saturday-clean on Brown's skin. White clouds, poised for greatness over mountains and hills in the distance, billowed soft in a deep blue sky. Just a few of the many things he loved about Oregon.

The trees and brush along the freeway showed no signs of a breeze; a signal the rainy weather might be letting up for a while. The freeway emptied out onto the east-west route. Time to coffee-up; Texaco Starmart brew was good enough. When he approached the swinging doors, a hippy kid held it open for him and smiled. Wow! That was unusual. A polite hippy?

The female clerk inside was friendly too, laughing at his wisecracks and wishing him a nice day. She wants me... he kidded, peering at his face in the rest room mirror. When he got back to the idling van, the pump attendant returned his silly grin.

Less than a block away, the polite hippy-dude trudged east with his thumb out, not even looking back at the traffic, as if hopeless or unconcerned that he would be picked up at all. Brownie passed without slowing. A quarter mile later turned around and went back; passed again. Was the guy dangerous? Hmmm... no backpack, or bundles of any kind. A weapon was very unlikely since the guy wore a sleeveless top and baggy cut-offs. What stood out most of all was his big, bare feet padding along on the surely, already hot asphalt.

Another illegal u-turn across a double yellow line set him eastward again. A surprised look from the hippy and an encouraging wave of Brownie's hand (a timeless gesture from one traveler to another) was all that was needed... there, or anywhere else in the whole world.

Maybe it was because of Feather, but he felt more comfortable now having one of these people in his van. A good mood increased his sense of hospitality too. In fact, he noticed that he was quite content not to exceed the fifty-five-mile-per-hour speed limit posted on the highway. What was the hurry? Besides, picking this kid up could be an opportunity to get some inside information about a continuing story he'd been following in the local newspaper for the last few days.

Lake City was situated at the upper end of a wide and fertile valley that opened up wider and wider, traveling from the south to the north. Rivers and creeks, from the coastal mountain range on the west side, and from the towering Cascades on the east, fed the large meandering river that flowed northward down the valley. Cities and towns had sprung up along its banks. The agricultural industry prospered from the water and from the fact that the rivers had overflowed their banks since the beginning of time, depositing rich, sandy loam. One of these rivers flowed right through the heart of downtown Lake City and another skirted its northern boundary.

Over the years the area had progressed from a logging community to a university town, and had in the last few years bulged with urban growth into a full-blown metropolis (due to high-tech and low-tech manufacturing).

All carefully monitored for environmental impact by the intellectual-set, connected to, and congregated around, the university. But the further from town the more likely attitudes regarding many issues would be quite different. Logging was no exception.

For almost a century, giant fir-trees were ferried down these streams by courageous men for a logging industry that now barely held on. Several generations of hardy American men and women had grown up on the banks of these two rivers. Their present day ancestors felt slighted, fearing their rich history and way of life were being lost and even ignored. Of course, logging techniques had changed with the times; rivers had been dammed-up for flood-control and for electrical power. Although the now tamed rivers flowed through Lake City, disappointment flowed through too. Even though people on all sides of political and civic issues turned on their lights with power from the same hydro-generators; drank water from the same stream; all tasted bitter and sweet and refused to see the light, even though it shone to one degree or another... at practically all times.

To Brownie (and those he talked with), the earth worshippers seemed to be lacking a certain conscience or awareness. Haters of everything that spoke of industrial America, free enterprise, and private property, they were sold out to the preservation of nature, hoping in the promise of a utopia, all the while blindly ignoring the blatant signs of their own diminishing human potential and spirit.

Their political allies and/or counterparts simply tolerated them as a means to an end and would no more have had them in their homes or cars than would the most adamant timber worker.

He'd found it a waste of time to get that involved with

the political thing. Whenever he saw the popular bumper sticker which read: Visualize World Peace, he couldn't resist smiling, because that summed up the whole farce pretty well. Visualizing was definitely not his bag. His learned, ingrained tendency of settling things out on the sidewalk, or in an alley precluded civilized discussions with practically anyone from a different camp, and at the very least developed into arguments... So, he'd left it alone. Chalked it up as a job for someone with better upbringing than he'd had. He didn't have bumper stickers either... well, actually he'd had one custom-printed that said: "I don't hate anyone... in particular." But he had opinions... and he could still be angry or disappointed. Who could fault him for that?

Yet, the kid who now sat in the seat next to him was probably oblivious to most of that and would be doing good just to sign his own name. And from all appearances, had absolutely nothing between him and starvation. Why, a sudden change in the weather could take him off the face of the earth, yet there he sat... peacefully watching the fence posts flash past his open window. Wearing a black, sleeveless, jean jacket, which had been shredded with a razor, or knife, in long slits along the chest, back and shoulders; this had caused the remaining cloth to roll around into a multitude of vertical ropes. His jean cutoffs were black too (shredding of their own accord at the knees) and had almost become the color brown from being unwashed for who knew how long?

Just as he'd suspected, his passenger was headed to the hot springs, which was further up the road another fifty miles; so he hung back, making casual conversation, not wanting to close in too fast with questions. But the kid seemed surprisingly open and in a talkative mood.

So Brownie piled right in, asking questions about the

newspaper story he had been following. It wasn't really news; it was more like a continuation of an ongoing saga. For over a year the tree-huggers had been protesting a tract of land about to be logged. It all seemed so foolish. Why would anyone care if trees from areas burned out by a forest fire were logged? Several protestors had been arrested (same old stuff) for trespassing on the site, or for obstructing the law, and were lodged in the county jail. Thirty or more of their "environmental associates" had been arrested too, during a demonstration protesting those same arrests.

The newspaper tried to be kind, referring to the deputies' impressions of these inmates as: "Not the usual; Not that interested in personal hygiene; Obstinate and unreasonable." A more comprehensive report in a subsequent article pointed out that at the arraignment most had refused to identify themselves beyond their self-chosen names... Sage, Starlight, Cedar... and were informed that it would be impossible to have public legal counsel without proper names and identification; such as drivers licenses, social security numbers, and whatever... A few of them caved in, gave the information and were released; others stuck with it. One plucky girl of eighteen absolutely refused to leave, "...'til they promise not to log the land!" The sheriff was unable to convince her, or the group, that this was a federal matter and they were just making trouble for themselves while taking up space in a jail that was needed for criminals. Their unreasonable answer to that was a threatened hunger strike. Basically, the county taxpayers had criminal-housing-problems, and now this worrisome group of misfits were on their hands. The kid knew all about it, but listened patiently while he was told the story. Finally winding down and catching his breath, Brown asked; "What's your name?"

"Shadooww..." the young man answered, with long O's and windy W's.

The air hissed out of Brownie's lungs in a short, "Wow!" He paused, letting the name sink in for a moment; "What do you call yourselves as a group?"

"We're just, heads... kids."

Kid? This "kid" had already said he was 24 years of age. But ignoring that, Brownie went on to explain that in his time the word "hippy" meant something a lot different than what he could see in this group of "heads."

The hippies of the seventies had been hopeful and had a mission to bring peace and love on the earth. Love was found all around, especially in nature, *because of it being so innocent and all...* Hippies of his day had the mission of turning everybody onto that love, and marijuana was thought to be the key. He finished with; "Do you worship trees... you know... nature?"

"I guess you could say they do. I don't know if I do, I really don't know what I believe: I believe in having fun, kicking back. I don't do any drugs, 'cept marijuana." While he rambled on, Brownie settled in, listening patiently and finally interrupted; "What about God... any god?

"Whatever you believe in becomes a fact. I believe in God and that's what makes him real."

"Hmmmm, you mean God is a created Creator?" maybe the kid would see the absurdity of his statement, but apparently it went right over his head.

"Yeah, he's real because people believe in him."

"Is marijuana real because you believe in it?"

"Maybe. It's a naturally occurring substance... gets into your system and changes your outlook on life. In fact, it lives through you by relating to the rest of the plant world, through your eyes, your energy. I guess it relates to the whole earth... trees, minerals, and everything natural. I'm not addicted though, I just do it 'cause it feels good."

Brownie studied him for a few moments in silence. He was a beautiful specimen of humanity. Thick, brown hair, no more than ten inches long, bushed out in every direction. A sparse, curly, reddish brown beard appeared to be classic in shape. His brow projected outward, emphasizing surprisingly clear, greenish-blue eyes. Most impressive were his feet: Larger than life, and perfectly formed, with marvelous toes that were angular and defined; each capped with bright, healthy, pink nails. Suddenly Brownie knew what it was about this guy that fascinated him. "You know what? You look like a statue of Plato, the philosopher..."

This pleased Shadow, who exclaimed; "Hey! I think that's what I want to be... a philosopher!"

Brown wasn't about to respond to this. After a few moments, while the youngster silently contemplated just what duties a philosopher might encounter, Brownie continued the conversation, tactfully encouraging him to visit the local library. The entire topic quickly fizzled... but it had led them to another one: Productive living.

Even though it was Shadow's opinion that there was no reason to work... just for money that is... it turned out he wasn't all flake. He had a job, kind'a self-employed, making head-jewelry that he shipped back to a Head shop in his home state, and he also sold it at the Saturday Market.

Brownie needed no explanation about Head shops; they were still around, and still sold pot-smoking apparatus, psychedelic posters, and tobacco products. And (for this "ever evolving" generation of hippies) weird, new-age crystals and minerals, believed to contain healing powers and magnetic alignments for the health of the human body and soul.

Shadow's ex-girlfriend-roommate worked with the city's grounds maintenance crew, but she was a weekend head who agreed with the hippy ideology, and tolerated the system for her own ends. According to Shadow there were lots of them; "weekenders," who returned to their "real" lives on Monday morning.

"So, there are transitional people amongst the tree-huggers?"

Shadow assured him that it was so, and showed no animosity to the tree-hugger label.

By this time, they had traveled up into the mountains, about half way to the springs. Brownie was very curious about how the kid had gotten his name; "At a party in my apartment, when I lived in San Francisco. Out of one hundred and eighty people, me and a friend were the only two who weren't busted! We went out the window and hung on a drainpipe for two hours on the third floor level. When everybody got out of jail, they said we had disappeared into the shadooowws."

Brownie thought about that for a bit. A shadow of his former self? Or a shadow of what is yet to be?

Shadow, obviously fascinated with his own name, was still going: "Now, man, I just disappear into the shadows. When I move around in the light, all that shows up is black… yeah, mysterioussssss…" then, coming down out of his reverie somewhat, he added; "All the kids have names… some of 'em cooler than mine."

Brownie shuffled in his seat and accidentally bumped the cell phone onto the floorboard; "Modern convenience," he said, flatly.

Shadow jumped on it; "Yeah and it's an *in*convenience too. They can find you anywhere in the world."

"Who could find me?"

"The government, man... I could do it if I had a computer. I have always had a way with computers. I saved my mom's from a virus once. I don't know how, I just did it. I could find you if I wanted to... just put me in front of a computer and I could find you."

"But I couldn't find you, right?" A little education was helpful at times: Brownie's computer classes had armed him sufficiently to tactfully inquire about Shadow's computer "gift," and with just a few questions was disappointed to find that the kid wasn't gifted at all... mysteriously or otherwise... just full of beans. Simply rationalizing, and embellishing the facts of his life in order to feel good about himself. He listened anyway.

"Right. Nobody can find The Shadow. I don't even have a picture I.D. The government sucks! They won't let me get one without a birth certificate. There's lots of us kids that came up on the street; we don't have birth certificates! Why should I have to prove that I'm alive? Can't they see that? I'm never gettin' one..."

Evidently this was a sore subject for the young man, but he had a good point. Really. Why couldn't the government help these street kids out with some sort of validation of their humanity? No wonder they created names for themselves and related to the earth so strongly.

He drove on in silence, wondering what might he hold onto that was tangible about this person with a mixed bag of contradictions; wanting to disappear, and on the other hand... be visible. Mysterioussss... right.

And besides, the kid had begun to cast a "shadow" over Brownie's day, which had started out just fine...

his thoughts had been mostly happy ones. He'd had it all figured out. All he'd wanted to do today was choose between the three options at the top of the "cone:" black, white or Brown?

The van picked up speed. He tried to put the conversation on the fast track; "So, Shadow, is there such a thing as right and wrong? What about the government and their facts; are they real facts, even though you don't believe in them? Or Charlie Manson? His facts were real to him, but they translated into death for others; and what about the guy that got shot the other night up at the springs, at Hippie Hollow? He was with his family... just celebrating his sister's birthday. Did the fact that the guy with the gun wanted the music turned down, give him the right to kill the other man? He went after that kid's music; believed it was right and now he's in jail... for a long time..." He wasn't finished but Shadow was... and looking straight up the highway... about to disappear.

Brown stopped talking, but was still thoughtfully and silently engaged; *Yeah, kid, the man with the gun is about to disappear... roll on out of sight... like just so much baggage that the state of Oregon will be forever hauling around. And you know what, pal? The people who pass you by in their cars? They're scared of you, and you stink. I don't care how much patchouli oil you put on, you can't cover stink with stink. You represent every fear they have. You have become a receptacle for their fears! You carry it in your pockets, and your backpack... Plato... even if you were butt-naked it'd still be in your hair and your pretty green eyes. I don't care how free you try to be; you'll still be loaded down with baggage, and a portion of anyone else's you come in contact with... probably more than you'll ever know.* Of course, all Brown could do was sigh... knowing that no matter how these thoughts were phrased, the kid wasn't ready. Hopefully someday he would be, and hopefully there would be someone there that would lay it out for him.

Miles back, he had asked Shadow if he'd known or heard of a girl named, Feather; He'd said he had, and described her as a tall girl with long blond hair, about eighteen or nineteen years old, but he hadn't seen her in months.

Several times in the last few days, and when reading the newspaper article, Brownie had thought about her and the strange names the other kids chose. Or possibly because of his instinctual concern for her as a child who needed a father; and though he hated to admit it, very possibly as a beautiful woman who'd said she wanted to take him all the way.

When he passed his mother's lane, he didn't even slow-down, feeling like a naughty boy at seventy miles an hour. The day had warmed up. Heat blasted through the van's open windows. Hepner's Country Market was the logical choice for a cool, fountain-drink. He pulled off the highway and coasted over to the gas pumps (Free soda with fill-up of ten gallons or more!). Two state police cars were just pulling out of the parking lot.

He was just about to offer Shadow a soda when Todd, (name on the shirt) walked up; "Help you?" It was immediately obvious that Todd was down in the mouth, and glaring past him at Shadow... who had just awakened from some dream and was looking around at where he was; then got out of the van, and yawned loudly. Brownie looked at Todd again, and when he turned back, Shadow had disappeared.

"Twenty-five bucks, Todd;" he said absently, closing the van door while his eyes scanned the parking lot; "What's up with the cops?"

"Ask Mom, she said not to talk about it with nobody."

The Hepners were an enterprising family with a logging history, who had seen the writing on the wall years before. While still involved in the logging business they'd opened a general store, high up in the foothills, just off the east-west highway. As logging declined they'd fine-tuned their commercial understanding. Since tourism had increased they decided to build bigger, and closer to the highway for more visibility. They'd made the right move. Offering more products and better service... business increased dramatically.

Even though the store was ten miles up-river from Brown's mom, he was on a first name relationship with the Hepners, as were many of the residents of the narrow valley. In fact, the stretch of forty miles or so, up the valley, was thought to be one community by most of the old-timers. They had the same high school; the same UPS guy served all of them, and many other everyday life services overlapped, reducing the concept of boundaries.

The corn-dogs barked at him the moment he set eyes on them... two for ninety-nine. Although he had healthier choices, he chose "Dogcatcher." The store was large and orderly: A testimony of know-how, and willingness to serve customers well. The nearest supermarket was forty miles down-river, yet the Hepners never tried to price-gouge. Brownie recognized their sacrifice. He waited 'til the gas console lit up with the amount owed. He was the only customer at the counter; "Did you guys have some trouble, Joyce?"

When she took his money, the expression on Mrs. Hepner's face left no doubt that, they had indeed. She looked to the back of the store. Brownie could see Mr. Hepner in the storeroom... fuming. She motioned for one of her daughters to take over for her, and walked with him toward the storeroom, explaining (and venting) quietly. She and Wayne were just about fed up.

The hot-springs crowd had become more and more troublesome over the last few years. Mainly the dreadlocks, who were often arrogant, and some were actually hostile. No social graces whatever, not only disrespectful, but dirty and foul smelling. Hanging out in the parking lots with their buses, running customers off with their bongos and primitive dancing, even after large, No Loitering, signs were posted. No. It was a problem all right.

And though none had been caught in the act, surely they were the ones who abused and vandalized the rest rooms. They weren't at all like the drunks, whose plain and simple, pickled-headed stupidity, and occasional stubborn demands one could normally predict. The dreadlocks were more complicated; harder to understand. They had two basic expressions: either a blank haughtiness, or a scornful, intellectually superior look, cast at anyone who dared to confront them about their behavior.

Aside from the fact that they went half naked with rags for clothing, skimpy scarves for dresses… full-grown women mind you… with dirty jeans hanging so low, that their pubic hair showed… They also disregarded the, No Shoes-No Shirt No Service signs; reeked so strongly of Patchouli oil that your eyes smarted; and they were so hateful! Disregarded any effort the owners made to be nice… all of this and more came tumbling out of the frustrated Hepners.

Brownie had to agree; they definitely had a problem, but; "Not all of these kids are dreadlocks. They're just coming in on the fringe, searching for a cause to identify with… not really committed like some… who are maybe, uh, terminal. Others are making transitions… you know… through life."

"Yeah, Myron, some of that may be true, but today was too much," Wayne looked tormented and weary as he continued relating the incident. It had been a close call. Somebody could've gotten killed. A bus load of them had come for gas and refused to move away from the gas pumps until they were good and ready. When Todd insisted, he was shoved aside. The other attendant came over to help and was pushed away even harder. The owner's son heard the commotion over the intercom and came out to help; three other men (loggers–unemployed loggers) who lived just behind the store overheard the beginning brawl between all three store-workers and twelve to fifteen dreadlocks.

All gladly jumped into the fray. Fists and hair flying like a scene from a cowboy movie: One logger brought out a shotgun and fired it into the air; this inspired a few of the dreadlocks to pile into their microbus and sputter off. But incredibly, two others rummaged around in their multi-colored van, found clubs and turned on the logger, slapping their naked chests and shaking their clubs like cave men, saying; "You wanna shoot me, go ahead… shoot me… " The logger with the shotgun (lower lip bulging with Redman chew) may have convinced them he would do just that if they didn't leave immediately. But the fact they had rattled off down the highway could have been because the State Patrol's flashing emergency lights could be seen a mile away, and by the time they'd pulled in… gotten the whole story… it was too late. Their search was futile; the van was nowhere to be found; not even at the hot springs. The Staters came back to the store, filled out their reports and left.

But then an even more incredible thing happened. Once the police and the loggers were gone, eight of the dreadlocks showed up at the store… again! All with clubs.

They had simply pulled onto a side road and waited it out, then went to their camp for re-enforcements; came back slapping the plate glass windows and doors, daring the store workers to come out... yeah... but the loggers came back too; tackled the one at the door and pushed his skinny butt inside... into willing arms.

Within seconds, the shotgun guy fired off a couple more... just over their heads... "Sure, a couple bird-shot ping-pinged, off the metal roof of the bus... and then, well, that was about enough for the other seven to give it up. That's when they slinked away... "'fore them logger-boys really got mad..." leaving the ringleader inside... captive... handcuffed in duct-tape. Charges were pressed and filed, but all doubted if any good would come of it. "Hell. Probably jes' trade out offenses... three shotgun blasts for simple disturbing of the peace... after all nothing was damaged, 'cept'n that beat up, old doodlebug van of theirs."

Brownie had listened carefully, feeling sorry for these folks; "Well, the rumor is the chamber of commerce is putting pressure on the county to shut the springs down; maybe that'll happen soon," he offered unconvincingly. The Hepners were in no mood to believe it. They scoffed and fumed a while longer. Brownie offered a few more garlands of peace, but it was useless. The emotional damage was too great. He left feeling powerless to help either side. His smile was gone.

The Hepners sat on milk crates, still discussing their predicament. The dreadlocks deserved the hate that was coming their way. It was time to get this settled once and for all. The entire up-river community was fed up with it. Where would they get their micro-beers and Ju-Jubes if the store wasn't there? "Heck Joyce, you know as well as I do, it was them kind that burnt the other store down...

cuttin' off their noses to spite their faces."

Joyce responded; "Even if they did, I don't hate 'em, I just want 'em outta here. And they'll never leave. If you run that group off, another one'll be right behind... we just have to put up with it," she finished with a long sigh.

But Wayne wasn't so sure; "Not if there's no hotsprings for them to come back to, besides, running that particular group off has a real appeal to me. Look how they treated us. You think this is the end of it? The law can't touch 'em... or it won't, anyway."

There was only one thing that would take care of it, once and for all... blow up the springs... just a little bag of "p... ppp... pow-pow-powder," as Wayne called it in a mock stutter; smacking his palm with his fist in rapid succession; "They come for nature, 'n nature's enemy can run 'em off... nothing like a little stump remover to build respect in a man."

Joyce was afraid somebody would get hurt; "Wayne, they're always there, day and night."

"We can run 'em off first..."

"How?"

"There's ways... " He looked knowingly across the yellow, sunlit, tiled floor; "At the last light, when the day-trippers have gone, and only the moon-gawkers are left."

A shuffling of big, beautiful, perfectly formed feet, might have been heard, had either of them stayed in the back room any longer. And, if they'd been looking at anytime during their conversation, they would have seen a mysterious shadow splayed across the same tiled floor further back, amongst stacked boxes of pickles and motor oil...

Back out on the highway, still aiming the van toward the hot springs, Brownie felt irritated. This day was not as happy as he'd thought it would be. Who was he kidding? And Feather. She wouldn't be up at the springs either; that was such a long shot, he'd had to be stupid to even think she would. With yet another illegal U-turn, the van was headed west once again... back down river. Time to narrow the cone choices down, Ready or not, mother, here I come; I'm either white and Brown, black and Brown, or black, white and Brown...

Just a few hundred yards from the store, he recognized Shadow. So! There he is... but he just honked and kept going. Shadow waved back absently. There was a pop-bottle sticking out each of his front pants pockets, and one was in his hand; he appeared to be looking for more in the ditch... When Brownie looked in the rear-view mirror, he had disappeared into the bushes. Let him look... work for a change; do him good to earn a soda.

Minutes later, the van wasn't even so much as a memory to Shadow who reappeared walking faster than usual, back toward the store with enough returnable cans and bottles to make a phone call.

Brownie tapped on the screen door to the sound of Wheel of Fortune, playing on Flo's television set. "Myron!" She exclaimed happily from her recliner,

"Come on in, son... the door ain't locked."

The heat from the sun was intense. A record high. Myron gladly pulled the door open and stepped into the somewhat cooler environment of the trailer's interior. "Sit down, Let's see if he wins the car," she exclaimed with childish excitement.

"It's hot in here, you need air conditioning," (Meaning that if he were any kind of son he would have provided her with it).

"Naaah, it cools off real quick at night cause of the river... I like the contrast. Shhhh... he's guessing, " she added and pointed the remote control at the gleeful contestant.

"Hee heee," she cackled, "he did it. Ooooh, isn't that great? He's so happy!" With a decisive aim of the remote she snapped the set off; "Want some iced-tea?"

"Sure!" He loved her iced-tea; pre-sweetened, southern style.

"You here alone again?"

"Guess so..."

"You aren't fighting with Maggie are you? You look a little down in the mouth."

Myron twisted around on the old Naugahyde couch hoping to curb the sweat rolling down his back.

Over the sound of clinking ice-cubes in the kitchen, Flo asked; "How's the headache? You feeling better?"

"Yeah, all better now," he answered trying to sound as cheerful as she did.

Returning with iced-tea in a quart fruit jar (just as he knew she would) and a glass almost as big for herself (no surprise either); "What cha' got?" she asked, arching her eyebrows, settling back into the recliner.

Myron took a big chug of the iced tea; "Mother, I am not here to make you unhappy..."

"Certainly not... What kind of remark is that anyway?"

"I don't think I ever asked you about this... why do

I look so much different than Dad, or you... or anyone in our family?"

"Oh? You haven't asked me that? About the freckles? Only a thousand times... up until you were four or five years old. Not satisfied with the answer anymore?"

"What was the answer? I don't remember ever talking about it."

"Well, it was always about the freckles. We talked alright; we talked until those freckles disappeared... and that was about the same time your dad disappeared... with another woman." Myron could feel his ears warm slightly. He'd heard about this before... too many times. Somehow when she said it he felt responsible for his dad leaving. Which brought up another subject; one he'd never asked about outright, but assumed that this was around the time she had turned to alcohol. "Do you blame dad for the drinking?"

Definitely a sore subject for his mom who stiffened a little, but answered with what appeared to be a determination to be honest; "No. I drank to please your step-dad, Bob."

"He made you do it?"

"No, but he liked it when I drank with him... and I guess I did too."

"Well, I didn't." Myron paused for just a second, regretting that this subject had come up, he was supposed to be talking about his skin color, but he went on in his haphazard spontaneous way, thinking out loud; ignoring any warning his conscience might have been signaling to him about the pain he was about to cause. His words were not given with anger, in fact they were as gentle as criticism can be; "I didn't like the drunken brawls the two of you got into, or the all night terrors of trying to keep you from killing yourself, or the stupid people that came around the house all the time, or the hell-holes we lived in, or the way I felt when you looked so cheap and low-life. I didn't like the fact I had to take care of you at ten years old, or the fact I was so screwed up by the time I was a teenager, I would do anything I damn-well pleased, as long as I could get away with it."

"I'm not going to sit here and listen to this, Myron. I've done the best I could for you... and all my children... "

This mystified Myron, how could she say that with a straight face? "Well, you owe me an apology."

That did it; her eyes became cold and hard, the pupils shrank to small, thorny points. He'd seen that look many times when confronting her about other things, but not for years; today it was very ugly to him. One moment she could be so wise and caring, but on the other hand, there she was, with that dishonest look on her face, and that telltale, prideful sniff at the end of her sentences that said; "I don't even believe this... and I'm the one's saying it."

The old woman's gaze tightened into a knot and repeated; "I don't owe you anything. I've done the best I could..."

His reply flew off the tip of his tongue; "Do you call being a fall-down drunk the best you could do?" As soon as he'd said it, he knew it would have to be swallowed... quickly... if possible.

But, oh how he wanted to press her 'til the juices ran clear, instead fear and defense oozed out in a muddy mixture, giving meaning to the wrinkles and fissures on her face, which were indeed like mud, cracked and dried-out from the sun. Maybe that was just the process: Her lies had to lay on her face, while the light of truth (that was all around for her to see, if she only would) sucked the moisture from them day after day... until what was left was cracked mud, and thorny, pin-point eyes.

Because he'd said more than intended... much more... and because shouting and posturing as he might've done years ago to cow an opponent was out of the question, tears of surrender came into his eyes; gushing tears of a child from the eyes of a forty-five year old man. "I'm just so disappointed, I wanted things to be so... so different..." While he said those words, a million thoughts ran through his mind: The loss of a childhood; poor performance in schools from a kid too troubled in heart to pay attention, and too many broken relationships to count... and much more went unsaid.

Though he finally hung his head in his hands, frustrated and tired, the blurred image of his angry mother had not escaped him... stooped over in a crooked, little-old-woman posture; hand on the bedroom doorknob... she was hurting, and fully laden with a past that was enough to stoop anyone over. Surely, she was ashamed of it... If only she would admit it!

Then something, a thought, or a memory softened her expression; her eyes filled with salty tears too, and a soothing stream ran down her cheeks... spreading into tiny creases and deeper fissures...not deep enough or soon enough to smooth out the wrinkles of seventy years, but the regret was sincere. She came back across the room looking very pitiful, sat down beside him and said while crying softly; "I did too son, I wanted it to be better, I was just trying to work out my own life... like so many other people..." Grateful for her tenderness, if not an admission of guilt, Myron put his arm around her. She put her head on his bare shoulder covering the word, "Brownie" (with three stars). For a moment they cried with each other as each traveled forever in the world of "if only," in their own silent summaries of opportunity lost.

Then Flo, sniffed loudly (and authentically this time), and was the first to speak; "That bump on the head did more damage than you thought."

This brought a dutiful chuckle from Myron who realized there could be a lot of truth in her joke.

"So." she sat up straighter, took a deep breath and said not so lightheartedly; "What is the question? Was there a nigger in the woodpile? Would a "yes" make a difference? What if there was? Would it change who you are? You're just getting a late start on this issue. You used to ask me about these freckles (she reached up and touched his face); I sang you many a song about freckles and skin, made up on the spot... with your head in my lap... don't even remember 'em now... must've done the trick though, you seemed to accept yourself pretty well."

Yeah, he had to admit there were times of peace and happiness: When his mother was beautiful to him; times when he was proud of her, and loved her more than anything in the world. But, the bad had somehow outweighed the good, and he'd become hardened, self-protective, refusing love, distrusting of others... and maybe it showed on his face as much as his mother's pain did on hers... just in a different way. He pushed up from the couch and looked at himself in a mirror by the front door. He'd mellowed over the years, didn't look particularly angry, but the man in the mirror did look tired and unhappy. He tried to smile but couldn't.

"I don't look like you... or dad."

"Maybe not, but you act just like your dad."

Whether this was true or not he couldn't say, he'd not been around the man enough as a child, to find out. And, no one had heard from him in twenty years or more; "I just want to know... for other reasons..." he said, thinking about his job.

"Well, get over it son, because you'll never know, neither will I. Sure I could guess... or lie... but I won't. You decide. And then do whatever it is that will make you happy," she finished speaking and slouched back onto the couch.

Myron could easily see that not only was she old, she was tired and beaten down by all her life's circumstances; with particulars that he would never experience or understand; after all, it was her life. Time moves on and so do the problems of each generation. Without the heart to press any further he pushed opened the screen door preparing to leave.

"Mother..."

"Uh huh?"

"Didn't you know I would ask you about this someday?" He moved his free hand around his face in a vague circular motion.

"Like I said, you're gettin' a late start..." And then, while patting a bible on the side table with one gnarly hand, she added; "But so did I..."

At the end of the long driveway he stopped short; switched off the lights, trying to decide; which way to go? Back down the mountain to Maggie, or somewhere else entirely... maybe even up to the hot springs to Feather's camp (this time just to be alone).

Still impacted by the two distinct sides of his mom's personality; the compassionate and wise, versus the bitter and dishonest; he decided that she would never recover from her defenses. Which must be the price she has to pay. Not unlike most people, he guessed. In the dimming light of the sunset, he saw Feather's poem, first up, on the pile of trash on the dash: flicked on the cab-light; found his reading glasses; picked it up and read it again, then folded and flipped it into the glove compartment. A slight breeze blew into the window of the van. He could hear the deep rumbling of thunder further up the valley in the higher mountains. Before long the silhouetted forms of the mountain peaks would stand out with lightning flashing against a blackened sky. Typical and exciting on hot summer days, but potentially very destructive to the forests. Rain may or may not accompany such storms, but the thought of heading east was even less attractive now.

Feather. What was up with that anyway? She had been in the back of his mind for sometime now... Wait a minute, she said she was going to Lake Community College, a place he was quite familiar with from his vocational training days. There was a good chance she could be tracked down there. Probably a lot easier than catching her at the hot springs... he might even do a little sleuthing in the admissions office for a home address. He started up the van and headed west, and as predicted, lightning flashed across the sky. Home to Maggie... it had been a long day.

Florence had gone into the kitchen to clean up. A look of determination could be read on her face as she stood in front of the sink, washing dishes and looking out the window. The faint rays of the setting sun cast a faint mustard glow onto enormous, thunderhead clouds gathering in the mountains. The tops of the giant fir trees in the back yard swayed gently; a flock of tiny birds were urgently cascading up and down the limbs of one of the trees. She paused, letting her thoughts wander:

"I don't want to die. I am one of millions filtering down

from branch to branch on a tall tree. We drift down in groups; I am but one speck, my generation is the rest. We flow together... gracefully. When all have collected on this or that branch, a speck or two starts the trickle downward. We all follow. Like little birds in unison, we are caught in the joy of activity, hopping after insects and cones. Eating, always eating.

"Our thoughts are growing wide like the branches of the tree... into a canopy so huge. Our minds expand. Above the branches we see sunshine. Below are shadows.

"We continue our journey pulled by gravity. We near the lower canopies and see the deep darkness. Voila! We are young! We fly to the top to fall and flutter again, pecking and finding what was left over the first time down. Plenty to see, plenty to eat. The bottom comes up to meet us. Too soon... we laugh and fly to the top again. To the other side of the tree... maybe. Over and over again we cascade with life. I don't want to die. I don't understand the bottom. I have never been.

"I see others who are too tired to fly again to the top. They let go with their wrinkled toes. They are gone, with scarcely a sound. Perhaps a glint of sun on their lusterless wings catches the eye. The dry crackle of dead branches breaking from their scant weight scares my soul. I stay on the lower branches longer these days. I watch my little fresh kid-birds dart up and away. I am inspired to follow. I live through their happiness. I go many times to the top.

"I am left behind with my generation. We watch them, the kid-birds, pass through our branches again and again. They are lapping us on the track. It's okay. We live through them. I don't want to die. So, I'll hop and flutter to the top into the sun, but I will feel the great force pull my feathers to the ground."

—◇—

Down the mountain a ways, as soon as the colored

lights on the cell phone blinked that a consistent reception was possible, Brownie checked in with Maggie: "It's me."

"Pick up some bread and milk."

"Don't you want to know where I been?"

"You told me this morning didn't you?

"Did I?"

"At your mom's, right?"

"Oh yeah, I guess I did... " But I don't remember it. *Hmmmmm... the pain killers, or old age?*

"Don't forget to stop at the store... I may be in bed when you get home."

The line went dead. *Uh oh... momma ain't happy. Guess poppa won't be happy either... tonight... again.*

—◇—

Brownie

by

Kenneth M. Scott

– Part Two –

- Chapter Eleven -

Walking into the supermarket he automatically grabbed a shopping cart and pushed his way along the aisles amongst all the other shoppers. "Pick up some bread and milk," reverberated through his head. Even so, his nose led him right to the deli-case, piled high with Jojos, potato salad, boats of crisp broasted chicken, sliced meats, succulent whole roasted chickens. Whew! Short of breath, he managed to walk on through the bakery section ignoring pies and rolls, tossed a loaf of wheat bread into the cart. The white bread would have been his choice, Maggie insisted on wheat. Always. Oh well, he took one last look at the white bread, and slinked on into the fresh fruit section where he found it impossible to ignore the bright reds, yellows, and greens; so bright they made his eyes hurt. He snapped a grape or two like a hungry gold-fish, fumbled a hand-full of trail mix (with M&Ms) from the bulk bins, made a right-turn, and with a smart flourish of parallel parking, pulled up to the dairy case... reached past the whole milk and grabbed the two percent... which is all she would allow.

He brooded about that for a moment. Seemed like there was never anything to eat in the whole house when he was hungry. Why was that? He could open the fridge a hundred times a night, and it would always be the same. Nothing to eat. Not when he looked, at least. But, somehow, Maggie could find an entire meal when it was time to cook. When he complained she'd say; "Tell me what you want and I'll get it when I go shopping."

He'd say; "Stuff. I don't know, easy to find - easy to fix. You know, stuff."

She'd say; "Stuff is too fattening, and too expensive. Eat a carrot."

He'd say no more.

He'd longed to get whatever appealed for decades. Well, this was his chance. He'd denied himself too long, always tip-toeing past the gourmet dept, the seafood case, fancy fruits. "Today is the day..." he mumbled to himself "...It's over!"

So, from the Gourmet section: Sardines, smoked oysters, little crackers. Then, ice cream: Ben and Jerry's. Heck yes! Just load it up to the top and then head for the checkout stand. Just do it. Not finished yet... first go to the meat department. Wow! Tenderloins, shrimp, fresh salmon, halibut, scallops.

Yeah... Okay... he would bring the stuff home to Maggie... yes sir!

"Do you like cookies?" He'd made a full circle and was in the bakery department again. From behind a cake display, a woman (whose pinkish blond hair was just a shade lighter than her faded, pink bakery uniform) strolled toward him. Something in the way she'd asked him if he liked cookies made him wonder if she'd spotted his overloaded cart... as if thinking, *Since this guy's loading up, how about some of these babies?* Of course, he liked cookies. "We've got a special on oatmeal-raisin," she said smiling big, holding out a floppy paper plate mounded with broken bits of cookies.

Upon looking closer, here was another face reflecting harsh experiences tempering a friendly smile with sadness. He felt sorry for her. Took a sample. "Good huh?" she twinkled, and held out a plastic bag; "Dollar a dozen." he took the bag and placed it on the pile. Her eyes roamed over the cart's contents.

"You having a party?"

Hmmm, maybe she was coming-on to him. "Nope, just stocking up," he said and leaned into the cart trying to avoid further eye contact and any guilt he may have had about not being able to invite a lonely lady to a party; *Bet she could use a little fun.*

"Nice evening..." she called out. He pretended not to hear; rolled on toward the deli section, pushing a cart that was already bulging with ten million calories and enough fat to grease every wheel in Lake city.

The contents inside the deli case, which he had bypassed the first lap around (in perfect obedience), now occupied him so completely that at first he failed to notice the woman standing just a few feet away. Gradually peeling his eyes away from the Greek olives, coleslaw and sliced meats, he cocked his head and stared at her.

Could she actually be offering a perfect profile just for him? Really? It had to be so, there was no one else around and she obviously knew she had his attention. Black dress, cut just above the knees, perfect shade of dark stockings, high-heeled shoes. Her body was not sleek, it was rounded, and comfortable looking. Supple was the word that came to mind. Brownie calmed down and watched with what he hoped was discreet admiration. Maybe not so discreet though, because in an obvious move she rotated her body toward him so that he could see the full (what she must have hoped was the beautiful) frontal view. He felt as though he should do or say something. Surely she expected it. Almost as though she had prepared herself for him, and was simply waiting for a response. She seemed about to place an order at the counter, but might just as well have placed herself inside the case with a sign that read: GIRL SANDWICH. He remained silent, waiting politely for her to tell the attendant what she wanted; sure enough, she ordered sandwich makings. Shopping for such mundane ingredients seemed out of place for the creature. Cheapened her somehow.

Strangely, she ignored him the whole time. Didn't look at his cart. Didn't smile. Didn't bat an eye. Took her stuff and walked away. Wow! Brownie had no heart (for the moment) to place an order and shoved off, brooding about womankind; how could they do that? A left turn with his cart took him down the cereals and dry pet food aisle. Terribly bored amongst such bulky boxes and bags, and desperate to rekindle his mad-shopper mood, he practically ran to the far end of the lane, barely able to stop the fast moving heavy cart even with both feet sliding on the linoleum. Narrowly missing catastrophe, he made it around the corner and with a sense of celebrated relief tossed a large jar of capers and two jars of pickled pigs feet onto his pile... but now his rekindled mood started fading, rapidly being replaced with guilt (of all kinds). *Forget the woman. Take the stuff home. Forget the stuff; take the woman home. Forget it all. Go home!*

The lines at the checkout were long. Girl Sandwich was in one of them.

He edged his cart into another line and loosened his grip, flexing fingers that were stiff from holding on too tight. He had imagined a very proud feeling when going through the line with such a load, but curiously, he was actually feeling embarrassed.

Girl Sandwich, had an enormous cart full too. Seemed as though her choices were about as extravagant as his own. Hoisting and stacking items onto the conveyor belt, she was aloof, oblivious to the stares of envy and the critical looks of other shoppers around her. Brownie wondered if he could detect disdain in her smoldering eyes. Did he even have the nerve to unload his groceries?

Were they all wondering how this woman could afford all that?

Rich mingled with the poor in supermarkets all over the world... by appetite. But at the checkout, it was as if people withdrew from each other. Stopped talking, and pretended not to notice what each might be taking home. *Some kind of unspoken social rule?*

But man! She was over the edge. And so was he. The other shoppers may each have had a treat or two in their carts, but nothing like his and Girl Sandwich's mother lodes. Certainly at one time or another he'd felt the same way they must be feeling. Rich people were audacious to flash their hundred dollar bills at the checkout stand, laying their wealth out within reach of working mothers, the down-and-outers... and unemployed airline workers... who had to settle for Kraft Dinner and Kool-Aid. What, other than a vague hope that someday they would be able to have it too, kept people from waiting in the parking lot and hijacking shoppers?

This train of thought was having an effect on him. He had to bail out. Call it quits. But could he actually just leave the cart and walk?

Girl Sandwich, Visa in hand, had just about finished... That's what he'd had in mind too; simply flash the Visa, just once in his life, and then... *Maggie'd have a heart attack! And then a hissy! Nope. Put it all back. Hah!* That would take forever. He could just leave it, but the cart could be there for days... The food would spoil. Naaah, he couldn't be the only one who'd ever done such a thing. The re-stocking crew would take care of it that very night. Okay... okay... He could have all this stuff... anytime he wanted it. With a sigh, the decision was made, Just knowing that it was possible was almost as good as doing it. He'd had his thrill.

Out in the parking lot, a pouting Brownie tossed his one paltry bag of groceries onto the floor of the van trying to forget Pink Bakery Lady's questioning look as he'd left the store. He leaned against the van's side door and watched Girl Sandwich load her outrageous haul into an older, red Mustang.

A smashed front fender (which she apparently couldn't afford to repair) somehow made her seem cheaper still, and added substance to a theory developing in Brownie's mind: Possibly the load of groceries she'd just put in her car was paid for with an illegal Visa! She was dressed to kill in order not to cast suspicion on herself, and her posturing in the store had simply been her way of trying to look dignified... to whomever. No telling where she might be heading now. He decided to talk to her, vaguely comforted by the thought that she might be as crazy as he was

Hurrying across the black-top he arrived just as she was squeezing into the driver's seat... She looked startled and then seemed to recognize him. Trying not to show how nervous he felt, he said; "I'm William, I... uh, saw you in the store, and uh..." *Crap!* (He was blowing it), but she smiled. *Whew...* "I just wondered if you're having a party," (sorry, Pink Bakery Lady).

"What if I were?"

"I saw you in the store, and just thought I'd ask..."

"Well, I could have a party, I guess." Her eyes seemed to narrow a bit; "If I did, would you and your wife like to come?" Oops, his wedding ring.

Brownie pushed his hands into his back pockets; "Maggie doesn't like parties, how about your husband?"

"Oh, he likes parties... he's buying," she held up her visa card; "but he's not invited."

Uh, oh. Now what? "How come..."

"He's having a party of his own... the son of a bitch!" her eyes smoldered.

Ah hah! She was on the make, after all. *Careful, Brown. Back off, and go home.* "That's a lot of groceries there..."

"Yeah. What happened to yours?" She hadn't missed a thing.

"You remember me from the store then?"

"Sure."

"And you saw me watching you load up?"

"Mmmm, hmmm."

Sheesh... Women! They were so amazing. Brownie's head was swimming; *Run, Brown, you're getting in too deep.*

"What happened to all your groceries?"

His reply was sheepish; "I couldn't find my Visa... actually, I got carried away... chickened out at the register."

"You wanna' use Teddy's? There's lots of power left in this one... and I have a whole stack of 'em to go through." A foot long, plastic accordion of charge cards flopped out of her wallet. Brownie leaned in for a close look, read the names on a few; "Are you Bonnie Burger?"

"Mmmm, hmmm."

"And Theodore Burger?"

She folded it back up; "Guess...."

"Husband?"

"Yeah. So, are you ready to party, or are you just foolin' around? Cause I'm just gettin' started." Decisively she rolled out of the car, flashing mile-long gorgeous legs with grudge potential reaching to the sky. "This is your lucky day, William."

"Really?" She was already heading back for the store. Brownie had to hurry to keep up; "You mad at Theodore?"

"Very definitely. If Teddy can have parties, so can other people."

"This would be a good way to get back at him?"

"Yep..."

Pink Bakery lady looked on with understanding and envy when Brownie walked back into the store with Bonnie.

The cart was still where he'd left it. On their way up to the register, Bonnie grabbed another cart and piled it with anything her hands could find, and then topped it with Redbook, National Enquirer and a wide assortment of impulse items lining the Check stand approach lanes. This time embarrassment never entered Brownie's head. Bonnie-B... had the most delicious look of abandonment and revenge in her eyes he could ever imagine. They were putting on a show–center-stage–and both were enjoying the part: Multi-pack boxes of 35mm film; an entire rack of Ronson cigarette lighter flints; forty-eight rolls of Certs and enough Eveready batteries to run that rabbit to Mars and back.

Teddy's Visa approval snapped back through the terminal as though the bill for sixteen hundred dollars and seventy-two cents had been no more than an ice cream cone.

Brownie and Bonnie cracked up all the way out to his van, then he sobered a little; "I can't take all this stuff."

"Sure you can, my cars loaded, and this stuff's not going back in the store," with that she grabbed the handle of the Van's side door, slid it wide open (with seemingly superhuman strength) and then, in a grandiose gesture, waved her hand from the cart to the empty space; "Fill 'er up!"

Good enough. When the last bag went into the van, Brownie turned in time to see Bonnie getting back into her car. Sprinting (and puffing) over with a Redbook and a People magazine for her, he asked; "What now?"

Her words touched him with sadness as well as relief; "Go on home, William, stop fooling around. I got some partying to do..."

"I'd sure enjoy that party..."

She appeared to harden; steeling herself for whatever it was she would do next. The Mustang fired up. "Might get too rough for you..." She backed slowly, looking behind and craning her head around for one last look at him, every hair still in place; "Have your own party..." and she was gone.

Brownie could now imagine a dozen scenarios that may have caused the fender bender. She was out to impress in a world of surface reality. And though she would play her hand to the best of her ability, her troubles would only lure more trouble. Boys, booze, bars, and Bonnie Burger... Not only was she a Girl Sandwich, she was hot and toasty; very definitely wrapped in plastic; and very appropriately named! *Whooo wee! Good luck! Bonnie Burger...*

In the store he'd cut loose pretty good. Doing the black jive thing now and then for Bonnie's benefit. She was fun. For short intervals they'd really been able to get down. Now, driving along the short stretch of freeway to Carlos', the inevitable black rhythm cut in: Popping the steering wheel and dash with fingers and palms, feeling good he composed aloud;

Bonnie Burger and Brownie Brown,
Doing up this lazy town… they're foolin around…
Fooling with the locks, fishing from the docks
Got sloppy shoes… got saggy socks,
They're fooling around…
She's an all girl patty, hot off the grill
Brownie Brown's ringing the till…

Oops! better stop right there….

—◇—

Except for half a gallon of low-fat milk, a loaf of wheat bread, and two jars of pickled pigs feet, the rest of the booty was left at Carlos' house in the garden shed and in the back-porch freezer. Thank goodness, he wasn't at home, 'cause really… Brownie didn't feel like telling him why he needed a place to keep all the food.

A note, "Brownie's Stuff," pasted onto the freezer door would be explanation enough for now. And, after many trips back and forth to the van (carefully detouring around the much respected TRAILMASTER tower), another note posted on the door of the garden shed, written on a brown paper sack with a red marker pen, wrapped it up.

He arrived home at around eleven p.m. Maggie, still not in bed, fired questions at him in rapid succession, killing any hope he might have had when he saw her in her nightie; "What good is a cell phone if you don't know how or when to use it? I work an hour and a half at the cannery for two jars of pickled pigs feet? Where have you been all night? Are you aware that you are out of work? Are you hungry, or did you have a burger?"

His answer; "Almost…" was dangerously close to the truth.

"What, you almost had a burger, or you're almost aware that you're out of work?"

"Both..."

"Well, there's a tuna casserole in the oven. I'm going to bed. Some people have to get up in the morning... and some people are fully aware that you're out of work, Brown."

That night, while watching the late, late show on the tube, W.M. Brown ate pickled pig's feet and brooded about his life: Fully aware that he was out of work, had no Maggie Brown to cuddle or confide in, and no Girl Sandwich, but then he wasn't eating a carrot, was he?

—◇—

After Myron left, the rest of that afternoon was a very busy one for Wayne Hepner. He spent an hour or so (in the house behind the store) talking with Mark, Cliff, and Dorman.

Working together since they were big enough to carry a chain-saw, in a dangerous, mutually life dependent profession at hard, honest work, there was no question of trust. Going to bed at or before sunset; getting up at two or three in the morning and meeting at the shake-roofed LITTLE RED BARN, where men and boys shared their thoughts and gathered the courage to fall giants, fortifying their day with coffee, and homemade biscuits smothered in sausage gravy.

All dressed about the same: Rugged jeans, caulk-boots; durable, grey, pin striped shirts, and suspenders of red, black, or yellow. Their jeans were purposely cut at boot-top height in order to negotiate the logs as well as detect untied shoelaces which could be deadly... among many other constant work related dangers.

While it was still dark, six or eight would pile into one crummy (carry-all), to ride for an hour or more over the steep, narrow, precarious and winding dirt roads... high up in the Cascade mountains. Some would catnap while others joked or told story's often at the environmentalist's expense; "Hey, who knows what a Bald Eagle tastes like? Kind'a like a cross between a Spotted Owl and a Great Blue Heron!"

When they would arrive at the "cut" in the first light, the forest might be dripping wet with morning mist, or white with powdered snow. And men, dwarfed by towering fir trees, would depend on each other for life the rest of the day. Watching out for widow-makers (dead limbs overhead) that might crush a skull, or a runaway log that could leave more than one man dead-flat in it's rolling path.

After their eight to ten hours of scrambling up and down steep hillsides and over log after log, yanking and dragging cables, hooking up choker-chains, bucking thousands of limbs from fallen trees, their day in the woods would be done. Daylight down the mountainsides in mid-afternoon allowed them to appreciate the beauty of the canyons and mist-shrouded hills all around. Often they would pass crummy-loads of hoedads; a job only for the young, who were more goat than human and able to climb the steepest hillsides with picks and their quivers full of seedlings... to be planted at so many per square foot. Federal regulations required clear-cuts on national forests to be cleaned of all tree-slash and replanted within a few years after logging. The seedlings easily grew two or three feet a year, with an almost unstoppable atomic force due to the abundant rains of the northwest,.

The return trip afforded a time of true appreciation of nature, where elk and deer grazed fresh grass on the slopes and meadows of the clear cuts. Bobcat and Black Bear were occasionally spotted, with shouts and general admiration, but an unwanted disturbance to those who were too tired to stay awake on the long ride back. The men of the woods returned home smelling of gasoline, tree-sap, and gear oil. Tired, tired, tired... and happy.

Wayne and Dorman grew up together in the woods. "Hell yes! I'm in, Wayne, just consider it another shotgun courtesy."

Wayne insisted no guns were to be taken along; "But we do need your tanker truck... Do you think you can get it started?"

Dorman was not insulted. Both men knew that the dilapidated water-truck, had been trailered to jobsites for the last few years simply for cosmetics, in order to satisfy the Feds requirement that a fire truck be at every site in case of fire caused by the hot engines of chain saws... but rarely caused by cigarettes... all chewed tobacco... to the last man. The dummy-truck would be empty but left conspicuous, as though ready for action.

So, yes, he still had it.

"Good" Wayne smiled with satisfaction.

While the rest of their plans were being laid, two of Dorman's grown sons were dispatched to "fire 'er up."

"Jimmy still working at the Ranger station? We'll need his help too."

—◇—

When Monday rolled around Brownie awoke grateful that he was on sick leave, and with the thought that he might as well go to the college... for old time's sake... and who knew? He just might run into Feather.

Taking a walk around the campus seemed like a good idea. Instead of going right to the admissions office, he walked around identifying with faces and places for half an hour or so, and then sauntered into the cafeteria (where else?). Nothing had changed. The smell was the same as ever. Sprawled around the room were twenty or more circular, yellowish, Formica-topped tables, each surrounded by eight or ten plastic chairs.

Not intimidated in the least by the crowds at every table, he made his personal pick, and wedged himself right in with his egg-salad sandwiches, potato chips and two cartons of milk. He was accepted immediately. No questions asked–no credentials needed. Looking around the room was a trip. Could he actually recognize faces that were there five years ago? Or were they all just from the same old boring recipe? Macaroni 'n cheese is still, macaroni 'n cheese, no matter which oven it comes from.

Many were there doing the mummy-walk, learning very little and yet stupidly believing a piece of paper would furnish them with a future. Some were aimlessly showing up, day after day, simply for the pleasure of being a part of the education subculture, contentedly encased in a protective envelope of federal education grants, supplemented of course with some means of support (a hopeful parent or wife). There would also be the budding intellectuals, with opinions on everything society suffered or achieved... while they hung back waiting for that unspecified day (which would never come) when they would "fix it all."

But, turning his attention to the immediate table, he scanned the faces: On his right, two young adult males in deep discussion about something; across from him, a middle-aged, very curly-haired, blonde lady anxiously spinning chirpy conversation with a muscular paraplegic, who seemed so full of energy he could've easily performed Evil Knevil stunts on demand in his wheel chair. On his left, a quiet, introverted type who could've been an intellectual or an idiot for all Brownie knew... only by opening his mouth would the mystery be cleared up... and from the way he sat there, eyes glazed over, that wasn't likely.

Three men in blue shop coats, who smelled of machine oil, and other unknowns, brushed past him, and on toward the exit; hurrying through the pods of feeding, gibbering sardines. There! Those were the real achievers. At least the industrial training department had some practical focus. Unlike himself, those guys were probably having a ball making something with their hands that they could actually see, or touch; after which they could put it out in the open for everyone else to see... sure... then they could take the praise for what they'd achieved, or the heat for where they'd failed.

Trying to see the face of every girl with cropped, blonde hair, occupied Brownie while he ate his food. The memory of Feather's face was very clear and once or twice, he thought he'd spotted her. After a bit, keeping his eye on the entrance for newcomers he decided to ask around.

Shouldn't be too hard to pick those who were most likely to know her: the less fortunate (to use a phrase); the shabbily dressed; not to mention the unkempt and poorly complexioned ones, none of whom were likely to gain from the bottomless taxpayer resources, nor from Lake College's valiant attempts to educate them.

The conversation next to him had become louder. A discussion about mathematics? They were actually learning? Oh well, there had to be exceptions... these were the kids whose parents were smart enough to take advantage of what their tax-dollars had already paid for. And perhaps allow their kids to decide for themselves, if or not they would continue on to university after junior college. Hmm... he took another look around the room; maybe there were lots of serious kids there after all.

While tossing sandwich wrappers and milk cartons onto his tray, preparing to move-on, chairs being pushed and bumped aside with great commotion hailed the arrival of yet another wheelchair (complete with electric motor) thumping into the space where the chatty blonde had been... beside the silent paraplegic. The man in the new chair was a more severely impaired quadriplegic with helpful gadgets and levers which were ingenuous... costing about a million dollars... attached all over it. Somehow, with whirring sounds and metallic clanks, a lunch was placed on the table and he proceeded to eat. Using both of his grotesquely twisted hands, and emaciated arms to grasp odd shaped utensils, he speared and spooned at a salad, two sweating wieners and several perky dinner rolls. An extra long straw poking up from a Pepsi Cola can, threatened to stab him in the eye each time he twisted his head to catch the food (nevertheless expertly aimed at his mouth). He seemed quite unconcerned about any spectators. Brownie hoped he was successfully averting his own eyes, glancing only occasionally at the scene... But, he was fascinated; the apparatus reminded him of the beloved TRAILMASTER Barbecue Tower. He settled back for a minute; listening to the conversation between the two handicapped men, apparently taking up from where they had left off sometime previously.

"So, Eddie, how's the ego?" asked Quadra-Man.

Eddie looked offended; "Will you get off that, Louis? I've heard enough a'ready... eat your lunch." He placed his strong hands on the wheel rails of his chair, ready to shove off.

"Wait a minute... have you ever considered loving your ego instead of battling it all the time? You're a rolling contradiction, guy. You play hoops and roll street races to win... don't you?"

"I do it for the exercise... " Para-jock snapped back emphatically.

Louis allowed his head to flop over onto his left shoulder, rolled his eyes toward Eddie and said through, what must've been an unsightly mouthful of food; "Maybe. But I say you're in it for the ego too, and that's not such a bad thing. I've spent too many years battling mine. Better take time to love it. It's one of life's greatest sources of satisfaction and personal pleasure."

Eddie rotated his chair to face Louis; "Man, you're as full of stuffing as a Christmas turkey," but obviously he was listening, and sat there waiting for Louis, who wasted no time in continuing; "Why not get yourself a bumper sticker for that wagon of yours? One that says, PARA-JOCKS DO IT THE BEST THEY CAN. Eddie!! Listen to what your ego is trying to tell you. If you've got something to be proud of, then enjoy it. Besides, getting to know it is more fun than running from it. Who knows? You might learn something."

Louis looked over at Brownie whose ears had perked up a bit too, thinking; *Sheesh. This is different.* Louis apparently figured Brownie agreed with him so far and nodded a friendly, hello. But the two guys next to Brownie had heard enough and so had the introvert on his other side. They left together. Louis' voice rose a bit louder, making it obvious that Brownie was included; "Love it like you'd love a woman. Make it a courtship. Then if you decide you really don't want the relationship there's plenty of time to plan the murder... but believe me, plan is all you'll ever do."

"Like looking at an ugly woman who appears at the breakfast table, morning after morning, and you thought (hoped) she' be dead when you woke up. But you forget, she cooks the meal, she makes the bed, and she manages the checkbook. My point is that you can't live with it and you can't live without it. If she goes, you go. So... might as well get along... and she'll shower you with her favors. Make you feel good about yourself. 'Cause in the first place she knows what she is, and you don't, and you won't... 'til you know her intimately. She knows that what she sees in her mirror is a reflection of all she's tried to do to make you feel good about yourself. If you learn to love her, she will become more and more beautiful... and then so will you. Works like a lazy Susan: You put a little bowl of kindness on, spin it around to Susan, she takes it off, puts a little something on there for you and spins it back. When a happy woman tells you that you are handsome, strong, virile... it's worth a hell of a lot more than when an unhappy one does. Love your ego, son, it's not as repulsive as you've made it out to be."

Suddenly Louis hung his head further-out over his chest toward Brownie and said; "No pity, pal, just treat me like you would any other freak." Brownie was embarrassed. Had no idea how to respond. Maybe his mouth had been hanging open or something. He'd been wondering if Louis had a woman, or at least a caretaker somewhere.

Eddie stepped in to comfort; "No big deal, he's this way with everybody."

Brownie decided it was time to go and stood up with his tray; "Well, I'm outta' here... "

Louis smiled, turned back to Eddie and said: "See?

Ego..." And then, completely unconcerned if Brownie left or stayed, he went on; "The ego doesn't believe for a minute that it's number one... it only wants to be told that it is... to help ease the pain a little.

"There's only one time you were ever in first position, anyway: For a millisecond, at the moment of your birth, before someone else, somewhere else, popped out of the womb, you were the freshest, youngest human on earth... everybody is in first position at one time... spurting out across the earth in the great race. The great human race that is. Blood pumping red... fired up with oxygen."

"For a while, you're living the dream. The good part. Running the race almost effortlessly. Others are living a dream too, but theirs is a nightmare. They can see what's just up ahead... the finish line. There's no kidding any longer, the race is coming to an end. They're just stalling, hanging back, bumping into each other, hoping someone else goes over the line before they do. Oh, yeah, they're still in the race, but suddenly nobody wants to win. They're looking back and realizing that it was all a matter of perspective, was it ten pounds of ugly fat, or ten pounds of beautiful fat... just without the nipples? So, love your ego, buddy-boy and cut the crap! Put those nipples on there and get that scrap-iron moving..."

Brownie had stayed put and had heard it all. Eddie sighed, shook his head as if to clear it, and then said sadly to Brownie; "He's got a point there... don't ya' think?"

Louis waited expectantly for Brownie's answer... which, after a moment, came out with a little more anger than he had intended; "Yeah... but it's kind of a depressing one, damn it! Obviously Louis knows all about egos. Thanks a lot Louis! See you around, I'm headin' for the finish line before it gets too crowded."

"Who gives a shit?" Louis called after him, as Brown weaved expertly through the tables and chairs.

"That, my man, is a good question," Brownie called back over his shoulder, and pushed on out the swinging doors.

But not fast enough to miss; "Asshole..." This was what he heard, and shit-head is what he thought to say in return... didn't, but wished he had as he realized; *Hey, that works out kind'a nicely; don't ya' think?*

For a while, he moseyed around the campus asking whomever, if they knew Feather. They didn't. The admissions office was no help either, especially since Brownie had no last name for her. They looked at him as though he might be a pervert looking for someone to rape or kidnap. *Damn!* He was leaving there in even more of a foul mood than when he went in. Maybe the prescription painkillers were demanding a payback.

Oh well, he had one other place to check out. The Saturday Market was a prime place for Feather to hang out. She'd been pretty excited about it. He headed for Carlos' house.

—◇—

Chapter Twelve

Thomas O. Purdy, whose only vocation was to satisfy his appetite, lived intimately with the Jordan's as a permanent guest. The Jordans seemed to accept him and his routine; in fact, found it to be a comforting daily chore to keep an eye on him and his whereabouts.

During the daylight hours he perfected the art of lounging, taking luxurious naps by the pool, or casually strolling around the estate.

Often Carlene Jordan would make a purposeful detour on her way about the property, "accidentally" bump her shovel or clank a rake, knowing that he would rouse himself and playfully stalk her when she puttered in the vegetable garden or tended her exotic plants in the greenhouse. Though it would be a stretch to say that Thomas was interested in horticulture, he was very interested in Carlene. She made it known that she cared deeply for him too.

The greenhouse was enormous. Carlene inevitably left the door open so that Thomas could follow, silently slipping in and out amongst the large leafed tropical plants and orchids with delicious anticipation. Some days, it was too much to bear for both of them. The lovely and delightful woman could hardly pause long enough to pluck a leaf, or turn a pot; Instead, she and Thomas clumsily bumped branches and stirred the gravel floor with shuffling feet as both hurried to the center of the greenhouse. There amongst the dense foliage, Thomas would end the audacious facade and pounce upon her with utter glee. The cooing and mewing was shameless while they fumbled and fondled one another amongst the terra cotta pots and tuberous growths... for what seemed like hours... supplemented only momentarily with aphrodisiacs grown by Carlene herself. She smoked hers; Thomas preferred to eat his. A perfect combination of euphoric results: Carlene, relaxed and indulgent; Thomas, rowdy and masculine.

A.B. Jordan, who was very lean on affection anyway (preferring less demonstrative encounters of love), actually encouraged the relationship between Mister Purdy and Carlene, reasoning that his wife deserved all the happiness she could find in this life... The one thing he insisted upon was that Thomas O' could not share their bedroom. Hospitality ended when the Jordan's turned in for the night. "Good night Mister Purdy; Hello Carlene–Good night Carlene."

This was just fine with Thomas, for that was just about the time he started feeling energetic and adventurous. Nights were not a time for lounging, but carousing. It was just a fact of life that everybody gets a little crazy after about ten thirty p.m. He still enjoyed walking about the property (which was very large), and even occasionally napped in the guesthouse. However he definitely paid visits to neighboring houses with astonishing regularity. Carlene had no delusions about his faithfulness to her (she was very practical in that way) but she could never have imagined some of the predicaments he found himself in. He fought at the drop of a hat: Gorged himself on delicacies, whether offered freely, or snitched when the opportunity arose; accosted females right and left, and impregnated many to his own inflated pride. During the day he was quiet, wordless really, but night brought out the angst and the irony in his soul. He tormented himself and others with what might have been mistaken for singing, whereas in reality he was simply venting what was within (screeching might have been a more accurate choice of words).

At any rate, he returned in the wee hours of the morning, often bruised and bloody, to clean himself up, eat with the Jordans and then rest in preparation for the coming night.

Violet (of Violet and Carl), who did housekeeping for the Jordans, knew very well what went on with Carlene and Thomas. She knew Thomas better than he knew himself, and perhaps she could have said the same about Carlene, but she chose not to offer opinions or exercise control in any way. This, a natural part of her own character, helped to produce a peaceful spirit and a generous smile which served her and her employers very well. The pay was pretty good and the work agreeable to her, but she took no nonsense whatsoever from Thomas O. Purdy.

It was only natural that she would have mentioned Thomas to Carl. He had listened more than once to her frustrations regarding the "relationship," saying things like; "Ain't none of my business how she carry on with that Mister Purdy!" But then she would continue talking as though it were. From her descriptions Carl knew Thomas was black, handsome, virile, and irresponsible... and (though careful not to show it to Violet) he admired him and secretly looked forward to occasional reports of his character and escapades; "That Thomas Purdy come dragging round to my kitchen this morning, looking like he won't live through the day. It's hard to believe he push hisse'f so hard, fighting and carousing all night, night after night. I tell you it's a wonder he ain't dead. Handsome is, as handsome does... and how he ever manage to keep his black self so handsome? I cain't begin to tell you. He can look so pitiful some mornings (n' I jes' have to feed him when he look so beat and drug out). But, den' he always look dapper by the afternoon... stretching and struttin' here and there."

On one such occasion Brownie overheard snippets of the Thomas saga while standing on their back steps with a cup of Violet's awesome coffee, thoughtfully observing the Barbecue tower. Noticing that it had begun to weather nicely, taking on a soft rust color throughout, which only served to enhance the design, allowing the eye to travel along the curves and appendages without stopping at the blackened welds. "Nice," he concluded; "Smooth and flowy-like."

From inside the house Violet was adding the final touches to her makeup before leaving for work and as usual was scolding Carlos; "Jest look in the refrigerator... it's in there! Open yo' eyes. I won't be back in time. If you wants supper then you put it in the stove like I tell you... three o'clock-at three hundred degrees; what's so hard about that? You lazy as that Thomas Purdy, and jest as useless," she chided.

"How is my man, Thomas?"

"Oh he ain't no difference than always. He need a caretaker jest like you. I don't know how Mrs. Jordan can stand to leave him for that Californian house six months to a time. She love him so!"

"Well, he there when she come back, ain't he. Must be able to take care of hisse'f jest a little."

"They lock's that house up tight before they leaves every winter, and from what I saw today, I hope they don't lock him out of that greenhouse of theirs."

Brownie sat down on the steps, trying to imagine this Mister Purdy.

Violet's voice rose and fell as she moved back and forth from the door of her bedroom to the bathroom where he could just see her coloring those bountiful lips a beautiful red, and rolling her soft round eyes up at herself in the mirror.

Carlos was intrigued; "What about that greenhouse?"

"Wha's that?"

"Oh, nuthin... " he said casually, knowing that if he showed too much interest Violet would find herself in a fit of guilt for gossiping, and then he would never hear the rest of the report. And, knowing also that she'd heard what he said, he waited for her to continue.

"I seen 'em carrying on. He'll do anything for that stuff she grows out there..."

"What stuff?" Ooops... Carl had blown it, and he knew it. Too much interest.

"There I go gossiping... never mind what stuff. I ain't gonna say."

"You ain't be gossiping... you jes' talking... " Carl added hopefully.

Brownie paused with his cup at his lips, ears perked, waiting for Violet to continue, but Carlos knew it was over, walked on out to the back porch and sat down next to his friend who still had his cup poised. Both men looked at each other with compressed lips and lifted brows, and then turned away, gazing in silence at the Tower. Carlos sighed.

Brownie sipped. The name, Jordan, was a familiar one. Just the night before, Carlos had asked him if he would be willing to lend a hand with an on-site barbecue for the Jordans, and forty or fifty guests; "Brownie, how's yo' head doin'? We got a gig. This'n pays pretty good too. We gonna play tunes, cook a barbecue, and serve them very same cookin's at a party for Violet's boss, Mrs. Jordan."

Brownie asked when, and it was really no surprise that it was to be in a few days. Knowing that Carlos was the last-minute-man... always... he knew better than to jump right in; scratching his chin, eyes rolled back in his head, cautiously and a bit haughtily he'd asked, "What d'you want me to do?"

"Help us serve."

"Why?" suspicious of any sentence containing the word, serve.

"Cause you can play the blues harp and talk out of three sides of yo' mouth at one time, son," and then Carlos tacked on for good measure; "Violet would appreciate the help... " But this added pressure was not enough to force his hand, he'd wanted to think about it overnight, especially since Carlos with his finger tapping gently on Brownie's chest, couldn't resist one more tact; "and you're one smooth colored man."

So, now, days later, he chose this moment to give his answer, as if the conversation had never been suspended for hours; "I guess I will, if you still need me."

Carlos looked around at him with a confused expression.

Brownie pointed at the Tower and said; "Jordan's... the barbecue."

"Yeah... yeah? Good. Tha's good," answered Carl, not in the least surprised, but Brownie was still lost in thought trying to visualize the greenhouse; meeting Mister Purdy at the party would be icing on the cake as far as he was concerned. Carlos, who may have

been thinking along the same lines concluded; "Party's
tomorrow... have to be there... five-thirty."

—<>—

On the Jordan estate, underwater lights from the
pool and the nearby landscaping cast an elegant glow
on what appeared to be a monolithic Egyptian ruin, but
actually an outdoor barbecue made of bricks and mortar.
Mysterious fumes trailed from one of the columns,
strategically and intentionally tantalizing taste buds
with the smell of barbecued chicken and baby-back ribs
for several blocks around the exclusive Lake City Hills.
An assortment of magnificent homes on hilltops with
plenty of acreage. Sounds of laughter, and clinking silver
on china, magnified by the swimming pool's smooth
surface, helped muffle Carlos's whispered advice to
Brownie; "You cain't talk like that to no whitey... not
here."

Brownie laughed, wondering if he looked as
ridiculous in his cowboy hat and shirt (Carlene's idea) as
Carlos did; "All's I said was, '...those are nice breasts...'
that's not a bad thing. She knew I was talkin' 'bout that
chicken, pardner."

"Yeah, unh hunh... but you gotta' be careful... her
man'll shor' take you up about it."

Brownie's eyes narrowed; "We're not on the
plantation, Carlos; we're out west and this is the
eighties... and we're cowboys" he said with a grin and
a flick of his hat brim.

Carlos flipped a long slab of ribs in return, with even
greater emphasis, then deftly slathered the blackened
surface with his sauce; "Unh-hunh, and all those folks
out there... who's cooking for who?"

"Tell you what Carlos, if I take this apron off and put on my Tux, most of these folks will treat me as nice as Mrs. Jordan treats Mister Purdy."

"Tha's 'cause you borderline black. C'mere... " Carlos reached up under the hood of the barbecue pit and grabbed a handful of soot; stepped over behind the Sarcophagus. Brownie hesitated only a second, then followed him.

Carlos, smiling cynically and holding up his normally pink palms (now black with soot) said; "You... are on... brotha,"

Brownie, staring at Carlos' palms as though a faith-healer stood before him, thought, *Hey, why not? This could be fun and Carlos might learn a thing or two...*

Characteristic to their relationship, Carlos read the silent "Yes;" then smeared and smudged away at Brownie's face; "Now, you's a tar-baby too... " he grinned, adding a final touch here and there, and finished with; "Ten bucks?"

"Yeah, ten bucks..." they slapped hands and it was on.

Brownie chuckled nervously and headed for the van where his rented tuxedo (furnished by the Jordan's for the band) waited for the after dinner performance. Crouching and stooping over, he managed to make the wardrobe change in the back; emerged with a feeling that only silk, sharkskin, and starched linen can give a man; casually meandered toward the house, slipped through a side gate, and strolled in through the utility entrance.

"Thomas Purdy you got nuthin' on Brownie," he declared aloud, admiring himself in one of the Jordan's full-length, rest room mirrors. He and Carlos had already determined to keep their eyes open for the legendary Thomas O', and that alone helped bolster his confidence. And Carlos may have been correct about racial prejudice of some at the party, but surely not where Mrs. Jordan was concerned; he was pretty certain that she loved all black people.

—<>—

Carlene and A. B. Jordan were not your normal snowbirds, even though they had a home in Palm Springs and this one in Lake City Estates, they had at least one other in the state of Louisiana. A.B., had made his fortune there, and so had Carlene's parents. The barbecue party was in honor of her brother, Palmer Phillips, who happened to be visiting the area on very important business: His new motor coach, manufactured locally and now glistening in the driveway; hopefully generating massive curb-appeal for everyone in the fashionable community... and for that matter, any royalty and all angels above, that happened to be passing by.

Brownie strolled out to the entryway. If Palmer Phillips had a flare for flash, then flash must have run in the family. The Jordan's entry looked like something from Planet Hollywood, plopped right out of Los Angeles. A Harley, resplendent in dazzling chrome, gleamed and reflected gloriously in the polished, black granite floor-tiles. A three-foot by five-foot poster in glossy black and white, triple matted and framed in bright chrome, hung on the wall just behind the Harley. Featuring none other than Carlene, smiling sexily, dressed in leather, and sitting on the front saddle clutching the handlebars as though ready to ride. A reluctant, A.B., sat behind her on the sissy-seat, arms around her waist, looking entirely out of place in his

Hell's Angels' jacket and tattered Levis.

—<>—

On the back patio, elegantly dressed guests still gorged themselves with the best barbecue any had ever tasted. Carlene basked in her accomplishment. Well, sort of her's, she did have the good taste to bring it all together. Of course that was all that was expected of her from her guests who gave full credit without question. All except for brother Palmer and his wife, Nicki. Especially Nicki, whose taste buds ruled her very being; "Pahlmer... Pahlmer!" she whispered into an obedient ear; "Deah, you know, the man who prepahed this meat must be around heah somewheah's, won't you get the recipe for this sauce? It is simply too gooood."

"The cook [pronounced perhaps a bit dryly] doesn't seem to be at the grill thius moment deah, but I will do what I Caen..." Palmer assured her.

"But, he's right theah turnin' the ribbssuh... " she protested

"No, I'm shua it's the otha' one, that lightah skinned cowboy? He's in chahge... "

Nicki, resigned to find out for herself, looked around for Carlene... Palmer was so slow and "pecuhliah" in how he went about things... *Hmmm, but then so is Cahlene,* she reasoned with a low and prolonged sigh; *I just don't know why Cahlene would be in the kitchen... that big, colored woman seems so capable...* The sweet, petite, and "deahlicate" Nicki, lips and fingers smeared with sauce continued separating sinews along a full rack of ribs draped across her plate... *Unaware* that Carlene, in fact was not in the kitchen. Violet was indeed capable and doing just fine... humming right along.

Carlene, on the other hand, had momentarily slipped out (with a plate of barbecue) to the guesthouse, where Mister Purdy had been instructed; "Please, stay in here, dearest, I'll bring you a plate." Not that she had any problem with the fact that he was black, but for one thing, his table manners were proven to be atrocious, and for another, he would have been unable to make conversation suited to her guests. Faithful, easygoing Thomas, was content to receive the food and a moment of her time. After a brief cuddling, Thomas set about the business at hand, and Carlene was gone; thinking about how her stunning evening gown was wasted on such a scalawag..

Palmer, sensing how important the sauce recipe was to his wife, stood up, adjusted his cummerbund, and excused himself for a look around.

Brownie, a sucker for Harley Davidson motorcycles had climbed onto the expansive black leather seat very carefully; placed his hands on the handlebars and closed his eyes... imagining Maggie perched on the back, her arms wrapped around his waist. This machine was way out of his reach, and so was Maggie in a way. *If she would only lighten up, t*ell him she loves him... *every... single... frigging... day.* He had a picture in his mind of how it would be. She'd be holding on tight; head against his shoulder, and her (still gorgeous) legs spread out all around him, and baby! They would just cruise...

Palmer, peered around a column out into the entry and upon seeing the "Negro" in a tuxedo and on a motorcycle, laughed involuntarily, correctly interpreting the expression on Brownie's ever-transparent face: dreaming about things he could never have... *for uh... whatevah raisons.*

The rude, scornful chuckle snapped Brownie out of

it; and while climbing off, he caught his sleeve on the handlebar, felt even more foolish and then stood there, pretending he hadn't heard the laugh.

Palmer, feeling as though he should not have been so mean, walked on out into the room extending his hand to Brownie, saying in a more than civil voice; "Hello, I'm Pahlmer Phillips, Cahlene's brothah?"

Before he could take Palmer's hand, and long before he could reply with his own name (he was struggling to come up with exactly what that might be), Palmer dropped his hand and continued; "I'm looking for the chef, that theah bahbecue fellah? Seen him?"

"He's out by the pit, I believe... wearing a cowboy hat, and an apron."

Palmer craned his head back, and then to one side; "Wait a minute, yo'ah the otha' one... the otha' bahbecue fellah, only dahker."

Well crap! he was busted; "Yeah, I'm the Chef," he lied, and in hopes of salvaging a bit more dignity; "... and also a member of the band," pointing to the tux with the index fingers of both hands. And, then, waving one hand in a small circle around his blackened face, he added; "Next costume..."

"Oh, I get it. Costume... Well, if you can play like you can cook, we're in for some tasty music."

"I just play the harmonica and sing a little, the rest of the band should be showing up soon..." with that, Brownie walked over to peep through a transparent flower petal in one of the stained-glass windows facing out at the circle driveway.

Palmer was convinced immediately that Brownie was admiring his Motor Coach. Which in reality was adding as much reflected color onto the stained glass window as the glass itself. Seizing the opportunity to show it off, and to pursue his goal, he opened one of the cherry paneled doors, and taking Brownie by the elbow; "Come on, I'll give you a touah. I didn't get yoah name..."

"William Brown."

"Wait'll you see this, Willie... "

(Uh ohhhh, easy Palmer... that would not be the best choice of names...).

Entering the motor coach was like stepping into another world. There was no way William could fully grasp it, except that it felt *reeealllly* expensive in there. With soft music, plush leather upholstery, marble counter tops, mirrored walls (to expand the feeling of spaciousness), and subtle recessed lighting directed to just the right areas, it appeared to be a small, very elegantly furnished home. Palmer led the way pointing out the marvels of storage, hidden beds, showers, closets, closed circuit security, and features ad-nauseum... "Would you lyke a beah, Willie?"

"No thanks, Palmie." If this distortion of his own name lodged anywhere close to impropriety, Palmie, didn't let on.

But regardless, William was not impressed... not even with; "Nine hundred, fifty-five thousand dollahs'll git you one jest lyke it," Palmer boasted while simultaneously dumping himself onto the leather couch. This time it was William's turn to laugh. How perfectly absurd; beyond comprehension that something with such cramped space would cost so much. He'd had no idea.

Palmer revealed his disappointment; "Well, I know

that's a lot of money to some people..."

"That's a lot of money period, I better get back..."

"Wait, Nicki wanted me to ask you for yoah bahbecue sauce reahcipe."

It was a small thing to Brownie, but at least he might have something this man's money wouldn't buy. "Sorry; old family recipe. Never give it out."

"I'll give you fifty dollahs, Willie..." he said reaching for his wallet.

"Gotta go, Palmie."

"Nicki will be very disappointed. Okay, how much then?

The wallet was out and William could see what looked like a cabbage patch of one hundred dollar bills being fanned by Palmer... very tempting for sure, but he didn't know the exact recipe anyway, "Sorry..."

"Why, pshaw man! A thousand dollahs, then?"

William stopped with his feet on the lowest doorstep. Could he make up a recipe? He looked back, with that, oh-so-transparent face of his... Palmer said; "I'll need confoahmation, that it's the true reahcipe, though... "

"I'll think about it..."

"C'Mon! name yoah pryce, you rascahl!" Palmer was beginning to enjoy himself.

William held onto the chrome stair-rail to keep his hands from shaking; "How long you gonna be here at the Jordan's?"

"A few moah days..."

"Can I call you tomorrow?"

Palmer decided not to push any further; "Fine, I'll be

waiting. "He stuffed the wallet back into his pocket, and then followed Brownie into the house, past the Harley edifice, where Brownie had paused again.

"At's a greaht Byke, eh Willie?"

"Yep, I used to own one just like it," he fibbed.

"Ryhte, " Palmer said over his shoulder as he passed on through the room.

Brownie waited a few moments. Maybe he'd never owned one before, but then he'd never met anyone who liked barbecue as much as Palmer Phillips either. The chrome on the Harley seemed to shine with promise.

The other three, black tuxedoed, authentically black-skinned band members walked through the open front door, laughing and excited to see Brownie. "Hey! You spendin' too much time out in the sunshine, B.B."

"Ladies and Gennemens," Carlos said in his smoothest, big band leader voice, "We gonna bring out the ban' with a number cooked up by The Cowboy Cook his se'f; B.B. Brown..." regardless of Brownie's suspicion that this could become a very embarrassing moment... the incongruous posse of black men in cowboy hats and tuxedos, clip clopped musically over the marbled floor in a most engaging black shuffle on out into the spacious room; bringing with them a vision of red-dirt trails, and Saguaro cactus silhouetted against smoky blue mountain ranges... Arizona drifted into the room, winding and resonating from the top of the formal, ballroom staircase to the bottom of the lonesome hearts of the hardest hearted... straight from the soulful hearts of Carlos and Brownie... as they sang their first number together:

"I can't tell you how many times a cowboy loses hope... or
how many times he trips over his own rope.
All I know is that most of the time, he thinks he's at a
rodeo,
Settin' on his high horse... and he'll be glad to tell you so.

The view from the Cowboys horse, can be blowin' with
dust 'n smoke,
But the view from his saddle is... preferred by every
cowpoke.
The dust from a long hard ride, can gather on an old boy's
hat,
But he knows how to brush it off, and then... how to put
the thing right back.

He takes a lot of pride, in a solo ride... underneath a
starry sky.
And when he's on his own... he feels at home... and he
don't like long good byes.

I can't tell you how many times a cowboy loses hope, but
I can tell you that most of the time he's hanging onto his own
rope.
Comes a time in a cowboy's life, he has to put a good horse
down, but that's just part of the price... for living outside of
town.

There's times the sun git's way too hot...

His throat git's parched with thirst.
But that's just part of a cowboy's job...
I guess things could be worse.

Jes' take a look at the way things are in this world of pain
and hurt.
Ain't nothing beats a good long ride, thru good old honest
dirt.

Puffy white clouds, 'gainst a deep blue sky; a sparkling pebbly stream.

Sure feels better than a bar of soap, n' it gits ya twict as clean.

Guess it don't really matter then... How many times a cowboy loses hope...

Just as long as he's got his horse, and as long as he rides in the rodeo-doh...

Da do-dah-day... and a yippee kai yai... Yippee kai yayyyy."

"Cowboy's Hope" was a hit and struck the perfect mood for a few subsequent western ballads until the musicians inevitably wandered in off the plains and onto the streets of big-city life (without the cowboy hats), playing the blues for an hour and a half... all according to Mrs. Jordan's previous instructions... fully intending that her guests enjoy an appetizer of western tunes and a very flavorful entree of earthy, backstreet blues. And broadened... really... by one of the most beautiful settings the great Northwest (and the state of Oregon in particular) could offer. There were no Blacks except the ones on the stage and the ones in the kitchen.

When the music was over, Carlene cornered Brownie, with Nicki at her side; "This is Nicki Phillips... "

Nicki was lavishly draped in jewelry and silk, her auburn hair twisted in a French bun affair that beautifully lifted it (except for a few tantalizing wisps), from her neck and shoulders, revealing creamy skin with tiny freckles; "Mister BB... I enjoyed yoah music so much," she purred; flattering him for several more minutes with a southern voice that was somehow perfectly matched to her sleek, emerald gown. Brownie suspected that she would be entirely comfortable talking to whomever... but something about her manner made him suspicious.

He listened gratefully to her compliments. Knew already who she was, if not her name. Palmer had sat next to her and dominated the dance floor with her during most of the music. Brownie was still aglow from what he considered to be his greatest performance ever. Immensely enjoying himself, certain that he had proven beyond a doubt that his lips were not hurt from the Tower collision.

He had also noticed that his soulful harp had penetrated Mrs. Jordan's world... her eyes seemed to have been searching his own more than once. She stood aside while Nicki had her shot, point-blank; "We've always admired yoah people; yoah colahful cultuah. Bahbecue in the south is world renowned, of coahse, but what you have done is bridge the gap from the Southeran to the Westeran, uh... ummmm... method. Thaht's a mahvelous piquant blend with peppahs and other things you've got thayah... and simply must be shahed with ouah friends. We have the Brunswick steww, fried okrahh, the Texas riubs... but this... this is so stupendous! I do hope you will shah the recipe with us... Mister BB?"

Brownie listened and was just about to tell her where he and Palmer had left off with their negotiations, when Carlene cut into the conversation; "Of course he will, Nicki..." This was no offense whatever to Brownie who had found it difficult to keep his eyes off Carlene all evening. Her stunning gown might have been wasted on Thomas Purdy, but it was not wasted on him. The low cut neckline drew him in like warm loaves of bread.

But Nicki, was determined to show her appreciation of him too; "I must say, Mistah BB, yoah cowboy song captchuad a certain spirit... Do you ride?"

"Beats walking, Mam... " he replied with easy bravado.

Carlene slipped her sleek form between the two and said; "Nicki, why not let me talk with this man a few moments... alone."

Nicki excused her tiny, elegant self; feeling quite thwarted and impatient.

Carlene walked gracefully out into the lighted grounds, glancing over her shoulder, staying on the concrete walk that led to the lighted greenhouse, glowing mystically with soft, pinkish fluorescents from the interior. Brownie followed.

"The greenhouse is one of my favorite pastimes. Do you enjoy planted things... leafy things?" she asked with a twinkle. Brownie nodded. "Let me show you a few," she said; pushed the door open; followed him in... closed it behind her.

Somewhat unsure of her motives, Brownie listened carefully, attempting to repeat the names of the plants Carlene called out; These Bromeliads... ('Bro... mealy... lads' ricocheted around inside his skull, pinging off into unexplored, stony recesses without the slightest hope of ever splattering out across his writhing tongue)... are some of my very favorites".

Exotic odors blended with an enticingly warm and humid atmosphere as they meandered through the botanical marvel. He waited patiently for her to show him what "other" plants he knew must be growing in there... somewhere. Yet the word, cannabis, was never spoken, nor did it appear.

Parting broad banana leaves and spiky fronds from very large ferns, she motioned for BB to pass through into an even more secluded portion of her private world. Wicker chairs with plush cushions bearing brightly colored flowers, openly invited them to sit. The floor, otherwise graveled in the rest of the greenhouse, was tiled in slate squares, and bordered with a large rectangle of bricks. Magazines on the beveled, glass top of a wrought-iron coffee table told Brownie that this was indeed her "special place." A Tiffany styled, stained glass, floor lamp completed the picture. Carlene motioned him to have a seat and took the other chair. She saw him looking at the mammoth wicker chaise-lounge across the table from them and said; "Sometimes Thomas and I sleep there together, have you met him?"

Unable to believe that she would be so flagrantly open about such a thing, Brownie answered while concealing his shock as much as he possibly could; "Violet mentioned him, he's black isn't he?"

"Mostly, but I would say he's about twenty percent white."

This was a statement that almost caused his kinky hair to stand up straight; "How can you tell?"

"It's right there on his face... and a little on his stomach and legs."

That certainly painted a picture; "Would it matter if he were a hundred percent black?"

"It might to some people, it wouldn't to me, though; I'd love him no matter what color he was," she oozed convincingly.

How comforting... even so, maybe she had a "thing" for multi-racial guys, and could be that's why she'd invited Brown to the greenhouse. He probed a little further; "What about me; what percentage black do you think I am."

'Why, you're not black at all, are you? You're pink, and sort of a speckly-brown; like one of those trout fishies from a sparkling pebbly stream."

Brownie had to laugh (even if it was a bit nervously), truly complimented that she would quote one of his song lyrics; "I'm no Thomas Purdy either..."

"No, but you could be just as much fun."

He chuckled again, still unable to believe that she would be so brazen, and said; "I don't know... was he at the party tonight?"

"Who? Thomas?"

Brown responded with a simple lift of his, not inconspicuous, eyebrows.

"No, I specifically forbade that... but he's around here somewhere." Then, apparently anxious to move things along, she opened the tiny drawer of a small, wooden, antique side table, which barely separated their two chairs. Producing a small silver box, she placed it between them. "Do you know what's in there?" she asked.

Feeling a bit rushed, but determined to see where this would go, he answered; "I have an idea..."

"Oh? Well, then open it," she said.

He did so, and true enough, inside was what appeared to be dried, crushed marijuana leaves. Instinctually he held it to his nose and sniffed.

Just then, a scuffling noise from somewhere nearby stopped him.

Carlene quickly eased his mind with; "Oh don't worry, that's just Thomas, he wants in. Don't worry. The door is locked. He'll circle the greenhouse a few times and go away."

"But can he see us?"

"Who cares..."

Wow! You are something, lady, Thought Brownie.

"Poor thing, he wants what you have there in your hands, he lives for it. I'm afraid it's my fault, I've addicted him."

Brownie thought of everything he had heard up to that point; imagined the sordid affair with Thomas, and was not surprised to hear her ask him; "Do you smoke marijuana, Mister BB?"

Before he could answer that, he had to ask; "What about Mister Jordan?"

Her answer was sarcastic; "Mister Jordan is more concerned about lumber prices, golf scores, cars, lawns, ponds, views of the mountains and so on, than this "rope-trick" as he calls it… but I assure you, he has no objection to my using it… if only he knew, or cared how it makes a person feel, I wouldn't be here right now." She stretched out cat-like before him; Brownie could almost hear her purring.

So, there he was. It seemed inevitable from the last few weeks of his life that he would be at this juncture. He knew she was asking him to join her in toking up. This "reality" he'd put behind him many years back; knew all the reasons why he shouldn't do it again. But, perhaps the mind grows dull after a while, even after such an obvious dead-end he had experienced with overusing the stuff. He wanted to do it… reeaaal bad. *To hell with all the reasons not to; what about all the reasons to… smoke just a little?*

Carlene produced a precisely hand-rolled joint, from her cleavage. *Of course, where else?* Brownie reasoned, placing the silver box back on the end table.

She sat, with legs crossed. Her gown fell open slightly, revealing marvelous, well-proportioned thighs. His eyes kept darting up the smooth highways of flesh. Both lanes.

He had never cheated on Maggie, but it seemed as though for the last few months he'd had more trouble than ever keeping his thoughts under control (like those racing through at this moment) prompting a distinct desire for road-trials, drag-racing, demolition-derbies... whatever!

She took a deep drag on the joint and handed it to him. He puffed, inhaled, and held it. Waiting for the old familiar feeling. Sitting there with eyes closed, a clear picture of Carlos's Tower came to him. He watched it collapse, almost audibly clanging into a heap of junk, losing all sense of form. A moment later, of perhaps walking through the pile looking for pieces of the Trailmaster, he lifted his eyelids slightly and saw the sea of green foliage surrounding him, and immediately thought; *Metal is not organic like pot, it takes shape with fire, while pot takes its shape from water.* Great, the old philosophic mode was upon him already; meaningless thoughts supposed to be so profound, yet so stupid when analyzed later. *But there is something about man that causes a love for form not supplied by nature, a love of endeavor and effort... a shaping of the land conflicting with or complementing nature herself.* Ooops! He was still doing it... tried to control his thoughts a moment to assess any other effects the dope was having. *Plants grow by metabolic processes while enterprise of all kinds happen at the hand of man...* Wow! Either this was powerful stuff or the twenty-year lapse since he had smoked it was causing a magnified reaction. *Man's efforts may in fact be organic too, on a different scale of time and results...*

Yep... I'm stoned. The physical thrill crept into his chest and then blasted right through his conscious mind, and trailed off into the stars. *My God!* Engulfed by the physical, it was only natural that his body began making demands. *Like that Harley Davidson parked in Mister Jordan's entryway...* Again, with closed eyes, he imagined confidently straddling the magnificent machine. *Whoa!*

Courageously cranking open his eyelids, Carlene's very direct stare answered affirmative. Bam! He was on the Harley! Gassed and ready to go... she swayed and smiled intimately, silently accepting his presence. Powerfully tempted to put his hand on her thigh... the highway beckoned... she was encouraging him, but instead he placed his hand on her bare shoulder.

With an almost bored expression, she glanced away, then leaned back, indolently returning his gaze again, with slightly lowered eyelids...

But now, Brownie's emotions were idling down just a bit, and too occupied with his own thoughts to respond further. Her skin felt foreign, thin, membranous, and clammy. He hesitated. Idled the engine even more. Her smell was wrong too... not unpleasant, just... not right. He had grown to love Maggie's smell; the garlic on her fingers when he kissed her hand, the smell of cookies in her hair when she lay in their bed, open and vulnerable to him; the subtle smells of body lotions. Skin with the perfect temperature, texture, and thickness.

He took another toke on the joint; maybe if he was ripped out of his mind he could ignore the one little fact that kept popping up: There she sat... Carlene... inviting him to mount up... settle on into that leather saddle... hit the throttle... the road was open. Not a cop in sight.

Although, in his mind, he had already been up that road a thousand times, he felt oddly restrained, held-back in spite of the powerful demands being made upon him... body and soul; There was no DETOUR sign, no BRIDGE OUT, no CONSTRUCTION DELAY... and definitely no mechanical problems; they had arrived at an intersection. A junction of highways. His hand slid from her shoulder down along her bare arm... brushed her fingers lightly... She didn't seem to notice. The engine with the classic slow Harley rumble... waited for throttle; he leaned back, arms folded across his chest, facing the dilemma: *Get off the bike right now, leave this glorious symbol of manhood on the roadside, or blast on through the intersection?* The answer though faint, was clear enough; *You know it... shut it down, dismount and walk away... from all the chrome; the pistons; the handsome, riveted, leather saddle; the eighteen-inch wide, teardrop shaped gas tank; the spoke wheels; the whole enchilada... This is not you.*

He slumped back onto the cushions. There was nothing else to do. He could travel thousands of square miles on that highway of flesh; explore as he might, ever searching for the perfect destination, but it would not happen. She was not his. That road led to a foreign country, and a language he had forgotten long ago: Ever increasing desire for ever diminishing return. And even if he crossed that border he would soon run out of gas. Then what? *Nope, better stay home...*

Feeling very foolish, his sheepish expression was wasted on Carlene, who had moved on, unaware of anything but stars visible through polished glass panes above... meanwhile, looming at the center of his galaxy, was the black hole of a bummer.

Then, for a moment, he saw very clearly, in another place, different from any place he'd ever lived or visited, a man he recognized as himself: an old, tired, worn-out, hippy biker, standing on a weathered, wooden dock overlooking a little bay of the ocean. Behind him were dilapidated buildings where old men like him lived. He could even see where his own shack of a place... an old storefront, the windows obscured with time and grime... connected to a small, run-down beer joint. Old men sitting at the tables looking out at the vast ocean, through dirty picture-windows, sipping mugs of warm, piss-yellow beer. They were all each other had (wives and children long since gone from their lives), and living now on a thin thread of companionship, watching each passing day... and each other... through the same dismal windows, while the white sails of the living skittered by on a bright, blue ocean... blown with the winds of hope. To places of worth; an ocean none of them would ever sail upon again, precluded by choices they had made at one time or another in their lives. He rubbed his eyes and shook his head trying to clear it.

One by one, the few remaining stars twinkled out of his galaxy. The euphoria faded while another perhaps subtle, but familiar, far more comfortable and solid feeling gradually settled in... now he remembered why not to smoke this stuff.

At that moment, a terrifying, screeching sound launched him upright onto his feet.

Carlene opened her eyes and gently tugged his pant leg, "Oh, it's just that nosey Thomas O. Purdy, singing. Here," handing him the silver box, "let him in, and give him some of this."

Brownie still had an urge to run from the greenhouse to the safety of home and to Maggie, but had to see this legendary Thomas... He took the box, walked back through the mini-jungle and opened the door. A very large cat, black... and about twenty percent white... meowed and ran in between his legs toward the center of the greenhouse, to the accustomed place for enjoyment of home grown cat-nip and his beloved Carlene. The cooing and mewing began almost immediately.

—◇—

Amidst the bustle of clean-up and packing-up of the band's instruments, Carlos, loaded down with pots, pans and leftover potato salad (but zero racks of barbecued ribs) sidled past Palmie, who had cornered Brownie by the kitchen's back door; 'Ah'll be waiting foah yoah cahlll... say... sometime around late afta'noon? tomorra? Willie?"

That Carlos had overheard was just as well to Brownie, who knew there were things they needed to talk about, and soon. Carlos waited for him by the Van; "You got any room at yo' house fo' some of these here leftovers... cause my freezer seem to be bulgin' over at the moment."

Ooops! "I'll come over first thing in the morning... and help make some room in there, Pardner."

"And I'm thinkin'" Carlos paused, taking a napkin from his back pocket, rubbed at a smudge on Brownie's face; "I'm thinkin' you owes me a few dollars on a certain bet there too... 'Willie'.

Mmmmm... "Yep, that too..."

"And is they sumthin' else? Pardner?" queried his long time trusted, ever faithful, oh-so-loyal friend, with an obvious glance back toward the kitchen.

Alright then! That too; " Yes, there might be something else we can discuss..."

Both men knuckled down to the job at hand, contentedly; knowing that tomorrow morning would come with at least a hint of sunshine, even though the cloudy skies predicted yet another rainy day in Oregon.

A.B. had slipped Carl an envelope of cash, and he'd handed it off to Violet, still going about his business, but keeping an eye on her as she rifled the bills. Her facial expression confirmed what he'd hoped... the Jordans had included a nice tip. Violet then passed around the dough (including B.B., of course), and Carl distributed the leftovers to the other band members... perhaps out of kindness to Brownie, but mostly because the thought of rearranging frozen foods on a Saturday morning? No, thank you.

Before long the comfortable thump, thump sounds of closing trunks and car doors; the relaxed "Good night nows" and "See ya' laters"; preceded the efficient starting of engines and a convoy of warm and happy friends coasting down the quarter mile of asphalt lane... canopied with giant maples, flanked by acres and acres of green grass, and laced with hundreds of azaleas and rhododendrons... at least two of the cars steered around one ugly possum staring stupidly into the headlights, and another barely missed a family of purposeful raccoons crossing single file.

B.B. Brown, the Cowboy Cook, watched as his windshield freckled up with the first of many raindrops to come. Most outward and inward signs of greenhouse "indulgences" were gone. All except for the guilt, that is. He was anxious to be back home, cuddled up next to Maggie. *No, of course not... at two a.m.? No one with a job at the Cannery would be awake, or want to be awakened for that matter.* Still, he wanted to be close to her. And with all his might hoped he wouldn't talk in his sleep... or while awake either. For the remainder of the drive home, he tried to take his mind off Car-*lene* and redirect it to Car-*los*...

—◇—

Considerate of Maggie's earned Saturday morning sleep, Brown rolled away from the apartment building with the effect of less than forty winks still in his eyes, confident that in ten minutes he'd have a cup of Violet's coffee and maybe even a biscuit with fresh blackberry jam...

She shook her head in condescending amazement at the two men; "Brownie, is it yo' special mission to git us all in some kind'a trouble all de days of our lives, honey?" This accusation of course was seasoned with more understanding than normal, since she had been present when Brownie mentioned A.B.'s wish for the sauce recipe. "Why, jes' gib it to 'em! Dey's gon' be long-gone back to Louisiana in two, three mo' days," was her advice.

No way... Carl and Brownie, both saw this as an opportunity of a lifetime... How much could they charge? Shouldn't they leave Brownie as the go-between, even though it was Carl's 'intellechal propity'? *Yes.... and is dey more to A.B.'s request than just some personal use? Mmmmmm hmmmm... you bet dey is,* Carlos mused, and then respectfully aloud; "Violet, this man didn't git dat house-bus by sellin' no newspapers on no street corner."

Violet gave up and turned on the television set, but only after the two budding "entrepernooers" persuaded her not to say a word; "... to nobody!"

So how to flush him out?

"Well, we got's to wade right in at first, pretend we're dumber' n a box of chicken parts; tell him dat recipe been in the fambly since slavery days, but dat you reckon you could use some money. Den.... once we strikes a deal... we come out wid; he got's to sign a promisorry paper; you know, outten respect for all dem what's kept it a secret fo' so long. And he has to keep it in his fambly; cain't sell it in no stores and such for the next ten years."

That was a pretty good plan to Brownie, including the added drama of playing hard to get; "Yeah, I like it... Stall; Take it down to the wire... 'til just before the Phillips' departure. And... and what's our price gonna be...?"

"As much as he willin' to pay, Pardner. And don't call him 'til around four o' clock either... so's you don't look anxious." They both grinned... yes sir; this was money in the bank, son... money in the bank!!

"Speaking of which, what's my take, Carlos?"

"Why fifty-fifty... minus the ten bucks you owes me, plus rental on the freezer, of course."

They shook hands. Brownie got up to go and then sat back down with a concerned look on his face.

"What's botherin' you now, B.B...?"

"Well, not much, Carlos... I mean... I met that Thomas O' Purdy,"

"Yeah?

"Yeah, I did. Didn't you?

"Nope... I didn't see no other black folks a'tall...

"Well, he's not all black anyway... 'bout twenty percent white... according to Mrs. Jordan.

"Really? Wher'd you see him?"

"Out by the greenhouse..."

"Tell me 'bout it..."

"I will! Son... but not right now... I'm supposed to pick Maggie up for lunch."

"Hold on, you can tell me anything; you know that! Come on... set back down here."

"Can't right now, but I will... don't worry... he's a cool cat."

—◇—

Brownie

by

Kenneth M. Scott

– Part Three –

- Chapter Thirteen -

What a liar, you are, man, Brown chided himself...
Maggie's not expecting you. "No, she's not, but I am going
for lunch to a place we go to now and then..." he muttered
to himself halfheartedly, relishing the satisfying truth
that Carlos would regret a certain remark about "rental
on that freezer."

In fact, Maggie would probably be up by now... Let's
see, what were her exact words about him not working?
"Out of work"? Well, she might be very surprised before
long.

As he waited in the van for his turn in the McDonald's
Drive-thru, he watched the gas gauge. "What?!! Are you
sleeping up there?!!" He yelled, jerking and cranking
his window up as dramatically as possible, wondering
which would be better... to die from carbon monoxide
poisoning or to completely run out of gas before he could
get to the station? Runnin' out of gas would be worse...
definitely. Which, of course he did... right in front of the
pick-up window.

After paying for "Super-sized" everything and
somehow managing not to blame his latest misfortune
on the cashier or anyone behind him (except for the idiot
who honked), he leaned his back into the rear of the van
and with legs fully engaged, pushed it out of the drive-
thru lane, crawled behind the wheel to eat his lunch...
then, straight away began chomping and calculating
his chances of successfully making it to the gas station
across the street... through five lanes of mindless, rushing
traffic.

His previous bravado with Carlos began to fade.

The money just earned at the barbecue gig would be considerably lessened after lunch and a fill-up. But even if Palmer Phillips wound up being tough... it seemed reasonable to imagine his share of the sauce deal would be at least five hundred dollars... and although that was sounding pretty good, last night's fun was catching up to him. *Man, a nap would be good after lunch; if only Maggie wasn't home. Best to power on through... hmmm... cruise around the Saturday Market? Yeah. And Feather... that too.*

Without a scrape or an explosion of any kind, he did his across-the-street-with-the-gas-can shuffle; fill-up-the-van-back-in-action scuttle, and was soon winding through and around the slowpokes of weekend traffic.

—◇—

The Saturday market was an event held on the County Courthouse-steps where young men and women from all over, gathered to sell their wares. Setting up booths stocked with leather hats and belts; beads on leather straps; polished brass bracelets; silver-wire-rings; (necklaces, stained glass, fresh flowers, dried flowers, pottery galore) and anything useful or pretty that could be made by hand or brought from the land and sold to the willing community.

On the drive over, he reflected (as he did every single time he visited the market) on how it used to be, back-in-the-day. In the early seventies it looked pretty much the same, but now the spirit of the whole thing had become something different; not only were the exhibitors in another frame of mind, but the attitudes and perspectives of the consumers seemed to run shallow, with an air of insincerity and less zest for the moment.

Even though, over the years, the town's population

had doubled, he was almost guaranteed to run into one or two people from those days (a time, whether vendor or not, the market had been a place to gather with others like themselves... their brothers and sisters). Thousands from all around the U.S. had gradually converged onto the town, found it to be good and planted themselves beside her waters to flourish in their own unique ways... freely.

Back then, it may have been a mild "them and us" or "we and they" kind of feeling, but that line of division had become far more distinct these days... His memories of the straight-culture were tempered with poignant, sentimental feelings and perhaps a sincere regret that all things must inevitably change.

"They" were established, with jobs, homes and traditions. "We" relaxed on the cushion of stability "they" provided, while questioning and rejecting many of their values. They came to the market to gaze in wonder at us... and to mother us. Sweet little old ladies, smiling and looking like they'd just come from baking cookies; grandpas, looking at the crafts and talking about the old days when they made things too.

"See? We're still here," they seemed to be saying. "You kids be good now. Won't you come over to our house for dinner? Ernie will show you his wood-working shop and I'll make you a pie."

They were the solid citizens who were a vitally important part of what went on each Saturday on the courthouse steps. Lights on an ever-receding shore, a connection with a civilization that, down deep, "we" really didn't want to lose sight of in spite of an obvious, otherworldly mind set. We were still fresh-looking... even with weird, tie-dyed clothes and the long hair; skin that was rubbery-firm and eyes bright with light and joy from a certain expectant hope most (if not all) shared: Love, for all mankind.

Now Brownie could easily see that the "we" had become "they." Funny thing about humanity's assumption of permanence when observing a place or an event that's well established. Such assumptions contribute to the disappointment when things or places gradually change into something else, or shock when such places or events disappear altogether. No doubt Brownie and many others would agree that the early days of the Saturday Market could have been some of the best times of their lives. A time of acceptance for all people, who somehow fit in perfectly as though a part of the whole. Making assumptions that all were seeking the same thing... although there were "those" who negatively rejected that idea, and did so at the cost of enjoying the precious present while it lasted... and whose outlook and influence surely polluted the future of an entire generation

Nevertheless, the crafts were truly refreshing in those days and there was a lot of laughter; a certain joy that was contagious even for the straight people. Now this generation had nothing as clear: It seemed that the laughter was shallower, the crafts were shoddier, the distinctions of character harder to detect, clothing styles mishmashed and generally hard to define. Brown had enjoyed so much the Dickens Christmas festivals of his day. However, top hats, clown clothes, or period dressing of any kind these days was very rare indeed. *Yep, that was an era...*

Occasionally an old familiar face from those times did make an appearance... obviously still "out there," or stuck out there... someone who'd never grown out of it. Maybe they *had* actually found what they were seeking. Or maybe they'd let it all hang-out and were satisfied with just leaving it out... but to Brownie, "Grateful Dead," had a certain ring of truth to it and might more appropriately be replaced by: "Lost at Last."

Twenty years had passed and most of the now "normal" looking (including Brownie), having made a transition back into productive society, would be unrecognizable... weight, wrinkles, and hair not withstanding... time and circumstance happens to all. And truly, W.M. Brown was learning that what goes around does come around, though very often disguised and in a manner quite unpredictable.

With all this said, the Saturday Market was still the best thing going... in many ways... as a place to monitor and gauge various transitioning cultures; no gated communities, no enclaves of sameness sequestered from the rest of "us." A place where hope still thrived, where fledgling free enterprise could flap its wings... where musicians, actors, farmers, professionals, (and yes, the down and out, and the otherwise hidden from view) all contributed their own pigment to the once weekly, colorful and evolving canvas. Basically a good place to visit even if you wouldn't want to live there

Brownie weaved in and out of the crowded aisles enjoying the sunshine filtering through nearby fir trees. Connecting amiably to groups of people lounging on the patches of mown grass; smiling and nodding at parents with toddlers, groups of teens, and as to be expected, a few weirdos here and there.

Interspersed between the crafts and food booths were stone planters with flowers and evergreen foliage, plus a large reflecting pool... all enhancing his overall, congenial mood.

Food booths of all kinds were grouped in and around

these civic amenities, offering vegetarian dishes, meat kabobs, fruit smoothies, various sandwiches and drinks, but certainly no commercial fast foods... the rule was homegrown if possible and definitely homemade. All established retail businesses, including restaurants and fast food shops were excluded on principle alone.

While it was true that amongst the craft booths much of the originality and the variety of handmade goods of the old days were missing, the market overall, was still festive and interesting here and there. Brownie had no use for the displays of crystals, minerals and other new-age paraphernalia; along with touted claims of healing and mystical guidance, nor for the clothing that almost suggested "rags" to him, but actually designed within boundaries; apparently meaningful to some of the potential customers milling about wearing similar styles; reminiscent of African tribal clothing (Massai, Senegalese, Zimbabwean). Especially prominent were the Haitian and Jamaican influences, complete with silk-screened photos of Bob Marley on T-shirts, as well as colorful, unisex, peasant clothing in similar themes.

Off to one side, in an area all its own, just beyond row after row of raw vegetables, fruit trees, and houseplants (but still in the midst of tall buildings, and sleek automobiles), about fifteen or more assorted bongo-type drum players were rapturously mesmerizing strangely dressed (some scantily) dancers who writhed about in abandonment... completely given to the moment, oblivious to appreciative (or disapproving) spectators.

It was evident that at least a portion of any meaningful enterprise at the Saturday Market was contained within this emerging and colorful, cultural phenomena... making themselves at home... meeting to sell to one another, as well as to the straight people. Here was a mixture of overlapping social strata, grateful for the organic fruits and vegetables, and many of the funky crafts... though quixotic and quizzical.

Home-remedies and health potions were for sale in abundance. The question was how could the vendors be hung up on a particular one? When suggesting to a customer that they should try this or that, certainly some of those customers would have wanted to say; "Here! This is a bar of soap, have you tried that lately?"

But maybe on this day, Brownie was really there for himself, for something other than the replay of what he could easily predict would be there each time he visited; something that had more to do with the hippy culture in general than with Feather in particular. Yes, he found it very interesting... as well as a bit disturbing... like for instance at that very moment he felt as though he were being stalked.

For several minutes, as he'd moved about the dancing area, he'd noticed (in fact found it difficult not to notice) that each time he negotiated a different place to stand, an eight foot tall performer wearing stilts and costumed in Haitian or Jamaican garb, closed in on him... him in particular... A Disney character of sorts, complete with a caricatured mask of a black man, in dreadlocks... dancing and jumping up and down stiff-legged... and a bit too near for Brownie's comfort, yet still remaining decorously within the peripheral spaces of the other dancers.

Time to confront this guy... Brownie stood still for a moment, then faked a move to the right, then did an about-face walking rapidly several yards in the opposite direction... it worked. Had he not known that a collision was eminent there would have been a pileup, but his shuffle to the left saved the Jamaican's bacon, who, unable to stop on a dime, of course, adroitly teetered and jiggled back to a solid stance nevertheless.

"Hey, man? Why'd you do that? You could've made me fall on my ass!" The voice was familiar... the name of the person it belonged to was right on the tip of his tongue!

Tapping in tiny steps to stay balanced, the stilt-man's feet were almost parallel to Brownie's chest... they were bare... and muscular... and perfectly formed... beautiful in fact. "Shadow?" Brownie huffed loudly.

The answer was delayed until Shadow with some apparent difficulty poked his head through the neck area below the mask, which was really riding on top of his head anyway, and emitted a loud hiss; "Tssssst! Not so loud... I just wanted to say, hi... don't use my name here."

"Why? What's the big secret?"

"I'm working is what... checkin' things out around the 'hood...' see what's goin' on."

Stifling his desire to laugh out loud; "I'm sorry..." Brownie replied unconvincingly.

"And I get paid to do this... which is cool... do you like the costume? I made it..."

An unlikely story was Brownie's thought, but he held back while Shadow continued.

"Yeah, man... the Shadow gets paid to hide out... how cool is that?"

Brownie had to agree the job was suited perfectly, and as he recovered his own composure, he realized it was good to see the kid. And was duly impressed with his skill on the stilts, continually tapping and balancing with short-stepping moves.

"Have you seen Feather since we met... is she here today?"

"Naaah, why do you want to find her, what's up with that anyway?"

"I don't know, maybe I can help her out..."

"Well, I could pass on a phone number, or somethin', maybe."

Brownie offered his cell number, but Shadow refused to take it, since he was operating undercover at the moment... but they could meet over by the fountain in half an hour.

After thirty minutes of milling about the Market, ever vigilant for Feather sightings, Brownie returned to sit on the concrete rim surrounding the fountain. True to his word, Shadow materialized at his side, not quite magically, but came upon Brownie from unexpected quarters... one moment the kid wasn't there, the next moment he was.

Brownie attempted to hand him his cell number, written on the back of Doctor Jack's business card.

Shadow, without looking at him, whispered; "Easy, man, don't give it to me here, it's too dangerous..." He began to sidle away and added; "You do look like a narc; ya' know that... don't ya?"

Brownie, exasperated with the continuing dramatics, replied; "That's ridiculous. I'm no narc, man..."

"Yeah, I know that... and I know who some of your friends are too."

That was enough; "Look, sonny boy, you go along and play now; I'm outta' here...."

When Brownie opened the door of his van, there was Shadow in the passengers seat... with a serious look on his face.

"What in the..." his words trailed off into silence

as he stared at an enormous and almost comical joint (unlighted) Shadow extended in his direction. He got in and shut the door, but didn't acknowledge the joint.

He noticed Shadow had a backpack on the floorboard between his legs; "Going somewhere?"

"Yeah out to my house, wanna come over?"

Shaking his head in dismay, the confused Brownie asked, "You want a narc to come over to your house?"

"Naaaaaah, I know you're not a narc, but you might want to prove it by lighting this up with me..."

The thought of seeing where, or what this kid called home was intriguing... and the idea of just a little puff or two also had an appeal; "You said you know who some of my friends are... who are they?

"Wayne, Dorman, Joyce, a bunch of loggers, and who knows who-all-else you run with."

So, the conversation was launched... a much needed one too. When spotting Brownie at the Market, Shadow had spontaneously and cleverly, if not tactfully (according to Brown), wanted to make friends with him in order to keep himself updated on the plans of Wayne and Dorman to sabotage the springs. Brownie, (who'd "apparently" left before the talk in the storeroom was over) unbelieving at first, was blown away to hear of their plans, but gradually convinced.

Shadow, obviously still half-suspecting that Brownie might be in cahoots with Wayne and Dorman, paused periodically; talking with sincere tones and an open face, but still asking Brownie to turn on with him... to prove that he was not mainstream.

Brownie, though very tempted, asked a few helpful questions. Shadow revealed further details about what the loggers were up to, but had no certain idea when it would happen; "That Wayne guy mentioned the best time for doing it would be when the crowds were gone..." Both heartily agreed that there was no "best time"...it would be a crying shame ever to do such a thing.

—◇—

An incredibly beautiful sunset had begun to dominate the sky, casting warm colors upon all the westerly sides of the downtown buildings. Shades of teal, pinks, oranges, and millions of tones in-between washed across the city; appreciated by many, unnoticed by some, but never purposely ignored by anyone.

It was after five o'clock and Brown was aware that he hadn't called Palmer yet. Shadow listened politely (hiding the enormous joint in his hair somehow) as Brown explained that Maggie would be expecting him home soon... "Saturday night and all ya' know... make some phone calls, watch a TV show, maybe get lucky..."

After persuading Brownie to "come over" the following Monday, the kid excused himself. Then, just before closing the van door he said; "We're not done yet... wait a sec... what's your name anyway?"

Maybe because Maggie was on his mind, but then, maybe because he just wanted to keep it short... thinking the kid might prefer it that way; "I'm Brown, man." was the quick reply,

"Good night, Brownman," Shadow rumbled in his deepest voice, bowing and side stepping at once behind a concrete pillar, but ultimately embarrassed since in his dramatic exit he'd left the shutting of the passenger door to Brownman.

—◇—

Two dollars in his pocket; Palmer's offer for the recipe seemed more reasonable than ever... The Brown man (thank you, Shadow) had now malingered from work, one full week with his head injury... Monday would be the proper time to reconfigure that part of his life. Maggie would certainly feel better about that, wouldn't she? And, after all, a steady income is better than nothing at all. Hopefully the quack psychologist guy had sent his review in by this time... *Hmmmm... a promotion! That sounds pretty good, doesn't it?* He felt himself sagging against the worn seat covers of the Van... not exactly feeling propped up by the idea...

The barbecue recipe! Palmer just might have been kidding, drunk, or... *or whatever...* but it was worth checking out! He grabbed the cell phone trying to find Palmie's number, while driving down the short stretch of freeway, watching for his exit. Good. The number was still in his wallet. *Good, good.* He tapped the numbers in... then just before hitting SEND, paused; too distracting... waited 'til he'd gotten off the freeway, pulled into the GET UP AND GO MINI-MARKET parking lot... pushed SEND... noticing that the sunset had apparently peaked a few minutes earlier and had now taken on tones of... *of BBQ sauce?* The phone rang at the other end... *sweet red peppers? Shades of glazed onions? And dried chili peppers? Definitely dried chili peppers!* Palmie's voice was unmistakable, "Yayus? Hyellow..."

"Mister Palmer?"

"Why, yayus... is this Willie?"

Oh Gawd... "Yes, it's me, Willie, how's it going?"

"Well, We'ah packing up for ouah trip back home, Willie, what's up with you all?"

"Are you interested in talking about that BBQ sauce recipe?"

"Well, I'm not shuah... what's yoah pryce today?"

"I'd kind'a like to talk about it face to face if you don't mind... how 'bout tomorrow before you head out?"

"Well, we'ah quite busy, you see, and A.B and Cahlene will be wantin' to go out to dinnah tonyte... perhaps in the a.m. would be good... Why, yayus, maybe tomorrah will work out; I'll talk with Nicki to see just how serious she is about this whole thing. Could you cahl me aroun' six-thuhrty in the moahning? We like to get an eahrly staht on trahvelin' days."

Good grief... "That's fine with me... but then, would we meet at the Jordan's?"

"Whyn't you cahll me... n' we can go from thayah, Willie...?"

"Well... okay.... Mister Palmer, talk to you in the morning..."

Dang! He hated to be left hanging like that... limbo was a dance he'd never been good at. But it was what it was... he'd just have to roll with it.

During the short drive home... Carlos was updated about the Palmie call. They agreed that two thousand was the absolute lowest amount they would accept. The recipe was already written down and a fresh gallon jug of the sauce was ready to go. The question arose as to whether or not the recipe should continue to be presented as solely Brownie's or could Carlos put both their names on the jar? The plot, if not the sauce, thickened: It would indeed be better to have both their names on the recipe; that way, when Brownie invited Palmie over to Carlos' house, they could double up on him for top dollar (whatever that sum might turn out to be). "Heck yeahhhh..."

Saturday night with Maggie was pleasant: Simple hellos... a simple dinner... catching up on the kid's lives... a few laughs with their favorite weekly sitcom... plus, Brownie knew enough to comfort Maggie with assurance that he would be returning to the Airline Terminal Monday (unless the headaches returned). They even dared dream a little about the potential of more income. Each considered themselves lucky that night.

—◇—

After a serious counseling session with Mister Coffee.... Brown found courage enough to make the six-thirty a.m. call... *sheeesh*....

Palmer was no fool, wanted proof that this would be the real thing. Which was the perfect time for Willie to suggest that he join him over at Carlos' house, who was "coincidentally making a fresh batch" that very morning. Then with a quick cell call, he notified Carlos of the coming visit and was sitting in a lawn chair beside the Q-tower a good forty-five minutes before Palmie showed.

—◇—

Carlos, after assuring mister Palmer that it was fine to pull his bus right on up into the yard, then assisted him with directions, shouting and pointing this way and that until the accommodation was complete; shook hands with Mister Palmer the minute he popped out of the bus. Palmer acknowledged him as one of the band members and then recalled that; "Oh yayus, I believe I did notice you doin' some tuhrnin' and flippin' of the riubbbs ovah' by the Egyptchuan Bahbecue. "

"True, true... yeah; come on around and take a look at

this Barbecue," Carlos invited, in earnest.

The moment Palmer Phillips saw the tower, he erupted into laughter, and unfortunately said; "That is one of the most outlandish things I've ever encountered, why I cain't believe it... did you put thius together? Say you didn't... pleahse... tell me you didn't."

Carlos' face sagged.

Brownie, not sure they'd been insulted, remained poised, hopefully still controlled, and looking relaxed in the lawn chair in anticipation of the serious negotiations that were about to begin.

Palmie walked around the tower, craned his head upward, peered inside... guffawing all the while.

Yes, expectations quite often breed disappointment; Brown rose to defend not only Carlos but the masterful creation which he too had somehow participated in with Carlos; "Hello, Mister Palmer, you bet he did... made and erected her right there on that very spot... and in that garage over there too," he added, convinced that due to the magnificence of such a creation every detail said or ever written about it, had to be correct.

However, Palmer, numb to his tactless commentary, crossed the line again and again, unaware of his racial innuendoes... comparing the tower with the quality of his motor coach... which could have been the ultimate scorn of the Q-tower.

His excitement was genuine though; "Ahh dew wiush Cahlene were not doin' her last minute shoppin'... gosh if I don't... But say, why not ahdvatyse these kinds of thangs with Road Quest mahgazine? Certn'ly thah would be othas who would enjoy such folk ahrt from yoah cuhlture, or why not open a chain of them across Ahmericuh? Evah one loves the black mahn's primitive natchure." These were great suggestions but, perceived as pompous racial jabs, were wasted on Carl and Brown.

Carl picked up the jug of sauce and headed for the back door; "You know what, Mister Palmie? You don't know nothin' about my culture or my nature. Now if you don't mind you can remove yo' self and that house bus with them fungus paintin's all over it (referring to the painted murals on the motor coach's exterior of graceful Cypress trees adorned with ribbons and strands of Spanish moss, romantically draped over a depiction of the endless backwaters and bayous of the deep south), from outten' my yard..."

Brownie's love for the Q-Tower, which had mastered him in more ways than one, watched in dismay as the deal fell apart.

And Palmer, mystified, prepared to leave... moving about the exterior of the bus rubbing here and there on chrome fixtures and checking tires... which Brown interpreted as a purposeful stall tactic... kept a respectable two arm-lengths away; trailed him around the coach, suggesting that he might be able to change Carlos' mind... admitting that Carl, "was behaving, just a tad defensive..." all things considered.

Palmer, somewhat mollified (could care less if Mister Benson wished to be friendly or not) was; "...ahctuahly quyte used to the schism in the white and black cultuahs." And... "Why, Bahbecue sauhce is raishully newtrahl... don't chu thank, Mistuh Willie?" he chuckled.

Brown smiled a little too, but kept his head turned from Carlos, who had been glaring out the front window the whole time. And when Palmer informed him that, now, if he really wanted to do this, his last chance would have to be on the other side of the Cascades in the town of Ridgline, he completely understood: The deal would have to be exclusive of Carl.

Willie countered (trying not to appear too anxious) that they might "more conveniently meet at Hepner's store," later that very day, "...which is right on the way to Ridgeline."

Palmer agreed... but added one minor detail... "Will you accept cahsh foah the deahl?"

With a simple, "Yes," and a shrug of the shoulders, Brown played his best-ever poker face.

Trying to persuade Carlos to proceed with the deal as planned was a waste of time: "This recipe ain't goin' nowhere." Neither was the jar of sauce. And the fact that Brownie was out of work, really needed the dough, didn't seem to matter at all.

"Take them groceries back... there's yo' money..." was the last thing he heard when he went out the back door.

—◇—

By the time he'd gathered ingredients for the recipe, functioning on memory alone (and almost perfectly since he'd seen Carlos and Violet prepare it many times); then, had taken all the stuff to his apartment to make a quart jar of the same (royally messing up the kitchen in the process), Ol' Brown was on the road, breaking every traffic law for thirty-five miles of scenic highway... and frazzled out of his gourd.

The gas guy at Hepner's described Palmer's muraled coach to a T... convincing him that he'd missed the rendezvous by thirty minutes; *But I've got the home court advantage,* he assured himself, *He can't take the winding old pass road with that bus, but I can!*

Needing every minute of the thirty he might gain by taking the short-cut, he would've peeled out of Hepner's parking lot if the old van were capable of such a thing, but even so, managed to express official urgency by grinding gears and swerving to miss an incoming car.

"Come on, Baby, Brownie needs the bacon!" he shouted over the rattle of the truck and the roar of its engine... arm out the window, whipping the drivers door... cowboy style.

—◇—

- *Chapter Fourteen* -

Fifteen minutes later, and barely out of the chute, Cowboy Brown was in a funk. Glaring at clouds of steam rolling out from under the van's hood, he was reminded of other similar bummers: Once in the desert outside Barstow, California; once on the Tejon Pass in the Sierras, and once on the Golden Gate Bridge. Hopefully this time would be different. He was no stranger in these parts. This was his territory. He knew every possible place within a fifty mile radius that he might call for help... and that would be a total of two... that is, if he could've gotten a signal on the car phone... and he couldn't. There was Wayne's place about twelve miles west, and an old abandoned gas station five or six miles or so back down the mountain... *Somebody should be along soon though.*

An hour later, only one, unfamiliar, unhelpful, car had passed. *Tourists?* Two hours later, he began to wonder if that one had been a mirage. Other cars didn't really exist, there was no such thing as other cars, other vans, other trucks; his was the only one in the world and he was the only person on the planet. The stupid water hose was shot; to drive the van at all would ruin the engine. Still, he waited. The sun gradually dipped behind nearby trees, which covered the steep hills next to the road and left him in the deep shadows. Reddish-golden, glowing bands of light were cast on taller hills in the distance. Snow-caps on the far away mountain peaks shone as pink coral and inlaid ivory, on granite silhouettes of black.

What about right now? Wouldn't a joint be the perfect touch to enjoy the incredible scene before him? Help him kickback and enjoy the moment? *Hmmm...* Almost every time his cars had broken down, he had been stoned on one thing or another, and maybe that was the connection that caused him to think about getting stoned right now. He'd thought of those days now and then, but even more so lately.

He kicked his feet up onto the dash and gave in to the moment: Door hanging open, head back on the seat, eyes closed. What the hay... he hadn't broken down since... what? Forever? The time on the Golden Gate was a clogged gas filter. Now, in hindsight, a breakdown at that particular moment was a good thing; he'd been so stoned he wouldn't have made it to the other end of the bridge without killing somebody or plunging over the side.

Blubbering through tears streaming down his face, while driving on a giant asphalt ribbon curling in the wind, he'd kept repeating over and over again; "God, help me. Take this away; I don't want it..." then the engine coughed and quit, just like that, as if God really were listening. The breakdown was miraculous.

He'd sat staring and immobile, quite oblivious to the honking horns, thinking of red rope-licorice and strangely attracted to the giant suspension cables swaying and weaving erratically against a blurring backdrop of pale blue sky.

It must have taken a while before the CHP pulled up behind him, because by then he was cool, except for occasional waves of minor distortion, which he'd learned to control by focusing on the fist-sized bolts and rivets most wonderfully holding everything together.

Sunglasses kept his pizza-sized pupils hidden from the fuzz, and maybe, just maybe, traffic-flow would be more important to them than the pleasure of locking up one more loony. Sure enough, after the briefest peek into his red Studebaker Rambler, and with the simplest of instructions, the cops used their oversized rubber bumper to push him on across the bridge. Brownie watched in horror through his rear view mirror as the ominous, black cattle-guard looking thing, tried again and again to shove him off the bridge into the San Francisco Bay.

But, with inexplicable control, one column at a time, (congratulating himself with each passing of yet another intersection of giant cables with steel columns) he'd held on, until they were across the bridge and onto the shoulder of the highway. The officers pulled on around him shaking their heads in disgust at his lack of driving skills. The sunset was glorious on that day too, sinking into the Pacific; kissing pink, cotton-candy-tufts on the way down... Candyland.

Wow. Life had been pretty simple up to that point. All he'd wanted to do was drop a little mescaline and go to a rock concert in Stinson Beach. Traffic in San Francisco was the pits; the drug kicked in quicker than he'd expected and before he knew it, not only was he hallucinating like never before, he'd gotten on a weird power trip. He could never remember what exactly had freaked him out, but that experience was the end of his hallucinatory drug days. Other times when he'd been waylaid for one reason or another, he'd just let it roll off his back. But on that day it seemed like providence when a guy who knew a lot about cars just happened along to pop off the clogged gas filter.

Yep, that was his last experience with that kind of stuff, and the few times he'd smoked pot after that seemed like such a waste, not worth the paranoia and feelings of inferiority.

Now today, watching the sun go down, there were other considerations. He had Maggie to answer to... did he still feel inferior?

Enough of this! He got out of the van, leaned inside and rummaged along seats and floorboards for misplaced or lost candy bars, cans of soda... whatever... even a lowly peanut would have been appreciated, but all he found was half a bag of very stale Doritos. *Depressing? Inferior? You bet!* He sputtered a mouthful of stale chips into the weeds along the shoulder of the road, tossed the bag back in the truck, locked and slammed the door and shuffled off slowly, hands in his pockets, resigned to a very long walk.

Characteristically, the narrow valley began to cool down rapidly due to the many ice-cold streams that flowed throughout. He could hear the muffled burble and clink of Chinquapin creek paralleling the road. Enormous ferns spiked upward under the trees and amongst the wild rhododendrons. Oregon grape and native blackberry pushed out toward sunnier areas next to the road.

Then, as he looked back up the road, there, before his lonesome eyes, in mid-stride, was what could have been his very own unfettered, dread locked self (except for the grace of God and his own protruding lips)! Unconscious of this at the time, he had an immediate liking for this blonde-haired, bearded man grinning from ear to ear; from whom (with arms wide open and a most generous smile) gushed forth the words: "Welcome home, Bro!"

Brownie could not (nor did he want to) avoid being enfolded into the man's arms in a brotherly hug. And, before he'd even stepped back a safer distance, the man said; "Tell me your name, and I'll tell you what it means."

Reduced to the very nubs of self worth, Brownie had no idea which of his name's to offer, so instead of a name he gave him a color..."I'm, Brown, brother," and meant it.

"Jacob!" the man shouted into the forest, and again... "My name is Jacob!" sounding more like a royal proclamation than an outright challenge to anyone who'd dare deny him *his* name.

Then, immediately, in a hushed voice as though reading from a prayer book, he made this declaration; And this is, Brown Brother; Hermano De Castagna... Brownbro... That's *easy*," he concluded, looking full into his new friend's wide opened eyes.

Brownbro eased right into it; "What are you doing out here in the middle of nowhere, Jacob?" (he'd wanted to say: "dressed like that," but refrained).

Jacob's body was tanned a warm toasty brown; wore only cutoffs, and on his feet, aging Mexican huaraches (soled with rubber tire-treads); "I'm local. This is home."

Thinking that this must be another guy with a camp in the woods, Brownbro hesitated to delve any further but had to ask; "Do you have any tools?"

Jacob, having obviously passed the van with it's open hood; "Sure, Mon!" he replied, "...just down the road."

In a rare moment of sanity, Brown asked the Angel of Deliverance to wait while he rushed back up the road to chock the van's wheels with chunks of brown basalt... plentiful in the area... returned in minutes and the two set off for "...just down the road."

Jacob soon made it known that this was indeed "home," by knowledgably describing the geological formations, the names of foliage, berries, mushrooms (including what was and what was not edible) and recalling what had happened in history, both ancient and recent. He left no stone unturned, and kicked a few off the highway as well... "Biker's nightmare..."

Brown was impressed, but it would soon be dark, and even though steadily downhill, he was growing weary of the walk. They'd been trekking for at least an hour, and he, familiar with a bit of the history of the area as well, asked; "That old gas station anywhere near your place?" knowing *that* alone was at least another two or three miles further on.

"Just past..." inserted the tour guide without pausing in his monologue: "The locals caught salmon right off that boulder, and dried them over there on racks of alder limbs... over here is where they left their dead on raised platforms... poles made from the Sacred Willow... and down here in this meadow? You know they had to be trapping rabbits; taking down an elk occasionally... giants of the forest... the local's dug pits... dropped boulders on their heads and slit their throats... yuah, Mon!"

In the fading light, the tiny gas station needed no words to deny service of any kind to Jake and Brown. The ghostly apparition might well have offered SERVICE long ago, to those who'd made the day's drive up fifty miles of winding dirt roads to this point... but the antique gas pumps had been removed (most likely to some car enthusiast's garage, brimming with restored Chevy's and Ford's) many years since. Now, the sagging portico weighted down by decades of rotting cedar shingles and mounds of moss, remained huddled over the graveled drive thru. The smaller building, just a shack really, had apparently accompanied a run-down, but still functioning, two story house behind it. The house had enough style and character to have approached "luxurious" in its day... perhaps having devolved from a stage stop, to a small lodge, and then to this: Simple shelter. A few smaller houses, huddled together along the same lane, proceeded on down toward the rushing creek Brown and Jacob had paralleled for so long.

While Jacob spouted on, Brownbro scanned the area for a place to sit. Jake casually and resourcefully reached through an opening, plucked a milk-jug of water from under an old shelf, gurgling it down with no hesitation.

Brown could feel his sweaty T-shirt cooling in the approaching darkness... "How much further, brother? I'm running out of steam..."

Jacob, peering around the tilted jug against his mouth, jiggled the index finger of his free hand down into the darkening cavern of trees lining the road; "Not far." Took another pull on the jug... handed it off... "Main highway's around the bend... almost there."

Brown, who'd found a crumbling wooden crate to sit on, took the jug with even less hesitation and swigged deeply.

Jacob made a move to continue onward but paused, looking down on the Brownbro... "Rest, Mon... jug needs filling..." and then glided off down the lane toward the creek, leaving him loitering in the gloom.

This didn't look good, and he was too embarrassed to show his wimpy side: chilled, beat, hungry; no way to get back up to the van to fix it, even if he'd had the tools; the last bus on the main highway had surely passed; "At the mercy of god," he muttered, quickly attaching a small (silent) request (just in case), "who'd please have some food stashed somewhere up ahead too?"

The routine began again; Jacob had done almost

all the talking so far, and Brown was too winded anyway. So now, they were off... at the same clip; but the descending twilight had affected Jacob's ability to see the roadside attractions and effectively muted (somewhat) his commentary... And if "just down there" had previously meant five miles away, then "around the bend" could mean several miles or more. But he couldn't bring himself to cross examine Jake, who'd instilled in him an odd sense of respect, in spite of obvious social abnormalities.

Finally, to Brownbro's relief, the main highway did appear just around the long, sweeping curve. They trudged on; walking in single file toward oncoming traffic (if there'd been any), and to his surprise he found himself keeping up most of the time. Jake's running commentary was at a minimum for the next forty-five minutes or so.

As the lights of various cabins and quaint fishing lodges began to appear, the highway shoulder widened and they were walking side by side. Whether Jake was tired or just reflecting, Brownie began to enjoy a slower walking pace. Interrupted only occasionally by the offensive lights of oncoming vehicles. A semi-truck barreled by noisily; Jacob was on it; "See? That was traffic. I used to go to the highway to look at trucks like that. Yuah... as a pup... go to the airport and watch the planes take off."

He gestured toward a dimly lit, almost hidden house back in the fir trees; "I lived there six years."

And a few hundred yards later; "I lived in those rental cottages for three years... didn't really get into this lower-river stuff until later. Yuah, I was mainly second pool... mainly second pool, at first, but hen I moved down here... used these rental cottages as a base. Which, people can put up with, you know, instead of having to live out of their car, or whatever. You know my parents are old... I had two old dogs, I let 'em die in those cabins over there."

Brown merely took it all in, asking no questions, waiting for the disjointed information to gel together, sincerely interested, and was only casually relieved to think their walk was about to end when Jacob said; "Around this corner (which was really a curve) we're just entering my valley. That's Redside Valley we're leaving... first pool," he said, tossing a thumb over his shoulder.

"That trailer back there? That's where Stephen lives, He's the guy trained me as a Rainbow Ranger–guardian branch (tree frogs croaking in the background); taught me metalsmithing too. He's an artist many times over... Lisa builds clothing. Hippy stuff–way hippy." Suddenly, he yelled, "Nahusha: Brazen Serpent!!!" Brown waited for more, but nothing further emerged...

Jacob continued with his monologue. There are colony's of people out here, whole families... they make their own clothing, they'll dress me in white if I want. Beautiful sisters will make my clothing for me. Beautiful sisters have given me most of my clothing."

By now, the river was again right next to the road with its ever constant, rushing and whooshing sounds. Jake, stopped abruptly; Brown, single file again, bumped right into him.

Jacob paid it no mind and when sudden barking clamored from a darkened, small house across the highway, he shouted loudly; "Hush now!" Then without missing a step, advanced quickly across and yelled over his shoulder to Brown; "This is the house!" The barking had ceased immediately.

Brown hung back and watched three large dogs, absorbed in canine bliss, wiggling, wagging and slobbering on Jacob... The yard and shabby house were washed in a cheap, yellow glow from a sodium-vapor security light mounted on a telephone-pole, and also illuminating a small dumpster, leaning ungraciously against it, with its lid flopped open.

Several mounds of split firewood here and there, waited in haphazard fashion for a nearby fire-pit surrounded with upturned bolts of wood for seats, and a few mangled, aluminum lawn chairs. There was clutter of one kind and another of course, but not trashy... really... and a wire or thick nylon fishing line stretched across the yard, decked out with silk banners and triangular flags (possibly borrowed from a car lot) adding to the impression that this might be a busy place now and then. An upturned kitchen stove and a few white, porcelain bathroom fixtures glared somewhat offensively, but would soon be completely covered by encroaching blackberry bushes around the perimeters of the yard.

Jacob waited on the covered front porch, which stretched along two thirds of the house, as Brown, in deep thought, closed the gap between them; *What have I gotten myself into now?* But instantly found himself actually believing the sincere; "Welcome home, Bro!!" from the front porch... and for the second time that day.

Once inside, Jacob, having conjured up a roaring fire in the overly large, river-rock fireplace, invited Brown to have a seat. There were two choices; he could sit across from Jacob at the outrageously enormous and aged wooden picnic table in the center of the room, or he could sit in the more appealing armchair next to the fire. A no-brainer... he snuggled onto the worn fabric, feet toward the fire.

Jacob was busy rolling a joint... "We got food, Mon... but first things first... do you smoke?" he asked, offering Brown, not only the perfectly rolled marijuana cigarette, but a Bic lighter with the same hand.

"No, but you feel free... and... you do feel free don't you?" He smiled convincingly.

"Yuah, I'm not ashamed of anything I do," He replied matter-of-factly, lighting the joint... and then with tiny spurts of air from the reservoir of pot fumes in his lungs, chopped his words out looking happily at the now roaring fire; "Something... I don't... have to worry... about. If you're a virtuous person... you just don't have to worry..." and then exhaling the remaining fumes; "Don't worry–be careful!"

Right, Brownie thought; *that's what I'm trying to do...* very aware of the tempting and enchanting odor filling the room... an odor that anyone who'd ever smoked pot would perk up for, if not lunge at, the remainder of their days.

He stared at the fire too, as Jacob continued puffing, obviously relishing the approaching high... watching, as previous to each puff, he touched the joint on or near his forehead and ritualistically lifted it on up toward the rafters... and presumably beyond... toward the heavens... a salute, or dedication to the gods.

With nonchalance, Jacob then rose from the table and headed for the small fridge in the adjoining kitchen... The entire front portion of the house was all part of one space... sort of... There were openly exposed, skeletal remains of walls, which one could walk through as needed... or go around... negotiating other partially sheet-rocked walls still in process of being removed.

Presumably, the two-by-fours that had not been removed were preventing the upper attic and the tin roof above from crashing in on them. Brownie felt no danger.

Jacob placed a platter heaped with what appeared to be previously cooked chicken onto the counter; "Yuah, Mon..." he laughed, and stuck his head back in the box; returned with two bottles of beer and several jars of unknown (as yet) condiments.

Brownie couldn't keep his eyes from the platter of meat; "That chicken looks goooood..." he said, just as Jacob plunged out the back door into darkness. But before Brownie could even worry about where to? he was back... arms loaded with green things... lettuce, zucchini, onions, and a gigantic, wrinkled carrot bobbing loosely from its bushy green top and flirting with gravity.

Jake dumped the whole pile into the sink, which was set apart from the counter and looking as though at one time it had been a utility sink; old and stained with the years, but made of porcelainized iron and firmly sitting... nevertheless... solidly upon a metal stand.

"No Mon, not chicken," he continued... as though he'd never left the room for the veggies "...Fool-hen."

"No kidding?" Brown replied doubting that this was true... and for once, knew exactly what Jake was talking about.

Regardless, Jake went on to explain; "Killed with a stick..." he exclaimed somewhat ashamedly, but continued anyway; "Just like the locals... and the early settlers... and the loggers..."

"And me..." Brown inserted, unable to refrain from a little white lie.

Jacob, looked doubtful, causing Brown to cave-in

immediately, yet still holding his own, claiming to have
at least seen "many a Fool-hen" in the deep woods...
though he'd never actually fooled one... not personally
that is; "I've seen lots of... Spruce Grouse," he finished
weakly, eyeing the platter with even more anticipation.

Brown'd had the pleasure of walking up on one or
two himself and was amazed at how close he'd gotten.
The colorful males were the most beautiful game bird
of the northwest fir forests and were either braver or
dumber than the females who were almost invisible.
He considered them to be very classy in appearance as
compared with the gaudy pheasants that were definitely
not camouflaged and most often found in the grasses.
He'd later decided that the reason for not running or
flying off was their overconfidence in camouflage. *Which
could be considered dumb... yeah.*

Jacob reached behind the stove and pulled out a tall
smooth, walking staff... pretended to lunge at him... as
though Brown were a fool, chuckled (tossing the stick
back toward the corner of the room) and grabbed a beer-
opener from the counter top. Brown couldn't help but
wonder about his own camouflage... and stupidity...
but that was only a fleeting thought as he watched the
developing feast.

The fact that Wayne and Joyce carried bean sprouts,
tofu, micro-beers and other hippy foods began to make
good sense as they drank beer and teamed up against the
salad: Splashed it with a soy sauce, sesame oil, and honey
dressing; crowned it with diced tomatoes (also from the
backyard); laced it with pumpkin seeds; embellished it
with wheat sprouts, then positioned it confidently next
to the fool hen.

As they sat down to eat, Brownie asked about the
tools, and was not surprised when Jake proudly told him

about his hammer, screwdriver, pliers and measuring tape... these were not what he'd had in mind, but didn't have the heart to say so; confident that a solution would come the following morning. He was also confident that such a meal would drop him like a rock into a deep sleep (all things considered), and had been looking around for where he might be allowed to crash, when to his surprise, Jacob offered a prayer of thanks and ended with, "... in Jesus' name."

The dogs were lying contentedly beside the fire while the men ate. Each ate respectfully and with few words until the job was done. The dogs had begun to mill about the table (politely), knowing that their time would soon be at hand.

Saddling his side of the bench, Brownbro faced the fire, feeling quite content to be zoning out, and away from any coming realities the following day might bring... vaguely tuned into the homey sounds of the crackling fire and to Jacob (with the "fixins" out again, putting the final touch to another joint) talking to and about the "dawgs," who were becoming more and more active. His tone of voice was peaceful, fatherly and proud when talking to them directly and perhaps dogmatic and philosophical when (more or less) addressing Brown.

"This guy is Norman, he's the ruler... Son of Gnarly!

"This one is the girl, she's only six months old, she's gonna be head of the pack... Christina, The Bitch Queen! He chuckled and continued "...she eats my books... tears out every page I read, and then the next day she eats where I read up to last... smells me on the pages (another chuckle); "...it's her literary phase. Norman went thru it. They all did!

"And look at him... Michael... ignored us all night...

he's the most!! He's my bud, the most developed, Cadillac Dog Of The World!"

Then abruptly, out of the blue, scanning rapidly around the room, he shoved Norman away and bellowed; "Hey! Did you eat my..." jumped up; walked over to the mantle and adjusted a bag of Ju-Jubes, came back and sat down; "Nope, I put 'em up high... dogs're glad to get the bones... don't worry... they think you've saved the best part for them."

Brown was wide-awake now... Jacob pointed at a single deer antler hanging crookedly on the wall; "Those bones are elk, from the Ochoco mountains. I'm going to the Ochocos, my mom knows that. And right now I'm preparing to go up there... and live. Like I said, the locals have invited us, so, I might as well."

Assured by now, that Jacob referred to Native Americans as locals and having quickly accustomed himself to the dog smell, he pressed further into the cushions of the old chair; "Oh, they have? Well, that's good."

"Yuah, That's pretty serious weather over there in the Ochocos... yuah. Yuahhhhhh.... That's weather," he puffed again, with an ear tilted toward the thunder rumbling in the distance, and partially exhaled with; "How serious can it get?" finally directing a haze up toward the ceiling...

"Just look around here. Besides, I've got these guys..." he laughed contagiously... "Three dog night. The song is true! And I can survive any night in the Ochocos"

Brownie didn't like the idea of losing touch with this guy so soon and asked; "Why would you go there?"

"Hot springs; I can dig out a hot spring. I've been in there... only nine miles from the little town. I can walk that, I know… if I'm really in trouble, or if my dogs need an emergency vehicle… or I do… or the woman I'm with… or whatever the horses are needin'… I know I can walk it."

That was definitely a given, in Brownie's estimation. Jacob went on; "You know, the ranchers that are part of the city council… have invited me out there. So we thought we'd move out there, place the Rainbow… guardians of that area. Greenpeace, Earth First… people like that… they're all Rainbows… Peace on earth!! Haa, haa… They are! We can walk into any church… yuah, Mon. Common land. I'm not a denominational; I can walk into a Catholic church, a Mormon church, any church, and if love is not given I can give testimony to that. That's easy…"

He instinctively handed the joint to Brown, who, not so instinctively accepted it and took a long drag… much too long, since at least half was expelled in a coughing fit, which Jacob ignored completely and stood up.

His energy level must've been off the charts… that, and perhaps the "Brazen Serpent" (apparently a woman) had coiled herself just a tad tighter around his mind. "Yuah, Mon! Stephen is the one you want to talk to: The best teacher I got out here, he trained me. I only started since '78, Stephen is like our High Hippy Elder out here. I could introduce you… he just lives right across the street (highway)…"

"So, he's a hospitable kind'a guy?"

"I think so… I think if I came over with you it'd be alright. Like I said he trained me, but (sigh) we haven't been much on talking terms, cause uh, he's with a woman that I lived with (aha! The Brazen Serpent)… he's not married to her, I lived with her two years and it's really hell… she's done things I couldn't figure out…"

Brownie's mind spun off wondering... what couldn't Jacob figure out?

"So, I don't know if he'd be willing to talk... things like that. She's worthy of great love... yuah, I wanted to keep her for life, watch her grand kids grow up.

"When you stand by high people out here, I mean big people, you're glad to stand by them, let alone be held in their hand. That's what I meant about Stephen, He's amazing. Stephen Canfield, out of Texas.

"This must not be the same guy I saw sweeping the parking lot at Hepner's?"

"Yuah, Mon! Got a ponytail? Scrawny?"

"Right..."

"Yuah. He looks kind'a rough. He can bust my butt over these mountains. Five minutes with him will change you. He'll only reveal himself when he wants, you know... powerful people you don't even know... are around you. Yeah, they're mostly quiet... and then when its time to reveal themselves, they will. Like I said, I'll show you where he lives, just across the street, around the corner here. Yeah, I won't lie to you. Hey, I could throw these dogs in the back yard; you wanna take a walk? I'll just show you where he's at. Still a little traffic out...."

Brown was feeling so fine, and heard his own distant voice say; "I'm up for anything..." he still had charge of the joint so he took another toke. *Nice... nice.*

Jacob demonstrated, once again, his self-control by saying; "Better put this food up, trust only goes so far..." (the plates and bowls of food joined the Ju-Jubes on the mantle) while he still chatted right along; "The best part of being a Christian is being in the present, you don't worry about the future or the past, the eternal moment is nowwww."

They walked out onto the front porch... noticed that someone had (recently? or not... who cared?) left five or six bananas on the stump steps, with half a quart of Busch Beer. Jacob asked if he'd like some Busch but had foolishly offered up the now, stubby joint. Then he chuckled at himself and took a swig... spit it out immediately "...SHIT!"

Brownie laughed insanely for a second or two, bending at the waist and holding onto a porch post, imagining the very worst for the contents of the bottle. Jacob assured him (twice) that it wasn't piss, before tossing it toward an already growing pile, simultaneously swished his dreadlocks into the air with a swirl and a tilt of his head and let out a wolf howl. From that point both men went into the friendly theatrics of stoned camaraderie... temporarily considering every word to be earthshakingly profound or hilarious.

They stood in silence as the moment dissolved, and then Jake whistled the dogs up; "Come on guys..." once they'd crowded onto the front porch he began handing out his benedictions.

"Norman... North man... strong and capable... you stay... protect the village."

"Michael, the Archangel, and the first messenger or aspect of God; Meek ka el. Michael... a reflection of light across the deep, like the smile on a child's face, the dragon slayer himself."

And finally his voice softened; "Christina, daughter of light, you're the girl! I love you." Simply said... and as heartfelt as any words Brownie had ever heard.

They carefully negotiated the stump-steps leading

down into the yard. The walkway, of rough-sawn wooden discs, were placed like lily pads for as far as anyone (in their condition) should ever attempt to balance upon.

Another long-haul-semi rolled by, casting a fine mist off the back of its trailer into the yellow glow of the sodium security light. Jake spun and pointed "See that rainbow!? They're everywhere!

"Trucks are smugglers; this is one of their main trade routes... ever since the locals... thirty thousand years ago... on the way from the great basin, down to the coast."

Across the highway they stood at the edge of the river for a moment... Brown suddenly with an urge to relieve his bladder (realizing that Jacob had already stepped back onto the asphalt and was walking upriver), hurried to catch up while zipping his pants.

Jacob seemed entirely focused on his mission; "We gotta' do a little dodging (meaning back and forth across the highway)... Walk. We're walking east. I was down on the rocks jumping in the river, this morning... forty degree water; I didn't get to the springs 'til late."

Although there were patches of fog and a slight drizzling rain, Jacob's perspective was; "Such a beautiful night... you know, the later it gets the more we own the place. Yeah, we can go walk right out on the highway and nobody'd bother us for forty-five minutes to an hour. Man, we could fall asleep on the yellow line... nobody'll even come by. Yuah, Mon; the dogs and I go walking at night."

Within five minutes, Brown, single-file, peeking around Jacob to see just how far they had to walk this time had begun to lose his enthusiasm, attempting to ignore the paranoia police who were staging a raid on his self-conscious; he saw very few lights way up ahead… had no idea what time it might be. *Ummmm…. Ummhhn. Maggie. His job. His life. His stupid, stupid life.*

Jacob, in order to maintain the straightest line possible between two points, and zero regard for the two joints, had again cut across the road… Brownie stopped; "Hey, Jake… how 'bout another time for Stevie?"

Jacob did a respectable about-face (military-style) in mid-stride… "Yuah, Mon…" retraced his route back across the yellow lines to stand in front of Brown; looked into his eyes, and without further comment led the way back toward the house; "Like I said, the best part about being a Christian…" Brownie had to tune him out; the paranoia police, in their pursuit of him had called in the hounds of heaven…. Or maybe they were just the hounds of Jacob celebrating the return of their master.

Bone-tired and feeling guilty as charged for everything his mind accused him of, aware of his loneliness for Maggie (who must really be mad at him for not calling) and very aware that he was in for a real butt-chewing, he eventually crawled onto a pallet of surprisingly fragrant quilts in front of Jacob's screen less fireplace. But how could he have called? There was no cell signal or telephone at Jacob's. And he was not about to wake up any of the neighbors. Nor were there any public telephones within six or seven miles in any direction.

So, as Jacob droned on for several hours, he'd given it all up and slept with the dogs… and dreamed dog dreams. He was one of them and it was such fun running along the river with his sloppy wet tongue flopping out the side of his mouth, and just lying around in the sun with his buds.

At the first hint of light, with aching joints, dry mouth, and clothing wrinkled from top to bottom, inside and out, he now knew without a doubt that a three-dog night meant three times the fleas (no matter what spin Jacob might've put on it) and he was itching to hit the road.

Surprised at how disinterested the dogs were, he quietly emerged from the weathered clapboard house into pouring rain... *great...* sloshed out to the highway, tucked up under the draping, wigwam-like limbs of a large cedar and waited for the bus... known to travel the longest distance of any city bus in the entire country (one hundred-plus miles, round trip). He reflected on this man, Jacob, while numerous log-trucks, void of any enchantment whatsoever, sprayed and splashed their way into town (intent on making at least two round trips before the day was done).

He liked Jacob, though it was hard to admit. Not long ago he would have dismissed him in a flash without the slightest effort of getting to know him... written off as a flake... now he truly had affection for him. Last night had been one awesome experience! This morning (despite getting stoned when he knew it was wrong) he couldn't deny he'd like to know him better. Nor could he deny that, even though he'd quit smoking tobacco and marijuana many, many years ago, a harsh, foul smelling cigarette would be so good right now... and a hot cup of coffee? *Gawd... would be fantastic!*

But his bodily discomfort soon rolled on over into an ever-recurring emotional appreciation of nature, as the rain, in rapid stages, diminished to a slight sprinkle, then a fine mist. The sun peeked over the steep hills and mountains, and on into the narrow valley. Fog trailed upward from the river in ribbons, revealing nearby bogs of skunk cabbage where the shadowy and gangly, yet graceful form of a great blue heron, as still as the log it stood upon, became silhouetted and magnified in the golden glow. Off in the distance he could hear the familiar pop and rumble of a log-truck's jake-brakes as it descended down to the valley corridor from one of hundreds of precarious and winding, mountainside dirt roads.

The bus rolled right on by his mom's driveway without his even noticing, and would conveniently go right past Schuck's auto parts store. The next one going back up the valley would be at two p.m.

This was still a bummer. Maggie was at work (not that she would help even if she were able); he felt like a traitor to Carlos; Julie had no car to come and get him, and Ol' Brown had no life.

A proverb of King Solomon, often quoted by his mom, "A man's hunger drives him onward" haunted his mind until he changed it up by adding..."Unless a bus takes him there..." and as usual he was hungry!

Next to the auto parts store was the HOMETOWN CAFE. Unshaven, wrinkled, and smelling like a wet dog, he found a place by the window, ordered coffee, and toast with his last two bucks. The toast instantly vanished, and now the white ceramic cup, and a flimsy, stainless steel teaspoon adorned the tan Formica (imitation?) tabletop. He mopped rain from his face and hair with a thin paper napkin. The smell of bacon grease and burgers filled the room. Thank God, he could dry out and there appeared to be an endless supply of cream and sugar... Sorry, Mister Coffee.

He sighed, flopped the drenched napkin down onto the table, then swiped two more from the table behind. His view in the window looked out onto the street. A smattering of early shoppers, mixed with a few smartly dressed businessmen and women hustled by the window, ducking in and out of sheltered areas with newspapers held over their heads, avoiding the rain. Aspiring types. They had no idea he was even there; couldn't care less what he was thinking: Subconsciously he had known all along that he was in a whirlpool, if for no other reason than the fact that the same stuff swirled before him time and time again: the same old movie plots; the same news stories; the same human tragedies; the same temptations to do the dishonorable; the same lost chances to do the good; always feeling more like a spectator with everything just out of reach... perhaps beneath or above him depending on his particular place in the swirl. Sometimes it seemed he was about to be sucked into the final dark hub, to disappear forever without ever having had a portion, or a place, in the true scheme of things.

It would be just as well to put an end to all the gobble-de-gook. No more laps around; no more wondering how it was possible for all that stuff to stay afloat with such foul smelling influential effluence on humanity; no more wondering what perverse miracle kept him out of the dark sucking center. And on days like today he was quite sure that the whirlpool could use a good flush; surely some cruel god daily spread his fat cheeks, plopping down even more of the same old stuff that refuses to go down.

Three men in suits plopped in front of the window for a moment, one backed up, pressing his wet, trousered butt-cheeks against the glass, right in Brownies face. *Sheesh... somebody send for a plumber!*

The three talked for a moment and dashed away. *Look at 'em! Still living for the unknowns, the slim possibilities; to become successful, famous, rich, powerful.* They needed uncertainty; thrived on it; sucked it down as their vital necessity. Sure. But just as the newspapers they held over their heads (full of forecasts, speculations, and bad news) were being soaked from the rain, their own dreams would someday become soggy from daily circumstances too. They were the types who refused to believe it would rain no matter what the forecast.

The human spectacle is too awesome to ponder, so don't bother. Where had he heard that?

He looked away from the mall and let his eyes roam. Places like the Hometown Cafe were comforting to him. There was something about these simpler folk who had enough sense to come in out of the rain. Folks whose ladder up had only one rung: Truck drivers, delivery men, down-and-outers, minimum wagers, and social welfare recipients. Yet their laughter was just as genuine and deep as anyone else's. They laughed at the same things he did; more frequently even... and basically content just to breathe in the known; *Take comfort in the facts... like the fact that this day will be like every other day. No surprises. No nonsense. Hell, what would they do with functional plumbing anyway?*

A thought swirled by poor Brownie's nose, like a rescue note in a bottle; *Many fears are born of fatigue and loneliness,* and was gone in a millisecond. Besides, what if he was prejudiced this morning? It was healthy and human. Preferences were spice. Of course he hated... certain people, certain types, certain foods. He certainly had a right to pick and choose. For instance, he despised the "terminally hip," who would never believe their (seeming) tolerance of others was superficial, nor that they were simply in a self-serving, survival mode. As long as they didn't look too closely, just floated along in acceptance, then they could cling to the edge of the bowl and never even feel the pull of the swirl on their dangling feet and legs.

But maybe what he hated was the "type" more than the person. Very rarely did he hate anyone he actually had a chance to talk with, person to person. Long ago he'd had a custom bumper sticker printed up which was still holding up very nicely on the rear door of the van: "I don't hate anyone... in particular." Now he was thinking seriously about adding "but certain people are beginning to piss me off..." Maggie would never allow that. She'd say; "What about people you do like? They'd think you were talking about them." *But people should have enough sense to know whose being referred to... sure.*

When someone was before him he always found something to like; for instance the older women who chopped their hair short, refused to dye the grey away, and wear make-up. He really didn't dislike them... it was just the spirit behind their actions or lack of action in that case... He knew for sure that they were refusing to spice it up a bit, simply to emphasize to all men that they had value beyond the physical. *And they do... but why sacrifice simple beauty? It would be so easy to put a little color here, a few curls there. At least then they might brighten someone's day... maybe their own.*

Okay, even Brownie could see he was confused. He felt widely separated by more than a little from the Terminally-hip. If he was black as night he wouldn't want their acceptance. Couldn't tolerate their tolerance... Their type was hard to describe even to himself. Hell! they weren't a type, they didn't even make the chart. These people were on another wavelength, up close and far away. Their consciences wouldn't allow them to openly hate him. Unthinkable! At least Palmer Phillips was more or less openly prejudiced. And William M.

"Brownie" Brown, Brownman, Brownbro was pretty sure he could convince these other politically correct boneheads that they did actually hate him... if he dared to voice his opinion about things. And how much more would they hate him if he came out as a black with the same opinions? Sorry. He was just not big enough to love them. His mother would shudder at the hate he felt. They deserved his hate. How unchristian of him... He was no Christian, but now that he thought about it, maybe that was what bugged him so much. He wanted everyone else to be what he wasn't.

He recalled (yet again) what this town was like twenty years ago. It was friendlier. Sweeter. It had been a simpler time, but things were changing even then, with tradition slipping from the souls of the rebellious like harnesses and halters from horses and mules... all running wild and hating real work now... Had it ever been different? Nothing ever stayed the same, but these days it seemed like the pace of change was quicker. There was a stampede for the unconventional. Now, everything was "global," an international mush of new age this-and-that, laced with an obvious taboo against offending any race, belief, or gender. Brought on no less by the very technology upon which everyone so smugly accepted and capitalized. *Helloooo? Communications? Really? Are you sure? Is anyone listening out there?*

Brownie had to leave it alone. What could he do about it anyway? This entire town seemed to be on its own frequency. One day rising up to defend with a roar (in principle if not in deed) every last twig on the planet, and then the next day freaking when anyone even dared to suggest rules and regulations that might apply to them personally. No wonder they all looked alike... they were overloaded with acceptance of everyone and everything!

They honored all color until there was no color, absorbed every lifestyle until there were no distinct lifestyles to celebrate, gave "equality" to genders until the males and females no longer knew what to safely think about, or say to each other. The bumper sticker HONOR DIVERSITY was such a joke... COPY DIVERSITY is what it was saying... but copying it until it's no longer diverse would not be honoring it... would it? How could there ever be diversity in a community of sameness where there was just no distinction between peoples?

For some reason, today at this juncture of complete uncertainty about almost everything in his life... right there at the Hometown Cafe, the slippery edge kept him from even momentarily forgetting the spectacle, or finding pleasure in just "being." In fact, he was unable to look at, speculate upon, or consider the madness of the human spectacle any longer. *Way to go Palmer... compared to some of these nuts, you're not so bad after all!*

The rain had let up, the clock read one-forty-five p.m. *Guess I might as well go on back up the river and dig on a little genuine acceptance from mother,* he mused. Swigging down the last drop of his fourth cup of very heavily creamed and sugared coffee; he grabbed the flimsy plastic bag of assorted parts for the van, and inched out onto the sidewalk. Within minutes he was boarding the bus. *Rain... again? Still.* He tossed the parts bag onto the seat next to him. Schucks, printed in bold letters on the bag fit his mood perfectly.

Gazing out the window with a critical eye for everyone in sight, his morose mind set glazed over, allowing thoughts from a gentler place to surface: Feather, Carlos, his mother and then to Old Joe, one of her neighbors; maybe Joe would give him a ride on up to his van. He'd written a poem about him just a few months previous:

OLD JOE HALBERT

Old Joe Halbert's about six foot eight,
Has to duck his head when he comes through the gate....
Smiling n' saying, hi to the folks,
Hopin' you've got time for one of his jokes.

Handing out veggies and all kinds of fruit,
Got a squash in his pocket and dirt in his boots.
Joe Halbert, he's the Picker man,
Tastes much better fresh than it does in a can.

Joe's a pickaholic now that's for shore,
Picking and a' plucking and asking for more.
And while you're in town roundin' up your loot,
Old Joe's in your back yard gathering up your fruit.

He gets up with the sun, and he likes it that way.
When the sun goes down he calls it a day...
Feels good about his self with a good day's work,
Found the love of his life when he found the dirt.

Joe Halbert, he's the Picker man, taste's much better fresh
than it does in a can.
Joe Halbert, Joe Halbert He'll pick it for you... 'cause he's
the Picker man.

You won't believe the stuff that he keeps in his barn...
But it's in his head that he keeps his yarns,
'Bout Tractors and trucks, buckets and jugs.
Horses and cows and spiders and bugs.

His truck is an old red one with junk in the back,
But most of what's edible's in a bucket or a sack.
That old red truck gets him down the road,
Carrying old Joe Halbert and his precious load.

Now, Joe, says his old truck runs great,
But won't say whether it's a six or an eight
Doesn't worry about getting her up to speed,
She's blowing down the road like a Tumbleweed.

To me the old truck sounds pretty rough.
But just like old Joe; they're both pretty tough
They're fit for the job that's close at hand... that old red
truck and the Picker man.

Joe Halbert, he's a Picker man, he'll pick it for you just
because he can...
Joe's a Pickaholic now, that's for shore, picking and
a'plucking and asking for more.
Joe Halbert, he's a pickaholic for sure!

Nothing's more beautiful than, Joe, in amongst the green
beans;
Picking and a'flicking... and a'clucking like a chicken...
when he gets it in full swing.

And when he gets down t'other end, he turns his hat around
and goes the other way again. Arms flying around like a flailing
machine... snipping and snapping, flipping and flapping... up
and down and in between. My God, he's a picking machine!!

And when you sit down to eat,
He's sure you'll think about him and know that he's sweet
Taking care of all your produce needs...
And just to think... it all starts with a couple of seeds!

—◇—

The knowledge that his mom had such friends as Joe,
was only temporarily comforting... Brown was jarred out

of the moment when a two legged something tumbled down the aisle and plopped in the seat across from him.

Without the slightest hesitation the thing, turned two shiny green marbles in his direction and said; "Hey, man... how's it going?"

The thing can talk? Surely not...

"My name is Rootwad," it continued, and a claw like limb emerged from beneath a bundle of, as yet, indescribable debris. Fleshly colored tendrils wriggled loosely at the end of the appendage in what might pass as a greeting, or a gesture of goodwill... on another planet.

And then it all made sense: Rootwad! Wasn't an illusion but a humanoid of some kind... with tangles of reddish-amber dreadlocks running helter-skelter in all directions... (some as much as a foot long) emanating from a central mass of dense wool.

The creature quickly shed it's coat of scaly something or others: oddly shaped dohickies and thingamabobs of every known material, all sewn or glued onto what might have been expensive suede leather at some point in history.

Brown stared briefly at the coat which settled nicely onto the red, Naugahyde seat as though it had a life of it's own. But to his relief it made no further movement.

What remained on the seat next to the coat was a tubular creature with a wad of roots and other debris for a head. He had no idea what sort of coverings the thing had arrayed upon it's limbs; for the moment, he was enthralled or at least engrossed with a search for meaningful orifices that could suffice for a mouth or nostrils.

The green marbles hovering independently amongst

all the shag seemed to widen and shrink with no apparent reason or predictability.

Whatever this being was, it seemed aptly named: Rootwad. Perfect for someone or thing with hair (and a head... if one was there) beyond anything Brownie had ever encountered. A jumbled mess! Had it been the thing's own idea to mingle bright, flashy lures and tangled fishing line through-out the mangled and matted mess... or someone else's cruel joke? Talk about diversity!! This was the kind'a guy that if you'd seen him once, but had never heard his name... when you did hear it... you'd know exactly who was being discussed.

With no idea of social distance or formalities... It had just began talking as if continuing where the conversation left off seconds before... "Yeah, like I said; normally I wouldn't be caught dead on a bus... " but this time he was desperate; gave up hitchin'; couldn't understand why nobody would pick him up; not even the "heads!"

Gradually, as the being continued its monologue... about a morning of woes... the bad kharma likely to fall upon all who had misused him that day, and finished up with the so obviously contradictory statement (if not an outright lie) about how things like this never stressed him out... "It's cool, man... it's all good... I'm set..." Brownie was at last tipped off to the fact that this really could be a human being... but barely bridging the gap between humans and foliage, nevertheless.

When asked if he was bound for the hot springs, the creature said that as matter of fact he was, but more importantly intended to broadcast pot seeds in a few likely places... "creek sides, meadows... just about anywhere there's dirt and water."

As mangled as he looked he was surprisingly

coherent, explaining that just as birds carry seeds in their beaks, heads carry and plant the seeds of their nurturing mother.

"How so?" Brownie inserted.

"Just through everyday living: Talking about pot, with people like you... straight guys."

At that particular moment Brownie had been gazing out the back window watching the lane to his mom's place shrink and then rapidly vanish as their bus rounded the next bend heading on up the river. The idea of catching a ride with Joe flew out the window as easy as one, two, three... besides he was known for *spontaneously* changing his mind... even abruptly at times.

His attention was quickly diverted by Rootwad's hair, cluttered with curious and colorful little steel lures, dangling and flashing with the lights of the bus interior. Enticing feathered and furry fishing flies, plus reclusive beads and bobbles tucked away or embedded over time, most of which he recognized, and was suspicious that some might even be from those he'd lost while fishing the gorgeous river for many years.

Nevertheless, Rootwad, shook more and more accumulated debris from the tendrils of his mind; "... and you're one of the living souls of mankind too... right? Right?? A part of the continuum of space and time?" *Uh-ohhhh* ... "Well, it's like the physical and spiritual combine together to form a union... Marijuana is physical and spiritual too, man."

Grudgingly, Brown heard about the philosophical and agricultural potentials of hemp all the way to Hepner's Market. Disembarking from the bus, he could hear Rootwad still rambling on as though someone was still listening; and then the light went on... When people started a sentence with "Like I said," maybe they really had, but not necessarily to the person they were speaking; *Yeah, now I get it... like he said...*

The store was crowded as usual, but Wayne who really just owned the place, readily agreed to give him a ride up the mountain to the Van and to trust him for a hot-dog, chips and a candy bar... "Oh, and a large Coke too?"

"Sure."

It felt like the old logging days, being in the crew cab with Wayne, who could afford to drive anything he wanted... but this is what he drove and nobody asked him why. Myron chowed down, like the hungry bear he was, without a word spoken, but once he'd finished and stuffed all the garbage behind the seat (as customary) he briefly described Jacob and asked Wayne if he'd ever noticed him in his store.

Sure, Jacob was well known and well liked by all... a good customer in fact... Hepner's cashed Jake's support checks from his mom on a regular basis; "The man is some kind of ambassador of peace, amazing to watch his style with all the hippies. Wish we had more like him."

"Well, then... he wears dreadlocks too, Wayne... are you sure they're all alike?"

This fact seemed to register, but Wayne made no reply, which was no surprise to Brownie... not much had changed from back in the days when they had logged together.

Wayne, quiet and solemn by nature... had always avoided any conversation that might challenge his judgment. Even so, on the rest of the ride up to his van, Myron fished and fumbled around the subject of the hot springs, even alluding to its coming destruction, but

Wayne simply wouldn't take the bait.

Brownie, frustrated to be left out of the loop on that one, gradually realized that a powwow with the hippies would necessarily be forthcoming. Somehow he had to prevent what appeared to be the inevitable.

For the hippies, to go to the law would be out of the question. Even in the best of times, they weren't on good terms with the police; routinely regarding most authority with the utmost suspicion. Nor could William, Willie, Myron, Brownie, Brown, Brownman or Brownbro go to the law; he certainly didn't want to be the one to get Wayne or any of his old logging buddies into hot water (pardon the pun). Many scenarios, some absurd, some frightening, played across the overused screen of his mind as he entertained the likelihood that the hippies would probably be forced to take matters into their own hands. He'd tried, but made no inroads toward finding out Wayne's timing.

—<>—

Brownie

by

Kenneth M. Scott

– Part Four –

- Chapter Fifteen -

The hose repair was a simple one. Wayne waited to make sure the van would start. And it did! Then, both men, each in his own vehicle, thinking his own thoughts, sashayed down the mountain to the rhythm of the twirling road, through "God's country". And of course, with the usual respect and appreciation of the ancient peoples, or "locals" as Jacob called them: The physically sturdy pioneers; other men of renown such as famous boat builders, fishing guides, legendary loggers, and a billowing cloud of unnamed or unnameable persons... all wholesome and faithful to the human spirit.

This contemplative time helped Brown to see that his meaningless job was... *yeah, meaningless:* He seriously considered the idea of driving on over to Ridgeline, but decided that would be foolish... he was burning out... might never find the man. And he'd still not given up on the idea that Palmie might call him on his car phone... He kept his fingers crossed, resolving to broach the subject again with Carlos... *And that would be best all around... come to think of it...* hopefully he'd cooled off by now.

He also recalled that while stranded on the old highway shuffling through papers and assorted junk on the dashboard, he'd studied the receipts from the Bonnie Burger event, all the while reminding himself aloud: "There's no point in imagining any of the particulars about that whole thing." But somehow, he'd still felt a lingering and unreasonable feeling of loyalty to her; ... *because of her kindness and all.*

Carlos' suggestion to return the goods wasn't exactly brain science. He'd known all along there would be some ready cash waiting there (but thanks anyway Carlos); he'd just grab the stuff and return it... (sigh)... after all.

When passing Jacob's house, he did his best not to entertain that world... for now... there were plenty of other things to think about.

Within fifty-five minutes, he drifted into his own homestead's parking lot; walked across slopping wet grass to the apartment, all the while dreading the coming encounter with Maggie. And, he was right, she truly had had it! Came unglued... off the wall... and uncharacteristically so. There was yelling and name-calling, certainly regrettable to both... but most devastating was the mutual exposure of canine teeth...

When a man bares his canines it's not so unusual but, in Brown's opinion at least, *when a woman snarls back it's time to hit the road...* which he did.

Maggie was unaware, of course, that her added pressure was pushing Brownie into... *finally... almost... just about... making his decision. Not about being black, but about finding a job...* one that he might even like! He slammed the door on his way out, not sure that he would come back for a long time... or ever. Maggie had her own outlook and would have definitely been in agreement about that... for now.

The primitive encounter with insensitive, coldhearted Maggie, confirmed for Brown... again... that he hated, actually hated, his job at the airlines, probably more than he'd ever hated anything. It was completely meaningless, an insult to his manhood. His humanity! Why couldn't he just go with this freedom for a bit? He'd be paid for the sick time and if he remembered correctly, employees had a right to be sick for a long time after sick pay was used up–without being fired for it–didn't they? *Yeah, get off my ass, Maggie!*

Zigzagging the van out onto the freeway, Brown yelled an obscenity out the window at an idiot driver... *Damn! They're everywhere...* caught the reflection of his own face in the rear view mirror. He'd seen that ugly snarl on his face before, but shuddered... unable to shake the memory of Maggie's canines. He repositioned the interior mirror and bared his teeth, making faces. Opened his mouth as wide as possible... jutted his chin forward... vicious. Then, after a few more facial tweaks and near misses on the road, mellowed out a bit and thought about dental health.

He'd needed his wisdom-teeth pulled for over a year but had delayed, dreading the ordeal. Besides, he needed all the wisdom he could get, not that they had been of much use, so far... Why were they there in the first place? Maybe he should have his canines pulled instead. He was getting pretty tired of ripping and tearing his way through this world.

Hmmmmm... wisdom-teeth are way in the back; hard to get at; rarely, if ever used; often rotting from lack of hygiene; or growing in crooked, impacting other teeth and could actually ruin a good smile... if left unattended.

No. He wouldn't dare say he was wise, and he certainly didn't know how to keep his mouth shut. Otherwise he might've passed for wise innumerable times. Yes, he heartily agreed with the phrase: Less said-less mended, and studiously repeated it all the way to town; "Less said-less mended; Less said-less mended; Less said-less mended; Less said-less...

Open wide; wider, please.

No.

As wide as possible... Atta boy! What? You don't have your wisdom teeth? Well... you sure as heck can't be president of these United States!! Next in line, please...

What? You want to get married? Open your mouth...

What? You want this promotion Mister Brown? Open your mouth... no ... on second thought, you'd best keep it shut. Just fill out the form... check one of those little boxes there... anyway you see fit.

Oh, and if you'd like, we could file those canine's down a bit...

His mom had a framed definition of wisdom on the wall in front of the toilet:

Wisdom:

The timely application of knowledge to present and future circumstance. It is the ability to make the best use of "information" in order to bring about peaceful and harmonious results. It is the tool by which man positions himself to cope with revelation about the universe, both within himself and without. Wisdom is expedient to economy. It is, the maximum use of the least of things known... resulting in a conservation of energy and a readiness, or a capable positioning, for the, as yet... unknowns.

© *1978 Ken Scott*

Wow.... That made more sense than ever; maybe it wasn't too late... he resolved to try harder.

Not only that, but he needed to watch out for the "Flake" syndrome... according to some and confirmed by a recent car phone message; Shadow'd essentially informed him that if he didn't want to be thought of as an irresponsible slacker, then he should meet him at the, "...same place as previously arranged... same time tomorrow, which would be Tuesday, Brownman, at two in the afternoon." Click!

Irresponsible slacker? Maybe so. He had spaced their appointment... for some reason, oh yeah, the Palmie thing. Well, he'd accommodate Shadow's wish for a re-do. Tuesday was another day, and sick or not, it belonged to him, Damn it!

He cruised on in the general direction of Carlos' house... quite conscious of not eating since the hotdog, and that he was flat broke and dead-dog tired. His only option was to make the grocery raid at Carlos' house... "raid" being his choice of words, since he had already imagined Carlos doing a little raiding of his own. He dialed the number, pushed talk.

Although Carlos wasn't there, he felt slimy anyway... sure that Violet would be peeping out the window, but knew also that in the classic wisdom of womankind she wouldn't interfere with he and Carlos' dealings... The reload took about thirty minutes. He'd arranged apples with apples and oranges with oranges, so to speak. Frozen goods separated from canned goods, and so on... most of the breads and pastries he didn't bother to load at all... reasoning that they might be rejected for lots of reasons.

The store manager informed him that the frozen items couldn't be returned since they may have thawed and been re-frozen. This seemed unfair, but from all the strange assortment of goods spread out on the counter he felt kind'a like a criminal anyway, and unless he'd been willing to tell the whole story (which, he wasn't), arguing would only arouse more of the same. He accepted the ruling and the nine hundred fifty-six dollars... successfully resisting the urge to do a jig until he was outside in the parking lot... behind the van.

There was no way he could take the frozen food back to Carlos' freezer. Now what? No longer flat broke, but still hungry, tired and homeless... and likely to remain so... *Unless I wanted to make it up with Maggie, and who says she'd be willing?* Thoughts about how that would go down raced through his mind, but none of them rang a bell... then, suddenly something did ring his bell... *Mom has a freezer, she loves me, and...* that was all he needed to know. The van had already started itself, and headed back upriver.

Thirty minutes later and with barely enough energy, Myron loaded his mom's freezer while she heated up leftovers. By six p.m., in the tiny spare bedroom, he drifted off into a not so deserved, but much needed sleep. His overworked brain and body had refused to shut down without the help of endlessly repeated affirmations: The thwarted Palmie thing was for the best; the hot springs intervention is vital; Jacob is someone I like; Maggie is really a sweetheart; the thwarted Palmie thing was for... that, all-in-all... all-in-all... the... all-in.... zzzzzzzz...

—◇—

He awoke at ten p.m. to the sounds of his mother's snoring, intermixed with the antics of some ancient "I Love Lucy" re-run from the fifties. He had an idea: Scribbled a large note and pasted it onto the TV screen; Mom, don't worry, I'll be back in the morning...

Twenty minutes later, an uneasiness about intruding so late at night washed instantly away when Jacob received him with another warm hug and the same effusive, "Welcome home, Bro!"

The dogs recognized him without a bark. Norman, offered his paw; Michael explored the darkened yard with his coat of white (like a reflection of light across the deep); Christina led him into the castle in search of her crown of royalty, and Jacob handed him a freshly broiled trout.

Perfect. He sat down while Jacob piled on the fresh salad greens and boiled potatoes. "Yuah, Mon!"

The radio was tuned to light rock music and the fireplace had just the right sized fire burning... so far.

His host was preoccupied... puttering and digging around in boxes in the adjoining portion of the downstairs main room... and the upstairs... not at all frantically... purposely... as though this was his normal nightly routine.

Brown began to settle in comfortably... fascinated with the assortment of oddities displayed on windowsills, or leaning in darkened corners. Slowly it came to his awareness that the music on the radio was Christian... hip stuff, though... but with predictable lyrics... if one took the time to decipher them above the instruments.

In characteristic, understated hospitality, Jacob appeared just in time to take away his empty plate and; "What you need now, Mon... is this and a beer." he said, proffering a rolled joint.

Perfect again. But he'd already made up his mind about the pot... determined not to lose focus for why he'd come in the first place. So the joint he refused, but accepted the beer. Hoping to ease into the "conversation" by making small talk, he stood beside the fire with an elbow draped on the mantle, enjoying the bottle of cold beer.

Jacob, ever alert to the periodic monologue of the radio announcer, would either cease his wandering ways, hang his sinful head, or lift it (and his amazing sky-blue eyes) heavenward... sometimes smiling, other times offering respectable commentary or disagreement... as though the living God was visible through a hole in the ceiling.

"So, that's a Christian station?" Brown asked, certain that this was a stupid question, but anxious to kick off the conversation.

"One-O-nine... on the a.m. dial... Yup, folks... that comes right out of Cordwood, Oregon. Those are the Baptists; they're real strong here in Oregon. It gets rocking too... heavy metal... I call it nail music. They go thru the Bible eight times in a day... different parts of the Bible. Yeah, they're explaining and scheming... so I wait for that." He continues his sojourn around the room, overlaying his own monologue upon the music in the background. Gathering enthusiasm as he goes... though not boisterous or loud at all... pointing and commenting on different books on shelves or about the colorful paintings and drawings on the wall... many on canvas, but all unframed; "That's the Jewish Menorah, the tree of life, a rabbinical oral tradition."

Brown nodded and burped, enjoying the tour...

Jacob gestured roundly to the familiar symbol of medicine painted on a large canvas, and proclaimed with audible reverence; "The staff of Asklepios." But it was far more than that. The staff, the overall dominant subject, paired with coiled snakes and angelic wings, hovered weightlessly within a Grecian looking temple surrounded in a landscape of lush foliage. Snakes in elaborate colors and patterns were everywhere... some seemed to be intently observing or approaching the temple... wiggling and hissing almost audibly; waiting perhaps for their go at the staff.

Jacob pulled it out from the wall and said; "I studied this, but I quit a month before I graduated..." then re-hung it, backside out, face to the wall

Brown put two-and-two together; "Because you got discouraged with society?"

"No, hah, hah... with medicine. See I was trying to understand! I'm a biologist (as though he were the only student out of hundreds enrolled in the program), trying to understand the best biology we know. In an anthropocentric society, that leaves man, right?

"I found out... you know... we don't know much... We don't know SHIT! (the one foul word he'd so far allowed himself... loud and chopped... broadcast perfectly into the ether as no one else on earth could have)." Then calmly continued, ignoring the digression... "No. I know a lot of people do... do know... a lot of different things... about plants; how to bring things out of plants; how to use those to stay healthy. And so, what is that thing Christ says... uh... 'Physician heal thyself...' what do you think he meant by that? A lot!

"Yuah mon, like that guy, Buddha," pointing at a tiny, gold-painted statue of Buddha sitting alone in the dark, "Heal yourself before you try to heal someone else. Cause the one thing I couldn't understand was, what was disease? I put in for an extra year in pathology; used the electron microscope to get right down to what was up. And I found out! Ohhhh..." he crooned somewhat deviously, "I don't need things in front of my eyes to see what's there... I don't need glasses... I don't need microscopes. I can see what's up. Disease means not at ease... illness.

"I couldn't quite understand what we were naming, or what we did know, and I realized we were naming something we don't know... and in a lot of different languages. I started using other languages, to find out... Chinese, Japanese." With this information he rotated his body, arms waving around the room in an all inclusive gesture; then stood up, pointing out beautiful calligraphy written everywhere... on the overhead beams, the window moldings... and some of the remaining sheet rocked walls.

"See... The Japanese..." (in a formal, booming voice, as though making a proclamation to the world). "Nam meyoho renge kyo, that's jewels in the lotus... chant that all day and your life is different." He continues on around, dodging in and out of two-by-four walls, ducking through openings in partially sheet rocked areas, acknowledging certain displays (Brownie shifts positions by the fireplace, craning his head this way and that, paying close attention... flabbergasted, as Jacob went on); "That's from the altar of the '97 gathering... that's the altar... this too... all that stuff's from the altar." (*Rainbow Gathering*, Brown assumes and makes a mental note to come back to the alter later... though not on bended knees).

Jacob, stopped, gazed around the room intently... then picked up a conch shell lying on a windowsill; "This is how you call the Counsel; a conch shell, blown North, East, South and West... in that order. That's how the locals did... to call the warrior brothers and uncles of Quetzalcoatl... I think he was the Morning Star, the Christ symbol of this continent."

Which, regardless, brought them back to the root of Brown's original question; not so stupid after all, given the all-inclusive scope of Jake's interests; "So... you're a Christian... or what?"

"I'm a member of the Rainbow tribe... and sure... I'm a Christian, but not a canned Christian... or a cookie cut-out."

"How does a person get to be a member of the Rainbows?"

"Anybody with a bellybutton can be a Rainbow... say you wanna be a Rainbow, and you're a Rainbow. Yuah, Mon, anyone with a belly button. A pretty loose organization... no merit badges yet. The secret password is, agree."

Brownie has already seen a picture of what looked like a younger Jake receiving his Eagle Scout merit badge.

"Are Rainbow's Christians?"

"Not in so many words... many are, but others're deciding. I name 'em... sometimes I baptize 'em."

Suddenly he jerks his head around and points (as though he's never seen it before) to something over the lintel of one door. Set apart from everything else, adorning the walls (a place of honor?), was a beautifully inscribed canvas with strange symbols in bright colors; "That's runes from Stephen's family; he's from Iceland... they're Christian Druids. I was trained by a Minnesota Druid."

Stephen Canfield... Brown automatically deduced, but his mind was in serious danger of overload by then. He needed Jake to focus if they were to get anywhere that night; "Name 'em and claim 'em?" He coaxed.

"Yuah, Mon... I ask them to tell me what their name is and I tell them what it means. That's our job you know... I had to find my own name, so I help where I can... but I only help the willing."

"You mean you found the name, Jacob?"

"I took that name for myself a few years ago... I was reading Isaiah... I like Isaiah... and Jacob... who became Israel. Anyway, there was all these names for one guy, I realized this guy was me! And then I saw that, hey! God was speaking to me!! Through writing! So if he was talking to me, I should start from the beginning.

"So, that I did! The whole thing is about names. Sign me up! Light is good. Adam had three things to do: dress and tend the garden, name everything, and love God. Words!

"So I'm about that. Rainbow Ranger, guardian of the hot springs... naming people and things in the garden... and baptizing. I ask 'em two questions, I ask 'em what they're full name is, tell 'em what it means, and do they believe in a guy named Jesus Christ. And then I baptize 'em."

Brownie was losing confidence in Jacob's sanity again; "How do you do that?"

"I tell them what I'm gonna' do... I give 'em ten minutes.Ask them to bring me water. Then I tell em, I'm gonna get-em-wet... baptize them in the name of the Father, Son and the Holy Spirit. I tell them they'll be following... and then I give 'em a Bible, cause that's what they'll be following... what they'll be looking at is the gospel, the witness accounts."

He bounced over Norman, hauled a cardboard box over to the fireplace, peeled the flaps back; hurriedly loaded his arms with books and stood up... Brown had no difficulty in recognizing that they were Bibles; leather covers in brown, black, red; stacked up to his chin. Many embossed with gold letters... others were paper-backs... several red-covered New Testaments slid off onto the floor at his feet: "This is the Vietnamese Vet's Bible; This is the King James; Those are Gideons... they're good. This is the living Bible, just plain talking in here..."

Brownie cut him off; "You ask them if they believe that Jesus is the son of God?"

"Well, no, they don't have to believe any of that, all

they have to believe is that there was a guy named Jesus Christ... Issha, in his own Aramaic language... It's up to them, I just say read the witness accounts, and listen to what He says. And that's what they're doing.

"Baptism is not necessary for Salvation. It's just what will happen... when people choose to do it... and really look at it. We all doubt; I'm doubting... with an open heart..." he says with bowed head.

"They'll doubt too... do it for confirmation... You'll be baptized, first by water, and then by fire. How does baptism by fire happen? By the spirit, the furnace of affliction will bring you forth purer than gold... and silver. The furnace of affliction will bring you forth, where your bondages will be burned away... not your hair, or your body, or clothing. This is in Isaiah.

"I don't have favorite books in the bible. I need to know all of the Bible in order to understand Revelation or Job, or Daniel, 'cause its deep... deeper than I can understand, or all of us can understand. Deep. I can't understand it all. There's no way. But it's my job to get at it. To know the times and seasons, to be able to name all those things that God brings me... in this garden not planted by human hands..." his head bowed again, chin on his chest. His words had become a chant; sentences running together, with little rhythm but burbling and cascading like a mountain stream...

Making his way over to the single mattress (Jacob had somehow produced from the shadows along with a worn pillow and tattered blanket), Brownie at first sat on the edge, but soon reclined and began nodding out... gazing up toward the ceiling at the strange letters and symbols slowly fading in and out of view... He caught bits and pieces of the recitation... wasn't sure if he was listening or dreaming... whether he actually heard, or would remember, the rest; "... that was made for me, before other things that were made. To be inhabited, even before you knew the face of God was love... Before you were created, before there was light! It was known that you would be drawn to it; that you would habitate the house of *Gawd*; That your only three jobs are to name everything he brings you in that garden; to dress and keep that garden... and to love him... and that's it.

"Yuah, Mon, I was like, sign me up! I was given the same jobs that Adam was given. It's right there in Genesis; That was the man of God... the one that was in the forest... the ultimate Big Foot!

—◇—

Brown awoke with the sun in his eyes, groaned and shifted position on the mattress. There was Jacob, standing at the foot of the stairs.... smiling at him... a cup of steaming liquid in both hands...

What day was it... *shouldn't I be doing something*? The days all seemed to be running together... Had Jacob been there the whole night? "Have you even been to sleep?"

"Yuah, Mon..." his oft' repeated words... always sincerely uttered... though this time slightly compromised with chewing, and swallowing (ugh! humanity...).

A portion of dignity was salvaged though, when a hand passed a cup down. He tried to close Jake out of his mind, but the smell of coffee changed all that. The guy was weird but he couldn't be crazy with such consistent hospitality. "Thank you, Jacob..." he muttered, and couldn't help but break out with his own smile in the presence of such genuine joy. Then, forthwith, rolled over onto his side, yielding like a pitiful slave to Mister Coffee... slurping and wishing (like all humanity) that he too had something to chew.

Jacob sat on the stairs and sipped his own coffee... neither of them spoke. Then, for no apparent reason, erupted into almost contagious laughter... Brownie remained stolid... unable to go quite that far.

He chose that moment to roll off the mattress. Jacob stood and stepped aside, allowing him to make his way through the narrow passage to the bathroom, which he gratefully did; splashed water on his face, glad there was no mirror present. Then, when leaving the bathroom, nearly tripped over Christina, who'd come to bless him with her royalty... *Arrrrrh, too early...*

The fire had reduced to glowing embers, but was still inviting. The front door was open and sunshine bathed the whole world in gold... casting a warm and inviting carpet of peace onto the scarred wooden floor... right to the very edge of Brown's feet. He had an urge to take off his shoes, also scarred, but character filled too... *just like this floor...*

Then he got it... the moment he'd opened his eyes, he'd been reacting the way he thought he should or would feel, but he actually felt good! Surprisingly good. The radio was on very low, still tuned to the same station. Now, where was that Jake?

The back door creaked and clunked shut. Norman and Michael burst around the corner and were all over him, vying for attention. Jacob made noises in the kitchen that could easily be interpreted as promising. The unmistakable muffled sound of silverware whipping around in a bowl meant... *eggs...*

Eggs had a mind of their own... almost... Brown began to make little snapping and clucking sounds with his tongue and substantial lips... swaying, shuffling...

making his way around the fireplace and into the kitchen. Jacob paid him no mind... Brown picked up a large, brown (of course) egg: maneuvered it over the stove inches away from Jacob's face... the moment Jake acknowledged his presence... he pulled it back and got it on... popping and locking, making it up as he went:

Now, an egg is honest, an egg is true...
He keep his eyes open while he's talking to you!
You know where he's coming from!
You crack an egg open and you drop him in the pan...
He's looking right at you, like a man to man!
An egg is honest, you know where he's coming from!
An egg has courage, yesiree! You'll never see him begging
on a bended knee.
He's not a chicken or a cock a doodle, doodle, doo do!
He's a good egg! he's honest and true... cock a doodle,
Doodle... doodle doo, do, do! Do... doodle do 'n do 'n ...
Do do do.

Brown was lost and loving it... spinning around, jerking his hands, rolling his arms in most unnatural ways... with a not too bad mechanical-chicken bit. The cock a doodle doos had a hold on him.

He's a good egg! He's honest and true... cock a doodle,
Doodle... doodle doo, do, do! do doodle do 'n do.
Chicken house, cackle berries, barnyard fruit,
Cluck, cluck, cluck and cock a doodle doo do!
Please don't think that I'm trying to be crude
But he's one of the few guys... that look good in the nude!
He's a righteous dude; a good looking dude... when he's
in the nude!
Cock a doodle doodle... doodle doo do!
He's got integrity, he's not just a shell

And there's more to his story that I've got to tell.
So many ways to use him you could write it in a book!
And when you get together baby, you're gonna" cook,
cook, cook!
Sunnyside up, scrambled or fried... Quiche Loraine,
omelets, or meringue for your pies!
One egg won't be enough for you, you won't be happy
with just a few...
Have to get 'em by the dozen! You'll have his sisters, his
brothers, his uncles and his cousins.

Fearing that Jacob was about to tackle him and stuff
a dish-rag in his mouth, he finally relented... breathing
hard and sweating profusely... A happy man. Nothing
else in his life gave him more pleasure than letting loose,
especially when it paid off like this. He had no doubt that
the "band" would swoop down on it like chickens on a
June bug.

Overcome with happiness he found himself bowing his
head (slightly), about to say 'Thank you Jesus,' but stopped
just in time. *There's plenty of that stuff goin' on without help
from me...* he reflected, somewhat embarrassed... *Whoa...
slow down here...*

Jacob was obviously impressed, possibly even
awestricken, and showed his pleasure (as he always did
with everyone) by including them in his world; "Dawg...
water?" he said, with a smile and a nod toward the back
door.

Brown, took the cue, practically lunged out the door,
looked around on the back porch, then spotted the dogs
who were now milling around a bucket conveniently
located under a spigot near the corner of the house... of
course... easy. *Dogs are so easy... someday maybe Maggie and...*

The deep rumbling noise he heard was unmistakably

that of Harley motorcycles... two or more of them... and sounding like they'd stopped out on the highway. Right in front of the house! Still revving their engines... *Those guys're rude... showing off...* but the trembling of the earth and increased rattling of the windows... changed it up: What the?

All at once, two motorcycles spun into the back yard... mounted thereon were two of the roughest looking guys he'd ever seen. As if this weren't bad enough to freak him out, Jacob popped from the house, completely naked! And grinning like an idiot; "Welcome home!"

The two goons dismounted, with their bikes still idling. Some might've called it purring... ca chunk, ca boom-boom, ca boom, ca chunk... But this was no time for romance... or was it? Brown was stupefied in so many aspects: The seismic activity continued... inexplicably... actually becoming even more violent; But the Bro's and Jake were oblivious; embracing, slapping hands, and hugging; a ridiculously bizarre scene that no one would ever believe, and he wished to God he'd never seen.

When a small fir tree hit the ground with a swoosh on the opposite side of the house, the men glanced over calmly, unconcerned or ignorant of the earthquake. Neither of them looked in Brown's direction. Another tree fell; this time a small maple crunching to the earth, limbs gouging into the soft dirt.

At this point, a yellow bulldozer shoved its way over the fallen trees, past the house. Brown slumped down onto the porch steps, cradling his head in his hands... all thoughts of country living and honest eggs had ceased... The guy driving the dozer smiled and waved while the ominous blade impertinently dared anything or anyone to get in the way.

The goons removed leather chaps and jackets, helmets and gloves. Revealing dew-rags, work clothing and boots made for walking ... or kicking-butt, or anything else... soon, both were buzzing chain saws and dragging limbs to a pile. "Bonfire this fall, Mon... Yuah," Jacob gushed, passing on into the house; "breakfast is on the table..."

Breakfast?! All brownie could see was swinging private parts, acres of skin and mountains of embarrassment at the thought of entering that house. Not to mention the questions of hygiene ricocheting all around his now shattered composure. He chose a safer, wiser, saner route; walked around the house, making haste for the safety of his van... and a possible escape.

But Jacob had passed on through the house and now sat in the front yard, cross-legged on a quilt in the bright morning sun, with a yellow can of Top Tobacco, rolling a cigarette; still naked, but obviously there for his morning tan ritual. This slightly sane scene helped a little... Brown began to regain composure... *sun tanning is normal... the guy just has no... what? Rules...?* He walked over, and sat on an upright bolt of firewood, one of several surrounding the fire pit.

Jake was completely unconcerned about cars and trucks passing along the highway; about the guys clearing his property; or whether anyone had a need to be anywhere else rather than wherever they might be.

"What's going on?" Brown asked, with a toss of his chin eastward, where blackberry bushes, at least one toilet bowl, numerous car parts, and other objects de arte' (or de basura) were twisting up into a ball with the briers and weeds.

Jake's explanation of a new drain-field for the septic-tank toned down his nervous system somewhat further, and the news that these were neighbors, who were also loggers, was very interesting... and besides, the dozer lived there... or right next door anyway.

Then, Jacob's statement; "Ol' Wesley, love's dropping his 'blade' more than anything! Mon...." brought all sorts of images to mind, and the fact that the clearing crew were also ex-loggers, he still couldn't wrap his mind around.

Calmer now and reasoning a smoke would help, he, accepted the rolling papers and began fashioning a cig of his own, for old time's sake; inserting a question or two in between licks and grunts. Trying to ignore the noise and the nakedness.

Sure, as the guardian of the hot springs, Jacob knew all those kids; Shadow, Feather, Rootwad, Striker... as well as their Christian names (and the meanings thereof no doubt).

"So, how 'bout dreads?"

"Yup, lots of 'em."

"They seem to be trouble makers..."

Jacob looked surprised at that remark; "No, Mon... they're High Christians..."

Brown continued; "Not everybody thinks so... they've been up to no good at the store for a long time. Wayne and Joyce are not happy with 'em... that's for sure,"

Jacob smiled slightly; "What some interpret as arrogance is just separation... nonconformity... unwilling to function inside the usual social order. And..." he paused with a steadfast look into Brown's eyes; "... dreads aren't the only people come to the store... there's a high-school too, a few miles away."

That was true, Brown thought about that for a few

moments and was quite aware of possible scenarios unsupervised teenagers might entertain... his own teen years for example were sufficient to get the point... So, changing-up his strategy he went on, hoping to be as tactful as possible and to describe accurately what had occurred recently at the store. Jacob seemed to be listening, with his face upturned to the rays of the sun, eyes closed, nodding his head as though he'd heard all about it... until he heard the "filth and perversions" part...

What had been a gentle and kind face stiffened, and all the air seemed to escape from his lungs... his eyes remained closed but had tightened. With concentrated effort like a person born blind... he shifted around for maximum sun exposure... to the right, back to the left a smidge... He opened his eyes and looked directly into Brownie's; "That's neurotic stuff... anal... not hippy behavior... I know that... I know lots of things. That's juvenile... high-schoolers, Mon." then satisfied, resumed his Hindu, meditation pose.

Brown could see they'd gone full circle anyway... remembered actually being accused of doing those very things in the seventh grade himself, and although he'd been appalled at the very thought... he'd never forgotten how crude and twisted, and sneaky some kids could be... and, yes... the store was a juvenile setting at times; "I'm just saying what Wayne and Joyce said," he offered gently.

Jacob, still poised for maximum sun, replied; "Like I said, if all you've got is a hammer, everything looks like a nail. So, you know... of course we look contrary, we're not carrying a hammer. Our hair's not dirty... gets washed... but not combed. True dreads are committed to simplicity... devotion... renounce the traps of vanity in society... have few possessions, great respect for creation. Yuah, some are even Christians. Hammers and nails... Okay? Black and white. That kind of thing. Once you get beyond it then you realize that there are variations all over, all different directions. Extremes are what the Greeks called paradox, the truth is actually beyond opinion. You realize that all language is polar; that all things speak in polarity. Positive-negative, black and white."

Ohhhhh no... Why can't I get away from that quack psychologist?

"Actually the truth lies between those. Real truth is a paradox... or a doorway to the even realer truth. Nice!"

The dozer backed up for yet another run at the earth; hit a rock or a piece of metal with a clank, apparently breaking Jacob's line of thought. Brown stood up, quite sure that otherwise the monologue would have gone on and on... and suspected that he wouldn't mind that at all. But Jacob seemed to divert; his body language had changed; obviously more revved-up about getting the place cleaned; intently surveying the job at hand.

In a short amount of time, tons of blackberries have been scraped off, yet there's still at least half an acre of them left. A portion of a sagging wooden fence has been revealed, dividing his property from the one next door; the rest of the fence is still covered in berries and stretches back to who knows where; Jacob has rolled another smoke; "That fence belongs to Wesley... he let me know that long ago... I haven't touched it since." He took a deep drag, obviously enjoying the cigarette. Offered a book of matches and the "makings" to Brown, who readily accepted.

The dozer kept pushing. The metal tracks clattered and clanged as it backed up with increased speed for yet another run, or alternately, an approach.

Enchanted with freshly exposed dirt, the pungent odor

of crushed grass, leaves, and berries, the two watched for a few more minutes, silently smoking their "rollies"... appreciating the mechanical grind and squeak of metal parts as the ultimate icon of construction and destruction rolled back and forth.

Jacob stand's, assumes the position of a traffic director, points one hand, palm-up, toward the river; the other hand parallel with the decrepit fence; "The property line goes out past the driveway, across the highway, past those big granite rocks, and out to the middle of the river. This is the original property-line of the valley. The highway is permitted to be on my land... I can close it any time I want to for a parade.

"From the records this is the original house of the valley. There's a horse-trail out back. The guy that lived here was the one who started those drift boats that are sold all over the world. There was a wildlife preserve sign back there too, I pulled that out. It's a carved one from the old National Forest.

"There's like twelve foundation houses here too. There's a grandfather clause in Oregon that says If you've got a rock that was a foundation for a house you can rebuild."

Jacob bounded off. Brown, certain he's about to fetch a rock or a plot map, looks away, not about to watch any naked man romp around the yard, but Jacob returned within seconds; collapsed onto the blanket with a small tin of... what else? Began rolling a joint... finishes in seconds... fires it up... blows ash off the end, lifts it up to his forehead and then towards the heavens. Inhales deeply. Offered it to Brown... The dozer has moved out of view but still clanking away behind the house... Brown lifted his hand, shook his head, "No thanks, Mon."

Jake smiled with understanding, took another big toke and headed for the back of the house; Brown realizes that he's feeling a bit sad or frustrated... noon already... time to head out. Hitched up his jeans, rubbed the stubble on his chin... slapped the pocket of his shirt (buttoned, consoling bulge of cash still there); felt around for his keys... yep... The old van looked as though it had found a home, or a friend, sitting silently beside the dumpster.

Across the highway, the river sparkled amidst emerald greens and shades of blue, mixed with swirls of silver and splashes of white; making no excuses, shoving its way onward to the never-ending next...

Damn! His coat was in the house. His turn to bound away, somewhat less free than a naked man... but feeling quite at home once inside. It's now quiet; the dozer has been shut down for some reason... a break, or whatever. The temperature is slightly cooler than outside but very comfortable. Summer. Inviting. The house, smelling of wood smoke and incense along with a pleasing something (herbs and vegetables from the kitchen?) presents a calm darkened space. The heavily timbered picnic table rests solidly in the middle of it all... a comfortable ambiance for whatever seems good or opportune... certainly not what many would imagine for such a place as seen from the road... there is even an air of purpose, ingenuity, imagination, maybe even resourcefulness... and undeniably, proven hospitality. Somehow, the faintly acrid smell of smoldering ashes from last night's fire adds just a hint of comforting reality to the whole scene.

The coat he'd sought was on a nail near the stairs. He could hear the men yakking and skylarking. The one room he hasn't seen is in the hallway next to the bathroom. The door (the only one remaining inside the house) is closed. He can't resist... pushes against it, but has to turn the knob.

The flooring is gone entirely... exposed two-by-six floor joists spanning the darkened crawl space immediately evoking visions of open graves, now abandoned. On the still Sheet-rocked walls there are murals... overwhelmingly large and hauntingly familiar. One side of the room depicts men and women in various poses of defense or explanation, arrayed before a white-robed panel of angelic beings, who seem bored or amused. In the lower background, a night sky of stars and constellations... further on up, swirls of galaxies and majestic nebulae are depicted upon a background of deep blue...

The upper fourth of the wall consists of a graphic layer of soil and rocks separating what's below from the heavenly remainder above. The wall gradually brightens to a sky blue and laced all around the edge of the ceiling are scenes of animals, foliage, and naked humanity playing, studying, sleeping, strolling along paths... holding hands... carrying babies ... or ushering youngsters presumably to where they should stand or sit to be taught... apparently of things that had occurred or were occurring elsewhere.

A black band running vertically, framing or separating both side walls from the center wall disappears into the horizontal darkness of the crawl space... or is the darkness flowing upward? Within each band are alternate columns of the Hebrew alphabet in red... the Greek alphabet in blue... the letters solid and authoritative... many of which duplicate and spill out onto the side walls in torrents, or whirlwinds... some morphing into books, billboards, encyclopedias, dictionaries; some into buildings (schools, churches, temples, synagogues, skyscrapers). Still, others disappear into (or emanate from) computers, keyboards, telephones and other obvious forms of electronic communication (televisions, telephones, radios) all relating to man's ability (or desire) to communicate.

Who could stand there and absorb this in one setting? *Not me...* Brown decides, and forces himself to scan the whole instead of getting lost in the incredible details.

The side walls are less complete than the central, but even so, the whole has already been outlined or roughly designated with scrawled, vague, almost decipherable figures and objects for future vignettes of expression... Human beings, sketched proportionally and accurately, though some, waiting for missing limbs or articles of clothing, were interspersed throughout... all actively involved in forms of communication, and all a part of what is an orderly, flowing, and very captivating design.

The dozer coughed and started up again, breaking Brown's trance. The house trembled more violently than ever, the menacing yellow contraption rattled by very close to the window, heedless of his fixation and suspicion that the dead would be rising up from the craw space any moment.

"Yuah Mon!" Jacob yelled, sprinting up the stairs naked as a jaybird, presumably not to be left behind in the resurrection.

The Harley's exploded into life; menacing leather-clad riders whipped their machines around a full one hundred eighty degrees, expertly negotiating massive areas of freshly exposed earth all around, and vanished, leaving only devastation behind; very likely unaware that the long awaited Final Day had arrived... and... sigh... that they were the ones who were being "Left Behind."

Wesley splintered right through the decrepit fence as though it weren't there and didn't look back.

Reverently, and quite aware that he has no idea where he might fit into the overall picture, Brown, backs out of the room and discovers that Jacob has manifested beside him... a changed man... fully clothed and in his right mind... or at least mindful; "Careful, don't fall through those timbers..." he cautioned... "I'm still working on that..." with no fanfare at all, as though he were talking about mowing a lawn. Brown shut the door quietly on a world haunting and beautiful.

Jacob, now sitting at the picnic table, pointed at the crunched fence: "Wesley said he'd do that... It's his fence..." then, with an all inclusive sweep of his arms; "He made all those logging roads," (perhaps meaning every logging road on the planet).

But stretching how far, where to, and how many, depended solely on the knowledgeable. From the valley floor The mountainsides had a limited number of visible roads, with their stark, earth-cut, side banks. But these represented only a tiny percentage of the Oregon total. Many, many more existed through out the entire resource, normally concealed from everyday viewing by trees and more trees... except from the air.

Loggers had first hand knowledge of the fact that thousands upon thousands of square miles of mountains and valleys (all without electricity, running water or voting booths) had roads interspersed throughout, lacing and intertwining like an enormous net.

Their perspective was one of unbelief at the "supposedly knowledgeable," who were content to cluster together by the hundreds of thousands in less than one percent of the inhabitable land in the beautiful state of Oregon; giving orders, making rules and regulations. Why? Either way, they would continue consuming things they had no real use for; vying for positions that meant little or nothing in the long run; bringing up little ones who would live the same... and whom with a growing naiveté of the true spirit of the woods, could actually become the "endangered" until eventually nature herself would consume them, instead of vice versa...

Though entirely sincere in their desire to protect and conserve, the "cultured and civilized" nevertheless locked-up the entire resource while a way of life and its important history was ignored or belittled. Generation upon generation of valiant, hardworking men and women (and their accomplishments) were washing down the now protected streams and rivers...

Sure, pristine was important, but nature regenerated naturally and forcefully... especially in Oregon's Cascade and coastal mountain ranges. Much of the westerly slopes (and all the way to the Pacific Ocean) was simply blessed... was practically a rain forest for half of the year. There was no denying it: Southern Oregon to Alaska was a zone where trees grow with atomic force.

Management was a good thing, but pristine should apply to families too... far more finite... and fragile... pressed within lifespans of a few short years... creatures ensconced in unpainted dwellings of wood with moss-laden roofs of cedar shingles, deep within the forests, accessed only by way of graveled roads and sometimes miles of rutted, dirt roads. Just as much a part of their own localized ecosystems, and even more likely to vanish without a trace as the "endangered" that were supposedly being "rescued." All eventually subject, nevertheless, to the ultimate organic statement of time immemorial... to be dissolved by the nutrients and microbes ever about their business of processing foliage and flesh.

The enmity between the "enviro-nuts" and the loggers had arisen from a smoldering spark and subsequently broken out in sporadic, real-time conflagrations, throughout the northwest, many or most of which, were never heard about... Brown was extremely aware of that first spark almost to the day, long after the advent of the drug culture of the sixties... when substance invaded substance, organic-upon-organic.

So much had transpired since then. Barely escaping the drug culture himself, he'd followed his mom to Oregon and taken up logging with Edward, his new step-dad. Once the propaganda had taken hold it was too late to do anything but roll over without protesting to anyone but their fellow loggers, many of whom had been "relocated" with jobs too... and most, if not all, wished for the good old days and lived far below previous standards... financially and otherwise.

Now, for the last week or so, the kettle was being stirred. Brown was revisiting his earlier convictions about everything, reconfiguring mistaken impressions and conclusions, staring full into the face of those times and their effects. Yes, there was a spiritual element to all of it... but only if one believed in such things.

His encounters were tempered with his own life's critical mass... challenged from every direction, forced to make decisions, important only to him, and faced with something larger than he could explain.

Brownbro watched as Jacob (looking entirely content) ate the untouched cackleberries and barnyard fruit (good eggs honest and true) breakfast that he had been too aghast to eat. And he was dressed (somehow tastefully) in cut-off jeans and a faded, tie-dyed t-shirt (curls and dreads more orderly than usual) and had turned up the volume on the radio.

With a mouthful of food, he spins off in an explanation

of why pot is one of the biblical things to do. Declaring that it does no harm at all, in fact it stopped people from contentions; violent crimes; and was used by the Persians (the largest empire in biblical times); "In Revelations it says, 'the herb that will heal the nations.... One tree for every nation. Yup it's also in Genesis, all the way through from where pot first started. God will decide the fate of man and sits within the house of Gawd, the garden not planted by two hands." The clatter and the noise of the dozer diminished into nothing.

Now, Brown realized that if he were to meet Shadow on time, no way would he be able to stop at his mom's; "Jacob, I need your advice on something."

"Yuah, Mon..."

"What if the springs were in danger of some kind... like a fire, or an earthquake or something else, maybe from people... men?"

"Hah, ha... Those things happen... already have... The locals dug those springs out by hand... more than once."

"But I'm talking about today, or soon. With explosives."

Jacob's eyes widened... his entire face altered... tensed, lips tightened, "No, Mon... evil... bad... "

"I want you to take a ride with me," not even sure if the man was at all okay with being in a car, "I can explain on the way."

Jake had risen, both hands on the picnic table... "I can walk up to the springs."

"No, into town... meet with Shadow."

This was a preposterous suggestion.

"No, Mon, my job is here..." by the look in his eyes,

Jacob was obviously now beyond reason; he scanned the room, spotted his shoulder bag. On his way out (practically running by now)... picked it off the floor... stood momentarily on the porch, "Dogs, stay!" and was off in a sprint across the highway and soon out of sight.

Brown made sure the dogs were all in the house, and as he started up the van was forced to decide: "East or west? West!"

—◇—

- Chapter Sixteen -

He drove across a succession of bridges that allowed an immense lake (one of many near Lake City) to flood the backwater bogs and grasslands on both sides of the raised highway... Brown had enjoyed fishing this area years ago, but somehow fishing in general had passed him by. Maybe he'd get back into it. He remembered a time when Julie was about six; just the two of them had been on these very banks fishing for Crappie. A bright silvery pan fish, with hundreds of black spots all over, and protruding, transparent lips like cellophane paper. Other lazy, but optimistic fishermen were there too, enjoying the beautiful spring day, all with folding aluminum chairs and plastic five-gallon buckets to be filled with fish.

He and Julie found a spot of their own, away from the crowd, and within seconds, Brownie caught a fish. Julie, bright and excited up to that point, was sitting on their overturned bucket, but when asked to give it up, her attitude headed downhill. Grudgingly, she sloshed some water into it when asked, but refused to put her own fishing line in the water. The fish were biting like crazy. One shiny beauty after the other was flopped into the bucket to Brownie's utter delight and to Julie's gradual deeper and deeper disappointment. When he declared; "We're gonna have a fish fry tonight!" she finally hit bottom.

"No, Daddy," she said tearfully.

"Why not?" he asked, wondering why she looked into the bucket with such sadness.

"Fish are people too. Please don't kill them."

"That's what they're for... that's what people do. We're

supposed to eat them," he explained.

But Julie refused to accept that; "Well, I won't eat them. They've got feelings too. Just like you... see the freckles?"

He could not argue with that; dropped the line in again... immediately felt a tug on the tiny, feathery lure. So exciting, to yank back on the pole and set the hook; to anticipate the size of the fish from the pull on the line. Just basic fun but, poised with the fish over the bucket, he couldn't deny what was there before him: Freckled fish; she was crying, and he was cruel. Not only were the fish in black and white, so were his two choices; "Turn 'em loose then... " he said bravely. The look of happiness in her eyes was one he could still see, and after so many years, had to admit he could also see that bucketful of beautiful fish sliding from the upturned five gallon bucket back into the brown muddy water, emphasizing once again that it's the one's that get away whose memory linger the longest.

This poignant recollection slipped away from his mind when he spotted the grocery cart market situated on a small mound of packed rock and dirt, extending out into the lake and connected to the adjacent highway by an asphalt parking lot. The raised two-lane highway interspersed with small bridges and ran for several miles straight across the backwaters of the reservoir. Shadow had told him to park in the lot at eleven a.m., and that was all he would tell about where he lived.

Just about to go into the market, he heard a whistle. A solitary figure waved from an old aluminum fishing boat. *What?* He waved back but just to make sure, opened one of the glass doors and panned the store aisles. Fishing tackle, soda pop, wiener rotisserie... all intriguing of course and well within afford ability, since he'd pocketed more than nine hundred bucks the previous day; *ah,*

Bonnie B., the pipes are calling...

Another whistle... he released the glass door and again looked down toward the boat landing.

The figure in the boat waved at him with a motion that meant; Well... are you coming or not? So, he obliged. Sure enough, it was Shadow; shirtless this time, but still wearing the same old black cutoffs he'd worn the first day "Brownman" had met him.

"What is this?" he asked, gesturing at what looked more like scrap aluminum than a boat.

"It's my boat... "

"Yeah...? I thought we were going to your house."

"We are... this is your limo-service. Get in."

"Are you sure my van will be alright there?" he asked, hesitating, feeling stupid and vaguely aware that this kid, who didn't even own two pair of pants, had no idea if or not the van would be okay

He tried to relax in the front seat, as very old wooden oars strained against murky water, under the (somewhat) expert handling of his guide. The youngster steered the boat under one of several low bridges, gliding between creosote-coated pilings. Brownie crouched down to keep from bumping his head on the beams, the sounds of trucks and cars rumbled overhead. Shaded from the sun, the fresh morning air underneath felt good. Mud swallows darted out from under the bridge into the sunlight and back up to their nests plastered onto wooden beams, chirping at the top of their tiny voices and even diving brazenly at the boater's heads. Brownman, was captivated by the little babies' wide open, yellow-lipped beaks incessantly begging for food. A log truck loaded down with fir-trees from the coast mountain range rumbled overhead; one of the nests dislodged and fell into the water... fortunately it was still under construction and empty, but he felt sorry for the birds who had worked so hard.

Within moments, they were out in the hot sun again, gliding silently through an alleyway of water lined with tall reeds. The alley narrowed as they went deeper into the slough. Shadow smiled knowingly at Brownie who was obviously enjoying the ride; "I had no idea this was so beautiful out here, it's like a scene out of 'The African Queen.' Did you ever see that movie?"

Realizing that Shadow had no idea what was being referred to, he dropped it. There was too much going on all around to talk anyway. Canadian geese honked and hissed from their nests atop huge piles of decaying, grey and brown reeds. Red-winged black birds, clinging to the cattails at forty-five degree angles, emitted their unmistakable calls, which sounded like prolonged plunkings of high-pitched bedsprings.

The alley of water gradually became a narrow path... Suddenly an enormous splash deep in the reeds caused Brownie to look around for the source of the sound. "Carp," said Shadow. "They're spawning. Some of 'em weigh fifty pounds."

"Wow... "

"But they're not fit to eat... except for the Chinese. They know how to get the bones out and take the mud stripe off 'em."

As they continued, the water became shallower and the splashing was much more frequent. Brownman could actually see dorsal fins and wide mermaid-like tails flipping up out of the water. *Whoa...* If only he could get his hands on one. With each churn of the water, the urge to jump in and pull one out by the gills was practically irresistible. He made a mental note; *Gotta bring Carlos out here... he won't believe it either, and it just might be he knows how to cook these things... people like him, know how to make do.*

Finally, any sign of a channel through the reeds had disappeared and they were on a sea of bright green grass interspersed with clumps of cattails in early bloom. The only signs of water were occasional small clearings (where for some reason the grass hadn't grown), splashing carp, and the slogging of Shadow's oars. A hundred yards away, far from shore, several legless, black and white cows could be seen up to their udders, nipping and grazing on the sweet, tender tops of the grasses projecting above the water.

Shadow stopped rowing, stood on the seat and used an oar as a pole, first on one side and then the other. Not at all sure where they were going, Brownie hung out over the bow and helped the boat along by grabbing and pulling on the clumps of grasses and reeds. He turned to ask where in the world they were heading and found to his surprise that Shadow, who looked a bit embarrassed, was now in the lake up to his hips pushing the boat. He explained; "It's not that hard with just one person. Plus the lake is at it's highest... normally we'd be walking by now." Brownie offered to get out, but no, Shadow insisted he stay in the boat; "It's just over there," he said. Brownie moved back to the rear of the boat to help elevate the bow. But the last thirty feet or so he had to walk anyway... in mud up to his shins...

Once the boat was pulled up onto dry land, they were immediately walking up a small rise on pasture grass (in the opposite direction of a nearby house) toward what appeared to be a dense grove of overgrown Christmas trees. Shadow picked up speed and then stopped for only a second when he reached the dense wall of green; flashed a smile back at Brownie and then disappeared (*of course*), apparently swallowed up. Brownie slowed for only a moment and then plunged in right behind. Shadow re-manifested almost immediately; leading the way through a long, twisting tunnel of very low branches, and occasional rotting tree stumps, presumably from days-gone-by when the trees were still being harvested. By the time they were out the other end, Brownie's back hurt from bending over, and from holding onto his knees, walking like a duck. Grateful to stand upright again, he looked around. They had come out into a one hundred foot diameter clearing, hidden deep within the thicket of trees, surrounded by a wall of twenty-five-footers in need of thinning and now too rangy to harvest. The hushed quiet increased the feeling of seclusion. They could have been in a Canadian forest, or an Alaskan wilderness. *Nice.* Shadow stood proudly aside like a fourteen year-old, still playing house, dodging the real adult thing... motioning for Brownie to take it all in. He did, and thought of Feather; He looked around; "So this is where you live?"

Shadow, who understood some of what he saw on Brownie's face, said with a little embarrassment; "I'm only here when the weather's good, or if I have friends sleep-over... " then felt even more embarrassed as he heard how that sounded: *Friends sleep over... that was not cool;* he laughed a bit nervously and tossed a stick onto the fire-pit. Grey ash, charcoal, and a few stubby, black sticks of unburned wood made it obvious that the pit hadn't been used in quite some time. "Most of the time I sleep in the barn... or the house," he added pointing in the direction of the house they had seen moments before. *Ah-hah!*

Browman had expected Shadow to live in a warehouse in the heart of town, or why not in some dark basement, or perhaps an attic with only one small window overlooking City Hall, a federal building, a national guard armory, a county building, or at least a highway maintenance facility; anything he could secretly keep an eye on?

This was so much better. Up above, a giant ceiling of bright blue sky framed one lone, white cloud drifting eastward. Surveying the camp, the most notable object was a shabby, olive drab tent, sagging from a few makeshift poles, in the very center of the clearing. One corner of the canopied entrance flapped loosely; a shoelace that had once held the flap up, dangled... Knee high, green grass concealed more of the short, rotting stumps, certain to trip anyone who veered off the meandering, trampled paths that were all around. Plastic Grocery Cart bags and empty beer bottles scattered here and there diminished the enchantment considerably.

Shadow grappled with two, canvas, folding campstools for a moment and then collapsed into one of them. This was just what Brownie wanted, a chance to rest. But it dawned on him that this might be like one of those missionary deals, where the civilized get to know the primitives. Not that it had been a problem getting Shadow to open up, but he *was* smiling and did seem to feel pretty secure where they were. He promised to take his guest on over to meet Arnie and Annie as they talked easily for a few minutes..

That this spot was where Shadow might bring friends for pot smoking (and whatever else Arnie and Annie didn't approve of in their house) was Brownies take, and within seconds proved to be correct.

"This would make a great pot farm," he confided to Brownie, and then went on to explain how he could make numerous, five foot mini-clearings through out the grove, where hemp would thrive under the hot sun passing

directly overhead. "The sun shines right here, man...
" he said, waving his arms in a big circle. Proud of the
fact that the area wasn't subject to highly toxic chemical
sprays used in modern forestry, "See?" he concluded with
obvious pride; "This would be homegrown organic... and
best of all, it would be un... de... tectable!"

Brownie knew it would be useless to discuss the
negative aspects of this "ingenious" plan, so he changed
the subject to one that was of more interest; "Do all you
guys have hideouts?"

Shadow jumped right in. He preferred the word,
camp, and wasn't sure he liked the term, "hideout," but
lots of kids had very cool camps around the countryside:
Deep within old growth forests; in remote canyons;
along the creeks. He told him about Striker, (AKA
Justin P. Swancutt) whose eyes had "...a real hard look"
(most likely developed by hours of practice in front of a
mirror was Brownie's guess).

One of Striker's hideouts was a cave, which was
actually an ancient lava tube within the lava beds
high up in the mountains... way past the hot springs...
almost to the pass. Although Brownie knew precisely
what a lava tube was, most people in Oregon didn't.
In fact, the lava beds were one of his favorite places to
hike at least once each summer, but only then, since the
beds were under snow in the winter. And there were
lots of lava beds left to explore... more than enough for
his lifetime.

He could easily understand how a person with a name
like Striker, would be drawn to such harsh and abrasive
terrain. But having explored some of them himself, he
knew that it was also a place of wondrous beauty. Just
to walk in a hundred feet from any of several highways
notched through the beds, was like going into another

world, or stepping onto another planet.

The entire Cascade mountain range, stretching all the way up into Canada was nothing more than a chain of extinct volcanoes... and a few that were not extinct. Most had erupted one time or other in recent history. There were still ancient Jack pines that were scorched from the lava flows, but had survived... others were left with their smooth, accusing, white trunks and appendages pointing cadaverously toward the heavens.

There were hundreds of islands and projecting peninsulas, completely untouched by the lava where for one reason or another the volcano's fiery fingers had gone in other directions. The islands were mini-ecosystems, places of deep seclusion where no doubt the plants, and any creatures inhabiting the area, had looked the same for thousands of years.

And as though planned by the same deity of destruction, there were elevated walkways of crumbling lava encrusted with eons of crunchy ochre, orange, and sage lichens; growing merely fractions of an inch in the ideal spring thaw, only to bake mercilessly in the dry summer heat, and finally to sleep in deep silence for up to six months under thick mantles of winter snow.

Just underneath the harsh terrain were thousands of tubes that might even run for hundreds of feet or more. Some were created when the lava had rolled and folded like a blanket loosely tossed across a bed. Others were created while the lava had been flowing hot and heavy, evaporating flesh and foliage, trapping gases, and pockets of air, and then in the midst of wild turbulence, had suddenly cooled and solidified. The tubes weren't always easy to find, but once he'd found a few it had become a fascinating past-time to search them out. Absolutely certain that he had gone into some that no

other human had ever set foot in. It was always a thrill
to enter through some small opening that became much
larger, sometimes circular, sometimes more tubular, but
always with obvious swirls and waves of a once white-
hot liquid now written in stone and frozen in time.

Brownie looked down at Shadow's beautiful feet.
The abrasive crust would reduce them to shreds within
the first hundred yards. "What about you? Have you
ever been there?"

"Naaaah, but I might this summer."

He could not imagine Shadow walking barefoot
on the clinking cinders. "Well, you'd better take some
shoes."

"Yeah, that's why Striker likes the location."

Striker. A good name for a kid living in an
environment that was flint hard. He hoped to meet him
someday.

He followed his tour guide up the slight rise toward
the small farmhouse. In the shade of a giant maple
tree, within a tiny, low, wooden fenced-yard, two small
children played with gaudy plastic toys. The door of the
house stood open. There was no screen door.

"Come on I want you to meet Annie and Arnie,"
Shadow said proudly, "This is their farm."

—◇—

The Thompsons, he recognized immediately; had
seen them at the market. Now, there they were washing
dirt from freshly dug red potatoes in a big galvanized
washtub. Brownie and Shadow stood outside peering
through a large doorway into a dimly lighted shed. A
woman with dark hair and faded Levi's (presumably

Annie) had her back to them. She shook the potatoes around in the tub while Arnold sprayed the dirt off with a hose. The fragile red skins rubbed off in splotches, revealing white underneath.

The shed was connected to a sagging barn whose weathered, gray cedar boards (probably never painted) were beautifully adorned with pale green and rust red lichens. A rusting, galvanized-tin roof baked in the sun. Brownie leaned against the warm wood; sun-dried lichens crackled under his fingertips. He studied the scene. It was wholesome, and simple. Annie dumped the muddy water from the tub and then rolled the potatoes onto the hay-strewn floor; for some reason he wished he could run his hands through the piles of red potatoes. Thirty feet away a pitchfork still upright in freshly turned earth tugged at him heart-and-soul to join in the fun. *What is it about the dirt? It spits us up one at a time. These potatoes are red... I'm like an old potato, a little fat and kind'a red, you can dig me later or you can take me to your shed ...*

Apparently, the Thompsons hadn't noticed the two, as yet, because the woman looked up in surprise when Shadow stepped away from one of the dark walls, (also a surprise to Brownie, who thought he was still right beside him). He spoke in a hushed voice and pointed toward Brownie.

Annie looked over and smiled, revealing somewhat crooked, white teeth. Warmed instantly by the smile, Brownie waited for them as they walked over; Arnie headed for the pitchfork and more potatoes. In the time it took Annie to travel the twenty feet or so that separated them, carrying herself in a way that totally put him at ease, Brownie felt entirely welcomed. He had come upon the living, breathing, pinnacle of earth-mothers, the sole expression of nurture and hospitality. She was opulent, round of limb, bulbous of buttock, and cherub of cheek. The fact that she was a female was not what particularly impressed him (a surprise to Brownie). It was something else. Something he may have seen, right under his nose all his life, but had never really appreciated 'til now. What he saw was an open book, inviting anyone who could... to read it. Someone who was definitely female, and apparently very content to be so. He would have been surprised to know that as a younger person, she had been more militant about what it meant to be a female person; siding with a radical element of women who were in the early stages of redefining themselves in relation to men and the earth.

She still loved the earth intensely but no longer agreed with some of her "sisters" who were convinced that a man could never be, among other things, an effective ecologist... Their reasoning was that since the earth was female, women were the only ones who could truly understand how to nurture her. But gradually, after birthing and nurturing several children, she recognized the codependent relationship of male and female. The rubber had not only met the road, but had left tire marks, with her very first child.

She no longer gave thought to the fact that she was a bit masculine, instead was thankful for the extra strength in her body: When giving birth; for strong arms when she needed to move a stubborn cow around; or toss a bale of hay. Theory be damned... She was off the drawing board and engulfed with the serious business of living. Her children needed her ample breasts. No time for armchair hypotheses, male this, female that... She now suspected the possibility that a subconscious envy of women who were slim, and sweetly feminine (back in the day) might have influenced her to associate with those like her slightly rotund self; those who may have felt the same kind of envy as she did, and perhaps even more so.

Now, old slogans such as, "The only thing I'd need a man is to protect me from other men," were nonsense. She needed the man she had married, even if he was a strange duck. Perhaps had married him for that very reason. People sought each other out to reinforce their own misconceptions and weaknesses... maybe she had done so with Arnold. But what was done was done. She had grown up. And maybe Arnold would too.

Glancing over at Arnold, he was his usual quiet and sulking self. Bird-like in appearance. A stark-white, balding pate as smooth as the potatoes at his feet, glared above a black crescent of thin, limp hair which sagged over his neck and shirt collar. She turned back to Brownie, with that killer smile.

Realizing he'd been staring open mouthed, licked his lips, consciously shutting it, not once but twice. "So, you're Brownman? We've heard how nice you've been to Shadow. Can you stay for lunch?"

He glanced over toward Arnold, who'd seemed to ignore him except for an occasional grunt and glaring glance from the potato patch.

Sweet Annie picked up on Brownie's hesitancy; "Oh don't worry he's always a little slow at warming up. Come on, you gotta eat somewhere. You can earn your meal by helping with the potatoes, okay?"

Sweet. How did she know that he wanted to get his hands on those potatoes? "Uhh, sure, I guess; if it's no trouble."

"Nope. No trouble."

It seemed the most natural thing to squat down onto the hay and drop potatoes into the bags held open by Annie. "That's enough for this one," she coached, then opened another bag for him to fill: "O.K., that's good...". Then, another bag; "Hey, we're a good team..." she bubbled encouragingly. "Wanna weigh 'em up Shadow?" And there was a miracle wasn't it? The kid was actually working.

Annie began passing the filled bags over to Shadow, who placed them in the metal tray of an old spring-loaded scale hanging on a rusted chain from a ceiling rafter; then she'd take out a potato or add one or two, as needed... "We weigh them at five pounds and then tie this around the end," she said, explaining that these would go to the Saturday market in a few days. The needle of the scale bounced back and forth with a comforting, seesawing squeak from rusted springs.

Arnold wheeled in with another load. Potatoes rumbled into the washtub. Annie offered the introduction; "This is Brownman... " They shook hands. Arnie's handshake communicated a bony boredom; "Meetcha..."

"Pleasure... " Brownie replied, wondering if it really was, and when without further words, Arnold turned the hose on the potato tub, decided that it really wasn't.

The uncomfortable silence was broken a few minutes later though, when Annie sidled over to Arnie and gently took the hose from his hand: "Why don't you dig and we'll wash and bag? We've got a system going here... "

Arnold gladly yielded. He had (at times) watched with somewhat confused admiration the changes his wife had gone through over the years.

They had lived by the lake forever it seemed like... were not pot smokers, but had many friends who were. Both he and Annie had smoked enough in their day, but now (except for very rare occasions) that pleasure was replaced by responsibility of family and farm. And the farm was theirs without mortgage; a direct inheritance from his own ancestry, handed down to Arnie from his parents, who had owned the land long before it had become lake frontage.

The lake was built as a reservoir by the Army Corps of Engineers for flood control. And (thanks to the annual rainfall, two large rivers, and many other lakes) rarely if ever did the city need the water. The excess water went over the dam and continued on northward as a small, slow, meandering river to join another river and yet another until all eventually joined the mighty Columbia... and emptied out into the Pacific Ocean.

The property owners with lake frontage were allowed to use all the water they needed for irrigation and livestock. Arnie needed it for both, making full use of his 200 acres; raising milk cows, Christmas trees, organic vegetables, and fruit. He loved being on the farm in the late spring and the early summer when the lake looked like a wildlife sanctuary, with cattails and reeds extending for miles around. He and Annie recognized many of the very same migrating water birds returning to nest each year.

As the waters receded in the summer months, the sun warmed the lake until it was almost tepid. The annually recurring ecological phenomena of algae, rotting grasses and fish-spawn served as a natural fertilizer for the already rich soil, which reappeared as the water level dropped.

They took advantage of the fertile soil by planting various types of lettuce, cabbage, broccoli and other vegetables that could be harvested right on into the fall and sold at the Saturday Market. The black and white milk-cows Brownie had seen were Arnie's and Annie's. And these Annie willingly tended for milk, butter, and cheese, for sale and home use. And they had chickens whose eggs were also sold to neighbors and at the Market. The summers were productive and busy, if not always happy.

The winter months were a different story... perhaps not causing, but at least paralleling, Arnie's mood. Since the lake was a means to control annual flooding it would be drained in anticipation of days-on-end of gray skies drip-dripping rain; gradually the immense body of water, though regulated, was almost always reduced to a small meandering stream. The floor would become a moonscape of visible, blackish-gray mud, even as Arnie's mindset did (to Annie's great disappointment).

Mud-cats estivated in the mire, while other fish; Carp, Bass, and Crappie, moved up and down the stream to the remaining pitifully few acres of pond that was once square miles of lake. By late spring all would be well again, and though enhanced by the Corps of Engineers, it was an established and dependable cycle,

The busy summer months not only kept Arnie's hands busy but equally improved or placated his otherwise dark moods, which inevitably and cyclically ebbed and flowed with the levels of the lake. He meditated, philosophized, and opinioned with himself for days, weeks and months at a time, with very little human interaction, not even with Annie.

From the Grocery Cart market, situated conveniently near one of the public boat launches and picnic areas, the Thompson's house was about six miles away... that is if you went by the road that squiggled along the lake's boundary. But if you were to walk on water you were only about one quarter of a mile away. Arnie couldn't walk on water, but he could walk on mud... aided by an old pair of modified snowshoes. He was a skinny man whose legs, without the devices, would've (and actually had once or twice) lodged like two popsicle sticks in the mud.

In the wintertime he slogged through the lake bottom, back and forth as needed. Occasionally, protesting Great Blue herons squawked and sailed off, only to settle a few hundred feet away resuming their frozen, stick-like pose.

A favorite thing to do during the interminable rains was to go early in the morning to the Grocery Cart for pecan cinnamon rolls and hot chocolate. This was entirely contrary to his "religion." Being skinny was a part of his self-concocted belief system, devised from first hand experiences. Self-denial was big. He never told Annie about the indulgences.

Anyway, he often stayed for a while, rarely completing two sentences with the bored owner, who considered him to be strange, but decent nonetheless. Years back, during the Christmas seasons, he'd allowed Arnie to sell his trees in the parking lot.

After hauling his precious crop of trees over by truck, and stringing up the obligatory colored lights, he would then day or night make the trek back and forth to his house... through the mud flats... In the daylight he wandered amongst the hummocks of reeds, digging out fluorescent fishing lures and the ubiquitous red and white bobbers, which he and Annie would clean up and sell in the spring. He had an enormous collection of arrowheads that also faithfully and annually revealed themselves on his daylight walks, some outright, others only when he mucked around in the mire. Mostly he found the tiny, white ones made from flint stone, or milk stone, appearing as white specks in the grayish black mud and surely used by indigenous tribes for marsh birds. There were numerous others of black basalt and obsidian, large and small, but camouflaged in the muck. He kept the collection as his private connection to a better, although more primitive time in man's history, when earth's inhabitants survived on the birds, fish, deer, and who knew what else from the size of some of the arrowhead specimens. They were deadly sharp, beautifully crafted and now they were his and his alone. Perhaps the beauty escaped him though... since he kept them hidden in a secret spot away from the clumsy hands of children and nosey adults... and hidden particularly from historians and hobbyists who in the last year or so he'd seen more and more of, trudging out in the bog.

During his walks at night, images of birth and death rose up with the real and imaginary mire. He had reasons for the thoughts that squished up from the lake-bottom around his webbed feet. When he was a teenager, his parents died within months of each other from diseases associated with obesity. Very old grandparents were unable to keep him on the farm, which had been handed down through several generations. But after quite a few years on the streets, he returned to the farm with Annie Foster. The grandparents were both dead now and the farm was his. When they'd finally married, Annie kept the name, Foster, to remind him that the marriage should have happened before the death of their firstborn child. He could see that.

Responsibility for his family and the farm, the notions he had picked up on the street, his hatred of obesity, and his bitterness toward life in general had all blended to become a belief system, a structure: The resulting philosophy could've been entitled; "The Trough of Existence," but would've been impossible to present with logic from beginning to end. Instead his thoughts were merely responses to an ever increasing slurry in which he dipped and dipped whatever came his way, by circumstance or purpose, until it was coated with a blobby unrecognizable form, then placed on a shelf to dry rock-hard, to remain forever with the rest of his conclusions. An earthquake, or at least a jackhammer, would be needed to dislodge the original material from his mind.

He needed the tree-lot to pay property taxes each year, and was grateful for the Saturday Market, although that was as far as he would ever want to go in the commercial world. The market was also a place where he could share opinions with fellow marketers and their children. On rare occasions he might develop a train of thought that others could follow (or try to), and at times he might even sense even a certain agreement, but inevitably felt hints of rejection instead of the recognition he'd hoped for.

In his darkened mind he saw the human condition as pitiful. And perhaps as a way to justify his own pathetic outlook found fault with others and they in turn found him to be disgusting. The deeper his feet sank in the mud of despair the more he considered everyone else to be in the slop. Thus, manufactured with criticism and sustained with a closed mind, he'd coined the term; "Trough of Existence."

At the trough, flavors blended, and even though it was possible to root around in the trough after your favorite flavor, folks could not taste one thing without tasting everything else... One of his grandpa's frequent replies (when someone asked where somebody else might be) was; "He went to take a shit and the hogs ate him." That alone said enough about the nature of pigs. It was possible to become so slathered with the slop that you could be mistaken for slop too, and be devoured. You never left the trough without being a little dirtier, and looking a little more appetizing to the other pigs. A devouring spirit was bloated and ugly, looking for what could be consumed next. Corporations fell into that category very easily. Whatever was taken or left at the trough eventually fell to one pig or another. Greed was a way of life.

In the corporate world, from the smallest wood products industry in Oregon, to the commodities market somewhere in New York, the trough was an open exchange. And whether they knew it or not, each carried its own portfolio of treaties and alliances with cronies, and associates that must be satisfied... buying and selling, crop after crop, and countless soul, after soul.

However, the old growth and rain forests were not a crop, but essentially the Mother's glory: Her flowing hair. Removing these was as insulting and as shameful as shaving the head of a beautiful woman; It might reasonably be said that these sacred zones were more valuable than people. But his Christmas trees were mere peach fuzz, the mere stubble of a beard... he'd planted– he could harvest... just do the math. People believed "things," without knowing why; needed an excuse for their own existence, but he had it figured out.

What was life all about anyway, if not appetite? All living creatures were ruled by appetite. He and Annie spent most of their waking hours working to satisfy someone's, or something's, appetite. When Annie pulled her breast from the baby's mouth, the contented sucking action seemed automatic, and continued even in sleep... without the nipple. Seconds later she might be out in the yard pulling dirt from the toddler's mouth. Adults had no one to pull the dirt from their mouths (or whatever it was they found appealing), and were destined to bite, chew, and swallow 'til the day they died.

The eyes were hungry for the first light of day. The ears for compliments. Arnold may have been resigned to the drudgery and the shame of his part in all of these things, but he lived for the little victories of mind over body. He fasted often. Delighting most when the hunger pains gave up, and the starvation-high set in. Spiritual insights came easier then.

Whether he was beat from work or fasting, when the day was over, he gave it a rest. Sleep was welcome, but make no mistake, the trough awaited. Oh! How he hated fat things... things that gathered around troughs. Pigs! (wouldn't have one near him, or raise one of the filthy "rooters"). How disgusting to become so much mindless fat to be sold by the pound and rendered into tallow. Simply for burning in human candles, lighting paths that would only lead back to the troughs from whence they came.

Why not step back from the trough for a moment, allow others to eat? Why grab every good deal that comes along just because you can. Why not allow someone else to prosper when you've filled your own gut? Even though he asked this of Corporate America, he knew the answer: Because the hunger is just too great; always there. Aside from fat seeking fat, that other part of self was always there too. The part that would love to be fed with honor and recognition (among other things), and even if it were to do a good thing, a wise and noble thing (such as stepping aside from the trough and allowing other pigs to eat) it would remain at the trough for selfish reasons.

This tirade he might fling at the wood industry, but it was not exclusively for them; every motivation of man, whether greed, sexual prowess, scientific achievement, medical research... all were a part of the dynamic. And all added their flavors to the slop in the trough. Mother

Earth on the other hand humbly gave, and gave. He worshipped the Mother. Strongly convinced that he who walked the lightest blessed her the most. Sometimes in the winter, if he happened to be under one of the bridges on the lake, ducking a downpour, his soul quaked when loaded log trucks rumbled overhead, even more than the long abandoned Mud Swallow's nests splashing into the pitiful little stream of water at his feet.

So Arnie dug potatoes and all but ignored Brownie... except for his paunch that is... He'd seen that immediately and jumped to a thousand conclusions about the man's spiritual condition: A glutton... and a redneck too, no doubt... if he were to believe certain information the kid had imparted just the day before.

Sweet Annie would not have been the first woman in the world to have somehow overlooked the severity of her husband's flawed personality and character. She had intertwined with him so devotedly and perfectly that his every flaw was shored up by her own strengths. He, on the other hand, thought he had her fooled, or that she was incapable of seeing in him what he may have otherwise been embarrassed about. He walked proudly in her world, gracing her with his wisdom while she actually endured him, hoping that someday he might grow beyond what he called, intellect and spiritual enlightenment, but what she knew to be a tangle of barbed wire. She couldn't touch it, or extract it, but there it was ...

Although very familiar with Arnie's "appetite thing," she had another perspective, but had never bothered to put it into words. Eating was just a part of living. Obviously. Serving their children and livestock, she knew this firsthand; not only that, but those she served, served her as well (or wanted to anyway); all they needed was just a little bit of encouragement and understanding.

The phenomenon of service to one another included wild animals, who lived and died too, without questions or complaints in instinctual cooperation, innocence, and humility. She was in no hurry to judge Brownman... she had given in long ago to the adage: "Believe nothing you hear and only half of what you see."

Maybe, because her's was a clearer vantage point, she walked lightly, in the center of her strength; her station was the common contact point for all existence. Neither man nor beast could really know the other without it. Exhibited in its purist form, sacrificial humility was the very opposite of appetite, in fact it would've been the antidote, if only it could be fed to the soul... instead of learned the hard way.

A child's cry from the yard diverted her from the chore at hand; "Why don't you and Mister Brownman finish the potatoes and I'll go get us some dinner," she called to Shadow in mid-stride.

Arnie rolled in with another load; "Catch any fish?"

Brown immediately envisioned his hands wrapped around a big carp, wrestling it into the boat, but fortunately said: "No, but I know where they're at..."

Arnie, may have interpreted that as a wisecrack, but smiled anyway; "Plenty out there... I guess," and rolled out for another wrestling of the earth.

The next few loads were delivered without conversation. Arnie slipped out the door on his spindly legs; Shadow shook potatoes around in the washtub: Brownman sprayed them with a hose... completely content with their tasks. Before the weighing and bagging could begin again... the wet potatoes were rolled around in fresh straw. Arnie, left the last load in the wheelbarrow, stood for a moment watching, then was no more, presumably onto another chore.

Brown kept a wary eye on Shadow, half suspecting him to vanish, should he make the mistake of turning his back. The work went smoothly. The bagged potatoes were increasing in number and absolutely beautiful... lined up on a wooden cart equipped with bicycle wheels... their earthy, red skins speckled with ivory.

Annie's melodic; "Time for dinner..." fit seamlessly with a timeless and universal appeal.

Washing up, children chirping and tripping around, moving chairs, assigning seats... other timeless acts... were perhaps lost on certain people in the room, but not Brownman.

He was awestruck by this woman, and repulsed by her husband. There, in black and white, were the two extremes of existence: Not that he could've put it into words, nor perhaps could Annie, but the dynamic was in place,and it would take more than all three of them pulling together to unseat it. Annie pulling with the earned strength of wisdom, Brown with lighthearted, spontaneous and childlike humility, and "the other one" with a disturbed warped and darkened soul of pride.

But perhaps progress toward humility and wisdom could be found in the mouths of babes (three who were at the table): Shadow (though he'd never agree with the description), Kylie and Eden. The adults, might have done well to pay attention to the children who were there in their own worlds and no doubt quite comfortable. Annie monitored every move and every bite that entered their mouths... casually encouraging independence and self-sufficiency while poised for any teaching moments that may arise.

Arnie, stiff and crystalline in his own world... was

largely focused on Brown... and all but oblivious to the lessons to be gained at that moment... while innocent charm, grace, and beauty were evidenced all around the table in his own progeny and in the childlike, unsophisticated soul of Shadow. Even so, all the children were aware of tension in the room... yearning for nothing more than meekness and humility; the prime atmosphere for make believe, and discovery... in other words, *play*.

Arnie may have experienced such in his own childhood but any evidence or residue was buried beneath a mud-caked consciousness. The "children" were in process, subject to future definition, the hallmark of which (according to Annie), would be humility: To be teachable without reserve; open availability to be loved; and in return, innocently and freely giving whatever love is available to anyone who needs it.

A quality, of course, lacking in most adults, though widely imitated... ironically by the proud... as in Arnie's case, who had already been defined. Selfish pride: The very opposite of humility; appetite for self, without regard to others; a closed mind; a predilection for hidden agendas, centered around selfish interpretations of circumstance. That thing which we hate, we become.

And then there's Brownman... happily spooning mashed potatoes onto his plate while eyeing further delectables upon the table. So far, no one had "discovered" him... although Annie was certain she had tasted something savory; Shadow suspected he had found a friend (another kid... like himself... somewhere in there), and Kylie and Eden waited... digesting... almost certain (with the instinctiveness of ready-play) that a new toy was in their presence, seated comfortably at their kitchen table, and they would have known this, even had Brownman not earlier-on clicked his tongue at Eden (the youngest), or secretly made a goofy face at Kylie.

The evening meal proceeded. Hospitable chit-chat from Annie. Cautious diplomacy from Shadow; measured portions and calculated results computed by Arnie (with every portion positioned just so, upon his plate), and Brown, happiest with good food in play... in hand, or mouth... his happiness swelling proportionately in that order, was anxious for the "fun" to begin. Yet had not missed the fact that Arnie had also calculated everything he'd piled on *his* plate; "Food looks great, thanks for inviting me, Wow! Straight from the farm to the table," he offered with little hope of response from the statue at the other end of the table.

Arnie's eyes had glazed over with the first morsel in his mouth. But sweet Annie smiled; "Of course, go ahead, Brownman, enjoy your meal," she said, completely relaxed but in total control of the universe.

Yeah. And so he did, with grunts and mutterings indecipherable, except for a delighted expression on an ever- transparent face.

This lasted for several minutes; homey clinking and clanking, thumping and scraping noises, interspersed with friendly gestures and eye contact.

Brownman knew from certain occasional glances by Shadow what was about to be discussed, but had already decided that it would be useless to predict what tone or tact the conversation would manifest. Yet when Arnie blurted; "Mister Brownman, why are you gonna blow up the hot springs?" the fresh peas fell from his fork, sputtering across the old fashioned tablecloth.

Uh-ohhhh... Mister? "First thing is, I don't want to blow up anything..."

Arnie's expression altered slightly from stilted to

firmly dubious... "What do you want to do, then?" he asked with the tiniest tilt of an eyebrow.

"All I know is what he knows..." Brown replied looking directly at Shadow... "Why would you... "

But Arnie cut him off.... "Shadow didn't say it, I'm just asking."

"Well, you should smile when you ask things like that Arnie..." and slowly pushed his chair back, with a look on his face that asked, "Is this meeting over?"

Annie, stood before Brown could complete his move, ushered the children out of the room. Arnie stood too, and Shadow looked as though he was about to disappear until Brown, still half out of his chair, leaned onto the table and said, "Wait a minute, did you tell him I wanted to do such a thing?"

"Didn't say you was–didn't say you wouldn't..." came Shadow's weak reply.

Brown slumped down again...

Arnie, leaned onto the table, and repeated, "What *do* you want to do?"

For a brief moment, Brown's head filled with many answers to that question, completely unrelated to what Arnie wanted to know: *What do I wanna to do, or what do I gotta do? Get out of Dodge, or get a Marshal's badge... Rob a bank or get a job... Get a Harley, or make it up with Maggie?* Yet he came to his senses and managed to get on the right track... even looking quite normal, while a trainload of fragmented thoughts whizzed on by... boxcar after boxcar; destination unknown. Whew!

Arnie had no idea he'd just avoided a kitchen full of scrap iron. What did impress him was a soft answer embodying enough humility to impact even his own awareness. "We've got to stop this," Brown said calmly and peacefully, "before somebody gets hurt, or killed..."

Whether divine edict or universal law, in this case the proverb: "A soft answer turns away wrath..." was evidenced. Arnie sat down. Shadow chilled. The conversation began.

Dinner was finished up with good appetite; every possibility of good digestion; and with something slightly akin to a new friendship.

Annie was blessed to have such civility and a potential "something," (she wasn't sure what) underway in her range of influence... in fact the evening finished with a glass of homemade wine, and an invitation to spend the night... which Brown accepted, but only if he could "sleep over" with Shadow out in the tent area.

—◇—

Maggie returned to the apartment to discover that Brown had been there; not only because the pickled pigs feet had been finished off, but the empty jar was sitting on the kitchen table with seven hundred dollars underneath... and a note. She sat there for a moment hating the damned lid to the jar for some reason, and the glare of the light over the table... for good reason... the same glare she'd hated for years and nothing had been done about it.

Work at the cannery would soon be over, harvest happened all at once and it happened fast... had to happen fast... food won't wait to be processed. She sat down at the table, afraid to read the note.

She'd had "the talk" with Julie, who refused to accept that divorce was even an option, but agreed that her dad was a goofball. And when she mentioned the mid-life crisis option, her mom responded with; "What again? Has he ever *not* been in crisis?"

Maggie left their session with the promise to keep Julie informed and vice-versa for Julie, if Brown contacted her.

Of course Maggie had friends at the Cannery who'd worked beside her since the first season she'd worked there. Some of whom were single... some who were single moms, single grandmas, or unhappily married... Rarely if ever had she actually connected with any who were contented in their station or circumstance of life.

The noisy canning machinery precluded depth of conversation in certain workspaces, sorting areas were quieter... the pay was the same in all of them... but with seniority one could choose...

At the beginning of the current season she'd purposely volunteered for the noisy section to avoid the endless whining (though often couched in humor) about men in general, as well as the outright mumbling and grumbling about the dreary servitude associated with married life. Most pathetic were the crudely expressed yearnings for companionship. Either way, it seemed overwhelmingly evident (as she watched the pears and apples pass through the labeling machine) it was just too much work, for too little in return... no matter how you sliced it.

Now, as she looked warily at the note, the thought of working at the Cannery made her want to scream. She realized that it really didn't matter what the note said as long as it didn't say goodbye. So what if Brown was like a windup toy on a tile floor careening from wall to wall, pantry to fridge, sink to garbage can... smack! smack! 'til the spring winds down... then someone or something winds him up and he's off again. Somebody should give the poor guy a helmet... probably should've had one since infanthood... sigh.

She slowly peeled the note open:

Maggie,

> *I'd rather starve than die from boredom at the Airlines. Pay the rent with this, and don't worry, there'll be more when we need it. I'm not mad anymore.*

Brown

P.S. No charger for the car phone... I really don't know what else to say anyway.

Where is he? What's he doing, now? Is it legal? The kitchen clock said 3 PM... he could be anywhere. She picked up the wall mounted phone; her first guess would be Carlos' house. Promising herself that if Carl or Brown answered she'd hang up, Carlos and Brown had a way of confusing the truth... always. She dialed the number; Violet, answered. Good.

Yes, Brown was seen just that morning loading his van with groceries "of all kinds!" Violet knew that much... otherwise he hadn't been around since the meeting with; "...dat rich man in dat jungle bus. Maggie, honey, dat was a circus lookin' fo a place to happen. Why, I jest cain't understand them kinds of things... whyn't dey jest join a circus and git it over wid?"

Maggie fully understood the difficulty involved as Violet tried to explain Carl's frustration with that whole fiasco, and was not at all surprised to know that a squabble had broken out between the two nut-jobs...

"No honey, it ain't all dat unusuable, dey is always up to somethin' or 'nother, dat only dey unnerstands."

Maggie found herself nodding as though Violet could see her head bobbing up and down, and then said aloud; "I know... how well, I know..."

Carl walked in from the garage; "Carl honey, is you seen dat Brownie?"

"No, but I sure want to... is... is that Maggie?" he asked, thrusting his hand out; "...let me talk..."

But Violet, before handing the phone over; "You be nice..." she whispered, and then reluctantly obliged; "Here's Carl... honey."

Carl very politely asked Maggie for Brown's cell number.

She relayed it, adding; "But the thing's dead..." and then, trying not to sound frantic, asked; "Carl have you seen him lately? I'm worried. He hasn't been staying at home, I thought he might be with you."

"No. And you n' me ain't the only ones... Mister A.B. called here, he lookin' for Brownie and that car phone too."

"Well, maybe he's been stayin' at his mother's... I'll try that." The conversation paused long enough for both to realize nothing more would be said. They agreed to pass along each other's message and hung up.

Next, Maggie called Florence, who wasn't exactly frantic about the current "no-show" Brownie had pulled, but griped of course about the note on her Television. She offered to call Hepner's, but Maggie assured her he had been by earlier that very day; "... took a shower, and changed clothes."

"Did he take any extra clothes with him?"

Maggie answered in the negative...

Flo's final words were only slightly consoling; "Well, that could be a good sign... at least we know he's close by... let's just hang tight, we'll find out soon enough what he's up to."

With no other choice, but to wait it out, she busied herself around the house (as so many women know how to do, and so many men haven't a clue).

—◇—

With the Thompson's kids tucked in bed, all humane solutions (and otherwise) for the hot spring problem were exhausted. The only concrete decision was to gain more information as soon as possible... but how, remained to be seen. A slight breeze from the lake cooled the house off as usual. An invitation to sample homemade blackberry wine included the tacit suggestion of *every man to his own tent afterwards*. While Annie busied herself pouring the wine, Arnie puttered around the living room; drawing curtains; bumping toys out of the foot-traffic zones; Shadow faded from the room. Brown had considered making a Maggie call... but there was no phone... Arnie's preference no doubt.

Well, she would be asleep anyway. Rising at 4:30 a.m. was the worst part of the Cannery job, although early was routine back in the logging days. And somehow seemed easier and more purposeful all the way around... Maggie was friendlier... hopefully he was too... the kids had taken up a lot of the slack that might otherwise have been there.

The wine was a vintage from years previous; more like a fine liqueur and tasted fabulous. Annie was way ahead of Brownman's worry about sleeping comfort and assured him that Shadow had by now taken care of everything.

Goodbye was far more pleasant than hello had been with Arnie, and a hug from Annie sealed the deal.

Shadow was at the foot of the porch steps with a kerosene lantern; "This way," he said with a sweep of his arm toward the thicket, still discernible in the fading twilight, and then proceeded at a fair clip across the pasture, occasionally remembering to swivel the lantern behind him for Brownman's benefit... although not needed until they were on the narrow and much darkened path, twisting through the thicket.

A small fire was burning happily in the old fire pit. Shadow was obviously glad to have company. The camp had been picked up and he'd even gone to the trouble of placing a bottle or a can on each of the stumps (which may have accounted for fifty percent of the previous clutter). The tent had been altered; with all the sidewalls rolled up, looking like a mini carport.

The small campfire dispersed its feathery cargo of incense... sweet aromas of sugary pine and dry grass lingering momentarily low to the ground, twirled up in and amongst the low branches of the surrounding thicket, wafting through the tent... lacing the faded canvas with fragrances likely to loiter long after the advent of the morning sun. But morning would have to wait. An enormous harvest-moon further engaged their senses... rolling up from behind the distant foothills, all glazed in creamy amber and pot holed oranges.

And because the scene was heady and enchanting, Brown found himself stricken with loneliness... and even more so, as he collapsed onto a freshly washed, flannel lined sleeping bag and cradled his head on a soft, cotton cased, sunshine-sweet pillow spread upon the grass floor of the tent... obviously placed there for him.

The short-sleeved shirt he wore would soon be insufficient against the chill moving in off the lake; *drawn to the sun warmed earth,* he mused.

Tired to the bone, but still feeling an obligation to show thanks to Shadow for such hospitality, he rolled onto his side, propped his head up on one elbow. The kid was sitting quietly by the fire in one of the old collapsible aluminum chairs with his beautiful bare feet resting on a stump. He may have been feeling a bit lonely too... or perhaps awkward in such close settings with a relative stranger.

Brown cleared his throat, "Brother, when I was your age..." *no... that was canned...* the kid didn't move but was listening. He tried again; "Back in Georgia, we'd be fighting mosquitoes and picking the sand spurs out of our feet, camped out here like this, and that lake would be crawling with snakes, and maybe even 'gators, depending on which part of the state we were in..." Shadow glanced over smiling slightly. Good, he had his attention; "But we'd be getting ready to go out frog-gigging too... never on foot, always in a boat or a skiff... snakes as big around as your arm... no... my arm... ready to ruin your night if you stepped on one. They're in the water too..." Shadow had by now, twisted his chair around, Brown could only guess at the expression on the youngster's face, obscure because of the contrasting campfire and the gloriously bright moon behind him... but he continued; fully determined to blow the kid's mind if possible.

"We used flashlights to locate 'em... their eyes shining bright yellow in the dark... always throwing the gig... you know what a gig is... right?" Shadow may have nodded his head, yes or no... Brown couldn't tell, but went on to describe the three pronged, barbed fork tied tightly to a long shaft of bamboo; "...or cane of some kind, with a long rope wrapped around your wrist in case you'd lose your grip. Bullfrogs big as your head... Anyway, you'd always want to aim for just behind the eyes."

Still on the pallet, reclining on one elbow, he held two fingers up, and then suddenly thrust them out! Toward where he imagined Shadow's eyes might be, and who nearly fell backwards in his chair. But in Brown's estimation this wasn't quite enough payment for such hospitality, so he continued; "Trouble is, there's snakes on the banks and in the water too... You see, what you did... was throw the gig out and yank it back as quick as possible... works most of the time..." Brown, now on his knees, posing with an imaginary gig... let fly one or two and yanked them back... "Like that," he said. "Then, you whack their legs off and throw the torso's back in the water... legs in a bucket still jumping around. No big deal after a while... you get used to it. Fried frog legs taste like a stringy chicken... batter 'em up just like you would a chicken too. Delicious around a campfire.

"I was just a little guy in those days, but soon's I was strong enough to hold one, they let me throw the gig. We'd take turns holding the light... wasn't easy in a boat rocking around. You had to be quiet too... Now, certain kinds of frogs are strange, when one shuts up they all shut up at exactly the same time... and when one starts to croaking they all start up... all at the same instant... " He let that sink in; "But bull-frogs are different. With them it's one at a time, and gradually the rest join in. And son, the voices are deep as a well."

Shadow had stoked the fire and was now standing on the other side of the pit... Brown could see his eyes, glassy and glowing in the firelight. "I practiced with the gig in the yard at granny and grandpa's house, 'til one day I was ready. We always had ourselves a fire too, pretty close to the boat, you know? So's not to step on any snakes as we went back and forth to the camp... Oh, and we made sure there was no sticks or branches laying around, so if you saw what looked like a branch near the fire you'd know it was a snake instead... n' everybody had to have a flashlight.

"The grown-ups wore shoes but the kids didn't... cause they didn't own any. Never crossed our minds either.... feet tough as nails" Shadow began to fidget around the fire pit.

"I stepped on one in the daylight that was laying across a trail by the lake. When that branch (bout as big around as one of my little legs) moved, I must'a been airborne, cause the next thing I knew, I was back up at the house sitting on that porch shaking like a dog shittin' peach seeds! Unh! Son! I can still feel that thing contracting under my foot." With this he flopped forward onto his elbows wishing he had a big stick to wiggle in the grass, but that wasn't needed. Shadow vaulted backward as if Brown himself were the snake.

"Well, like I was saying, the time came for me to throw the gig... in the bow of the skiff... uncle Will, holding onto my pants. Grandpa and another uncle, with flashlights panning the water and the reeds (frogs'll just float in the water all spread-eagled, eyes and nostrils peekin' out). I wanted so bad to do good. Perfect night... frogs hard at it. You never heard such noise... like a symphony of tubas... deep... deep... but thumping and reverberating too... like a long drawn out kettledrum... coming up out of the earth... brrrrroooomp... boooommmm.... Bommmmp... must'a been late spring, early summer.

"We'd drifted along without the lights for a few minutes... but the minute the flashlights came on, that was it... they all stopped their music... no noise... but man, there were eyes everywhere! We had two gigs, but only one man could throw at a time, the other was a spare... just in case." Brownman, now on his feet, outside the tent, had worked his way around the fire, facing Shadow. With a sweeping motion out into the darkness with his left hand, and with his right, pointing from place to place with two fingers for eyes; "there, there... and there." Shadow could see the frogs, and so could Brownie; the firelight reflecting from the cans and bottles placed earlier on the stumps, did the job nicely. And he'd surmised correctly, Shadow had placed them to indicate where the stumps were, but now they were amphibians... floating silently... staring...

Brownie, stepped up onto a rotting, makeshift, log bench... waited for a moment with the gig poised overhead... Shadow grabbed his waistband; then, ten-year-old Myron Brown drew back and... thunk!! Yanked the frog into the boat behind them... but... "Snake!!! My god!! A water moccasin!!!" The real thing could not have been more tangible; curling and twisting around, with the gig slightly piercing its body about six inches behind the head... the vile creature's mouth was wide open, fangs protruding from balls of cotton on each side of its jaw... eyes evil and murky yellow.

"Look out! It got off the gig... it's off!"

Shadow manifested instantly beside Brownman, completely absorbed in the drama... laughing from the belly like any other-ten year old. Even went so far as to put an arm around Brownie's shoulders and yelling; "Kill it Grandpa... Get him, Uncle Will!"

They lost their balance and sat down on the log. The laughter tapered off but they sat there, silently gazing into the fading fire for a few moments longer. Brown finished up the story (which in reality they'd portrayed just as it had happened so long ago). His mind wandered along sandy country lanes, chicken yards, sagging barns, and giant Cypress trees with sphagnum moss trailing from their limbs... then he got up, groaning with the effort, and walked back to the tent... slid onto the pallet... asked Shadow; "Where's your bed?"

Right there in the tent... too many snakes out here, man."

That was fine with Ol' Brown... who'd found a familiar notch on Maggie's shoulder and was soon fast asleep.

—◇—

Brownie

by

Kenneth M. Scott

– Part Five –

- *Chapter Seventeen* -

Dinner with Annie and Arnie had been meaningful but every attempt at a solution had run aground... it was agreed by all that the main thing to do would be to mount a twenty-four hour surveillance, and should any loggers show up, try to talk them out of their plan... In the meantime, perhaps Arnie and Annie could talk with the Hepner's. After Brown had described Joyce, Annie was certain she had seen her appearing faithfully at the farmer's market every Wednesday... Perfect!!!

Yes, they knew Jacob... not as well as some, but agreed that he would be the prime agent for intercession. And a meeting was important... Joyce, at least had Wayne's ear, but more importantly had ears of her own. But would she share information?

The Thompsons were off to the Market early the next morning, and Brown was up with the sunshine, but Shadow lagged behind by about two hours. Maggie would be at work anyway, so there was really no hurry to get back to the apartment. Arnie agreed to leave a note on the windshield of the van (if it was still there) for the owner of the Grocery Cart Market. A jar of peanut butter, a bottle of water, a loaf of bread and three bananas was a great find for Brown (although he had to fake the whole process with a spoon instead of a knife). PB&B sandwiches never tasted so good!

Aware that one or two streams fed the lake, the mouths of which were on this side (maybe even within walking distance to the camp), Brown managed to find a trail leading in that general direction, and sure enough, found one of them. It was a small meandering river with no detectable movement to it... the trail hugged the banks for the most part, and was no doubt maintained by the boots of fishermen. But blackberries, donkey-tails, ferns, scrub-willows by the thousands, and an occasional maple or fir tree... some large-some smaller... threatened to take over any moment. Brown picked his way through numerous blackberry vines growing across the trail, characteristic to the specie's perpetual thorny nature.

It was still very early in the morning; his wristwatch was tucked under a corner of the sleeping bag. There were no highway sounds, although once or twice he'd heard the boisterous and thoughtless sound of a speed boat warming up from somewhere on the other side of the lake, miles away.

The water had an amber tint to it, but that was only due to the iron content of sandy soil. The landscape could be the same as it had been for thousands of years. The air was still cool with a contrasting warmth on his head and shoulders from the intermittent rays of the sun, and certainly the phrase "old as dirt" could have crossed his mind, but not today. Instead, "cock of the walk" would've been far more appropriate; *for the first time in... what... Years?* He felt very alive, and completely at ease...

Time for a swim... *ahhhhh... refreshing.* With the water up to his chin, the sand and mud mixture from the bottom of the river squished up between his toes. It was chilly at first but he'd quickly become accustomed; ducked down to the bottom and cupped a handful; popped back up, absently rubbing himself down with the stuff. Then he spotted a tiny rivulet of water seeping into the river from the nearby bank... dog-paddled over and immediately was entranced by the miniature world before him... in perfect detail. The stream had gradually carved out a small spring in the river bank, complete with tiny, colorful pebbles resembling an idyllic mountain lake; the shores of which were lined by several larger stones that could easily have been giant boulders to an ant, or the perfect place for a tiny fairy to relax in the sun. Miniature Maidenhair ferns resembling palms and tropical plants leaned out from other areas and reflected with perfect detail in the crystal clarity of the pool. A small cove with a sandy beach further invited his imagination (as if he had not already succumbed!). He allowed it to be so... to be transported into the privacy of make believe, and for a time he experienced perfection as only a child could.

Sun, filtered and danced across the water as maple leaves so directed from above. A teensy overflow, spilling through a small channel into the river, beckoned his mouth but he decided to refuse that honor for a time while he ran along the shore of the tiny beach; scrambled around on terraced boulders; dove from the lower one and circled back only to climb out and up to the highest (reasonable) point; stood for a moment and with a precise swan dive, arced back into the darkest, deepest part of the lagoon.

Then he began to cry, gradually erupting into profound sobs of loneliness... but happiness also... at such beauty... as visual elegance mixed with his poignant, aching heart, "God if you're there, have mercy on me... I'm just a man... I'm just a man," he repeated again and again... blubbering with his big lips, wiping tears and snot from his freckled face unashamedly. Eons and mountains of disappointment erupted from his heart for all things bad, until finally, with a purged heart, willingly tumbled in absolute free-fall toward what was (as yet) a tiny laser-bright desire... for all things good. Nature had done her work. From this little world of innocence, a land where only a child could have entered, he stood up a different man; naked as the day he'd been born... if not as innocent. Nevertheless, something had happened, and it was good.

—◇—

Conscious of being part of the earth... yet something transcending even that, something entirely unique... he slurped from the rivulet. Raised his head from the tiny pool with eyes clear and bright and the faintest of smiles, recalling that the hope of finding a clay deposit had originally drawn him to the little spring. Now a simple mud bath seemed an appropriate ritual... *spiritually speaking.* Gently, he scooped from the bottom of the pool... *yes...* brought up a handful of exquisite silt and clay, grayish black in color and of perfect consistency... slowly and reverently rubbed himself, retrieving the emulsion from it's source, little by little, mindful not to disturb the miniature world.

Sunshine, filtering through giant maple leaves overhead, eased on into the glade with gradual late summer blessings for all flora and fauna below. The coming day would be a hot one. But for now, the perfect temperature slowly heated the clay, shrinking and drying the thin layer, simultaneously stretching the skin underneath. Soon, considering himself to be sufficiently battered, he ceased applying and stood ankle deep in the river, rotating with arms awry, legs parted, seeking the sunshine. But unsatisfied and perhaps becoming bored, aware that ideally the stuff should be caked on and left for a good hour, he dropped back onto his knees, enlarging the enchanted pool, expecting it to run out with each handful, but no, the deposit ran deep and kept on giving. The clay had become a rich and thick emollient. He continued applying, aware of the increasing weight upon his frame. This was definitely a good feeling. He packed a goodly amount on top of his head (anticipating the added benefit of hair restoration for his balding pate), then raised up from the ground... a man of clay (except for ankles and feet). "One hour, minimum, should do it," he grunted aloud; tumbled up the dirt bank and shuffled along... like a mummy from the mire.

Within five minutes he was skirting the lake's shore again. The carp had begun their wallowing in the reeds, and he continued his waddling, clothes scrunched up in one big fist but with his shoes back on his tender feet. In full sun by now, and crusty... maybe even crunchy... he was comforted by the fact that water was near anytime he decided he needed it.

In the thicket, visible across some twenty yards of well-grazed pasture grass, Shadow was no doubt lurking around in some inconceivable dream scenario. The idea of duck-walking through the bows and branches to wake him seemed a waste of good clay. Besides, he had already lost patches and splotches... the thought of revealing himself or playing some trick on the kid, had fizzled to almost nil... the blob of clay on his head would surely be dislodged and certain parts of his anatomy might not appreciate certain aspects of a certain trail. So he crumpled and folded his earthy-self onto the pasture grass, feeling the prickly aspect of that move immediately.

Discomfort gave way to the only logical thought possible to any man of clay. At this particular point in time and space, the time was now–and the space was nature's own Carp Wrestling Arena!

Really? Really? Yeah! I'm doing it... The view from behind would have been more than most anyone could endure as two gigantic cream-puffs galumphed and shimmied erratically into the aquatic arena, flinging flakes of fudge-icing left and right.

His intention was to take the several large specimens by surprise, aiming for where the body of the largest one would logically be, all things considered (the shape of the tails and their juxtapositions in relation to where the other contenders might be). The result was that he actually splashed right into the midst of three or more lunkers... all thoughts of wrestling vanished instantly with the reality of slimy fins and muscular tails, thorny projections and bony scales engaging his primitive man-self and invoking talents unknown to modern mankind: A man of the marsh, harking from ages long past, intuitively grasping, diving, plunging, leaping, slapping, and making actual physical contact with prehistoric holdovers from who knew how long ago.

Apparently due to the extremely clever forethought of covering himself with clay, the fish were none the wiser... he was just another fish competing for spawning ground... and managed to engage several groupings with zero luck before running out of energy and breath.

Who knew? Given time to hone his talents, he might have caught one of the suckers. But finally, with kinky-haired head tilted all the way back 'til it hurt, gazing upward to the blue sky, opened eyes rolling toward the back of his head, he lurched backward with a huge, and final splash...

While still in the lake, entirely contented with the outcome of the mud bath, he finished the scrub, shook out his clothes, spread them out on the grass and situated himself upon them, basking in the morning sunshine.

Clay. One of the most basic of materials, dating back to the first civilizations, but still in use all over the world. His seemed to have been of high quality. The Bible mentioned in several places how people are like pottery; some made for honorable uses, others for more menial (or even dishonorable) and all according to the potter. Some vessels found their way into mud huts and used for slop; others would be used in palaces, for the finest of wines, rarest of perfumes, exotic ointments and spices from faraway.

He'd certainly put the clay to very good use, and would never forget the day the man of flesh had become a man of clay. But there was a problem, he'd noticed multiple scrapes and small punctures from the fish-fins not felt during the wrestle... now becoming painful; some just beginning to swell, others bleeding slightly. He calmly accepted these as marks of honor... at a small price... well worth the discomfort, and he'd gladly do it again. Maybe someday Carlos would join him. The carp were wallowing again...

—◇—

After stashing the old, aluminum boat in the reeds across the highway (opposite the store) and then continuing by way of a much too long and needless route (according to Brownman) but necessary "to throw 'em off" (according to Shadow), it was ten o'clock. The van was still there: Thank you, What's Your Name...

The apartment would be Brownman's first stop, to change clothes and apply antiseptic to what had now become marks from fish-fins and teeth. He urged Shadow to come inside, lest he disappear before they could get up to the springs. While he took a shower, the kid flipped through a magazine; made and ate a sandwich; vanished and reappeared a couple of times; yawned and stared out the window.

Finishing up in the bathroom, the unsinkable William Brown, threw a few toiletries (including more antiseptic) into a paper sack; caught his reflection in the mirror and rubbed his chin; *I've never actually had a beard... wonder if it'll come in kinky?* Next, he tossed a razor in the bag (just in case); poked his head through the doorway and offered Shadow a spare toothbrush.

"Nahhh, I'll just lose that, man."

Well, the kid's teeth were his own business, and he had to admit they looked ten times better than his own.

They'd already concocted a plan of sorts at Arnie and Annie's. Shadow was to hang out at Hepner's to glean any information he could about the timing of the hit; Brown would appear now and then (as often as possible) to snoop around and such. They whizzed right by Florence's trailer, stopped at Jacob's house; there were no people around. The dogs were outside, so Jacob must have come back; but as they headed on up to Hepner's, Brown realized that the open floor in the mural room was a ready made exit... and entrance, for that matter.

Shadow confirmed that he knew Jacob. And what's more, Jake always called him Shadow, but could also tell him his real name any time he asked for it (which wasn't very often), but it was a good idea to ask occasionally; "Cause what if I forgot it someday?"

Cool.

They passed the hot springs turn off, and pulled into Hepner's; parked in the shade of a big Maple. When Brownie rounded the van, Shadow was nowhere to be seen. That was okay, the kid had his car phone number (just in case the charger turned up), his mom's phone number... and ten bucks for food; "And this is really important, Shadow; My car phone might not work at Jake's, anyway, but even if what you've found out is super urgent try to make it to Jake's house before calling Mother... walk, hitch-hike, whatever." Then he said, "Look at me. My mother is our last resort. Our fallback position. Do you understand, corporal?" Shadow liked the sound of that military jargon and shook his head affirmative.

The weather was back to normal for August... clear skies and the hottest time of the year... often reaching one hundred degrees during the day, but quickly falling to the mid-fifties most every night in the narrow valley. The further up the mountain the colder the river. Even on the hottest day, relaxing beside the river was a sure fix. However, swimming simply wasn't an option, except for crazy people... and Jacob.

Who, as The Rainbow Ranger, was at that moment guarding the hot springs... doing his very best to make certain everyone picked up after themselves... and torn between the need for information and to keep a diligent watch.

Brown loitered around the store enjoying smells at the fresh deli counter... and the delightful heated display cases with chicken-tenders, jo-jo potatoes, and what could have been crispy, mini-burritos. He kept his eyes on Wayne through racks of red wieners encased in glass and brightly lit... slowly rotating... bubbling grease and dripping cheese onto the aluminum foiled bottom of the rotisserie cooker. Wayne was in conversation with a sweet-looking young woman (without dreads) in a flowered, full-length skirt and a cotton blouse barely covering her breasts; mid-drift exposed, as was typical.

Their voices carried easily. The reason for the increased (hippy) business at the store was the imminent Rainbow gathering... at least a three-day drive further eastward. The springs were a natural stopover and most of the crowd would be gone by Thursday.

Ol' Wayne was musing aloud; "So, the weekend won't be very busy around here either..."

"Not really..."

"Good, I might do a little fishing, catch up on some chores... but how 'bout Friday?" he tossed out there, as she headed for the door.

"I doubt it, maybe a few locals from town," she replied cheerfully, "but the State Fair starts Friday... so..." and she was out the door.

Brown played poker face with Wayne when he paid him back for the previous loan, plus one additional (particularly appealing) hotdog and the giant fountain coke in his hand. He was also keeping an eye out for any signs of Shadow, but then, the fact that he couldn't see him meant he was there... somewhere... what a kid.

Normally a gasoline fill-up this far from the city would be out of the question, but the Hepner's were artful in their pricing... always reasonable enough not to exclude the likelihood of soft drinks, or snacks... also reasonably priced. Wayne and Joyce, pillars of their community would ideally be respected and appreciated by everyone (sigh)... *but that wouldn't be life on earth, now would it?* Brown pulled up to the pump almost gleefully.

"How much, Myron?"

"All of it, Todd" he replied, meaning fill 'er up... and glad to be able to say so, for a change... thank you, Bonnie.

Enjoying the smell of gasoline... a bit of sadness pricked his heart. Every small community had its divisions and whether subtly or sharply there would always be problems. Inevitably falling somewhere along the lines of religious or political mind sets of course, but basically resulting from small minds... some of them very small. Sometime ago he'd thought about this and came to the conclusion that not only failure, but success could breed respect or contempt... from either side of the equation... envy and jealousy from some on the outside, and a condescending spirit from those on the inside... but not always.

Obviously the Hepner's had remained intact and more so. They had learned in every way the responsibility of "having." Which meant faithfully managing their own affairs and the privilege of responsible giving to others from their own abundance... that, and true graciousness, which could only be learned or refined from being accused or abused by others when undeserved.

Jacob was gracious, but perhaps he functioned on a plane other than those who had to earn good character by first hand experiences. People were born with a certain temperament (a natural disposition to be optimistic, cheerful, considerate) like a gift from the gods... or The God... whatever. Unshakable optimism and courage was one hell of a combination... couple that with intelligence and, wham! You've got Wayne and Joyce, and a coming generation of serious potential for good. Just take a look at their kids, mostly grown ups and thriving in plain sight.

So, that's about all Brown could take for the moment, but he knew many of the small minded in the community. Little clay pots; some cracked, some in need of washing, some missing handles, others chipped and poorly glazed from the day they were born... and the very moment the phrase "without a pot to piss in" came to mind, it took on a new twist: These poor souls took pleasure in pissing in other people's pots! For whatever reasons... reasons aplenty–excuses none.

So, without plunging into despair with all those infinitely sad details, just what were the reasons? This had
bothered him for so long, but today it seemed obvious.
Jacob may have hit the nail on the head when he said; "If
all you've got is a hammer, everything looks like a nail."
It looked to Brown like everybody had both nails and
hammers... fully capable of producing one or the other as
the situation arose. Hammers and nails are good things,
but never to be used on pottery of any kind.

Todd took the cash and continued on with his "Hepner kind of day." Brown scanned the area for Mister Clan-
destine... who was still doing his job very nicely.

The drive up to the springs was slower than usual due
to the increased traffic. When passing Hippie Hollow he
noted that there might not have been even one space left
for parking.

Two Forest Service enforcement vehicles were cruising the road... mostly displaying their presence, and
quite capable, should anything "unlawful" arise. Brown
scooted into a space in the overflow parking area, located around the next bend some distance from the actual
trail leading back to the springs; if Jacob was on duty he
would have no trouble spotting him.

The springs, consisting of two pools, were crowded as
to be expected... About half the people were completely nude, others only partially, but Brown quickly set his
mind free from "all that" and studied the demographics
of the tiered pools. The warmest of course would be the
upper, and so on... but there was a size difference too. The
lower was actually larger than the upper and almost deep
enough for shallow diving. This seemed to be where the
less "serious" bathers congregated; and possibly many of

the youngsters belonged to parents who were in the upper pool. Characteristically, as in all swimming holes, in a stream of any size, bathers had piled hundreds of stones on top of the overflow, which provided some increased depth... and better diving. The water gurgled through the many openings and proceeded on down a quarter mile below; through a culvert under the road and into the reservoir. Only one of several along the watershed providing flood control for the enormous and fertile valley, fifty miles away.

The lower pool seemed to be the most crowded, but traffic between that one and the upper, much hotter pool, indicated that it was used for cooling down. Though the upper was smaller in size, there was consistently more sitting room in that one.

The smell of sulfur common to hot springs was not too overpowering, nor did there seem to be the expected stringy and slimy residue clinging to the edges of either pool. Sulfur is a natural disinfectant, but visible sludge brought to mind toxicity (even though congealed) and this prevented many from enjoying the benefits. Brown could only imagine the difficulty of skimming such goop from all the pools. Not to worry though; today Jacob had been doing an exceptional job. Hopefully he recruited helpers as needed.

He chose to perch on the hillside, a bit removed from the rustic lean-to provided by the Rangers... U.S., not Rainbow... As far as he could tell, Jake was nowhere near.

He thought of Feather... decided to keep his eyes open for her. Thought of Arnie and Annie... Shadow... thankful that all had agreed to the necessity of keeping the whole thing quiet for as long as possible; wisely choosing to isolate rather than escalate the problem. Shadow promised he'd not told another soul, which was very hard to believe. Yet, he was a strange and unusual young man. Time would tell.

Right now, though, there was an urgency to talk with Jake. And who could say what his reaction had been after running off like that in a panic? If this thing were kept a secret it would indeed be a miracle... By now everyone in the valley knew of his association with Jacob. Even Wayne had seemed a little "distant" today. Yep. Everybody knew about it, or would very soon... If not from Wesley the Dozer, then certainly from one or more of the occasional carryalls passing by Jake's place, loaded with hoe-dads, choker-setters, and slash-crews... all networking (though they'd never call it that) at Hepner's. And for sure they had seen him there. In fact it was said that if you farted in Glenwood, they'd smell it in Trailbridge long before anyone heard it. Yeah, the "valley network..." no matter what they called it... was invasive, destructive and punishing. Venom with but one surefire preventative... kill it, before it grows. And there was no antidote; insidious and silently killing or inflicting its victims with great harm.

The day was heating up... If the weather held as expected, all logging would be called off... all of it... topping, falling; setting chokers (attaching cables to fallen trees); yarding (mechanically dragging logs up the mountainsides), and loading logs onto the trucks, many of which carried a "pup" (extra trailer) riding on the back of the main haul-bed until at the log loading site, for increased capacity on the trip back to the mill.

Even subsidiary aspects would be suspended. Replanting by the hoe-dads, clearing and burning by the slash crews... road maintenance... all would wait 'til conditions were perfect... regardless–even in winter months. Yes sir. All would be cancelled... and that was good with Brown.... gossip was bad, but fire was worse. And either one could stop paychecks, dislocate families, and ruin habitat (including human).

Feeling somewhat like a hidden squirrel or a fat chipmunk... Brownie relaxed even further, enjoying his view of the springs, which were located in a ravine, heavily forested in all directions. Access trails were cut into the steep inclines and went no further... the surrounding hillsides were strictly for the strong and adventurous... and that included Ol' Jacob... whose current descent down the opposite hillside became known to Brown only after he'd made it halfway down. The man was strong, sure footed, half-naked of course, smiling as always, and making use of the tree trunks. But his main stabilizer was a bark-free, wooden staff. This he plunged into the lush banks of moss, fir needles and ferns... expertly... like a three-legged animal of some kind.

The "chipmunk" waited as still as could be, while Jake slid on his butt down the four feet or so of steeply cut bank and landed on the path as agile as a deer... upright of course. Once positioned: leather pouch adjusted; dreads shaken into place; standing erect (not pompously but as dignified as any almost naked man could possibly appear); he held his staff out like Moses, and said in a voice sufficiently loud enough for those who wanted to hear; "Welcome home, Welcome home..." then proceeded to circle around the backside of the springs, smiling and pointing the staff at various bathers whom he apparently knew, calling out their names, embellished occasionally with the meanings thereof. Occasionally he pointed the staff at others, offering: "Tell me your name, and I'll tell you what it means..." and once he'd told them, without fail (as though not to be rude) finished with; "My name is Jacob!" adding almost inaudibly, "I'll let you find out what that means."

After making his rounds, gazing down on his flock, he abruptly pointed his staff up the hill, right at Brown (who'd all along thought he was hidden) and said; "And this is Brown Bear..."

"Hello's" came lilting up to the astonished and embarrassed... Brown Bear?

Wow.... liking the sound of that (couldn't have thought of a better name for himself), he waved a few times, then slid on down the hill and unashamedly hugged Jacob... "It's good to be home," he found himself saying (with just a tinge of doubt).

Then, Jacob made it a point to look him square in the eyes... with an unmistakable expression.

Brown Bear silently and correctly got the message; *Really... do I have to? Are you sure?* A slight nod and an unmistakable twinkle assured him that if he didn't, he might have to be renamed. He tried to twinkle back; *Renamed? So soon? So easily?* But the smile on Jacob's lips was gone, replaced by a stern expression that said, *Come on! This is so easy... why not?* All the while slowly edging aside, allowing room to pass on the narrow trail and on over to the changing shed.

The Brown Bear lumbered over, carefully positioning himself behind a waist-high, log wall; removed his shoes, pants, and shirt, then had no choice but to remove his pathetic undershorts. Certain that everyone would be waiting for the unveiling, he came out... ta-daaa... no one paid him any mind. *Goody.* He chose the center pool and sank down to chin level; found the temperature very much to his liking. Cautiously glancing around... no eye contact... *good...good...* maneuvered over to the side of the pool and was surprised to find the perfect stone ledge to sit on... next to a person he was pretty sure had on a bathing suit. The pleasure was undeniable, and he almost said so to the "possibly" naked person but changed his mind. After a short soak he scrambled across the dam to the upper pool (God help anyone watching that) and knew that the brief, pre-heat in the lower pool had been a good idea. Early on into this final soak, he spotted Jacob sitting upon the hillside, like a shepherd watching sheep.

After five minutes, the possibility that he might soon be overcooked (boiled peanuts came to mind), convinced him to saunter with great confidence back to the changing shed... sincerely hoping he'd preserved even the tiniest bit of dignity. While dressing he vowed someday to be back at this place; miraculously wedged into a cathedral of towering trees... almost holy in fact... and enjoyed by many people not that much different than him... Not really.

Once dressed, he climbed up the bank, sat beside Jacob, who said right off the bat with a sweeping, comprehensive wave over the pools; "That's hot water... but if you want to cool... there's a waterfall just over there... over the hill." Then he went on describing the rock formations and the pool, almost big enough to swim in... how beautiful and how nice it would be if the two places were right next to each other... "Cold... hot... alternating... ya' know?"

Sounded great all right... and an invitation to "...take you there, Mon, right now!" seemed so brotherly and generous... how could he refuse? From where they were sitting, making it to the top of the hill didn't look to be particularly daunting... and it wasn't... not exactly. But from the top of said hill, descending to the falls in the gorge below? Why, even a goat would've given it second thoughts.

There was a path of sorts, ending abruptly at times, only to resume later if one were to negotiate a boulder or scoot down a log, or slide down steep, dirt embankments hand-over-hand.

See them go: overcoming terrain by holding onto stout vine maples; denuded sapling fir trees, or clinging to exposed roots... down, down, down... watch Brown Bear fall on his furry butt (more than once)... see strong Jacob... spring like a gazelle from boulder to log.

Hear Brown Bear's thoughts... *No human should ever do this, I'll never get back to the top, even if I do make it to the bottom.*

But eventually his bottom did make it to "the" bottom ingloriously, but deservedly at the very least (considering his whining and fears).

He'd never been in a more beautiful place. Under as little as half an inch of water were multi-hued, solid rock-slabs... ten–fifteen feet wide, stretching across the full width of the creek, interspersing pool after pool. Knee deep or neck deep... pools edged with stone ledges as though placed there by God himself for any visitor... there, only by direct invitation... or at least those predestined for such sensual delight. "Those with eyes to see and ears to hear..." the ebullient praise, the chattering, the uplifting laughter of yet another masterful composition of nature's own voice in full symphony.

The falls! Accompanied by musical splatterings, patterings, and mistings upon rock, fern and moss. Each of which, could but contribute (if only drip by drip... droplets, rivulets, trickles... from the highest point to the lowest) to the pleasing allegro tempo; accredited if not in fact, at least in spirit, as being the prevailing impetus for such a sensational performance by all members of the orchestra at hand… in a never ending crescendo.

The natural inclination was to advance up the creek, to stand as close as possible to the living veil of man's greatest need on earth. Drawn by osmosis or by sentient attraction, the Bear ambled along, undulating his great mass, delicately if you will, in full appreciation of his surroundings.

Jacob must have gone behind a tree or an outcropping to take a leak, or else he was hiding somewhere. Bear, having saved the falls to share with him, was a bit disappointed, but resolved not to be distracted; focusing on the marvel at hand. He was unable to see where the falls began, but they were at least thirty feet high, and probably emanating from yet another pool above, perhaps stair-stepping right on up to… the Living Water Himself… if one believed in such things.

And it was very hard not to praise someone for such beauty; "Nice job," he said aloud… still facing the falls, but pitched so low that he could barely hear it. "Nice job!!!!" he yelled. And even that was muffled. *Okay…* he smiled; Then, at the top of his lungs; "Way to go!!!" At that moment two hands penetrated right through the veil, at eye level, as though God Himself were reaching out for him.

Brown managed to stay right where he was… facing the falls, five feet away.

The hands obviously attached to the naked Jacob gradually preceded his full body; emerging, bit by bit, allowing the water to lengthen his beard in streams of water… his dreads appearing to be three feet long… and when completely out… lifting his hands upward, for all the world looking like Moses… and of course, he shouted, "Welcome home!!!"

His voice may have resounded to the heavens or simply drifted along the happy creek, on around a jutting
portion of the opposing hillside, and eventually flowing
under the lakeshore road and into the reservoir.

The logical thing to do next... is exactly what Jake
did... stepping backward gradually until only his arms
were jutting out, then just his hands... then turned them
palm upwards and motioned for the Bear to give him his
paws...

The space behind the falls was quite roomy. Not a
cave, unfortunately, but a solid rock wall concaving just
enough for two or three people to stand comfortably
side-by-side. The fact that it curved outwardly on both
outer edges made it the perfect hiding place. How many
human beings had ever stood there in that exact spot?
One hundred? A thousand? No more than two thousand
in all of history. And of course, it was entirely possible
that the area had been hand chipped, but without direct
sun or an artificial light... No matter; it was an honor to
be there. The sun had definitely passed the daily merid-
ian, and might never hit the falls directly at any time of
the year. The Bear took it all in, but was soaked and time
was wasting... they needed to talk.

Although he'd hoped for something much different,
he wasn't surprised to find that Jacob had alerted several
of the brothers to keep their eyes and ears alert, but wanted Brown to tell him more. Brown obliged, to the smallest
detail, and realized again that he didn't know very much.

"Don't worry Mon, the Rangers are ready... twenty-
four-seven."

Brown wanted to know who might be the lead ranger
for the area if Jacob wasn't? Jake had never even considered the need for a lead ranger. And what about leaders

in general? There were none per se' … apparently "agree" had never encountered "disagree" at this level.

What about Stephen Canfield, the high elder?

He was gone… left days ago, already at the gathering with other elders.

When asked if he would be willing to have a meeting with Wayne, Jacob refused, saying; "The hearts of the sons of men are fully set to do evil… unless punishment is swift."

This vague and indirect response was beginning to sound familiar, causing Brown to suspect that he himself might really be the only one who could make a difference after all. "I gotta get goin'…" he said with regret.

Jacob made sure he helped the ailing Bear back up the mountainside, down and around the backside of the springs, and all the way to the trail head parking lot. That was cool, but Brownie was beginning to wonder why this whole thing should be so important… his life was tiny compared to so many others, and it was unraveling like a poorly woven pot holder.

Nevertheless, before parting he tried to assure Jacob that the hit wouldn't happen before Friday and that he should just come on back with him, but Jacob refused to abandon his post… Sheeesh!

Well, would it be alright if he and Shadow hung out at Jake's?

Of course it would, but would he please keep feeding the dogs, and make sure to give them love?

No problem… Was there anything he should bring next time he came up?

"No. The sisters are taking care of me, Mon."

The Brown Bear's last words sounded confident enough for even him to believe; "We'll let you know the minute we know... and don't worry, nothing's gonna happen to the springs... nobody in their right mind would do such a thing,"

—◇—

Back at Hepner's, there was still no signal for the car phone! He tried the pay phone; no Maggie.

Thankfully she'd found the note on the fridge telling her that he'd bought a car-charger and had decided not to have his wisdom teeth pulled–didn't mention the canine teeth option–signed it, but then scribbled across the bottom of the scrap paper; "And don't worry I quit my job at the airlines (though he actually hadn't... just trying it on for size...). It looked pretty good in writing. God was talking to Jacob "through writing," why not try that with Maggie?

So, in hopes of information either from Shadow or some hapless logger, or even Wayne, he cruised Hepner's one more time.... inside and out... no Shadow... no hapless-nobody. Hopefully the car phone would work down at Jake's. For some reason he just didn't want to face his mother with this. She could become pretty frantic at times... especially when she couldn't have complete control of a situation... very stubborn. Or would fearful be a better word?

Maggie had returned from work, found the note, ignored it as long as she could, and was sitting at the table with coffee in one hand and note in the other. "Eloquent, Brown. Little more than a dozen words and you tell me about your teeth. Taking time for dentistry, but no time for me?" She realized that she was talking to the wall...

or more specifically, the phone on the kitchen wall as if Brown himself were listening. She raised her voice half an octave; "What? You quit your job?! God! How could you? Are you out of your gourd?" But of course he was... and so typical. And what about the teeth? Why should that be so important to write? It was a full-time job for her to read between the lines in that man's mind. *He's up to something...* How much more of this could she take? She had to get out of this suffocating apartment. The ringing of the phone nearly floored her. And it was Joyce Hepner–of all people! They'd developed a sincere relationship in the last two decades; "Maggie, I was wondering, honey, if you and Myron were alright."

"Actually I'm glad you called Joyce... I have to say, Brown has been acting strange, which is normal, I know, but even more so..."

The conversation progressed rapidly to the particulars from Maggie's perspective. She finished with; "And he hasn't been home much."

Joyce brought her up to speed; "Myron's been hanging around the store a lot the last few days and word has it that he has converted... or maybe not... been seen with hippies of all kinds. But look, I don't think it's true... and the "hot line" has no mercy... I wanted you to hear this from me... and sugar, you mustn't tell a soul."

Maggie, thinking this was no big whoop, started to thank Joyce, but Joyce continued; "Because Maggie, there's more; promise you won't say a word to anyone else... "

"I promise, Joyce, what's going on?"

As the story unraveled, Maggie began to put the pieces together. That Brown had met Jacob, she already knew... he'd told her that much. And now that the whole picture came into focus, she could understand why Brown wouldn't tell her this part... yet there were still a few missing pieces: Like, where had he gotten the money? Who was this Jacob character really? Even she'd heard things about the man who'd long been grist for the gossip mill... She could select any scenario–from drug dealer, to schizoidal maniac...

But the part about the dynamite... that was serious stuff. Wayyy... out there. Joyce then followed the whole story up with the, "Annie experience," at the Farmer's Market; "A really nice lady, but that Arnie? Her husband..." she trailed off momentarily speechless, then; "They just last night heard about the dynamite... and... and from Brownie, apparently..."

Joyce was too kind and tactful to say it outright... but Maggie got the picture and filled in the blanks; "If he's out there shooting his mouth off, all-out war could erupt..."

Joyce agreed (without saying it aloud), and went on; saying essentially that preparations were no doubt underway with a counter-defense... if not an offensive; "That Arnie guy looks capable of almost anything."

Poor frustrated Maggie's hands were trembling. She was on the verge of tears and wished that Joyce had started this whole conversation differently; maybe with the fact that there was still a sliver of hope... instead of tacking it on at the end. Joyce assured her that she and Wayne (after much "reasoning") had worked up a different plan. What that was, she wouldn't say, but assured Maggie that it was far more gentle; "Nobody's gonna get hurt."

Maggie pressed that one long enough to realize that Joyce had said all she was going to. In order for the new plan to work, it absolutely had to be a secret. Obviously Wayne's honor was at stake, and now even more so, all things considered: Why, he simply had to react, not only to the burr that had been under his saddle for "way too long..." but his manhood was now at stake... and that was all there was to it!

The one thing she could tell Maggie, but only after she'd sworn again (this time to God almighty) was that the thing was scheduled for Friday afternoon.

What was also said, but already understood, was; "Please keep Myron at home..."

—◇—

The valley opened up quite a bit wider at Hepner's, and in the past had made not a difference in the least to Brown, but now it did... a signal for the car phone would've been helpful... but no go. And Jacob's house was squeezed into one of many narrow passages in the valley. No signal-no problem to the Shadow Man, and he regretted he hadn't connected with Maggie... (sigh)...

His life had already gone to the dogs... they were all over him, but at least they liked him... Should he go on down to his mom's? A slight breeze swished up from the river gorge, cooling his worried brow. Norman offered his paw, Michael laughed at his plight, and Christina seemed to be hanging back... waiting to be recognized. All was quiet around the house; he could feel the heat of the day radiating from the clapboard siding; some of the blackberries were attempting a comeback from the recently scraped yard... fibrous nothings, merely sticks... drooping as though embarrassed at their impotence... though for sure a temporary state... unless further punishment was swift.

The rumbling noise Brown heard from inside Jake's was thunder... he'd noticed thunderheads forming over the distant mountain peaks. Well, that would or wouldn't happen... there was no real predicting thunderstorms... the clouds could form and fizzle or drift on eastward where they would most likely dissipate over the immense high-desert which covered at least half of the state of Oregon. The one major influential factor of weather was pressure... high and low. If the atmospheric pressure was high, the clouds could pass on over, but if the pressure was low, the clouds would be held captive long enough to drop their precious cargo... in the winter months this occurred more often than not... The natural beauty in the western half of the state depended on it... winter rains were a way of life. And if you didn't like it... you should probably move away... please.

The weather almost always came in from the west... And it was easy to predict dry weather, if and when the wind blew from the east or the south... Oregonians were like landlocked sailors; everyone kept their eyes on the weather and didn't mind talking about it.

But summer thunderstorms in the mountains? It was anybody's guess. Lookout towers perched on lonely mountaintops were there for just that reason, the men and women staying awake all night if necessary, alerting the Forest Service about lightning strikes... hundreds of them arcing and snapping... but not all strikes found combustible materials, many never contacted the earth at all. Firefighters were on call all over the state, thank god.

Brown dutifully checked out the dawg's water... rummaged around 'til he found a large sack of dried kibble. The clouds continued forming... he straddled the bench facing the window... the purposeful crunching of the kibble was impossible to dismiss, he even thought about moving the bowls onto the back porch... but resolved to stick it out... how long could they eat anyway?

The west wind picked up, which could mean one of two things... the pending storm would pass, or rain would happen within the next five or ten minutes. Rain was his best guess... from the looks of it.

The room darkened... he spotted a candle but didn't light it. The dogs stopped crunching. The wind stopped... the pit-pat of rain on the front porch roof was unmistakable. The patter increased... and with it the wind... working in tandem as old friends or intermingling as lovers... The temperature outside was still warm enough to draw Ol' Bear out onto the porch. He watched as the lovers now involved every living thing in their passion... generously and unabashed. For a moment the intensity of water from sky... and wind from unknown places... whipped and spattered the leaves and branches aggressively, but then with a whoosh, both vanished as quickly as they had appeared. Perhaps only foreplay or merely a tease... progressing to a final and gentle romantic conclusion further on up the mountain... and hopefully not the beginning of a violent and emotional argument.

The rumbling continued further east. The sky in the west had lightened considerably, promising a lovely sunset over the coastal mountain range, seventy-five miles distant. Red at night-sailor's delight... But Brown, ensconced in the hills as he was, detected but a tiny wedge of pink. The filtering light revealed tiny spattered craters in the dusty yard from the indecisive lovers... tears or saliva... would be anybody's guess.

—◇—

Knowing that his mom's freezer was packed full of meats... wasn't a sufficient lure... thawing would take way too much time. Food. Now. The fridge offered eggs and a variety of vegetables... potatoes were on the floor in a box by the stove... a package of still usable flour tortillas on the counter set the cook in motion. Thursday would be a holiday... sort of... he could relax... surely he'd figured the timing of the hit correctly. Maybe he really was exactly where he should be... it certainly felt right. He promised himself that he would for sure, *call Maggie, tomorrow morning... one way or the other.*

Twenty minutes later he was at the picnic table feasting on the best meal of his life. Stir-fried vegetables, including tiny chunks of potato, were heaped on a platter... three eggs were lined up side by side (in wide-eyed honesty) on top of the mound. An iron skillet warming gently on the stove top was for more tortillas... as needed.

The front door was still open but would need to be closed soon... only after building a nice, cozy fire, of course. He hoped Shadow wouldn't show up, nor anyone else. This would be his chance to study the mysterious Jacob from the inside. Not that he intended to snoop...

There was nothing left on his plate for the dogs, and there would be nothing coming from the leftovers on the stove... of that he was certain.

Once the fire was built and enough wood for the evening piled against the chimney... he started checking around for reading material. Passing over magazines, novels, scientific sounding titles, expensive looking hardbound books in several languages... and a plethora of language resources... only some of which he recognized. The books weren't gathered in one place–not at all–but didn't appear to be disrespectfully scattered haphazardly either. Most were in boxes and others were stacked neatly in one corner or another throughout the downstairs area.... except for the mural room, which he would save for daylight.

He realized, before climbing to the upstairs, that this was a personal space... hesitated... but hadn't they crossed that threshold in their friendship? Sure... and besides, the guy was completely open, beyond childlike... if such a thing was possible... Angelic maybe.

Thirteen steps later he was flipping a light on in the upstairs bedroom. There was a window in both of the gabled ends; a mattress was laying on the floor under one window; stacks of books within reach against one wall, and a long wooden shelf (held up by concrete blocks) stretching almost the full length of the other wall.

With a desire to see everything possible, he looked around for another light. There was a small table lamp below the far window and on a nearby bookshelf were several candles. Thanks to a book of matches still in his pocket, shortly all were burning and glowing beautifully through their glass enclosures. The room had taken on the quality of a shrine. Immediately he wished Jake were there to guide him through each niche... apparently situated in vignettes of relevance.

He spotted a can of Top Tobacco, and as suspected the rolling papers were inside, nesting upon the distinctly familiar, shredded tobacco. The dreaded possibility of taking up the habit again was shrugged off as simply a desire to "roll a few;" he then cradled his butt onto the mattress and began crafting masterpieces... slowly looking around the space as he did so. Soon he had ceased rolling and was smoking. Perfect. Almost. He hurried down the stairs, grabbed a beer and was back before the spell of enchantment could be broken.

Noww then... he was no intruder... he had become studious, observant and respectful of the anthropological find. *Yes.... more like a colleague.* After thirty minutes or so (about two and a half rollies later) he opened the windows at both ends of the chamber, allowing the smoke to clear and no doubt the dust of thousands of years if not the writings and opinions of philosophers, scientists, lengthy mathematical formulas, and the published works of scholars from all around the world.

Though such profound possibilities were at his fingertips, these works would be available in libraries and such... 'til doomsday. His interest on this night was Jacob in particular... the finite man... whose notebooks were the only real clutter in the room. Just by reaching out in any direction he could have one in hand.

The first one was filled with odd hieroglyphics (maybe of Jacob's own invention) and page after page of symbolic hand-rendered animals... mostly four footed ones... and then toward the back, the drawings became very exacting; beautifully depicting aquatic creatures, including human beings, immersed in foaming seas or submerged in underwater worlds... how could one person have so much talent?

The next one he picked was a three-ring binder. Although the faded, cut-rate cover was illustrated with Disney characters, the inside pages were completely indecipherable, possibly written in Greek or Russian...

The third one seemed to be more approachable. He settled in with it. This one was a standard eight and a half by eleven spiral notebook containing portions of familiar phrases, underlined or intermingled with doodles in pencil, pen, crayon, perhaps even charcoal from the fireplace... anything that could make a mark on the spur of the moment... just meaningless squiggles until the subjects thereof suddenly materialized before his astonished eyes! Every line counted, not one was wasted and yet the whole was camouflaged masterfully.

By this time he was getting sleepy. Not wanting to waste the opportunity at hand, he propped his back against the low wall beneath the window to catch the cool air. Placing the notebook beside him on the mattress he gazed at the ceiling, intermittently closing his eyes while gradually realizing that his overall enjoyment and admiration was somewhat compromised. The thoughts, the doodles, the man's entire body of works, were very likely the brainchildren of marijuana. And to what extent the drug had influenced the rest of what he might see tonight was also in question.

But there was a difference here. Unlike so many or most of the kids in the pot culture (who had as yet to develop their talents), Jacob was an accomplished man prior to yielding to the substance, and very likely smoked the stuff for the very reasons he'd mentioned to Brownie: for self-medication. Not that there wouldn't be a downside for habitual use. As in any medicine, the benefit exceeded the potential negative consequences... of which there were plenty as evidenced in the provided literature accompanying all "legal" drugs.

Brownbro slid back down, fluffed a pillow, elevating head and neck, now looking all the way across the cluttered attic to the far window. He was beginning to understand the true and tragic, negative consequences of this herb. First and foremost, it should never be legal for anyone in their formative years, and that would be anyone under thirty years of age (at least in the current cultural climate of the United States). The lack of incentive and personal development in young people should be obvious... and the per capita use among older adults was nil for that very same reason: They simply had too much to lose... actually enjoying the application of their talents and the fruit of their accomplishments; this was no secret. What was needed aside from some sort of control, was an explanation, simple and believable. Maybe then there wouldn't be so much drama and sensational propaganda proliferating around it.

Simply put, aside from temporary physical impairment, the drug created such an intense awareness of true power and potential accomplishment, that the rewards thereof were consumed in thought before actual work began... if ever. The power was diffused... neutralized... and although simulated, still very "real" experiences at a psychological level.

With human potential, indeed breathtaking in scope... the satisfaction of such "discoveries" was enough for most of them to say, "Been there, done that," whereas in actuality they had not... nor would they ever... and interestingly enough, as ingestion and discovery continued, so would ever-decreasing standards and altered priorities... though perhaps subtly. And due to the amazing depth and scope of those experiences, reminders of previous "self worth" would be more and more necessary, though perhaps by then incomprehensible, or eventually too late; underscoring the truth that common sense diminishes proportionate to the effort required to use it.

Admonitions against pre-celebrating were simply another way to say; Don't count your chickens before they hatch. Brown was beginning to get a handle on what he had so many years ago run from in fear, but now could actually calculate the risk as an adult, and the basic answer to, "Should he or shouldn't he indulge as a lifestyle ?" would instead be a question: "What have I got to lose?"

The traffic had all but ceased on the highway, and the sound of the constantly flowing river was lulling him into greater relaxation. He imagined the handout that would accompany legalized marijuana:

Notice:

Actual physical harm has not been determined. However, research amongst a large cross section of longtime users, including the homeless, the imprisoned, the institutionalized and old hippies in particular, guarantees a diminished human potential, and a lack of accomplishment accompanied of course by an actual loss of time (and therefore opportunity) to recover what has been lost, as well as the realization of what might otherwise have been gained, attained or achieved.

Warning: Use of this drug, whether casual or prolonged, should be considered life-changing, and a waste of time and energy. The drug initiates an altered state of mind and may provoke enthusiastic commitments and or journeys unprofitable, unrealistic, or completely impossible. Symptoms may linger long after ingestion... Do not administer to children under the age of thirty.

Recommendation to Physicians: Prescreening of patients before prescribing is highly recommended regardless of age. Prudent outpatient care should include documented proof of personal resources and reassessed periodically. Regardless of age, inferred or actual promises, this drug may provoke delusional estimates of personal wealth and self worth. See PDR for further elaboration.

And then he drifted off, as did the approaching boredom (had he continued with the task).

—◇—

- *Chapter Eighteen* -

He dreamed he was in an air terminal. Lots of windows of course, with airplanes visible everywhere and stone walls, marble floors, escalators... but strangely there were piles of clay. Enormous mounds of brownish-maroon clumps and balls in roped-off areas, as if available for anyone to use. Some were in the process of being shaped into something by a person or persons in particular, although there didn't seem to be anyone working or shaping the mounds.

One was easily identified as the beginning of a pod of whales; another was towering upwards as though it could easily become some gigantic, two-legged creature. There were numerous tawdry items scattered throughout... small jars, pots of all sizes, animals, slabs of clay cut into profiles of men women and children... all junky... and, or, incomplete. And he saw what was obviously a man of clay, sagging over a waist-high wall of ill-formed clay logs... the man was distorted and carelessly formed too, but still retained the general shape. The surface looked to be hardened, but clumpy in texture, and the whole thing was freaky... as though there was actually a man inside (something no sculptor would ever do), but then he detected (imagined?) the eyes blink open for just the fraction of a second... and then close.

There were lots of other roped areas for clay... of various sizes... conveniently located near stairways, escalators, outside of restaurants, rest rooms and so on. But the terminal was otherwise neat and orderly. These clay areas seemed to be an accepted "normal" part of the surroundings. He grabbed up a handful of the stuff and massaged it around a bit; then looked about in amazement, wondering, "what in the world...? Clay?"

Then, snap!!! Just like that, he awoke... to the smell of smoke. He sat up, looking around the room, saw no flames, rushed downstairs trying to remember if he'd actually started a fire as planned... no, but the lights were still on and that was dumb... he had no idea how long he'd been sleeping... he looked around for a second... even opened the door to the mural room... no flames, no smoke anywhere... He relaxed just a bit but finished up quickly downstairs and bounced back up the stairs... no flames, no smoke... but only one of the three candles was burning... the other two had burned down to nothing and the last one had apparently just done so... a sniff of the glass confirmed the source of the smell as a dying wick.

And then he remembered the dream... which was vivid and in full color. Obviously his clay day, which began just that very morning was not over yet. He decided to go down, find something warm to drink and reflect on this by a fire (he would build after all).

The house heated up quickly. He sat with a dog in each hand, and Christina, the soon to be Queen Bitch, was in his lap. His chair was still the only one in the room... in the whole house come to think of it.

Cozied up by the fire, his thoughts returned to the dream: The most obvious symbol was that God created man from clay... just reached out and picked up what was readily available, already there, and came up with mankind, the most fantastic of creatures! And, for the moment, God (or What's His Name) breathing life into man was as good an answer as any; *And no doubt mankind is from, and of, the dust... in mineral content. Just add water— how poetic. What, or who else, could ultimately sustain mankind with such finesse and style? And as for humanity, how satisfying to come up with some wonderful and profitable invention or product from everyday materials at hand!*

So. No matter what we call it: an idea, a creation, a brain-child... whatever... all become entities we've created with lives of their own... inventions and projects that are sustained by our energies and imaginations. And man... created man... has continued to this day, and perhaps thanks only to the creator thereof. Again, he thought of a scripture often quoted by his mother ("... in Him we live and breathe and have our being."). *How interesting that our own little mini-creations (enterprises) come about, and are sustained in a very similar way... we hold them together with our own breath.*

At this point he had the notion (duly noted) that, *after the investment of resources, limited breath, and precious blood, our creations too may continue without us... some so perfect that little effort would be needed from our hands ever again... Such is the strength of good ideas and good men;* Methuselah came to mind, and the thought kept building; *And once we have "moved on," our ideas, though good ones, would perish unless someone else adopted them as their own and perhaps breathed the same or even more life into them... ignorance, misuse, or neglect notwithstanding.*

The room had become hot. Brown opened the front door and was practically knocked over by the dawgs escaping into the cool. He followed. Leaning against the front porch, another rollie hanging loosely in one hand and a freshly opened beer in the other... he was back on the dream scent... analyzing.

Clay. Just laying around amidst the hustle and bustle of our culture waiting for anyone who wants to... to pick it up. These piles could be ideas, plans or dreams that others have had but discarded... not just in airports... all over the planet. But why were they left available right out in the open instead of thrown out for gosh sake? Where anyone could pick up a wad? A wad or a lump... by the handfuls or the buckets... picked up by those

*who want to try their hand at someone else's ideas or creations,
or re-fashion the clay into something entirely different... their
own ideas spinning off from the discarded, or arising as original
and fresh... perhaps over months or years to come.*

*Hmmmm.... maybe some of those ideas were already
complete to one degree or another. Why, surely they were, and
available in an airport... the modern day crossroads of the
world! And if they were such good ideas... what if they were
taken to the limit? Handled by people with good work-ethics,
stick-to-it, get-it-done kind'a people... Wouldn't the resulting
creations take on identities of their own? Why, it happens every
day; Ideas and hopes manifesting in so many ways it boggles
the imagination. Dreams reaching fruition, indeed, becoming
entities rising from the earth just as man supposedly did from
nothing but clay.*

*Okay... not everyone would see potential whales in the
mounds, or other giant creatures. Instead, most wouldn't even
notice or have an opinion, while others would just consider the
piles an inconvenience to walk around (especially those little
clumps that may have "dared" to roll off the piles onto the
sidewalk, sticking to their shoes, interrupting their busy day).
If only they would pick up an interesting piece, then pinch and
fiddle with it... it just might become something worthwhile...
maybe even a blessing for all mankind.*

While having these lofty and delicious thoughts, he
tried to keep in mind that clay is, after all, considered a
lowly commodity... not ranked as highly as oil or gold by
any means, but a commodity nevertheless. In fact, clay was
the most basic of all commodities. The valley gossipers
pissing in pots not their own, was graphic enough, but
not having a "pot to piss in" would be an apt and graphic
description of ignoring or rejecting resources abundantly
available all around... And to have a cup that overflows?
Well, the cup would have to be there in the first place...

and pot or cup... both were made of clay.

Surely, the mud bath of only hours ago, qualified his continuing thoughts; *Clay holds together nicely with a consistent, cohesive texture, is sifted and refined naturally, comes together under unique chemical circumstances over eons, and is much different than mud.* And his experience just that morning confirmed as much and everyone knew that; *Mud is messy, almost useless; mostly inconvenient where man is concerned, and often the results of poor timing; occurring when water meets soil in an aggressive, abrupt and crude manner. Bricks, made with measured amounts of mud, mixed with straw and lots of sunshine have limited use. But clay, occurring naturally, is versatile and more of a direct resource or gift... from uh... What's His Name... than bricks.*

And as he grasped the scope of all this... completely immersed in a deep sky full of stars and just the sliver of a moon... all reflecting and dancing in the river, quite visible from the porch... a flood of emotion eased over him; conscious that this dream wasn't some abstraction, but a message served up just for W.M. Brown... revealing that prosperity in the marketplace also comes as a gift to those who have eyes to see it and are willing to "pick up" on the opportunity. Although real clay belongs in the hands of the potters and the sculptors who understand what it is (and can put it to use) symbolically it was much more abundant in the marketplace than he'd ever imagined; *Clay is there all around us... to be used by everyone! God is talking to Jacob through writing and he's talking to me through clay!!*

Suddenly he was struck with the awareness that even the color of the clay was significant... a deep, reddish-maroon... resembling the color of blood in a test tube; *And why didn't the clay dry out, lying out in the open like that all the time?*

The parallel was just too tightly woven to dismiss...
He tiptoed into this conclusion: *Like mankind, clay remains
in its natural state, and moist by divine providence. In the
dream it was colored with just a hint of blood as a reminder
from whence the blessing comes, and how it will be sustained.
That beautiful color of life and death underscoring the fact that
humans are like Gods and have been given the gift of creating
our dreams and desires, simply by picking up the blessings that
are wedged in all around us. Prosperity of all kinds. Enjoyment
of life, received and sustained could very well come by the gift
and grace of God... Yes. And the final result might even be
glazed and fired... fit for the highest use.*

The room cooled down. A glowing pile of embers was
all that remained of the fire, but the dogs refused to come
until the temperature was to their tastes. He cracked the
back door, leaned against the mantle, peacefully gazing
into the mysteries unraveling before him. Within five
minutes the resident canines strolled in... one by one,
as if they owned the place, and he feeling something
similar, shut everything down, including the coals in the
fireplace... for sure.

Bedtime. He cozied-up on Jacob's mattress... craned his
kinky head around for one last look into the heavens... the
dream, so rich and savory, had opened up a parallel that
stretched on into forever, and wasn't that fact reflected in
the stars? He'd had a wonderful, clay day. Miraculously
wonderful.

—◇—

He'd missed the morning sunrise but refused to
chastise himself for that... how much beauty could a
person take? And how much noise? The log trucks had
rumbled past shortly after daylight; the dogs'd heard a
prowling critter, or another dog, to bark at, and Wesley

had picked this day to demolish the rest of the old fence (yep... with the dozer), which was the final bell. He pulled the wristwatch out of his jeans; ten-fifteen. He knew of two things he had to do today... cruise Hepner's and take another soak at the springs... The dozer exhaled one last breath... Good.

The dogs were sniffing around outside, visualizing in a way that no human ever could any and all creature traffic passing through within the last five or six hours.

He took care of the morning ablutions... left the back door open, locked the front, and was outta there.

Gasoline Island was backed up to the street with hippie buses and vans tanking up for their eastward journey. Strangely dressed people of all ages trekked back and forth to the store, the outside facilities, and of course climbing around and on their vehicles checking tie-downs, tires, washing windows. Smiling, happy people. Although there were a number of dreads... quite a number of them... mingling with all the others. No one had seen the troublemaker's since the incident.

Breakfast at Hepners, to a man of less discerning palette, was good... excellent... Myron dragged the process on as long as possible; paid at Joyce's register; "What's the news?" he asked bluntly.

"News?"

"Yeah... you know... Wayne... the springs?"

"Oh, He's cooled off, you can go home now, Myron... er... Brown."

"Really?" he asked, wanting to believe her.

Carefully avoiding a second white lie, "I called Maggie, you didn't talk with her?" she asked.

But another happy person had moved up the line.

Perhaps he didn't answer or she didn't hear... Either way, W.M. Brown wasn't going home... this was his day off. But he'd best call Maggie when she got home from work.

He meandered on back to the van, fired 'er up and cut through a small graveled lane that would eventually come out onto the highway. Thank goodness, he only whacked a scrub fir-tree when Shadow popped his head from the back. "Holy Crap! Are you nuts? We could be killed with that..." but his voice trailed off... the kid looked as though he'd just escaped a dungeon. Skin, paled and wilting; hair a mess; smelling awful; eyes bloodshot and looking so disappointed to have blown his entrance... he stopped the van while the escapee scrambled around between the seats and sat down. Brown put his hand out... Shadow reached back... they clasped hands and Shadow smiled weakly; "Good to see you, man," both said in unison.

They joined the sparse westerly traffic on the highway... both windows rolled down... Shadow had lots to tell him.

Strange goings-on... lots of them, but Brownman decided it would be best to debrief at Jacob's before going on up to the springs. And though he was anxious to hear all of it, soap was the only thing he could think about. He asked the young man to "save it" 'til then.

After tactfully persuading Shadow to; "get your butt in there and start scrubbing while I douse your clothes with lots of hot water..." it was one-thirty. The day was in full sun and sweltering. If it was this hot here by the river, Maggie would be roasting in the apartment and once home from work, wouldn't stay there long. More than likely she and Julie would go swimming at one of several riverside parks... where this very same water would be significantly warmer. The idea of a note in a bottle crossed his mind; *What a crap shoot that would be...*

one in a million odds she'd find it, and one in two million it would actually make it fifty miles down river without breaking or lodging somewhere. But the romantic aspect was appealing enough for him to consider what he would write:

Maggie,

> *I don't know if there are such things, but if you get this note it will be a miracle. But if I hadn't smacked into the Trailmaster tower, where would I be today? Maybe everything is miraculous, and we're just used to it being that way... I could almost believe anything right now, and yet I wonder if I know anything at all. I'm afraid that believing in anything one hundred percent might set me up for missing the real thing... I want to stay miraculous. You, Julie and Cooper enjoy your swim and know that I consider you to be miracles too.*

Love, Brown

"Shadow, I'll be back in half an hour, buddy... your clothes are hangin' on a branch in the back yard."

That was good enough for Shadow, but Brownman made it even more inviting... "There's beer in the fridge and I fried some potatoes... fry a coupla' eggs. They're on the counter... Just get some rest, okay? We'll talk soon's I get back."

-◇-

Florence Wheaton... a k a, Mother, and who cares what else? was the thought crossing through his mind (for the first time in his life). Today she was different... more alive than he'd remembered, with an unmistakable look of concern that threatened his composure; "Two days later?

You show up two days later after tellin' me not to worry... you'd be back in a matter of hours?"

So the first of several apologies were given and maybe those were more sincere than any she could remember. "Son, Maggie is really worried, and you need to call her."

"That's... one of the reasons I'm here... Where's the phone?"

"Same place it always is... where you're not looking."

"Well, where ain't I looking?"

She pulled it from the top of the TV... handed it off... shook her head good naturedly, and headed for her garden; "You will be staying for dinner..." she informed him as she crunched along the pea-graveled walkway.

Yeah, maybe I will, he agreed silently, thinking that didn't sound bad at all; *That woman can cook, and she's not bad company either.*

-◇-

Maggie picked up the phone on the first ring and; "It's me," said Brown.

"Where are you?"

What? Is that all? How 'bout something like ... uh... uhmmmm.... sigh... well, what'd he expect? "I'm at Mother's."

"Come home."

Okay. Well, no.... of course he didn't say that, he didn't say anything... waited for her to draw her own conclusion and maybe show for once that she could think for both of them? *Uh... no. She'd been doing that for years.*

Should she say she was upset with him? *No. She's smarter than that; considerate and well mannered most of the time*... So, instead, he said; "I can't do that right now, but I would like to see you, how've you been?"

"What? How's your wife of twenty-five years... you moron?"

"I know, I know... (but actually he didn't)... look, I want to talk to you... can we just talk?"

"Are you on that stupid car phone, Brown?"

"No... " he said, and began to explain that he still couldn't get a signal, was at his mother's, and...

But she cut him off; "Well if you want to talk to me, you're gonna have to do it here."

"Then, that may be a while..."

"Brown, I know what you're up to. Joyce told me everything. I know things you don't know... in fact I talked to her ten minutes ago... said you'd been in the store... and she didn't think you believed what she told you. And it looks like she was right."

Brown emitted an audible hiss, ready to respond, but Maggie preempted his comments; "The hot springs thing is over, the hippies are headed out for the rest of the summer. Wayne's gonna cool off... school starts in a couple weeks, tourist season's tapering off... he'll wish he had 'em back, once the rains start... for the money... or at least to make life interesting up there."

That wasn't cuttin' it with Brown... "Well, uh, I'll call you back in a little bit. I just wanna confirm..." but he stopped... not sure what he wanted to confirm... "...and Mother's making me stay for dinner..." he added not too persuasively.

"Making you?"

"I want to stay for dinner... is that better?" He replied,

just a bit sarcastically.

Maggie backed off... "Call me when you're done with dinner. I'm getting out of this apartment... Julie's coming by, we're taking Coop' to the park over by the deltas."

He knew exactly where she meant... he'd been teaching Cooper how to fish there, off and on all summer, "Roger-you, on that..." he said with just the slightest hope that she'd read between the lines.

"What?"

"Never mind... over and out."

Florence knew how to cook. Myron (confident in at least this one fact) accepted her coercive invitation; adding that he'd like to bring a friend.

Thinking he meant girl friend, she raised her hackles. They locked horns momentarily. Florence pointed out that "bringing a friend" could easily have meant, a woman.

Brown very quickly backed down, hoping to cut her off before "her next logical thought" was linked to an endless "train of thought" as she so often did. No sir! Today was his day off... he didn't want to get on that train... certain he'd ridden it before. And that look in her eye–she was about to pour on the steam.

He zipped on back up the highway; anxious to find Shadow, but slowed to almost a crawl when that train came rushing through his mind anyway, express and ripping right along with so few cars he could barely count them. In less time than it would have taken to get the old van back up to normal speed that baby had chugged right on through. The cars flashed by like a filmstrip; The first scene was him with his mom in the kitchen; he said something... something... but he couldn't quite make it out... the next scene was so real he could smell the plate of cookies in her hand while the clikity-clik of hardened-steel wheels on bright silver rails beat out the cadence in his mind; She was smiling and speaking (clikity) responding to what he'd said (clak clak): "Son, those were your words, not mine. The answer to that question is right under our noses... she smiles, nibbles at a cookie... not so much what we put in, but what comes out... words... and how we use them. And when! Why, there's no end to how many actual words have been launched from here (she pointed to his mouth) much less from all of humanity." The camera panned her face; she twinkled and held a cookie out toward him... (The van slowed to a crawl). Mother's cookies! He licked his lips. The next camera angle clikty-clikity-clikity... clik-clik... brought him back just in time for the wrap up; "...plentiful than stars... yet rarely are the right words spoken. There's nothing more pleasing than the right words at the right time... spoken into or about someone's life. Words paint pictures, build castles, break hearts, heal bodies and wound spirits. Life is about words, son. And words are life... or death..." and with a final clikity... clik-clik... the train was out of sight, and the van was already back up to speed.

Myron shook his head... rubbed his skull... scratched it wondering; *Did I just have a vision?* Jacob's place popped up around the next curve and he was *onto other things... thing... uh... Shadow.*

He looked upstairs for him, peeked out at the back porch, went back into the front room and then had to chuckle... There he was. Like a magician, the trickster had played on the most obvious, "concealing" himself in plain sight on a pallet in front of the fireplace, wearing cutoffs and sound asleep, while Norman watched over him in characteristic nobility.

Tired as the kid must've been, Brownie felt it necessary to wake him, then chugged a beer while listening to the report on all that had been learned.

Shadow was glad to get it out. No. It wasn't over at all; "The thing's happening tomorrow at three o'clock for sure..." The house behind the store had been; "...crawling with loggers... in and out all the time." He'd managed to listen beneath one window or another; "but just couldn't hear anything... not really... only when they'd go in and out of the house..." catching bits and pieces of their conversations, but essentially figured that; "Wayne's the only one know's the whole plan." All the rest of them, about eight in all; "...kept talking in code of some kind... n' saying; 'I've only got section so and so,' or 'Stop right there; I don't need to know nothing elst...' Either that, or saying; 'Come on, you can tell me... hell, we been friends forever...' or complaining to each other how stupid it is that nobody could trust nobody... Yeah, saying things like that..."

Brown was amazed at how thorough the kid had been and wondered if he'd ever said so much at one time in his life.

Shadow flopped onto the picnic bench. Wrapped his report up with; "Man, Wayne was whizzing in and out all day long and into the night, in that funky old truck."

With sincere thanks and praise for a great job, Brownman popped another beer and swigged it while giving Shadow time to get used to the idea of going to Florence's house for dinner... and maybe they'd go up to the springs after.

—◇—

Myron, acted as tour guide around Flo's property,

considerate of the young "secret agent's" need for rest and maybe to help keep him awake. The chicken pen, vegetable garden, and river view, being the visual highlights, while the anticipated smells from the kitchen worked to a mighty finish.

The applause would be forthcoming and entirely sincere. Even though Brown had sat through hundreds of such performances and had become an aficionado, the pleasure of bringing a friend to such enjoyment.... Well....

Dinner was southern cooking, if not at it's best... close enough. Fried chicken, buttermilk battered ; Green beans cooked with ham-hock, garlic and onions; mashed potatoes, "just eat 'em;" a plate of sliced tomatoes and green onions sitting right next to a pone of corn bread... with a crispy, buttery crust... for "anybody that knows how to add two n' two." And iced tea, (presweetened of course) "sitttin' pretty in a pitcher with yellow daisies, dripping wet with condensation..." or, "with the evenin' dew... dependin' on how you look at it..."

Myron's concern for Shadow's ability to fit in was needless. His mom's talents were more than enough and masterfully arranged for a respectable portion of every dish to be taken to its logical destination.

Once the peach cobbler made its final encore, Shadow found great comfort on the couch in front of the television—which might as well have been blank.

Wisely, Flo, had not pried in the least, but both she and her son were aware that a conversation was imminent. So, once they were on the porch with their coffee, Brown willingly opened up about everything: Starting with the Airlines proposal to turn him into a Negro; his disappointment with Maggie not understanding or supportive; Carlos' stupid refusal to sell the barbecue recipe to Palmie (omitting his own shady attempt to close that deal... regardless); his fascination with Jacob (no mention of the marijuana); Wayne's nutty proposal and apparent intentions... right on up to the current briefing from Shadow.

Some of this, Florence, was partially aware of, and some of it not... the difficulty for her was the usual... not interrupting. Brown expected it, and had looked at her pleadingly several times and was impressed with her patience... all in all.

Her take on the Maggie thing was, not to worry, it would all iron out. Job dissatisfaction or not, money isn't everything, and a practical woman like Maggie wouldn't miss that fact.

That hippie man, seemed to be a pretty nice person, but she'd only ever seen him naked.

Wayne and Joyce were another matter entirely. Joyce had confirmed the rumor that Myron was upriver more than usual and today when she'd called for the second time, hadn't beat around the bush about "...steering Myron in another direction..." assuring Flo that the Forest Service had gotten involved and were taking care of it.

Shadow's sleuthing was impressive, but she found it hard to understand the depth to which her son had involved himself. Brownie waited patiently for her while she worked through the obvious implications and alternatives: The police, the dangers, the tourism, the negative publicity... and finally what might happen to the Hepner's if somebody really did get hurt... or killed... not to mention the victims. And him spending the night away from home... "What? Twice already? No. You'd better get on back down to Maggie, son; it looks to me like you've done all you can..."

They sat watching the late afternoon sunlight filtering through the fir trees... the chickens were still out, but would soon go to the pen of their own accord. And as always, before full darkness arrived, Flo, would close the gate. Brown didn't have the heart to ask where the old Rhode Island Red hen might be... speaking of victims.

"I'm not going 'til this is over, mother." There was no way he could describe the magnitude of all that he'd experienced in the last week... the ins and outs... the personal revelations about so many things. But made an effort: Somewhat bravely, following what looked like a vague path through familiar territory; other times by instinct only... he expressed himself as best he could to whom he now realized was his closest friend.

To return to his world of the last five or six years, with or without Maggie, would be a loss of what he considered positive momentum... things were rolling... he was happier.... So much happier... and realized that he'd almost forgotten what it felt like to be running his own life.

Like an explorer, this new land (yet old and familiar) unfolded before his eyes, heart, and mind; conscious of feeling almost like a man... for the first time... although he was well into his forties

Florence was a bit surprised to see this new stage of maturity appear on his face. She'd enjoyed similar times as her children grew up before her, somehow becoming new little persons... not specific changes... but truly new levels of awareness showed on their faces seemingly overnight. Myron's jaw was more firmly set, his brow more serious, and there seemed to be a twinkle of wisdom in his eyes she'd not seen before.

They sat there a moment while the clouds parted just a little further on the horizon. The colors that washed onto the clouds were the same as ever, but someone had replaced the canvas... just now... and had painted with tints of orange, deep rose and gentle pink in a way neither of them had ever seen. Florence, could almost taste the imminent and glorious sunset.

Myron had a far away look. Something his mother said, had not gone unnoticed. The Forest Service? He wasn't buying it. Those guys were far too scared and politically correct to make a move without orders from way, way high up the ladder. No sir. They'd done all they were going to do... of that he was certain.

He'd hoped to describe his wonderful dream and the events of the day that led up to it: about Arnie and Annie's farm; about Jake's Christianity... pseudo or otherwise; most of all, he just wanted to put his head on her lap and cry... for a long, long time. But the timing was wrong... Shadow pushed open the screen door, looking lost, trying to get his bearings...

Flo, insisted on packing up the leftovers for them. Myron had not missed the worried look in her eyes. The hugs were sincere. His final words were from the driver's window; "Will you call Maggie for me, Mother?"

"And say what?"

But the van was already bouncing up the lane.

—◇—

Both windows were closed on the drive upriver. The temperature had already dropped several degrees in the past twenty minutes.

The moon had begun the waning phase; creeping up behind the hills... misshapen, as it framed and tugged upon the earth's silhouetted horizon for the billionth time... ascending into the heavens.

Hours for using the hot springs were posted in all parking areas: Open Sunrise to Sunset. And on the sign at the beginning of the trail, the specific: No Foot Traffic After Hours.

That was plain enough. Brownman turned around and cruised slowly past Hippie Hollow... still lots of buses... hopefully most, if not all, would be gone the following morning.

He recalled with affection, the hippie buses of his era, drawing an obvious contrast between them and the bus-conversions of the seventies. He told Shadow how many of those were works of art, crafted to express a longing and even an optimism for what might be. Built by young men and women who had learned various skills from their pre-drug, productive lives and imported into their cultural revolution. Their buses made romantic, symbolic statements, while these run-down contraptions were doomed to rust... as were the spray-can painted slogans and political jargon written on the sides. And, from the same cans... occasional, haphazardly depicted suns, swirls and rainbows dashed with no artistic merit whatsoever, confirming the one positive thing that could be said... they were colorful. Their owners, many of them getting stoned since grade-school, had never learned the first thing about work... Theirs was an even greater emptiness without the satisfaction of personal accomplishment, or a job well done. They floated in an undefined, vague direction, content to celebrate their lives away, while deluding themselves that they actually had purpose.

All was well at Jake's house... the dogs enjoyed the chicken bones which Myron's mom had explained (long ago) was just fine for larger dogs as long as the spur on the leg bone was removed... it had a tendency to detach, along with the cartilage at the larger end, creating a potential problem if the slender spur went toward the wind pipe and the rest toward the esophagus... all un-chewed of course; *Dawgs... carnivores... nature... yup,* it made sense.

The day had practically vanished, yet it seemed as though much had gone on. *Sequence of event should never be measured against time... neither in importance nor intensity.*

Brownman had no trouble staking out his bed. Shadow had already affirmed his choice and was soon fast asleep in front of the fireplace. He felt a twinge of jealousy though... the dogs were curled up all around the kid... maybe they were comforting him in some primitive way... He looked for all the world like a boy who was being raised by wolves.

The only beer left would be savored in sips, and one last piece of chicken was respectfully escorted up to his (Jake's) bed... in case he woke up hungry in the middle of the night.

—◇—

Joyce's talk with Wayne had gone something like this: "You realize that if you do something crazy you'll wreck more than those springs don't you?"

"Nobody's gonna get hurt, Joyce, I'm goin' in at night... nobody's allowed at night."

"So you can see in the dark? How do you know everybody's outta there... soon's they see your light they'll be up on that hillside... waiting for you to leave... "

She had a good point... kept pressing... "We get lots of business cause of them springs."

True.

"And at the very least, Eisenhower, you'll be in jail before the smoke clears."

He hated it when she called him that... just like a woman to remember every word that comes out of a man's mouth and use it against him. Besides, she meant to say Einstein. And it wasn't everybody that could say they'd worked with him! Just because he mentioned (and it was fact) that he'd helped Einstein with one of his projects... she'd rubbed it in... accusing him of hoity-toity any time he took a stand about something she obviously knew not a thing about. And what was so punishing to him, is that she could never get the name right... ever. Well, this had been going on for years.

When as a kid... he'd moved some crates with Einstein's name on them into a freight car, he was excited about it. And maybe he was hoping some of the man's luck or brains might rub off on him. He'd told Joyce about it the very same day... they'd only been married a couple months... why, hell, she'd been excited too.

What had been a good day then, had turned out to be a sad one now. It had been a mistake, him saying; "Just think I helped Einstein; I don't know what with, but I did..." Shit! Forty years ago... He'd never heard the last of it and it had become a matter of self-respect; "Einstein, not Eisenhower, Joyce;" he corrected her every time now.

"Whatever..."

Damn! and she always said that! "Cain't you see? What they've done to us?"

"Not all of "em... they ain't. And don't say, "us;"

it's your pride, not mine. All I have to do is write the check, Wayne; cleaning up after people is part of the hospitality industry." He hated that too... talk about hoity-toity.

The other pressure she could put on him he knew right well... and he sure didn't want to go that far. He was a man who liked his comforts and predicting them at the end of the day was one of the things that kept him going, "So, what do you suggest, Florence Nightingale?"

With that, she outlined something that he had to admit would put the fear of God into 'em... and maybe he wouldn't go to jail (not that he doubted the power of a good attorney and his own good name).

So, he'd been preparing for the last week, almost, and had gone to bed Thursday night (with his wife by his side), reasonably sure that it would work. He'd done something General Eisenhower would be pleased with. None of the men he'd recruited knew the whole thing. All they had was individual notes, and were forbidden to compare them. He would put all the pieces together for them tomorrow. From that point on nobody would be out of his sight... and besides... he'd made it perfectly clear; "I'm telling you right now, just one of you blabbing your mouth'n the plan won't work. And if the plan works... n'one of you tell's... we'll all be payin'." He had given them a chance to "back out'n call it good... or put in... n'call it better."

They all put in. All had, one way or another been offended (or perceived it that way) by the danged hippies more than once. And it truly sounded like one hell of a good time. Wayne'd promised them as much, and they'd all believed him... He was Wayne Hepner, now, wasn't he?

—◇—

Brown woke up with the chickens... No. He woke up with one chicken leg on the pillow beside him... and he didn't even blink. Just made a mental note of the diminishing resource, put the chicken in his shirt pocket and checked the weather. Perfect... another August day.

He went to the John, and after a good toothbrushing, sat where he did his best thinking, staring at the empty toilet paper roll. Maggie could talk him into anything... and out of anything. For that reason alone, it had been good to stay apart. But with the awareness that she actually could... really could... talk him into going back to the Airlines–he should burn that bridge once and for all. It was only six-thirty a.m., he could be at the Terminal by eight easily.

Expecting to find Shadow on the pallet had been presumptuous... he was nowhere to be found. He called out several times and gave the kid fair warning... nothing. He scribbled a note saying that he would be back before eleven, and signed it, Myron... but than caught it, signed off with Brownman, and headed out.

The employee parking lot was at an inconvenient distance for a guy with just one thing to say... He pulled right up to the passenger loading and unloading zone... nodded at Griffith (who never had liked him for some reason) and didn't look back. Once inside, he bounced down the stairs to the employees lounge and dressing rooms. Emptied the contents of his locker into a shopping bag brought from the van. Ten minutes later he stood outside the office of personnel... He'd been in this area a few times, of course, but must have been unconscious not to notice how ugly.

The tile wainscoting was in weird colors: Queasy

metallic swirls and thin, spiky looking things crisscrossing in a matrix effect; the walls had various paintings of stuff that he didn't understand at all... in colors that were shocking... bold and slashing; no objects, just colors... panel after panel; The door of the office looked more like a shower door than an actual shower door... all glass, translucent and bubbly; big and little circles with streaks or waves of sandblasted areas running mostly vertical. Maybe representing flight, but it reminded him of prop-wash from an old biplane, in dire need of a tune-up.

Everything in the area looked sterile and dehumanizing. When he pushed into the office it was easy to imagine that he'd just entered a bee-hive. The reception counter was affixed atop honeycombed columns of stainless or aluminum, connected with horizontal copper strips weaving in and out of one another. The floor was the same tile as in the hallway... He didn't know if he was feeling seasick because of all the weirdness, or nervous about what he was about to do. Fortunately he could hold his composure by focusing on the fact that there really were planes launching off the distant runways. Several others had their noses right up against the smoky plate glass windows, wondering; "What goes on in there?"

There were cubicles and offices; all apparently situated to take advantage of the view. A carpeted path ran throughout in a fibrous labyrinth connecting them all... the pattern was simply incomprehensible, but had combined with the entire area masterfully; stating in no uncertain terms, "There's nothing to look at here... get back to work..." if you can find your desk.

Well, time to ring the little bell on the counter. Somehow, Ms. Fisher, the personnel manager, was able to spot him from some secreted observation point. And she was on it! The receptionist hadn't arrived yet... no problem. As manager she tried to ignore the clothing her "token" supervisor (W.M. Brown) had chosen. And the scruffy beard? that would have to go! She simply could not believe the shopping bag he'd placed on the counter *or* the smells emanating therefrom. Even so, she did produce a rigid smile, inviting him back to her office, "Well, mister Brown... looks as though you're feeling better?"

"Not too bad..."

"We have your paperwork from the psyche evaluation, and the new employment form, ready for you to sign..." The smile was still there, but looking actually as though she were posing for a dental x-ray.

Brown was very curious about the psyche evaluation; "How'd I do on the psyche part?"

"Oh, just fine...."

"May I see it?"

"Oh no... that won't be necessary... our policy is..."

"What if I insist? I do insist... "

"I don't think so..." she pulled the file toward her slightly.

"I think so!" Mister Brown said, and snatched it from her desk... swiveled around with his back to her and began rifling the pages... it was easy to detect the familiar scrawl of "Doctor" Marshal.

Ms. Fisher had come around from behind the desk while Brown instinctively responded by scooting the swivel chair on into the corner of the small room–face to the wall like a bad schoolboy. She'd have to knock the flimsy wall panels down or dislodge him from the chair to get to the file.

Oh, what a treat! The doctor had poured his heart into this one... in big letters. "Mister Brown: Negro. Heart and soul." A disturbed signature squiggled across the page erratically... ending with what could have been a blob or a leaking pen; or even a Rorschach ink blotch... a confused little rabbit came to mind.

Mister Brown had by now–using the chair like a cattle guard–worked his way toward the door; left the chair as a blockade... but ineffectively, because Ms. Fisher hoofed right on through. And like bacteria in a petri dish, the two feinted and dodged along the glass windows (under the scientific gaze of the jet aircraft), twisting past cubicles, and ignoring completely, the suggested path of the insane carpet.

His shopping bag... a pigpen in a palace... slouched on the silky, cherry-wood counter top. He dropped the file into the slop.

Ms. Fisher's facial expression alternated between stupid smiles and snarls, until at last, convinced that this brute really was taking the file... retreated slightly, shouting, "Security! Security...."

"I quit! See you in court, sister!"

This whole thing had taken less than thirty minutes... he sprinted to the van and pushed Griffith aside (currently in the act of putting a citation under the van's windshield). The van fired right up. He tossed the shopping bag with the file in it onto the passenger seat, and cautiously moved out of the busy passenger zone.

Only gradually did he realize what had occurred. He was overjoyed... and felt like a millionaire.

—◇—

- Chapter Nineteen -

William Myron Brown pulled right up into the front yard, squeezing past the big, deep-cobalt-blue, four-door Lincoln in the driveway. Carl loved that car, and so did Brownie, but he'd always told him whitewalls would make all the difference. Still would.

It was only nine-thirty, but Carl was tinkering in the garage... Three little boys, bare-chested and bare-footed, wearing shorts, were standing near the Tower, looking it over. Brownie was almost positive he'd seen them there before... more than once... oh, well, he admired it every time he got near it too. He tossed a wave at them but they were too deeply absorbed.

Carl pretended he didn't even know Brownie was there; Brownie knew different. The interior of the windowless garage was in deep shadow... gradually the stuff hanging from the walls and rafters made more and more sense. The wooden boxes of metal parts and assorted doodads on the bottom shelves, poking out from beneath the workbenches, stretching along the walls into subterranean darkness... would never make sense to anyone but Carl.

"Hold this B.B..." A piece of iron tubing levitated around in the gloom... while Carl, overly attentive to whatever... still hadn't looked at him.

Ahhhh, it was the smoker unit; he'd been working on that thing for the last week. Now, he was bent over it, still wagging the tube for Brown to; take it...

So whatever happened to please? He ignored it.

Another insistent wag....

Nope...

Carlos stood; "Okay... brother Brownie, where you been?"

"How you been Carlos" Brownie cooed in return, holding his hand out.

Nope. "You is one half-assed friend, Brownie Brown."

"You know I need money, Carlos, you blew that whole thing... you're the other half of that ass..." Surely, both paused for a second imagining what that ass might look like: two-toned maybe; depending on how you sliced it.

Carlos abandoned the visual as quickly as possible; "Not quite..."

"You mean I did? I blew it? Hey, I was going to cut you in, you know? Palmie thought the recipe was mine anyway..."

"Well, I know once again you done landed on your feet like a cat throwed up in the air."

"Palmie called?"

"Better'n that... A.B. called."

Carlos continued. Explaining that Palmie actually wanted to call Brown after the missed appointment at Hepner's, but had called A.B.; "Ah've... lost his cellulah numbah. You know? The leadah... thet lyht-skinned Negro's numbah?" and in the process had mentioned the Trailmaster Tower; "Thayat's an unbuhlievable work of true Geenyus, A.B."

Brownie accepted the metal tube, Carl let his end go, and walked outside for another look at the Tower. Brownie followed... still carrying the tube.

Carl was standing a bit more erect than usual; "I started to give him your car phone, but he wanted to see dis Trailmasser for his se'f... He likes it, B.B.... really likes it... said not to, under any circumstances, give our recipeep to Mister Palmie."

B.B., took note of the fact that Carlos used the word, "our." Lights began to come on in all sorts of long darkened regions of his mind, "Then what'd he say?"

"Didn't say nuthin' elst'... Onct' A.B. Jordan speaks, everybody bends over, shuts up and listens."

"So what're we gonna do?"

"Listen, tha's what."

"Say... wha'd chu'do wid all dem groceries? Take 'em back?"

"Like you said I should..." (as though he did everything his old friend told him to do).

Carlos wasn't quite that stupid; "Even the meats? They's a lotta' good barbecuin' n' smokin' in that haul."

Brownie reverted to his crafty side; "I left you all the pastries and breads... some produce... " lies of omission were fair-game in their peculiar relationship.

"Yeah, I wonder who you left them pastries for, pardner..."

They were off and running again; both feelin' the familiar warmth and strength of their barbed friendship.

"You talk to Maggie lately" Carl asked, deeply serious.

"Yep, we got it ironed out..."

"Tha's good... tha's good...."

The time was ten thirty-eight... Brown wanted to dig further into certain potentials... but had no more time; "Well, I'm listenin' too, pardner," he offered.

"Mmmmm hmmmmm... Tha's good... tha's good."

Carl's mind was roaming the Trailmaster's form... picking out the perfect location for the "smoker" add-on. No doubt there'd have to be some sort of dumb-waiter to raise it well above anybody's head... "and so's to shoot them irresistible 'romas out d'ere... mmmm hmmmm."

—◇—

Brown made a beeline for Hepner's... dusted right past his mom's place... checked around for Shadow at Jake's... not there.

Next, in the parking lot at eleven forty-five. Sat there for a while, no Wayne... no action at the logger guy's place either.

Joyce was obviously not pleased to see him... She abruptly came from behind the checkout counter and said, "Well... come on then;" pushed through the swinging doors leading to the back room.

She had no qualms about telling Myron to stay away from the hot springs, assuring him... "Nobody's gonna get hurt. The Forest Service's got it handled."

"Joyce, this is me you're talking to..." but what she was beginning to pick up was that, "me," was a man she might not be acquainted with after all. There was a strength about him that she'd never noticed... less tense, maybe.

Myron continued... picked it up where they'd left off earlier; "So, Wayne's working with the Forest Service now? And the eight or more loggers he's in cahoots with, have had career changes too?"

That was enough. Joyce had no reply; shook her head dismally and headed back for the cash register... "All I can tell you is nobody's gonna get hurt... we're making sure of that."

"We?" He called after her...

"Wayne..." she replied... to everybody in the store... just before the swinging doors wobbled shut behind her.

Brown followed, and as he passed the register, Joyce's word's; "Stay out of it, Myron!" found no purchase.

However, "Who in the hell is, Myron?" seemed to resound loudly, clinging to the very gates of heaven, even though Brownie had merely muttered them.

—◇—

A slight breeze, as old as enmity itself, picked up dust and candy wrappers in the graveled parking area and sent them scuttling out across the blacktop toward the blue waters of the lake. A noisy tanker truck rolled in next to an old school bus. A green crummy, crunched into the parking area right behind them. Eight men, all dressed in white body-suits and respirators, got out and grabbed their equipment from the rear: Backpack chemical sprayers, industrial strength weed-eaters (known as brush-cutters), a chainsaw, a backpack blower, and one leather-handled canvas satchel. A faded-blue pickup truck skidded in, bumping across the gravel.

On their way up, the guys in the pickup, having noticed more buses than expected at Hippie Hollow (a quarter mile from the springs) had made a daring and unscheduled stop. With expert skill, a dead snag, six feet in diameter was felled across the driveway. Escape was impossible. No need to invite more trouble. Thank you very much, wildlife habitat tree!

Aside from the pathetic bus, and the men with a mission, the only other vehicle in the first parking lot was a white van, whose owner had left just moments before the loggers arrived. He, like every living thing within a mile, had heard the noise of the aging, red tanker pull into the lot, and now stood in the trees just off the main trail watching the scene below with curiosity. The men piling out were familiar in form, if not in feature.

He had already taken serious note of the numerous hippie-buses still there as he drove past Hippie Hollow. The three men in the cab of the tanker had no inkling of such observations as Brown had the night before... about bus conversions, and comparisons of mood and spirit of their owners. Neither did the men now in the parking lot: None had ever been within a million miles of drug use or experimentation. They were mystified and estranged from even the thought of getting high on dope. Who needed it? Counterfeits. Bogus naturalists looking for a quick way to get in touch with what loggers had had all their lives.

Brownie squatted on a large boulder, watching with greater interest. There were sawhorses blocking all parking in the upper lot and a few were being placed at this one. Official, international-orange signs were being placed strategically: Closed for Maintenance.

He had no plan whatsoever... just hoped to dissuade Wayne by talking. The unfolding of the drama temporarily stopped him. Maybe they weren't gonna hurt anybody... how could they in those outfits?

Magnetic rubber signs on the tanker's doors said, U.S. Forest Service, and looked authentic. A closer inspection would reveal also that the labels inside the respirators; the patches on the "employee's" white disaster recovery suits, and most of the equipment in the parking lot, also had the Forest Service label. The word, Poison, was written in respectable, bold, white letters on the sides and back of the tanker truck's rusting cargo tank, although the validity thereof–anybody with half a brain would doubt.

And the same for the men in the tanker truck, all three had rubber respirators covering their mouths and noses. When they spoke, their voices sounded a lot like muffled Darth Vaders.

"Vis ib icht, I gubess... " one was (almost) heard to say.

The driver of the tanker stayed put, but Dorman and Wayne got busy with the black hose (standard equipment) reeled up on the back. A sleepy face looked out from the hippie bus' rear window; "Less strbp hrrre," Wayne said, pointing his hose nozzle at the blackberry bushes directly beside the bus.

Dorman nodded and proceeded.

White, cloudy liquid spewed out onto the bushes. A pair of sleepy eyes in the bus opened wide. Dorman, aware that he was being watched, turned around and waved at the young hippie, carelessly dousing one of the buses back panels. Horrified, the kid leaped off his bunk bed and ran toward the front door. Wayne had already put on his backpack pump-sprayer, and walked over to the opening door of the bus. Two authentic black and red canisters of bug-spray attached with duct tape to his forearms looked frightful. The labels said: Wasp and Hornet killer–deadly at twenty feet.

"Yuuu'd bttter..." he garbled... purposely allowing his sprayer to dribble onto the bus steps.

"What?"

At the top of his voice, which was almost as loud as an insect's, he said it again; "Muuv this buiss ottta hereb"

"What?"

The heat of the moment and the increasing heat of his de-con suit added up to one, hot reaction: Dorman lifted the mask and shouted; "Get the hell out of here, you little piss-ant!!" He emphasized this with a squirt right into the kids face, who, with an ear-splitting yell, bolted past Wayne, bounded across the highway and jumped into the lake, twenty five feet below, rubbing his face wildly. One of the weed whackers went chopping after him, plastic propeller blades flying, but Dorman signaled him back up the trail, toward the hot springs; "What th' hell you gonna do Ed? Jump in there with him?"

All the gasoline powered contraptions were running and revving as the ominous exterminators advanced up the trail single file or two abreast; randomly cutting and spraying the foliage lining the foot-worn trail. Hardly anyone paid attention to the fact that the wind had picked up a bit, and massive dark thunderheads gathered above.

By bumping his elbow against a canvas bag, cleverly attached to a leaf blower, one "technician" was able to dump white flour into the proper air outlet, sending a smokescreen of "chemicals" billowing out in a cloud of fake toxicity.

Brownie, sneaking along from tree to tree, began to get the picture... couldn't resist an audible chuckle. He'd seen the multiple empty milk cartons strewn across the normally litter-free, gravel lane behind Hepner's store. The men from the pickup had regular old cow's milk in their backpack sprayers! Their powerless spray was a bluff to run the hippies off.

The crew paraded menacingly around the springs' pools, chock-full of determined naked men and women. The look on their faces made it quite obvious that they, pre-informed, were there to protest and resist the loggers. However, none had anticipated the weapons that were coming at them. First they huddled together. One skinny man paddled forth to the front, rivulets of water ran from his heavy beard when he stood erect to speak; "We are here to stay, man... "

His speech was cut short by Wayne who lifted his mask and said, loud and clear, "Stay then..." His arm went up and down on the pump handle shooting a skinny stream of milky substance into the pool. Dorman and Mark followed suit. Whining sounds could be heard as stouthearted protesters laid their lives down sacrificially for their cause. Another yelp was heard up on the steep hillside.

Brownie, while ducking behind yet another tree had just collided with what he first thought was the mossy, squishy trunk of the tree. Squishy? The thing that hit the ground momentarily and sprang back up had two eyes, and skin covered with red, green and black patches in eerie patterns. And except for a loincloth, it was totally naked... "Yuk!" Brown's involuntary yelp, with a simultaneous, instinctive balling of his fist and a raring back to take a punch, sent the thing shuffling out into the clearing to emit a shrill, alien whistle.

Suddenly the whole forest was full of them. Coming out from behind rhododendrons, rising up from behind clumps of ferns, and from underneath piles of moss. They weren't all males, either. Some had female breasts swaying and jiggling back and forth with every movement, others had little nubbins, that might have been mistaken for men's chests had they not been much smaller in overall stature than the male forms.

But who had time to sex them, and who cared anyway? With yet another yelp, Brownie ran down the hill to his people. The ones with clothes on!

Wayne recognized him immediately, and hollered; "Hold your squirts, he's one of ours." The pump handles slowed for only a second and then resumed, moving up and down slowly; a steady stream of milk spewed out into the pools. So far, no one had sprayed any directly onto hippie body parts. Wesley adjusted his sprayer from stream to mist, and with a twinkle in his eyes, moved slightly upwind. That was effective. Even though it was milk, imagination goes a long way... eyes began to smart from the burning-hot "pesticide." Except for a few determined faces still in the pool's center... hips, thighs, naked buttocks, and shoulder blades began to line the pool's edge... accompanied with angry exclamations of protest, as hearty resolution gave way to self-preservation.

Increased noise and motion from the hillside provoked a staring, open-mouthed reaction as the logger's watched weirdly painted and creepy, moss-covered, dreadlocked men and women advance slowly down. Leaves, pods, and moss hung in strings attached to arms, legs and waists. Wreaths of the same, mixed with glass beads and other strange jewelry, were worn around heads in bizarre, otherworldly fashion.

For now, the loggers had ceased revving their equipment. The gas powered engines idled with an erratic; putt-putt-putt. The sound of their own air hissing from Darth Vader respirators provided sound effects to the eerie scene that only they could hear. Weird! A distant thunderclap momentarily caused everyone to look up at the black sky. Lightning flashed in the distance.

A few hippies (stark-naked) had crowded around the small gurgle of warm water spilling from the hillside into the spring, frantically splashing and rubbing it onto their bodies, hoping to remove toxins with uncontaminated water... In the lower pool, several had begun to climb out, heading for the changing shed.

One of the leaf-blower guys revved his engine and bumped the attached bag of flour, sending a cloud threateningly up the hill toward the freaks of nature; dangled the respirator below his chin and said with a growl; "Come on down, Wackos, and get dusted, or turn around right now, while you still kennn..."

As if in answer, a rhythmic, bongo drumbeat began. Another display of lightning flashed across the hillside, and a drummer picked up on the drama of the moment, exploding into an increased intensity of slaps and thuds... others, joined in, one by one. Silhouetted in the fading light... amongst the obelisks of their gods (darkened tree trunks)... Dreadlocks swayed and twirled. Thunder shook the ground while lightning bounced around the valley and hillsides like manic searchlights on steroids.

Chainsaw Guy (alias Shotgun Man) had had enough; a tale-tale trickle of chew oozed out from under his respirator, traling on down his jaw and neck towards parts unknown. He waved the McCulloch up into the air, walked menacingly toward the first drummer and revved the engine. The dancing dreadlocks paid no attention. They were caught up in their own theatrical spectacle, in a setting like none other in the world. Leaping and twirling as if their gods had intervened—and they were invincible! Either the drummer hadn't noticed, or was totally ignoring Shotgun Man's threatening chainsaw... who stepped right up and slit the bongo in half, from the stretched leather top, down to the drummer's feet. The thunder rolled on, but the missing drumbeat was enough to stop the dancing.

A downhill charge from the Naked Brigade, was inevitable anyway. The loggers all revved their equipment dramatically, but to no avail. Chainsaw man had no heart to cut anyone, nor did the man with the brush-cutter. Milk sprayed impotently upon enraged nakedness. At one point, in an attempt to put a stop to the whole thing, Brownie grabbed a pump sprayer that had been tossed aside and began pumping his mouth full, shouting; "Look! It's milk. It's milk!" gurgle... gurgle... But it was too late. The brawl had begun. It was time for flying facemasks, fists, fur and moss... and other things.

Brownie, somehow avoided any fist action by dodging and darting from tree to tree, shouting to both loggers and hippies... "Stop it! Come on... knock it off! Heyyy... Let's talk about this... Look! It's me... Brownman and I'm not mad at anybody. Let's be friends."

While doing so, he saw a creature that just had to be Arnie in drag, but had no time to wonder. And, almost certainly, the one hippie (and as far as he knew the only one) painted entirely black, running up the mountainside had to be Shadow! He started to chase him down, but was stopped dead in his tracks: "FIRE!" Someone shouted. Loudly at first, and then the same word, repeated again and again, trailed off into a whisper... "fire..." The upper hillside was ablaze. Men and women looked up from bloody noses, black eyes, and bruised fists.

For a moment they were frozen in time. Not a soul moved. Not even the sound of thunder interrupted what every creature (human and otherwise) was at that moment applying their senses to.

The wind was blowing toward the springs. The normally loved smell of woodsmoke was now sniffed in animal fear; and the reddish orange flames crackled out death and danger for anyone that dared stand in its path. Then, to the horror of some (and within seconds to all), flames from the crest of the nearest hill could be seen jumping through the tops of the trees. There must have been multiple lightening strikes. Warmth from the fire could already be felt or imagined on naked bodies... De-con suits weren't going to stick around to share the feeling. They gladly disengaged arms and legs from the creepy life forms as fast as possible and led the rush down the trail. The changing-shed was left sagging with the rush of hippies gathering belongings. Nakedness was not an issue but certainly clothing would be needed later. The trail could have been a fast moving parade of partially dressed models with ill-fitting apparel in a pathetic parody of style and fashion... comical under other circumstances.

So far, the fire on the crest of the hill continued on a narrow path; likely heading for the next hill toward Hippie Hollow, and no doubt fanned by the updrafts of cool water from reservoir and creek.

There was no time to waste. Lightning still flashed sporadically, further highlighting the subsequent circus of figures running down the path toward the cars and trucks... and toward Hippie Hollow. Thunder rolled and rumbled all around.

Brownie made it to his van in record time. When he crawled behind the wheel, keys in hand, others jumped in the front and piled through the side and back doors, heedless of anything of worth (hah!) that might've been in there.

The van was packed with as many hippies as possible (including the strangely arrayed dreadlocks), and with tires almost flat, the bulging vehicle swayed its way toward Hippie Hollow.

The loggers were loading up too, all except for one vehicle: The tanker wouldn't start; "Damn thing might actually be useful if we could get it going," Dorman mumbled as he pushed the driver of his own pickup out from under the steering wheel, up against a naked, bearded hippie. And in the bed of the truck, loggers and half dressed hippies were stacked on top of dirty toolboxes, chains and other greasy equipment with no complaint whatsoever.

To the surprise and outrage of the hippies, the enormous snag, purposely fallen across the entrance of the camp, spelled doom to all vehicles. The sound of crying tore at Brownie's heart; "Anybody got a chainsaw?" he yelled. Nothing. Again he yelled it... still nothing... although this time he was certain the question had gotten around; "I'm going back to get the chainsaw," he said to no one in particular; recalling he'd last seen it at the edge of the springs.

Dorman thought he was nuts; "Are you kidding, man? You'll be burned to a crispy critter!" He looked around for his buddy, Wayne, to confirm his statement, but he wasn't there; "Anybody seen Wayner?"

When he turned back, Brownie was already in the van, cranking the wheel sharply in the direction of the springs. Within seconds he was back at the parking lot and had hit the ground running. The heat was definitely closer, but the fire had taken a new tack... laterally. His head throbbed as he ran up the trail. The Doctor had told him he could go back to work, but to take it easy. Too bad. He had to do this. What choice did he have? When he got within fifty feet of the springs, Wayne almost bowled him over, heading in the opposite direction. "Get out of here, Myron! She's blowing any second!"

"What's blowing?

"The springs... " He pointed his chin up the trail;

"Dynamite!"

If that wasn't clear enough, the fact that Wayne turned and kept running–was. Brownie followed, hot on his heels. Before they had gotten thirty more feet, a mighty explosion caused them both to hit the ground and cover their heads. Dirt and rocks pelted from above... thunking and bouncing off tree-limbs.

Brownie, now with his face crumpled up against a boulder, looked disgustedly over at Wayne, who, while spitting dirt, explained, "...Pfffts... Short...ttt.. fuse."

Brown was astounded. The fool had done it! Even before attempting to stand, he puffed out; "You idiot, Wayne... you stupid idiot!"

Wayne, who didn't look too happy with himself either... scrambled upright; "Well, it's done now..."

Both men stood, dusting themselves off. Wayne, not thinking too clearly, started back up the trail to see the damage. Brownie had recovered his sanity enough to realize he hadn't seen Shadow or Jacob... didn't recall seeing them anywhere down at the camp. And where was Jacob? He would have stood out, even if not that danged Shadow.

He could hear the fire crackling and roaring in the distance. The wind was carrying smoke and ashes their way; he had to take a look around at the springs. Wayne was walking fast, but Brown pushed past him at a clip. A gigantic uprooted tree was lying across the gulley where the springs had once been; foliage so thick it was impossible and a waste of time to study the extent of any destruction. The damage had to be severe. And what? Had he expected his friends to be standing there, waiting for him to rescue them? Of course not, but where to look? They could be anywhere, even under the fallen tree, which had an enormous tangle of roots and earth at the base... a globular wall of exposed dirt and roots, jutting upward, conflicting with all reason. He yelled both of their names... separately. Waited... straining to hear.

The start of the springs wasn't in a gulley or a canyon, but oozed right out of the hillside... had done so for eons... Perhaps gradually carving the subsequent gorge that carried the overflow down the hillside toward what had at one time been a large factor in the overall watershed of the main river, but was now a lake for part of the year and a grotesque reddish-brown and ochre, crater for the other. Becoming an almost empty reservoir, but in all fairness, needed for flood-control in the expansive valley, fifty miles downstream. Stumps from millions of logged trees attested to the fact that the lake's denuded banks had once been a continuation of this very mountainside.

Only seconds had passed since he'd yelled, but Wayne must have had enough; "Let's go, Myron... that fire has a mind of its own." But Brown (not Myron, thank you) wasn't going, and Wayne wasn't staying; "Are you comin'?" No answer... The unmistakable sound of a tree crashing to the earth was all she wrote; "Stay then.... You're nuts!" and Wayne was history.

—◇—

Brown found himself crabbing his way through roots and branches to eventually stand on the trunk of the fallen giant cedar (blanketing both pools) scanning for any sign at all of Jake or Shadow. He could feel the warm air on his frame and particularly his balding head. After yelling and yelling for his two good friends he'd given up; released them to their own fate or destiny, and now he was alone.

Still standing on the enormous tree trunk shifting his weight from foot to foot, alternately grasping branch or root, gazing up and all around, the once confused man could finally see it all... very clearly. The past, the present, and the future... he was juxtaposed in time and space, but no longer important... simply an add-on... an accessory to something that had always been, and always would be. The great equalizer had shown up... with no need of invitation or explanation for its presence.

He could see the wall of flames responding to the laws of nature... calling to the winds... to come... and they surely would. Whether sweeping from the cool lake... or drafting in from who knew (or cared) where? Northerly, westerly, easterly... He thought of a scripture... one that he himself had read several times and pondered occasionally: "There be three things that are never satisfied, yea, four that say not, 'It is enough:' The grave; the barren womb; the earth that is not filled with water; and the fire that saith not; 'It is enough.'"

He watched the flames almost abstractly as they maintained their course, possibly to continue tracking north for a time, across the top of the ridge... toward the main highway. And due south... as long as the westerly winds buffered from one side, and the natural draw from the cool of the lake pushed from the other; and all this, as though he were not involved in the least...

Words had lost all meaning, even as many as there were, in as many languages as were imaginable! Time now meant nothing... never even existed. Space was but a concept, a relative term used by insignificant, animated bits of dust, stirring around as though opinion or analysis of anything actually mattered.

And feelings, as varied as they might be, or had ever been, were all at last reduced into but one—an urge. A desire to respond; a spark of something; a tiny inclination so subtle that it might have been missed in an entire lifetime... as faint as the forces of nature on the tiniest tuft of down, drifting aimlessly across the frozen tundra. Yet, as sure...

As in a coma, or a dream-state, he sensed words dispersing from his mind... into the air... white... pure white. At first in the form of paragraphs, phrases, sentences, fragmenting again and again into individual or hyphenated words, and then simply drifting and disbanding into letters as though blown by a breeze from the lake... block letters, script, italics, punctuation marks... gradually disjoining to become beautiful artistic strokes from a quill... folding and twisting in nonsensical, liberated cursive lines, like ribbons... in loops and whorls... wooly tufts and shaggy tails... whipped together creating the finest, tiniest lines.

Heavenly filament, lustrous and silky, filled the sky, and began to gather into a ball... as small as his fist at first, but rapidly accumulating and enlarging, spinning around in the sky... becoming a magnificent, shining orb.

Yes. Now he understood... a lifetime of words combining, spinning and shining, brighter and brighter, ever increasing and ever enlarging... had indeed been launched from his mouth.

William Myron Brown wasn't a man of clay, he was not a sagging lump or wad with eyes, looking out onto a world of opportunity... the mounds in the airport dream weren't clay, after all... They were words wasted or misused, combining one way or another, to become a force.

Words with consequence and more valuable than most would imagine... used by the passersby, the people of all races, and nationalities... with apparent disregard, or ignorance of the value of those words. Words which would never go away... words that would have to be accounted for, stored, recycled, or redeemed by someone... but words that would nevertheless, always be alive.

And that crumpling figure of hardened clay justifiably represented the dearth of words he'd all but wasted his whole life. A visual testimony against himself that he truly was just a man; just as he'd confessed on the riverbank to What's-His-Name (except he had called him God). There, in the presence of that oh-so-innocent miniature world, where, comparing himself against such perfection, his heart had been broken into a million pieces.

Afterward, he'd caked himself with clay. How amazing. The parallel with his dream was beyond coincidental! Now he realized that many of his own words, and those of others, had limited his true potential in a world of opportunity. Not necessarily an opportunity for money, or for fame, but for the sake of fulfilling the Creator's original intention when investing and entrusting Himself into yet another idea–William Myron Brown–with the power to become an entity... and to prosper in all things.

The people in his dream, bustling about the airline terminal, were "ideas in progress" and much more than clay... far more... they were spin-offs from the very first man and woman. A continuation of "someone's" very good idea! So good that it had been replicated and replicated into the billions and billions... and each with a singularity like none other. Entities of consequence... for better or worse.

- ◇ -

Just a few miles from the very spot where Brownie now stood, was a different "someone"... who'd basically gotten the truth of this... Someone who'd had their own private journey, fraught with challenges and disappointments, but had ultimately come through the fire with a crown of white... and had lived to tell about it.

Sitting perhaps now, alongside the river in her favorite place to think; on a bench Edward had created for her many years ago. As the years passed, they'd often sat as much younger people, side-by-side, holding hands, and had shared the beauty before them again and again. Entities with overlapping commonalities... shared the good and the bad... and on an ever-increasing level, yet, ultimately would remain alone, as all entities are... individual and unique... but living in a shared state of creation and creating.

And whether her thoughts were overlapping with Myron's at this moment or not, made no difference. Had she known what he faced, the response would be the same. This was simply his new beginning: An opportunity to start from scratch. To rethink everything, leading to paths of greater and greater understanding, while keeping it simple. Like a board game, with an arrow pointing to the first square with the words: Start Here.

Florence had no confidence whatsoever in fate; she was smart enough to know, that arriving at this critical starting point would not come with merely a roll of the dice. Circumstance may prevail in everyone's life, but the first step onto square-one was a divine invitation... a set-up really... designed for just that one decision. And stepping on that first square was not at all a religion... yet could definitely be a position from which to search one out... the depths of which would vary only according to the intelligence and integrity of each player.

While this might've seemed too simple. She had hoped the day would come for Myron, when simple was paramount... a need to listen to his own voice instead of the opinionated, clamoring masses of humanity. Yes, their opinions were valuable, but only to a point. As a parent she had finally realized that the basics of life are inherent within and common to all, by virtue of "design" alone. Individuals, poised to become singular and unique, charged with the task of discovering their own destinies and function or place within the whole. And luck was certainly not a lady, but a featherless bird in a leafless tree, taking credit for all that is good.

Ultimate simplicity: A sacred place. A reliable foundation upon which to build a tower of precepts and guidelines; a place of safety in adversity, and likewise, a haven from which to proclaim thanks... for the blessings of sanity.

Florence and Edward had independently made the connection with Jesus before they were married, and both considered their's an intelligent decision, based on the "idea" that Jesus is the actual Word of God manifested in the flesh. Who, knowing that human nature would follow its own course, nevertheless, amazingly and voluntarily, suffered and died at the hands of his own creation... and subsequently took care of business.

In the single, most courageous and outrageous move in all of mankind's history, He cracked the code, entered the doorway of death, and nullified the incurable illness of all mankind. Bringing not only the keys to that door, but the surefire antidote against death, once and for all! He returned as the first of an entirely new species: Spirit Man.

Resurrected as Spirit in a glorified body (the first ever completed human being), he confirmed what all men hoped for in their heart of hearts... that there is such a thing as true love and that death has no power over it...

True love had conquered death by the one unchanging, ever faithful, never-ending word of restoration: Forgiveness. THE Utterance... at the appointed time in mankind's history... had altered the course of each and every entity on earth forever.

A cleansing, fresh slate offered to all who would admit their need of forgiveness for their own wasted, useless, careless, hurtful words, and admit a necessity of daily cleansing due to further utterances sure to come... and their inability to change their hearts for the better, or make good the bad.

Put simply: The news that the old was no more, that all things had become new to whosoever would take full responsibility for their words and deeds... was good news two thousand years ago, and was no less good on the day Florence accepted the invitation.

She recognized that this cure for mortality was the only prescription of its kind ever offered, and generously included a fulltime physician: The Spirit of Truth would, in changing times and in real time, from century to century, lovingly confront and diagnose failures and mistakes and then administer true relief with forgiveness.

This cleansing would allow the Spirit to thereby infuse the physical, with a new kind of thinking. Natural man, thinking and reasoning without the Spirit, would instead become Supernatural man, thinking and reasoning with the Spirit. Hence, spiritual thinking: Spiritual beings applying spiritual solutions to physical circumstances, plumbing the ocean of God's wisdom for guidance in a world never accurately mapped... though filled with highways and byways, laced with billboards, road signs, hitchhikers and McDonald hamburgers.

It wasn't all that important to her whether or not there

had been a gradual progression from Neanderthal to Homosaphien. So what? The need for (and the appearance of) Spiritman was a great idea, and the more she'd studied mankind over the years, the evolutionary timing couldn't have been better. Perfect, in fact.

This proposition was in store for Brownie, at no charge. And yes, Brownie, fries and a coke would come with that. But (and there's always a but)subject to perfectly orchestrated timing, regardless of how presented–or by whom. Even God himself.

—◇—

Unbeknownst to Flo, some of her words (that may have been "just words" at the time spoken) had now done their job with Myron... and in an entirely unsuspecting fashion. Even in a compromised state of alcoholism, her words had rang true to his young heart, eventually piling in and weighing upon him and his failure to obey, and finally bringing him to his knees in honest confession. Instead of hardening his heart for a lifetime, he'd admitted an inability to consistently obey even the simplest of instructions... "Don't lie, cheat, steal, lust after another man's wife or goods... Son, in other words, do unto others, as you would have them do unto you. Just do the loving thing."

What was so hard about that? He'd agreed with all of it, but found it impossible to carry out... had never admitted it to anyone, not even himself... justifying instead, the fighting, the hell-raising, the heartbreaking inconsideration of the weak, and a truckload of acts too shameful to admit to anyone... ever.

This concept of being true to your own words and ultimately responsible for them (even if spoken to one's self), acknowledging them as the basic force behind all deeds good or bad, had brought him to this moment of truth. He'd been driven or drawn by a need to return to, rather than depart from, God... where all men and all words must eventually return)... to be weighed against one another–combined, sifted, sorted, measured and tested for intent, as well as result. And whether foolish or wise... all would be accounted for.

This, not the religion part, is where Brownie, now found himself. And all beliefs must start at the starting place... and move from there... with fundamental, basic tenets, subject to stand or fall upon their own merit and the depths of application.

Certainly Florence and her friends at the church had explored their beliefs to one degree or another, but most would've simply accepted the importance of their own words without such philosophical explanations or understandings.

Although words shape everyone's lives, that information might've seemed a no-brainer... Of course, words, whether careless or careful; concise; blustery, gusty and windy; condensed, coalesced, superfluous, supercilious... or just plain and ordinary; words in any language, written, spoken or otherwise... were just life... simply thoughts and intentions communicated... and wouldn't rank particularly high on a list of reasons leading to their conversion... perhaps not even make the chart as a reason for their life's crisis.

"Hmmm... but you know, Carla? Come to think of it, words, whether intentional and conventional; on purpose or by happenstance; suggestions real or imagined; white lies or black... uttered as blessing or curse... are sourced in the heart, and like the bible says, the mouth could be viewed as a fountain for the heart; spewing forth words both sweet and bitter. Yeah, words from the heart would rank pretty high in there, all right."

And for most, "salvation" was not an intellectual decision, but a matter of trust. Many of them had reached out as a last hope to the offer of a clean slate, and had heard enough about the life, the love, and the goodness of Jesus to step up; take a chance, play the very last card in their hands, held until there was nothing left at a table they had enjoyed as long as they'd had health, money, good looks, a promising future in business, entertainment–or all of the above. Calamity can happen in a flash, changing everything.

The church Florence attended, and perhaps every similar one nearby or globally... was filled with people who were looking to have their lives put back together... surely they had not shown up at these often despised and ridiculed places because they'd suddenly had an urge to be humiliated... to hang on a cross, to enjoy the pain of rejection from many quarters–and the pain sure to come from other believers. Believers who, while intending to do good, were shooting themselves in the foot daily, with one-track-chatter (albeit with joy) and an outdated message that seemed totally irrelevant to anyone in their "right" minds.

Even so, after all the loss of face, all the admittedly stupid actions and mistakes of their own, churchgoers would still gladly be numbered amongst the grateful, that the living Words of God are not forgotten and will live on forever.

Words, like the seeds of trees embedded on the forest floor, with residual power, ready to spring up under fire. Seeds. Pressed into soil containing billions of others, in varying stages of usefulness... whether lying shallow and vulnerable to the heat of life's disappointments or compressed over eons into a unified matrix of solid rock upon which the entire foundation of existence rests... have life within.

—◇—

Brownie was not out of the woods, yet. No. As a more complicated soul(perhaps even philosophical), such a proposition should be, could not help but be, tested, considered and reconsidered for a lifetime; because this, in itself, would involve flawed, inadequate language. How to find those words, when to use them (and with whom)would be the ultimate challenge and would also be one of the greatest satisfactions in life.

He, Brown, had experienced a paradigm-shift which would lead to at least this much: Regardless of one's convictions, or status... humble is the default position for all... naked we come and naked we go; choice happens in between. To be voluntarily humble is to be teachable (to stand-*under* a teacher or teachers), but if there were no teachers, there would necessarily be no *under*-standing.

William M. Brown had heretofore regarded himself as merely a physical being, but now the physical and the spiritual would be in synch and would work in tandem... forever. No doubt he would soon learn that the lessons humans want (and are wanting in) are the ones involving other human beings. Horses have bridles and ships have rudders through no choice of their own (although both are poetically beautiful and metaphorically convenient). Man, on the other hand, in his search for identity has set sail upon the uncharted sea of metaphor, laden with the ultimate cargo of poetry, and propelled by the winds of freewill to ports of their own choosing (if not creation)... whether that be Xanadu or "No-can-do" rests on many factors.

As children, all persons are destined for that journey with the first breath of oxygen. Little boats learning to be galleons, outfitted with cannons and lots of powder, charged with the unction to "become" at whatever cost. With proper upbringing there is a qualified chance that all will enjoy the pleasure of self-awareness and self-actualization... without self-detonation. There is no substitute for parental love: physically, emotionally and mentally. Parents are entrusted with the mission of teaching seamanship, defensive warfare, as well as how to employ cannonball and powder as tactical weaponry when necessary... all the while preserving and magnifying potential. Teaching and leading with example: How and when to be explosive; how to maintain that potential; how to reload and take on more powder, and never forgetting that this is done with words. Worsa uttered or written in any form, in any language, in complete sentences or endless fragmentations, all were designed and entrusted to the speakers and the hearers as a means of searching out and delivering one cohesive, simple truth–children to children: We are here to become... to be coming... to the awakening of self and the simplicity of home.

In terms of logic (and Brown loved logic): If God spoke the physical world into existence, including and supposedly because of mankind; and if that creation manifested solely by the power of a pure word, then from the moment that first word had been spoken, man was included... irreversibly partnered... with the speaker of that word. From there forward man's life would exist within the Word of creation. One all encompassing Word (World) would be his realm of existence... and as such and in such... he would be privileged to create therein. Explore, distort, destroy, build-up and break-down to his heart's content as an entity... but a created entity... a sub-god in effect.

With the power of life and death on his tongue, speaking with the power of The Alpha and the Omega of existence, he (mankind) would become (or be *un*becoming) with every letter or utterance that would ever exist... including every numeral from zero to infinity. He would be caught up in words, though forged and fused from the source, yet remain within the source of all source which was and is, the beginning of all beginnings, and the end of all endings. He, mankind would still remain within that closed system, and entirely dependent upon the unnamed owner of that Word (What's His Name). The ultimate integer (One) who by divine design and decree, granted all mankind permission to freely divide that one Word... for a time.

And had it not been? By these lesser entities? Whom, as yet in a temporal and deplorable state, were not to be trusted beyond a certain point? Had they not done so, in a quest for knowledge, but forsaking wisdom from the very first attempt to define it, and in their subsequent endless and valiant attempts to "re-fine" it?

Naturally, once unleashed into the hands of individual entities, the One Word would indeed have been so fragmented as to be impossible to reassemble the original intent of those words (complete with their own definitions) without the coordinated agreement and acknowledgement of those same entities. Yet, to bring all enitiies back to the full awareness of the Living Word (wherein they had been sustained) for an accounting would be vital, for the sake of truth... a necessary acknowledgement of that "One" solid and immovable, realer than real, unchangeable, knowable, yet unpronounceable Word.

But, considering the sheer volume and the foolishness of words spewing forth in a steady stream since day-one, the option of simply sweeping all under the carpet of forgiveness would indeed be gracious and make sense in more ways than one... And entirely possible for the I Am, the very force that had spoken them into existence in the first place. To take advantage of this option of course, would ultimately and necessarily be left up to the entities themselves in order to maintain freewill... the capstone of identity.

Of course, Brownie did not have the words for this, but would soon find it obvious that this accounting remained as yet to be concluded, in fact would not and could not be premature without compromise and great loss...

He would come to the understanding that the Keeper of Life (also at this same moment surrounded by flames), the creator and sustainer of those very entities in his dream, is also alone (all-one) even more so than he, and had not made a mistake... instead had planned from day-one to use that very firestorm of words to refine the gold from the dross in a process of accountability and recognition of (and for) these lesser entities. In order that they... a reflection of himself... might proceed on toward the great and glorious, inconceivable "next." In scope and depth, incomprehensible and beyond imagination, furthering a perfect and wonderful plan... unstoppable... and infinitely good.

And Florence might one day have been the one to explain her understanding of that plan to her son. Formally introduce him to the one with the power to bring it all home: The living Word, made manifest in flesh and blood, who dwelt among us (though we knew him not) was crucified, resurrected and is forever alive to save (through forgiveness), all those who come to him. The same yesterday and forever; imparting the living Word to ever-changing man, and desiring to do so in fresh and relevant ways; alive and meaningful to those who have eyes to see and ears to hear. Words that are Spirit; crafted to interface with every man, woman and child; born of, or being drawn to, Himself. And amazingly enough she would speak it as though it were the absolute gospel.

—◇—

But Brown was in the very midst of it and would not need a formal introduction. Smoke from the burning forest, billowing and roiling malignantly, contrasted the magnificent white ball... which continued to grow and grow.

Alas, it soon became obvious that the whirling action of the sphere attracted the smoke, which insidiously curled around and layered ever so thinly with the filament... contaminating and darkening... dulling the globe gradually... until it was a black and formidable mass. Absorbing all light from within and without. While the globular mass whirled and whirled, compacting tighter and tighter... until it had become an enormous sphere... as though it would surpass the earth in size.

Then, milliseconds before the sky was blotted out completely... before all feeling was sucked from his body; before all breath, and all senses were drawn up into the sphere... it stopped whirling. The weight and density pressed him to his knees. A weight, which had been there for a long time... but now he knew: Every word he'd ever uttered was his responsibility. And because he was willing to acknowledge those words, there was nothing left within: no excuses, no explanations, no questions... not really. All he had left within was that spark: That tuft of fluff... that teensy, potential response.

Then the flames from the burning forest filled the sky, consuming the sphere. So methodic and thorough that not the tiniest punctuation, not even the speck of a dot, was left.

A clean slate was before him! A conclusive, final and irrefutable fact. One that Brown was entirely willing to stand upon... forever... and that willingness had emerged from the tiniest ember... a mere spark. The cornerstone, true and perfect had been placed. From that day forward the click-click-click of mortar and brick, snapping smartly, would be laid upon that foundation... reaching all the way to heaven. An entity and an edifice with no end. "The old Brown was no more... he was an angel of light." And his new name would come from the One who had known him all along.

—◇—

Chapter Twenty

Dorman came back to the springs in his pickup with several of the loggers to see if anybody was hurt... all had naturally heard the explosion. From down at the parking lot, he shouted for Wayne.

Wayne shouted back as he rushed down the trail, pausing long enough to yank off the "damned De-con suit" and dust himself off... as if it mattered...

Several white-clad loggers made room in the back of the pickup for him... When he ordered them to take off the ridiculous outfits, they jumped to it. Dorman hopped back in the cab. Wesley wondered where was the chainsaw? Franklin asked about the explosion, but no one expected an answer, especially Shotgun Man who had stumbled and dropped the chainsaw into the main pool. And every last one of the men in the truck knew what the explosion was. What they couldn't know were the thoughts circulating around and around in Wayne's head... *What have I done? What have I done?* While his face, as calm as a professional gambler at a high-stakes poker game, denied everything. The great Wayne Hepner, simply said; "Myron's still up there..." The men looked at him questioningly. "He wouldn't come," he shrugged... Then abruptly stood up, pounded on the roof of the truck; "Hold it, maybe we could jump-start the tanker!"

Dorman thought that was a great idea... he'd had that old rig for twenty years.

Give a logger a piece of cable with loops on the end, assorted pulleys and a few minutes, and he can move anything. Wayne instructed Franklin and Curly to strip the signs from the tanker and to gather up the previously placed sawhorses and road signs. Then he, Dorman, and Wesley, rummaged around under the crummy seats and the toolboxes mounted on the sides of the old tanker. Pulling out mammoth bolts, nuts, hydraulic jacks (older than the tanker itself) empty tins of Skoal and Red Man chew, moldy Playboy magazines (centerfolds missing), dirty rags, and more than enough cable to do the job.

The men worked smoothly toward their mutual goal... as efficiently as thirty years of logging together would allow... which wasn't too shabby.

Even though the old truck was pointed uphill, and loaded with a tank half-full of water (though now spewing out white and milky to lighten the load), it was still a cakewalk. They hitched their tackle around a tree to the front axle of the tanker... and then to the trailer hitch on the four-wheel-drive pickup... in just a few minutes, the truck was turned around and coasting down the hill, with Dorman popping the clutch, pumping the gas, and cursing fondly; "Come on you old bitch, you can do it, you can do it!" she responded with a few coughs and then "cakewalked" on down the road.

Three Forest Service pickups rolled past them, headed presumably to the springs' parking lots and beyond.

While the loggers had been up at the springs, the hippies in the bus camp, about thirty in all, had gotten dressed (more or less) and had become even more aware of their plight... hemmed in on all sides... but had responded sensibly with three of their buses laying into the logs... their bumpers pressing as much as possible, yet had made no headway whatsoever. Some of them were huddled together near their buses, looking desperate and pathetic, while others were tossing things out windows and doors, preparing for the worst.

The few loggers, who had stayed with the crummy, stood near it feeling guilty, and waited impatiently for their friends to return. The De-con suits were still on, but the respirators were long gone. A few cars and trucks from campgrounds further on up around the lake slowed as they passed, but none stopped.

—◇—

The first thing Wayne wanted to know when they eased up in the tanker was what the Forest guys had to say, which was nothing much... that is, after Cal told them not to worry; "'Cause Ol' Wayne and them" had it under control.

They'd said nothin' about the De-Con suits... although Wayne had plenty to say; "Why are you still wearing them damned things? Get 'em off!"

With the arrival of the tanker, at first no one cared, but then as intentions unfolded, there were "Hoorays," and "Yahoos," all around the camp. Most everyone came over to watch... many offered to help, but soon most stepped back as they saw the loggers in action: The angle from which they were forced to pull on the tree demanded the driving of spikes into the log, to keep their cables from sliding off. They hitched block and tackle (two sets) to a very large, old growth tree and attached the cables around the smaller end of the snag. The three buses kept pushing (though in the loggers opinions they weren't needed), while in the low-geared tanker-truck, Dorman was coaxing and finessing the "old bitch," and successfully pulled 'er free of the driveway.

By this time, the fire could be seen on the ridge behind the bus camp. No time was wasted. Gathering up kids and gear scattered around the camp, the ragtag convoy was soon pulling onto the lake road. Loggers and hippies were waving "So long" to one another respectfully, if not joyfully.

The breeze from the lake was welcome on their bodies, but the loggers knew change could happen very quickly... "You never know which way the winds're gonna blow."

Sirens from down in the valley were growing louder, and that would be the volunteer fire department rallying with all hands possible.

Wayne hadn't forgotten Myron though, and neither had Dorman and Wesley. Something had to be done. They put their minds to it... the least they could do was tell somebody... the Forest Service for instance... yeah, but why hadn't they?

"Stupid." Was Wayne's take, and secretly, perhaps even from himself, glad they had been... suggesting that the crew, "...best get on outta here," He'd take care of it; "...unless, somebody's got a better idea?" Apparently no one had.

Dorman and Wesley began to gather up the cables and winching gear. Wayne, somewhat reluctantly drove off in the one remaining pickup truck... back up the road... hopefully the Forestry boys would not be in either of the springs' parking lots.

The storm clouds had seemingly moved on eastward, stacking up against the mountains. The sky in the immediate area was still cloudy enough not to rule out the hope of rain. The breeze from the lake had diminished to almost nothing. Wayne was torn with the knowledge that although Myron was up there somewhere, the fire would advance on down the hillsides toward the lake (but stop there of course). It would also be reasonable to expect the main highway to provide somewhat of a firebreak to the north and that would leave only the southerly portion to contain... If only the west winds would continue... and if there was manpower... and if the right machinery was available in time...

The Forest Service must have prefigured something similar. They had moved on south to where they would be needed most... there were no trucks in either lot. He did half a cookie in the upper one, snapped 'er out onto the road, and whipped her into the lower one... turned the truck off. All was quiet. Myron's van looked not only neglected–but dismally foreboding. That guy seemed like he didn't really belong anywhere... never did exactly mesh with the logging crews... but damn it... he was likable. Wayne rolled out of the truck, sensing an increase in the temperature around him. The breeze from the east was gone completely... There were no sirens, no birds chirping, no nothing, except the snapping and crackling of the flames.

He hitched up his pants, pulled a tin of Red Man from his pocket and stuffed a wad inside his jaw... aware of the energy it would provide, and he needed it... fifty-five years of hard work... most of it in the woods... he was feeling pretty damned old about now. Hiking up the trail to the springs had no appeal whatsoever, for many reasons. And he sure as hell didn't feel like running.

Wait. The van... he trotted over and looked in the front... hoping... tried to see in the rear, but wound up opening the back doors... nothing... at least nothing human. However, he did see an appealing box of pastries in the front and was ravenous. First he grabs one, and then, since there were only a few more, took the box 'n all; *Myron's done with these...* then goes back over to get his axe.

Looking up the gorge toward the springs, he could

see the fire clear as a bell. It was miraculous that it hadn't already come to the road. It was pretty too... he had to admit. He could see it jump through the tops of the trees, exploding the foliage in waves... sending white smoke into the clouds above, followed instantly by darker brown and black. Consuming fresh sap and resin... pre-drying the fuel, as it went along its destructive course.

Well, he had a job to do... With bear-claw number two in one hand, he reached behind the seat of the truck and pulled a double-edged axe out with the other... gulped the last bite... then allowed the Redman to drop down from the pocket of his cheek to his wetter, lower jaw. Shoved the pastry box to the passenger side, noticed a soiled envelope with Feather scrawled across it in big letters... stuck that in his pocket, intending to put it back in the van... Slung the axe over his shoulder, hand draping loosely over the handle, while his wrist held it in place... remembering his topping days. God, how he'd like to have the energy to climb just one of those beauties right now... feel the first jerk and sway as the uppermost section fell to the ground, whooshing through the limbs of other trees like an enormous blanket. And then him, hanging onto the remainder of the tree as it rocked and whirled in shorter and shorter arcs, ultimately decreasing to just the slightest shudder. Not one time had he actually believed his safety harnesses would hold... not really.

His pace quickened and was aware of the tendency to strut as he had in those days... as all of them had. The toppers, the fallers; the truck drivers, when they'd walk up to the yarder, yelling up at the operator. Everybody talking about things they knew about. Sometimes they'd get mad... sure... they were all dunderheads at one time or another. And there were times when the talk wasn't easy either. The bad news... about injuries, horrible deaths, squished bodies, maimed limbs, missing fingers or hands.

The unmistakable sound of a helicopter thumping in the canyon beyond, broke his reverie. When it arced high above the fiery ridge, the Man-of-the-Woods had already made it halfway up to the springs. And the helicopter was one of the big ones! Why, it was a military 'copter! He could see USA on the side and an American eagle painted on the underbelly of the forward cowling.

At first he'd thought it was one of those big freight 'copters; *Like the ones you'd see back in the days when people could actually sell a log or two, and others had a use for 'em right here in the United Damned States of by-God Americuh! Damn! She's pretty... swoopin' down over the lake with her giant bucket scooping water by the thousands of gallons in seconds, n' banking 'round like a... I don't know what... headin' to where it'd take hours n' hours for firefighters to reach... ever one of 'em men—real men! God bless 'em... n' they'd still have to hump their butts, tryin' to hold that line for hours and hours... yeah... real men... and some women too, now that I think of it.*

Invigorated and proud of the response and dedication of the people in his river valley, Wayne picked up his pace, now holding the axe at the ready, around the thick of the handle, just below the blade.

The helicopter was back. The water would be going to where it was needed and unfortunately there was no way it would be needed on this side of the hill... hadn't he already figured as much?

The fire was jumping from tree to tree, mostly staying higher up, but thanks to the wind, still coming right on down the hill. The ground-cover would burn too, but the fire would take a little longer to get to the lake... either way it was a done deal. He reached the springs; clambered over the fallen tree, looking behind the uprooted mass... trying to see past the dense foliage lying across the pools, or what was left of them... he couldn't really tell... He knew for sure Myron wouldn't be under there anyway, because they'd both been together when the dynamite blew. But where might he have gone? There was nothing. "Wait! Myron must've gone back down to the road already!! Sure he could have done that... while I was at the bus camp... but where did the fruitcake get off to? Maybe with the Forest Service?"

Anything was possible. He yelled his name only once... it was useless over the noise of the fire and the chopper... the heat was becoming more and more intense. He bumped over the tree and its enormous limbs blocking his path onto the trail... obstacles of his own making... *and Myron... oh, my god...* and what about those others he was looking for... Jacob's smiling face loomed up in his mind... "Oh, Lord... no! Please, no!" he whispered.

He could hear the roar of at least two fire trucks headed up the lake road... by the time he reached the parking lot there was no doubt which way he wanted to point his truck. Survive, he would, from the present position, but would prefer to do more than just survive. He backed around until his truck was parallel with Myron's van, facing downhill... and the main highway.

The Forest Service and the volunteer fire department knew how to take care of themselves... and all were no doubt willing to wait for the fire to burn out in the process. Any real danger they would face would be a pre-calculated risk.

He glanced over at Myron's van... remembered the envelope he'd planned to return... then had an insight... what if the van burned up? Maybe he should grab the registration or something? What about all that junk in the back? He opened the passenger door, yanked the glove box open, raked everything into a shopping bag from behind the driver's seat... reeking of shaving cream, underarm deodorant, and... Sheesh... he consciously piled other crap on top of the stuff already in the bag to bury the smell. "Is the guy living in his truck!?" The junk in the back was frightening... crushed MacDonald's bags, dirty towels, brake fluid, motor oil... For a second he had misgivings about the pastries he'd already eaten; *too late... long gone... keep rolling.*

The smoke rising from just over the ridge, slightly southward, was billowing white now... which meant steam. The water was having effect... the westerly winds must've still been holding, because now, the chopper was dipping water from further on up the lake, soaking the southern advance. There was reason for optimism. Barring sudden drops in atmospheric pressure, the fire would be contained. Of course, the firefighters from town would be needed to hold the western perimeter of the fire... thank God, for logging roads and a helicopter or two now and then.

The heat had become more intense. Wayne started the truck and edged out onto the road where the temperature was still tolerable and, still keeping an eye on the direction of the fire's advance... waited. Suddenly, the bushes on the down-slope of the springs' trail began to shake, progressively closer and closer. "Glory to God! It must be Myron..." he said aloud, then immediately began to formulate words of criticism to hurl at the man... mostly profane... but stopped the moment a brown bear emerged, limping on three legs toward the road.

Perhaps out of guilt... or some twisted subconscious awareness that here was the very totem of the man he sought, or just concern for innocent creatures impacted by the fire... he ripped the paper from a pastry and tossed it in the bear's path... but the poor thing ignored it completely and hobbled on across the asphalt toward the lake.

Now, somewhat hopeful and thinking; *If a bear can do it, Myron can,* he watched for someone on foot to come out of the woods and onto the road... promising he wouldn't say one insulting word this time; *Please... if only... please, I promise... Myron, you idiot! Ooops... No. I mean, Praise God! Myron! You're safe, old buddy...* until finally, when all reasonable risks to his own safety, and even beyond, had been taken... face burning hot... he flipped the key over, pushed the clutch in and silently rolled down the hill toward the main highway... determined to go the distance without popping the clutch... coasted over the rise at Hippie Hollow, reflecting proudly on oil and grease. Maybe he'd just needed the reassurance that he could've escaped if the truck had failed to start–somehow that'd seemed a good thing to do.

—◇—

Maggie had slept miserably; then had had a bad day at work, and now an even worse feeling about this whole thing... The minute she walked into the apartment she called Florence, who'd been watching for Ol' Joe (to get back from wherever), because she was; "...set on taking a ride up to those springs."

Next, she called Carl; "Carl, I'm worried about Brown."

At first Carl wasn't at all alarmed. As far as he knew, worrying had to be a lifestyle for anyone married to Brownie. But instead of saying so, he waited while Maggie explained what was up. Carl was impressed with her calm delivery... and surprised that he knew not the first thing about any of it. And, glad he'd gotten to the phone before Violet, 'cause she would have been nonstop, "Lawd," this... and "Child" that, and they'd never get to the bottom of it.

But she laid on the "Lawds" and the "Childs" anyway, just for the fun of it (since she'd already heard most of it). And insisted on coming along to help... while secretly, her opinion was that more people needed to see her in that Lincoln-car; "Lawd, honey... I look's good in that thing."

So, now, Maggie, Violet and Carl were sitting idly in the Lincoln... three abreast... in a line of waiting cars that had been heading east until twenty minutes ago; "No telling, child, how many cars settin' out here in this heat." That same heat purifying the thoughts of each... doubting their own reasons for being there at all.

Up ahead, Florence and Ol' Joe, had been one of the last cars to get past before the Highway Patrol "shut 'er down." And there was no alternative route eastward without backtracking fifty miles or so for a different route over the Cascade range. This wasn't the first time, and it wouldn't be the last, for the highway to be shut down... though no consolation to those inconvenienced.

Florence was frantic. Joe tried to keep her calm and simultaneously motivate the old red truck (a six cylinder, if it was anybody's business... which it wasn't). They'd been refused entrance at the hot springs turnoff, and were heading on up to Hepners. Both Joe and Flo had tried to throw their weight around, but there wasn't three hundred pounds between the two of 'em. Joe'd almost made it happen though, with his talent for telling jokes and spinning yarns to any and everybody. He'd even run for public office a few times, but had gotten "too emotional" when addressing larger crowds... startin' at say, eight or ten at a time (if anybody was countin' and they'd better not be).

Joyce had to admit, "Yes," Myron had most likely gone up there.

When the first of the loggers came driving into the parking lot, Florence and Joe met the truck before the loggers could pile out. All of them... to the man... had no idea what the old folks were talking about. They'd been up cruising for winter firewood... hadn't they!?

Florence had not heard the dynamite, but was entirely stressed out when others in the store mentioned it: "That was too loud for stump removal... don't you think, Dedee?"

"Eh?"

"I said that–oh forget it...."

Ol' Joe, instead of telling jokes, figured he'd, "...jest git out'f the way..." and had gone to inspect the produce; calculating (once again) how he might really do something for the Help-less-ner's if they'd only let him organize a supply line from all the home-gardener's, "right directly to the store." Joyce could sell (at a profit of course) and he wouldn't charge a nickel for the picking.

Wayne alerted the volunteer at the turnoff that it was; "...very possible someone was still up there at the springs... it looked like Myron's Van in the lot... almost sure it was... thought it would be a good idea to use that walkie-talkie there, and tell the chief... see if he's in any of the other trucks." Then he slinked on up the highway, passing fifty or sixty cars (noses pointed toward town) waiting for the road to open.

The Patrolman had said it might not be long, now... and for sure; "...nobody'd want to get heated up about the delay." Most folks had to think about that–and none of them laughed. The weather had cooled as the sun dipped lower anyhow, and it was easy enough to see that the clouds were building up darker and darker... laying tight against the mountains and stacking back; down toward the river valley.

"No doubt thisn's gonna be a corker."

"God knows we need the rain."

"Yeah, but the lightning..."

"Was that thunder?"

"Hell no.... that was a explosion of some kind."

"My windows was rattlin'..."

"My car shook."

"So... wasn't no thunder."

"Lisa, see if youc'n find that haif bag of M&N's anywhur back ther'..."

Of course the wait was an opportunity for many folks to enjoy for a change what they'd normally; "just whizzed by."

The river was so pretty; "I'll never get over how blue it can be at times and greenish at others... makes you wonta' drink it n' be in it, all at th' same time."

"You'd better just drink it... you'd freeze your ass off."

The blackberries were ripe and "mighty good" (some were picked for a pie, but would likely be eaten before they got home), and nobody ever seemed to remember, "How purple yer fingers'll git 'til it's too late."

"There's a silver lining to everything, Bea, those bushes over there's just what your bladder's been waitin' for."

Naturally there was some concern–serious concern– over the fire, but the; "Patrolmen'd said, they thought they caught it in time."

"Yeah... n' that about 'getting all heated up' about thangs."

There were plenty of tourists, hippies, and local folks milling about Hepner's, inside and outside... business was brisk... Joyce worried about Wayne; knew exactly what the explosion had been all about... and was irritated with everyone. The hotdog rotisserie had been reloaded; Becky was slapping ham sandwiches together and ladling potato salad into paper cups; the gas pumps were running constantly, and thank god, Todd was holding up.

Florence was circulating... all ears... wanted to talk to Joyce about that dynamite... Joe had finally cornered someone over by the potato bin... yakking away...

Wayne sauntered in, but picked up the pace with one glance from Joyce... started busting open boxes in the backroom, trying his best to formulate his story. The beer and soda cases were fillable from inside the walk-in cooler... but it looked like; "...nobody-wants-no-hot-nothing..."

Thunder was barely audible from in there, but his ears were still good, if everything else wasn't... rain would be so good, a downpour even better. He peeped out into the store through cans and bottles, again and again, shelf after shelf, watching Florence.

—◇—

When a few eastbound cars began peppering by, this was curious to Carl... "Why they going, and we ain't?" Actually he knew that could mean only one thing... they'd opened only one lane. But, shortly the cars trucks and campers had dwindled down to one or two...

sporadically... and the cars ahead of the Lincoln were just creeping forward. Some were doing "U-ies" and heading back the way they'd come... he got the message; they were turning around and going home. Maybe he wasn't so worried about Brown, after all.

Maggie and Violet got out of the car... stood over by the bank and watched the cars flowing by, and kept looking at the smoke and clouds in the sky. The helicopter flew over their heads. Maggie prayed it wasn't the Flight for Life 'copter...

Violet must've known more about helicopters than Maggie, because she knew for sure; "No, honey. That there's one o'dem army helmicopters." Both could hear it become louder... and then, quieter, as it dipped back and forth over the mountains. Suddenly she figured it out; "They's firefighters!"

—◇—

Brown had made his way to the far side of the upper pool... knew now, that wherever Jacob was, he had to go find him. He hadn't come this far to turn back... Shadow was such a trickster, he could be anywhere... Maybe that wasn't even the kid he'd seen running up that hill... "Hold on!! The hill! The waterfall. Over the hill!" he shouted, to no one in particular.

The fire was approaching... bouncing through the treetops, sending sparks high into the air. A mammoth chopper arced over head... it was military... USA insignias on the tail sections and the painted eagle on the bottom were nothing less than inspiring. He prepared himself mentally for what would be next... imagining the giant bucket opening its jaws, spilling blessed water... extinguishing the flames right before his eyes. Fantastic!

The danger would soon be over.

Within thirty seconds the chopper was overhead again, he could see water dripping from the bucket... but it kept going... *No! Oh, nooo...* Yes.

How self-centered and unimportant he felt. Presumptuous and stupid. The cavalry hadn't arrived to save the day. The cavalry was engaged all right, but from a larger, comprehensive sense. Every muscle in his body weakened with this awareness.

There was no way he could make it to the falls and back to the road; no one could've. He began his retreat toward the parking lot, scrambling again over the downed cedar... stopped in mid-straddle of the trunk... stood up, tried again to look down into the first pool, beyond the mass of green branches; impossible. How could he assist anyone at this point, anyway? There would be no time. He heard a chop-chop-chop behind him, and even without turning would have known that the helicopter was back... but he turned anyway, and what he saw appalled him. The prop-wash was fanning the flames down toward the lake... and toward the creek... and this was its third pass! Flames, bounding twenty to thirty feet at a time from treetop to treetop... were making their way toward the parking lot... would easily jump the creek canyon and the open space above it... and would soon have him corralled on three sides. Then, just moments later, here was number four pass; down to the lake and back, just as beautiful as the first one, with water streaming over the sides of the bucket... though in scant amounts... most evaporating before reaching flames. Sigh... What would have been the blessed solution was to be his undoing.

Now, there was no guarantee that he would even make it back to the van either... he was to be burned alive!! But life had just begun! Why, this was impossible! No God would be so cruel...

He thumped down from the cedar, scrambled through branches, and began the climb uphill again... tripped, rolled sideways two or three times before colliding with a small tree... and then from that position continued on all fours. Clawing his way upward, up the steep hill, leaving the springs behind. The heat was almost unbearable... there was little time to look, but he could easily see that the line of fire was coming down the hill from the ridge on his right too.

Winded, blowing in and out like a racehorse, he ascended... stood at the crest but couldn't see the falls below... this had to be the way... for a moment he was disoriented... then disregarded the thought... it didn't matter! There was no other choice, the flames were pursuing him.

Rolling and sliding... slamming into trees and skidding under logs and branches... the incline leveled off a bit and there was the creek... but where were the falls!?

It looked as though he'd gotten ahead of the fire... or it had taken a different tack... he was so far down in the gulley and amongst so much foliage it was hard to tell. Somehow he'd missed the "trail" Jacob had shown him. Backing away from the drop-off, he tried going upstream along the edge of the embankment, but the hillside was just way too steep, forcing him back towards the highway... until he'd found an easier slope down to the creek bed, and slid all the way to the bottom. He stood at the edge of the stream amazed. Why, from this vantage point one would have no inkling of a forest fire raging nearby!

Now what? No doubt the falls would be upstream... the lake road would be downstream... but he remembered Jacob talking about that as a way back to the road. It was way too hard to climb out... "like a box-canyon!" And they had even discussed the diameter of the culverts running under the road; "Big as a basketball... no bigger, Mon!"

He went up the creek, wading mostly... nearly breaking a leg before outfitting himself with a stout limb as a staff... and when he reached a sharp bend in the gully, he had a hunch... splashed and slipped his way on around... and it was true. There was the waterfall!

Jacob and Shadow were sitting on a ledge smoking, but didn't look at all like happy campers.

From this vantage point, still surrounded by mammoth boulders and overhanging branches, he could see no actual flames, but the woods on the three surrounding mountainsides were obviously still ablaze. Dark smoke and ashes blended with the cloud-darkened sky above. The helicopter flew over... still staying low... this time headed in a southerly direction. Both guys stood to watch the passing aircraft and remained unaware of Brown.

He decided to see just how close he might get before being spotted, but it was a half-hearted attempt. At any rate, his arrival was a surprise, just short of shocking to Shadow, whose imagination was such that this could've been anything... including the resurrected corpse of some legendary logger since Jacob had just been talking history, dating from the "locals," right on up to early, logging days.

Jacob, recovered quickly; the thought of an unhinged, lost camper may have crossed his mind but, "Yuah," it was Brown Bear, but barely recognizable... almost transformed from the last time he'd seen him. Walking right up with such confidence; standing there with an attentive air... maybe even holding his paunch in a bit and looking slightly rugged: Jeans ripped and torn; T-shirt hanging in shreds; scratches and scrapes all over... including one respectable scrape on his forehead. "Nice!"

Not that this all happened in slow motion. Once they'd seen him, he'd advanced rather quickly, anxious to advise them of the danger at hand. They'd seemed just a little too nonchalant. *Stoned?*

The "Welcome Home Bro," was slow in coming too, and though it finally did, the hugs had not. *Yep, stoned.*

It soon dawned on them that, Brother Bear Brownman, had come to save them... And Brownie wasn't about to change their minds; after all, he had almost come of his own accord.

At first, their story, about how they happened to be there, was plausible: Within minutes after the fire had started, Jacob, as the Rainbow Ranger, guardian of the hot springs, had come to the falls (instead of evacuating) to make certain everyone or anyone knew about, "...th' fire n' all... "

Shadow had seen him and followed, practically on his heels. Once there at the bottom, curiosity satisfied, they'd climbed back up, all the way to the top overlooking the springs and realized their chances were better back at the falls... Whether they could have easily gotten out at that point, Brown didn't delve into... in fact, he saw their decision as providential because Jacob might well have died while zealously defending the springs. Shadow though... well... once that variable was introduced, the logic of any further scenarios went out the window. And then, he took a step back... rethinking their story:

Something didn't jibe.

Brown knew for certain that Shadow bounded over the hill shortly after the lightning strike. He had personally watched him (painted completely black) pass right by Jake and disappear over the crest. And he'd spotted Jacob even before that, already larger-than-life as the quintessential naked man (without costume) half-way up the hill... and he had remained there for a time, in a characteristic pose: Arms stretched wide; elevated walking staff, like Moses parting the Red Sea; preaching maybe. Something... but words indiscernible over the yelling and grunting surrounding Brown, who at the time was focused like one of the Hebrews in retreat from the Egyptians. As the fight intensified, "Moses" gradually retreated uphill–eventually disappearing altogether–staff and all. So. That meant Jake wasn't being straight with him. He'd left before the fire had even kindled. Something else had taken him over that hill. It had to be the fighting... he'd been afraid, ashamed of the fact, and therefore had concocted this distorted version.

Brown wouldn't—couldn't—let those words be immortalized... for Jacob's sake... No sir! Not after his own fire-on-the-mountain experience, less than thirty minutes previous. And Jacob himself had said; "Words have substance, our bodies contain them... just vessels... we should speak the right ones."

He called Jacob on it–bluntly; " Wait a minute, Jacob, you left during the fight... you didn't even know there was a fire... you were hiding out. And Shadow? You were afraid too... weren't you?"

Jake takes a long toke on a cigarette, enjoys it to the absolute fullest, exhaling slowly; "This is how the locals give prayer... how they uh..." He stopped, tried it again;

"First of all it's easier to be around fire when you're on fire as well. When with the weak, be as the weak..." failing again, he paused for almost a minute.

Brown figured the conversation was over, but Jacob, just terribly embarrassed and tormented, said; "You know sinners are not excluded from heaven, it's just that they can't abide there... to the point where they're restless. Can't stay. They gotta' go!" This statement didn't seem to relate to the conversation at all... not until he followed it up with; "I got hit with a rock in this eye, so, now I don't see dimensionally, but I use other clues... overlap, shading... things like that. It's okay. It's now pretty much, snap! I mean I can't even be slowed down now, you know... But I don't fight..." a short pause, and then to comfort his sinful self; "Living with God you become a prince of power of this planet..." Then slammed himself, with more feelings of guilt; "And your self is SHIT!"

Now, Brown understood, and maybe Shadow had also gotten some of Jake's roundabout confession. No further explanation was needed, but both determined to hang-tight with their friend 'til he was finished; "... be good to your covering... your tabernacle... because it houses GAWD. Tell it to jump over a cliff and it will! It'll be sick if you tell it to be. Your body... it's like your dog. But it's also like, 'I can give up this cigarette, pot or any other addiction...' but it would be tough to do it with tomatoes. No 'maters would be rough... no pizza, no ketchup, no salsa."

Thank goodness, this time it looked like it was over... and obviously the confession had been very important...

As for Shadow, Brown, didn't press; he could've had one of a million reasons for vacating the scene...

including tailing Jacob. But then again... a kid that spends so much time hiding out? Fear might actually have something to do with that.

That they were about to die, however, didn't seem to matter in the least. Brown mentioned the debris mixed within the normally unsoiled falls, and the slight discoloration of the creek water... "mmmmm hmmmmm..."

He also pointed out the fact that flames were now visible along several fronts above them... "Whoa... she's blazing, Mon!"

Jacob reached into a crevice behind him and produced his rawhide bag, pulled a package of Top Tobacco from it, and once he'd loaded his paper, offered Bear the package. Bear, after loading his own, handed it off to Shadow. They sat there smoking; "Well, if this is the way we gotta' go... then I couldn't ask for two better guys to do it with," he offered rather weakly, not believing it any more than they had.

"Oh, we're not going anywhere... 'til Smokey gets done..."

"Yeah... this is the perfect hideout."

"What are you guys, nuts? The whole friggin' world is on fire... we're gonna burn to death!" but then he tacked on, "...most likely," wondering if maybe their odds had actually improved some with the arrival of the helicopter.

Jacob laughed... actually laughed... in his face; "Bear, Mon... you and Smokey are bro's... He's got your back!"

Brown began to wonder if there really were a Smokey the Bear... but only for a second; took a puff off his rollie, exhaled, and said, "Good deal..." Maybe these guys were really stoned out of their minds. On mushrooms or peyote... he looked a bit closer...

Their eyes were a little red, but his probably were too. Their pupils looked normal though; "What the hell are you talking about, Jake? Shadow, what's wrong with you?" he asked, tossing his smoke into the now grayish colored creek; full of little twigs and curled, toasted leaves.

Jacob compressed his lips, ratcheted his head back and forth slightly: "Fire burns up, not down... not on this planet anyway," and walked on over toward the falls.

"Yeah," Shadow agreed... pointed his finger upward in agreement... followed Jake.

The helicopter flew over again... neither of the wizards looked, but Brown did, surveying the hillsides. The flames were all around them now, but hadn't advanced... particularly... at least, maybe not.

Oh, he got the message alright. The theory was sound too; "Yeah? Well, who's gonna keep these hundreds of acres–of steep mountainsides–free of falling sparks?! Like those right there... and there?!" This he'd yelled over the sound of the falls, the helicopter, and the whirring in his own nerve-wracked brain; jabbing a finger this way and that, at the so far, harmless, spent ashes drifting down.

When he turned to face the nut-jobs, they were gone... and had apparently stepped behind the cloudy waterfall. The sound of thunder in the near distance, the 'copter going back and forth a few more times... accentuated the feeling of a war zone. Jacob and Shadow poked their arms and hands through the falls and made various noises that were almost entirely muffled... except for an occasional shrill whistle.

At this point, Brown Bear, presumed (correctly) that neither of these guys had associated the explosion with the springs. He didn't have the heart to tell them, and decided it would be best to let them find out in heaven.

Shadow "needed" to stay hidden just a bit longer. But Jake reappeared from the cleft in the rock; came on down and sat beside Brown.

Brown, now understood why peace-loving Jacob'd left the ruckus... but still wanted to talk about the springs. He asked; "No fighting for you 'eh Jacob?"

"No Mon... no fighting."

"Even as guardian of the hot springs?"

"Rainbow elders are about wisdom, bro..."

"Well, what were you saying with your staff raised like that? Nobody could hear you."

"Somebody heard me... yuah. Loud and clear."

"Who?"

"I'll let you figure that out."

"Well, what were you sayin', anyway?"

"I was bringing down the fire."

"Bringing the fire down? From the mountain?"

"Not from–to. To the mountain."

Wow... Brown could have begun a list of questions and rebuttals to this statement, but who could argue? The world was burning down all around them...

"Wisdom sends to you seven maidens and prepares a feast before you, before your enemies. Even in the midst of darkness... and she first sends, Joy... and that's pure joy... and that happens!"

"Okay, so then what"

"What?"

"What happens, then?

"You're tested. By a storm. A storm knocks you over because you're off the path, and you didn't even know it. Therefore the way is hard, and therefore the way is crooked and you can't see very far, and so what hits you are storms..." This must've included firestorms, because Jake swept his arms out... waving broadly... all around the mountainsides.

He went on; "Because you're off the path. So. When you know that... what comes to you then, is pure joy... cause you're being tested." He fixed Brown with a stern look; "Your father is no longer with you and you're walking by yourself. But Joy comes to you, because, you know that by your testing you can go thru stuff. What you gain is the second Wisdom..."

Brown interrupted; "Where's the first... you didn't say.... who is..."

Then, Jacob interrupted Brown; "Joy, is the first... I said that," he answered with a finger held up, but wide-eyed, as though he wasn't quite sure.

"The second maiden, she's the most beautiful of the seven... she works her perfect work in your body and your mind... so that you want nothing and need nothing. Her name is, Patience. Then, Hope, is the third. And because you've been thru the storm... when you see one on the horizon... you can tell people to duck!"

Brown wondered if he'd meant at that moment, looked around for an actual danger, but Jake went on; "And then there's Charity; Cheerfulness... there's all kinds of ways to love, and you learn them as you go... but these maidens are... like... used in the new and old testaments. I'm just learning them. Let's see: There's Diligence (something you have to use when you read); the three sisters themselves– Hope, Faith and Charity. So, Faith is your shield, the measure of your size… it's not by works… The bigger your faith, the greater the size of the shield. Your salvation is already here, but you're now working at being a godly-man, not just a faith-man. Yuah, now you're working at becoming godly… and so you have this shield… so your works are what you do to become godly."

Shadow sidled in beside them, quite aware that the fire had, in fact, dropped down the hillsides just a tad. Jacob put his arm around his shoulders, and went on. Shadow felt included and therefore pretended interest, if not understanding.

"Because that's all Christ gave… was the power to become the children of God… now you have that power and you're gonna use it. You are a prince of power… now… on this planet… with God… Isaiah: forty-nine. You are Israel, the living bread. You are, Brown Bear! You! A prince of power of this planet… Yuah! And so, you're gonna use that power. You are already. I can see that. What does that say for God? Is this love… look at all these transcriptions…" Brown didn't see transcriptions of any kind, anywhere… (assumed Jacob could though). "Look at all this time you spend with me. Most people, like I say, shun me like a leper. They don't know you man, they don't wanna get to know you, 'cause you're scary looking. That's true. 'Cause they prefer being afraid."

Brown began to understand. Thank goodness Jake was using "you," as in, anyone, not him in particular. He was losing focus, but trying to keep up; "I don't hate anyone… in particular," he parroted, remembering the bumper sticker on his van.

Jacob ignored that completely; "…afraid, cause they don't know how to pull out of it. So, they pick me up on the road, or they say, 'hello.' I had people yesterday, who are the parents of the wife of Willard? They picked me up for the first time… in the six years I've been here! And now they're happy and friendly. Now, they see me worthy. Yuah, Mon! They'll come to you. You don't have to worry. They thought I was calling 'em out into the parking lot… but I was going out for a cigarette…" (Brown, mystified for only a moment, realized Jake had changed scenes altogether) "They busted my lip and then I said, 'Why?' and they went back in and everybody in the tavern beat 'em-up… I just got my gear and left. Now the guys that split my lip are giving me rides, smoking me out, giving me pot, whatever I want… everybody apologized."

Shadow wished someone would smoke him out, and not with the stuff all around them either.

Jacob continued: "I rented a place at Woodacre cottages… before that I was living at the springs, but to make my parents feel better, I rented. My mom showed up, and said, 'Well, let's just get a piece of property.'"

Jacob, so confident of his prediction… continued spinning the gossamer… unique to him. Even as the earth burned all around, and perhaps to help everyone stay cool, he'd gone on and on.

And actually for quite some time, Brown, had reason to believe Jake's previous theory, but as the fire encroached down one side, and then the other… down and down… they'd been inching closer and closer to the falls, realizing all along without saying so, that this was their final position.

The fire was within thirty or forty feet of the embankment above them. So far, none of the burning trees had actually fallen into the creek bed, but they'd heard what definitely sounded like trees and limbs popping and crashing up the mountainsides. Shadow was sticking close and was the first to go behind the falls, sticking his head out the side-opening, urging the other two into safety. It was actually comfortable under the falls. Why, it seemed like they were gonna make it! Maybe...

The other two men stood silent and resolute... perhaps having said all that was necessary and amazed at what they were about to do–had so far done–still had to do. The helicopter could faintly be heard somewhere to the south... their eyes met simultaneously and both ducked behind the falls with Shadow.

To Brown's amazement, once behind the falls, Jake continued: "So, who are those maidens that come to us from Wisdom? You tell me. I'm working on it, man, and all these years I still have never been able to work on the architecture of that temple. They are the parts of the body... they are the ways of Wisdom. The six around the one, the Pleiades; The seven dancing women... the architecture that's been known since the ice age. Why can't I click into that? That's what I mean; we're all part of the body. I've been getting into the historical scriptures, the ones from the disciples of the disciples, of the disciples, of the disciples. The Apocrypha, the Vulgate... you'll never be satisfied... it always needs a little more polish. But it's good for rainy days..."

—◇—

For an hour or more, time out of time, the three men balanced on the narrow ledge and were grateful for every inch they stood upon, every nick and scrape behind them (and to think that someone, from centuries past had prepared this place... for this time... for these three). There was no question in their minds about what would be happening to them without the falls and the carved out space. The glow from the flames was intermittently visible through the occasionally translucent falls. Each counted the seconds, hoping it would soon be over; that the fire would finally burn down to tolerable. At one point, Jacob, wanted to make it clear that; "Human hair is the most valuable commodity we have as humans, and people should watch out for hair-nappers."

And also that; "The umbrella is a great invention. You can stand under it and be dry... roll a joint... in an area four feet in diameter (the bucket hunters'd taught him that)."

Brown, as a last request, wanted to know; "What the Sam Fat are bucket hunters?"

"Mushroom pickers!" Shadow and Jacob rejoined smugly.

Brown had a strong desire to tell the two about his new dedicated self to the One Word, but was too short of breath, and the moment to do so was long past, perhaps usurped by the well-meaning Jacob. Either way, that was it—talk was done.

Breath was becoming the "most valuable commodity." As they rotated their bodies, alternately contrasting the cool of the wall for the warmth of the falls... the only words from any of them (and so very few of those) were quipped commentary on the heat.

These three, in this moment of time, under a cataract of warm, blackened water and sludge (flesh and blood intact, breathing charcoal-filtered air), succinctly portrayed the full scope and spectrum of life. The spirit, the water, and the blood capsulized in a canyon; a cleft in a rock, covered as though by the hand of God, or coincidentally protected at the farthest periphery of fate... had indeed witnessed fire burning downward.

To Brown's disappointment and to Jacob's dismay, sparks and burning debris had fallen all around them, into the creek bed and onto the side embankments, igniting tinder of all kinds: Crisp lichens, brittle branches, twigs, pine-needles and leaves... dead things... no longer waiting for anything, but still subject to one word, the final utterance... to all that had ever been or would ever become: Cease.

—◇—

Chapter Twenty-One

When it finally started to rain, everyone gathered by the windows, or tucked under Hepner's extensive front awning. The westerly wind preceded the arrival of the downpour and eventually tapered to minor gusts. No one felt inconvenienced, or as though his or her busy day had been interrupted. On the contrary, this was perhaps the most welcomed rain any had ever known.

Sheets of water ran from the awning. Some huddled in their cars with wipers running, just for a better view; others dashed through suddenly formed puddles to get their windows closed; a number of hippies with upturned faces were dancing and whoopeeing in sopping disregard of protocol. Out on the highway, cars were forced to pull over or risk hydroplaning... or worse—being smacked by some other fool.

Of course, thunder and lightning provided the perfect dramatic touch, gaining respectful: "Oh dear Gods,"... "Holy Cows," and from certain, less-respectful townies... a few "Jesus Christs." Some of the boomers were so earth-shattering, parents in apparent control, were hugging and shushing screaming kids... even though trembling themselves... within.

Joyce eyeballed the coffee pots with mercantile fervor.

Joe furrowed yet another row in the fertile soil of his eighty year old cranial region: Blueberry smoothies for the hippies... maybe Hepner's would rent him some space in the parking lot... he could have fresh picked, quarts and pints, and no doubt, Mary Lee, would make blueberry tarts... if he asked her nice enough. But, shoot! Hepner's could make the danged smoothies inside the store (he'd still supply the berries). A man can only do so much!

Wayne went out the back door; If only... please God... or had it been too little, too late?

Florence had already picked up his scent, but was not closing in... afraid to ask... hanging around the dairy case, vacillating between the whole milk and the skimmed... finally decided she'd had enough skimmed to last a lifetime. Time for substance: "Wayne! Where's Myron?"

Hang-dogged Wayne's; "I looked for him 'til the heat drove me out..." was unconvincing, but he went on with the fact he'd reported the van to the fire department, but hadn't; "...heard a word... not yet... anyways. "

"You mean my boy is in them woods while you're here cowering in them bottles and cans... how could you? We've got to get up there right now!! Wayne, if he's hurt, you are in... deep... shit!" *Oh, God forgive me for saying that.* Normally she wouldn't have said it, at least not aloud... even if she'd had a mouthful.

The shit part was not news to Wayne... he'd already gone to jail, lost the store, and was waiting on the electric chair; "Well, I just got here ten minutes ago, Florence, it ain't like nobody could do anything 'til the fires die out... or died way-down, anyway." Then he went into greater detail about how he'd made absolutely sure no one was there before settin' the powder; how Myron'd thought there was somebody still up there; had almost run him over, just before it blew... "could've been killed right there, but then went runnin' headlong into them burning woods anyways."

"I even followed him, told him he was crazy; he'd better get outta there... I'm sorry Flo, no point in both of us burning up..." Oooops, he shouldn't'a said ANY of that.

"Oh, Jesus!" Florence yelped... already in tears.

Wayne, was white as a ghost, and terrified... but still an intact human bein' with compassion, wasn't he? He forgot to mention that Myron'd gone back to look for his hippie buddy.

"Who? The naked man?"

"Who?"

"That naked hippie, Joshua or..."

"Jacob??

"That's it..."

"Yep, that's what he said."

The rain continued, the thunder and lightning had moved on east... albeit greatly diminished.

Wayne steered her on into the back room... "Why don't you have some coffee, Flo... we'll get word soon... I'm sure this rain has made a difference."

Florence was beside herself, with no car, and not trusting Joe to do the right thing either; wouldn't ask him... no sir!

Joyce was back at the register. People were still watching it pour. That rain was a miracle... really. She motioned for Wayne to take over the register (which he did without making eye contact). Joyce then escorted Florence over to the coffee machine... poured her some coffee and slumped against the counter; "Oh my God," she'd been; "almost dead-sure (Oops, darned sure) Wayne had blown the springs," and she was mad as a hornet...

And not only Myron was missing, but maybe that nice man, Jacob... " No telling who all elst'... Oh God, help us." She had to go to the back room and sit down. In walked Maggie Brown, followed by two Coloreds... uh...

Blacks... no... nowadays they were African Americans.

Carl and violet may have been the only two "Coloreds" who'd appeared in the valley in years—literally. Joyce was long since aware of the evils of prejudice and this wasn't where she was coming from at all, nor were most of the fifty or sixty people at the store, waiting for the rain to let up. No. The two were merely unusual, different, colorful, impressive, interesting. Seriously. Whether in part or in whole, those were the words most would use.

The Lincoln rolled into the lot as an ancient steamboat might've... but competent... entirely capable of even higher winds and more daunting weather. Violet waited for Carl to come around (in the rain) and open the passenger door. Still sitting in the middle, she'd put her hand on Maggie's knee to remind her–they should wait. But Maggie piled out and darted under the awning... So, Violet complied; good-naturedly holding a newspaper over her freshly coifed hair, moving stylishly toward the front door... slowly... until Carl caught up and managed to modify her stride from stately to prompt. Yes... colorful people.

Maggie was first in the door. She passed Joyce, went right up to Wayne; "Where's Brown?"

Wayne was right in the middle of a transaction... seemed to ignore her. She slapped the counter, and said, "Don't make me come back there, mister!"

Mister handed the sale to the second cashier and made a beeline to the back room where Joyce had just gone (and where he thought he should've been all along). Maggie Brown was right behind him... Florence was bringing up the rear.

Carl, Violet and Joe were aware (as were many others in the store) that trouble was underway. Joe moved

around to the back of the counter; had waited... maybe
twenty years... for this moment, and looked completely
lost. Violet and Carl were trying unsuccessfully to blend
in. Joe bagged groceries, wiped the counters and deli
cases and otherwise got in the way... wishing he had
something more to do with his hands...

—◇—

Had a gigantic dead tree not fallen across the creek
above the falls, survival was almost certain. But it did...
and with a mighty crash. Lodging perfectly behind
another very large tree on the opposite bank. Pounding
deep into the hillside, the overall effect was immediate:
the falls became but a trickle. The waters accumulated
behind it... forming an instant pool with all components
necessary to become a thing of great beauty, classic to the
Oregon wilderness...

The three men still behind the curtain of water, had
periodically checked on the situation as best they could
from their refuge, but were unable to determine very
much. Brown remained as the middleman the whole
time, trusting in relayed information. Gradually they'd
agreed that the heat was lessening, and that the worst was
over. At first the fire, as predicted by Jacob, had burned
upward, racing up the mountainsides from each kindled
spark, and for a moment there had been an inkling of
confidence... but to the disappointed eyewitnesses,
sparks from a higher source had changed all that.

And when the water stopped flowing, it was just
unthinkable. Shocking. Jacob quickly got the basic
picture and directed everyone into the pool: Chin-deep
on Shadow; neck-deep on the Bear, and shoulder-deep on
Jake.

The outcome of the falls was settled. The surrounding, once pristine, foliage would require many years just to refresh, and decades to match the beauty of just a few hours ago.

The initial conflagration of burnable material along the creek banks had been consumed, yet the heat was still intense, and without the natural filter of the falls, every breath was contaminated with smoke. The several sludge-filled pools provided minimal, yet sufficient respite for their bodies. The silent, solid-rock floor of the pool, descending for perhaps miles into the earth, and impossible to alter by mere climate, steadily exchanged cool for warmth. Sadly, the smoke and fumes could not be avoided, nor could natural seepage. Without continual flow from up the mountain, the pool would eventually drain...

For a time the wind played in their favor, as well as a small rain shower which had followed; jubilantly received but disappointingly insufficient to make a difference in the life and death drama that was playing out.

The cloud cover, and even the slightest amount of moisture, had of course done wonders for the perimeters of the conflagration, allowing time for the establishment of man-made firebreaks. And even though certain incidental islands and atolls of green within the interior would be spared (for God's own good reasons), the inferno would continue as long as there was fuel.

Resourcefully, Jacob's training as an eagle scout provided at least a prolonging of the inevitable. Brown Bear's clothing was immediately ripped into portions as large as possible. Each man had a cloth to dip in the water as a cover for his head, as well as to filter out some of the smoke, which only increased as the wind and rain decreased.

Shadow hesitated to take Brown's underwear, so Brown traded and had to admit the undershirt looked better on the kid.

Jacob, with reluctance and far too much consideration each time he placed the seat of Brown's pants over his head, looked at the others with obvious embarrassment... So, the shirt had been ripped in half and would serve far better than the thick jean material anyway... for both Shadow and Jacob.

Brownman was quite aware that his boxers were a boon and a blessing no matter how silly he might've looked. Nevertheless, he kept a close watch on the seat of his pants, which had been tossed onto a nearby boulder (safely surrounded by water).

Scientifically and medically one could merely speculate as to the last few moments of consciousness in a case such as this, but in all likelihood, instinct for survival would dominate all others.

This is not to exclude however the thoughts of loved ones, or the mountains of overall regret one might face in his or her last moments. Brown began to conjure them up, but realized that most of that had been settled in his own personal firestorm. And after all, many of the choices and experiences up to that point had been instrumental in bringing him to his newfound awareness. God had given his best for Brownie's worst, time and time again.

Jacob may have been remorseful, wishing things had been better in his life... by far... but essentially felt as Brown did... it was all-good.

Little Shadow, frightened, and mostly speechless, looked frail and skinny without clothes; merely a faded impression of what he might have been—in another life. His hope was in the words he'd heard from Jacob. The pool, after all, seemed to be working, and this could otherwise have been a way of hiding out, but now, man! It was lots of work: Ducking under, holding his breath while cooling his head to merely warm–instead of hot! The comfort of his two friends was immeasurable. Both of whom (their own discomfort duly noted) had kept up at least the façade that all was well.

Sputtering and wide-eyed each time they surfaced, the three occasionally found a rhythm, dipping in unison... toughing it out as long as possible... surfacing; breathing through the rags; hoping each time for evidence that the air had cooled even a slight amount; looking with hope, while disguising their disappointment and maintaining a positive attitude for one another.

There may have been panic when the water reached an almost unbearable temperature, but neither would've mentioned it as long as they lived, no matter how many times they might tell the story... if they were to survive.

—◇—

The dunking had gone on for what seemed hours. The level of the pool had diminished such that the natural heat-exchange of the earth beneath, and the ambient air above, reached an imbalance. Just an increase of one degree in the pool's temperature was critical and literally meant life or death–starting with the weakest. Jacob had begun to hold shadow up while simultaneously proffering the wet rag and attending to the use of his own. It is uncertain if Shadow was conscious enough, or if Jacob was sane or idle enough, to discern the identity of the strange figure standing on the boulder where Brown's jean-bottoms had lain the whole time.

Perhaps it was the way the light played this time of

day, silhouetting a figure: Tall, with arms upraised, chin tilted up, jugular exposed in utter surrender... eyes rolled upward, burning red in color... The feet placed so solidly as to be made of stone or metal. And, with no urgency, the upper-torso rotated ever so slowly from right-to-left, left-to-right, facing north and easterly, scanning the dark sky; perhaps ignoring or completely denying the smolder and smoke all around. Because of their position and because of the angle of the light, the expression on the face was only momentarily visible... revealing an unmistakable, gentle smile.

Submerging again, Jacob must've wondered (and hoped) the figure would still be there on his return for air. And there it was... still the same. Now he scanned the pool for the Bear... saw no signs of him anywhere. Maybe he was dead already. He gave the kid a shake and said loudly; "Breathe!" Saw the kid's lungs expand as he gasped for more himself, and upon hearing a voice; "Take two fools dip 'em in water a hundred times 'n call me in the morning..." he responded with a sputter, and squeaked out an insane little laugh; poked Shadow again; watched his lungs fill, and then submerged noting the figure still on the rock. Upon surfacing again (resembling the Creature From the Black Lagoon) he still saw the figure (though faintly). The obligation to shake Shadow was by now automatic, only then did he realize the kid was gone... He tried to move his arm hanging loosely at his side... couldn't... looked around for the Bear; tried to breathe deeply, hoping for air enough to explore the pool for the two missing friends... realized he could barely inhale at all; turned toward the rock, pushing, lifting his one good arm to the figure; the single word that came forth was, "Help." and barely audible. His legs collapsed from his own weight and the sludge rolled over him.

The thunder increased in tempo and volume... rumbling and echoing over the mountainsides. When the clouds could hold no more water, when the winds could press no further, rain began to spatter, making dots and fat, promising blotches on the boulders, and plops in the pools. And of course, the earth opened its welcoming arms to receive all that was available. All... the only word she'd ever known... what she'd always given, and always expected... All in All.

The fiery mountains now sizzled, the scorched trees had hope. Seeds in the ground would begin to soften... ready and waiting for the message borne by water: Become... to be–coming. Seeds. Once concealed in a tuft of fluff, with a cargo of naught but a grain, blown by the winds of the Great Northwest, or wafted by a breeze across pond or lake. An ember as surely as actual fire... waiting to respond ... desire encased within a shell... waiting... if only.

—◇—

The hand that pulled him to safety was real, the rain spilling in torrents over Jake's body probably was not... but... but yes? It had to be... no... wait... he was under the falls! Again? Still? Whoever held onto him did so with but one strong hand clasped around his wrist. In a tangle of legs and arms splayed out on the rock ledge beneath the falls, he squirmed free of the grip... only to bump his head into the solid, rock-faced cleft. Oooops. Sitting upright he was able to confirm a profuse sheet of water spilling down before him. Automatically reaching out for what his feet kept colliding with... possibly small human arms... giant peeled bananas.... maybe water balloons... he pulled the sagging form of Shadow to his side (gratefully discovering that his own limp arm was now functioning), then pulled a significantly heavier form slightly closer... this could be nothing less than a fat bear... Brownbro... most likely. He sat back as the animated form shook and spluttered around on all fours, looking wildly about, until each (man or beast), reached out and touched the other, just to make sure.

Wordlessly, and in unison, both then reached for the almost invisible form lying nearby. Jake snapped into Eagle Scout mode, rotated the kid onto his belly and started respiratory procedures. Quickly, however, he paused from pushing on the back to check the airway... and a good thing... the removal of a chunk of bark (or some such) did wonders all around. Brown, unable to resist helping, continued gently pushing on the back. Jacob double-checked for obstruction, but was interrupted with warm water spilling from the boy's mouth; "Here we go!" he exclaimed with obvious meaning. Tears blended with wet faces and went unnoticed in the darkened cleft of the rock. The sound of crying was almost inaudible, but unanimous... and so was the question of how they had gotten there, under the falls.

Brown was the first to put his head out, and after shouting, "Rain!" was joined by Jacob. Never had either of them seen so much water coming from the sky... after a time Shadow slithered out beside them with weakened enthusiasm. All were elated and breathing deeply, floundering around, assisting one another, boulder to boulder away from the falls and slowly stood as one... completely upright and in full celebration; hugging and steadying each other almost to the point of embarrassment. Soon, each stood on his own boulder, wordless, scanning the hillsides, the sky, the creek and the steadily cascading waterfall, expecting the rain to stop at any moment while mixing hope and faith that it had arrived with a mind and a mission of it's own.

There had been an almost immediate effect from the downpour. The waterfall, the pool, and the stream tumbling by, were black with debris washing in from the hillsides. The sound of hissing coals was completely muffled, but in the opinion of three experts on smoke's color, taste, and texture... the rising steam from the forest floor was unmistakable, and you could take that to the bank!

—◇—

Florence and Maggie, exhausted, but with renewed hope... stayed on at the store. The deluge changed everything, lifting spirits and hearts in a giant, glowing column of smoke and steam right on up to the heavens. The crowd gradually thinned. All were grateful, and none would forget the hospitality and amenities provided by the Hepners, especially the locals... who lingered almost to the point of freeloading. Carl and Violet stayed in the background as much as possible, enjoying immensely all the "goins' on." Joe helped Todd and the other cashier keep the place somewhat safe with mop and broom, (only rarely knocking things from shelves and display islands).

The TV reporters had initially sensationalized the story of the "Raging Fire! Coursing through the valley threatening an entire way of life and ruining forever, pristine recreational resources loved by all." Now, as they watched their story fizzle into a mere sizzle, they prepared to leave... so far none had caught-on that the men were missing. Torn between joy and disappointment, two cameramen from different networks stood under the awning at the corner of the building, enjoying a final smoke before the hour's drive back to town.

Wayne had invited Maggie to; "have a word" on the porch of the loading ramp at the back of the store... unaware that just around the corner, the eyes of the sky, and actually the ears too, stood in tandem: "Maggie, I don't know how this's gonna turn out, but I do know that the things in this box were inside Brown's van. I stayed there until I couldn't take the heat no more, n' thought I may as well gather up anythang worth anythang, in case the van burned up, 'fore we could get back up to the springs there."

Maggie lost it for a moment; yelped loud enough to alert the ears of the sky, presently yawning under the awning; "Wayne, if Brown is dead, let me be the first to tell you; it's your fault, entirely..." and then when she looked into the yawning mouth of the cardboard box at the pathetic meaningless pile, fell back against the wall; "Pastries!? Pastries!" Shook her head, searching for purpose... anywhere in life... anywhere at all; "You're all idiots, every damned one of you!"

When she advanced toward him, Wayne stepped back, certain she was gonna whack him! Instead she held the box over the nearby dumpster, scattering the contents like ashes onto a sea of garbage... not really looking at any of it... except maybe the pastries. Finally she let go the box too, looked toward the western skyline and screamed at the top of her lungs; "Brownnnnnnn! You idiot! Come hommmmme..."

Wayne had heard animals screaming deep in the woods, but never had any compared to the horror of this... found himself literally clinging to a porch stanchion, shaking in his boots and alone on the dock.

Scanning the junk Maggie'd just released into the

dumpster (while upbraiding himself for being such a fool... or an idiot...) he calmed down and reached into his shirt pocket for some chew. The envelope labeled, Feather, was still there; at least he could make sure Maggie received that... depending. And in the meantime he'd best find a lawyer... not because of the pastries, but because criminal negligence had occurred to him.

When the eyes and ears of the whole world (maybe even the universe) returned to their cars and the waiting reporters, naturally, hearts responded and mouths spoke; "Hold on... this could go national!"

Maggie had now sequestered herself in the Lincoln, abject and ashamed. Wayne, spotted her purse by the phone in the back room; almost slid the envelope into the side pocket, but didn't; What the hell... it might not be a good thing... He then pulled out the stool, slumped down, head in his hands... unable to face the lights or the crowd beyond the swinging doors.

The ringing of the phone would've caused cardiac arrest in lesser men. In this case it merely shocked him from the stool, where he staggered momentarily, gripping the desk; "Wayne? It's Dorman."

"What the hell, Dorman?" he replied in his usual gruff manner.

Dorman, completely unaffected, continued; "What about this rain, old buddy?"

"What about it? Did you call to talk about the weather?"

"Yeah, I guess I did, in a way... whada'ya say we go back up to the springs, do a little lookin' around?"

This was like a cool rag to Wayne's forehead, affecting his entire nervous system; "That's not a bad idea... Dorman," he said, lowering his voice and looking over his shoulder, "Let's...

But Dorman cut him off... "We'll be by in ten minutes... in the tanker," and then hung up the phone before Wayne could reply.

The T.V. guys were back in the store, one peering out the window at Maggie, another closing in on the black couple. Joyce watched closely from a checkout register. The cameramen were back under the awning... fully locked and loaded.

The tanker rolled up to the pumps. Todd gassed it, while Chainsaw and Eddie piled in, also locked and loaded–with the usual–chainsaws and axes. They could've been headed to work as far as anyone could tell... dressed in red-suspendered, high-wader pants, cork boots and hardhats, jaws bulging with chew... bright-eyed n' bushy-tailed!

Wayne sauntered across the asphalt with his axe (sheathed), and had dressed down for the occasion as well, wearing greasy over-alls and a hard hat, hoping to blend in with the crowd. In fact, the pumps had been so busy most of the afternoon the guys were completely inconspicuous to all... except for Maggie, and she was tuned up like a jet engine on a runway... and would recognize that confident stride anywhere.

The patrolman, happy as a clam in his rain-gear and the fact that he was surrounded by luscious green trees, wasted no time moving the barricade; smiled and waved at the familiar truck and it's occupants.

The empty tanker zipped right up the winding road. The burn had taken most of the trees around Hippie Hollow. And that was hard to look at, especially in view of what it had been just hours before. Smoke still curled up from many areas and would need to be policed when the fire crews got around to this side of the mountain...

But rounding the bend to the spring's parking lot, the loggers were surprised to see the mountain was still green! "I don't believe it... How in the world?" And there was Brown's van! Sitting there virtually unharmed.

The four men were out of the tanker, checked the van for survivors and were on the trail in a jiffy. But this was not a nature hike. Although untouched in the near vicinity, they could almost hear the moaning of the burnt forest nearby and feel the sadness of the surviving trees and plants all around. They carried themselves with nearly the same respect and demeanor as pallbearers at a funeral... or undertakers.

What they saw at the springs couldn't have been more miraculous. Three naked idiots clustered around a chainsaw, taking turns at the rope-pull... and because of their attentiveness to this task, the idiots were taken completely by surprise.

"Hey, that's my chainsaw...." Might not have been poetic but was certainly enough to stop all activity at the base of the fallen tree.

W.M. Brown (aka god only knows), jerked up from his more than compromising position and broke into a grin... "Hey, Wayne... hey, you guys..." and then splayed his arms out wide, spun around like a demented male-stripper and laughed aloud.... Look! Look! Can you believe it? There is a god! Yes sir..."

Amidst exclamations of "How in the hell? Where in the hell?" as well as abusive but good-natured slurs, the first thing on everyone's mind was, maybe there is a god. And the second was; "...find some clothes for these guys, for god's sake." But this idea was immediately dismissed (since the nearest clothing would be miles

away), and countered by yet another idea... from Brown;
"We're not going anywhere 'til this log is cleared out
of here;" seconded by Jacob, "thirded" by Shadow, but
rejected by the loggers... at first... yet, gradually seen as
wisdom by Wayne in particular (in spite of certain visual
distractions)... and from there the motion carried down
to the last man. Naturally.

Five experienced loggers turned to the job at hand,
and not one believed in jawin'...'til the work was done.
While the men were scrambling for axes and saws, Brown
stepped closer to the base of the trunk, pointing; "Hey
you guys?" Waited for eye contact; "Whatever you do,
don't cut this last limb; somebody tie a handkerchief on
it..." He'd expected at least a question or two, but none
came; nor had there been certain other questions up to
that point.

Questions about their survival, or, "How's your
mamma and them?" could wait. Besides, they were
burning daylight. The work progressed quickly. One or
two guys bucked limbs with chainsaws, others piled
brush for subsequent hauling out to the parking lot
(or a more suitable, much nearer slash-burning area).
Shadow, happy to be involved, thrashed around in the
pool handing the butt-end of the limbs out to Jacob and
Brown, who pushed them on up to Wayne and Eddie.

After thirty minutes or so, Eddie, aka, Like-I-said Ed
(another one of those people who started every sentence
with, like I said–and never had), seemed to be slowing
down, but proved to be his usual thoughtful self: "Like
I said; we could cut that root ball off'n there and drop
that log right where it sets... but uh, like I said though,
we'd wanna git all them limbs off the bottom side first..."
adding... "Uh... 'ceptin' that last one."

Brown had already considered the fate of the

remaining log, which would normally be left as-is for the ODFW to use as they saw fit: for trail maintenance, bridges, erosion-control or whatever... and Wayne most certainly would have been thinking about a strategy for the cut. But Brown had a vision: Here was a ready-made bridge spanning the pool on a downward slope and at a slight diagonal; "Yeah and with a little ingenuity the log would make a fun way for kids and old folks to get down to the second pool," he said aloud and watched for stone-faced Wayne's reaction.

Wayne continued dragging the latest monstrous limb without even looking at Eddie (tangled up in the limbs and boughs) as they staggered along the bank. Chainsaw pops up from within the foliage (apparently there all along); "Hold on. Edward... like I said... hand me the saw."

Now there's a good idea, Wayne mused, and plopped against the hillside, ran his handkerchief over his head, studying the log from top to bottom while Chainsaw whacked away at the cumbersome limb. Good Ol' Dorman had fired his saw up again and was back at it... trimming; balancing along what would've been the upper part of the tree trunk, but now was the lower... considerin' gravity n' all.

Noticing Shadow and Jake were pulling the fall-offs across the pool to the far side, Wayne let go a shrill whistle and waved them back; waited while Dorman finished his latest cut. Then, two more whistles and Dorman shut the saw down, looking back at Wayne; "Git off there, D, let's get the rest of this cleaned up." D, began sidling back on the log. Chainsaw was in pause mode too (his machine idling with a sweet putt-putt-putt), eyes on Wayne, who said simply; "Go ahead at 'er, Shotgun."

Brown scrambled up to what was left of the trail,

sweating and grinning at Wayne's solemn poker expression... Dorman dropped down beside him. Both watched Wayne edge along the hillside and disappear behind the wall of roots and dirt.

Chainsaw finished his cuts... then he and Eddie finished the brush-drag without Wayne (considerate of the O' Man's rest-time). Shortly, the crew gathered around the base of the trunk and the mammoth root-ball... taking a moment to assess the pool and their heartfelt work. The brushing had revealed yet another miracle... the main pool was not damaged, but rather enhanced (by no stretch of the imagination). Less than eight hours had passed since Wayne's devious plan (though crude) had gone haywire... this was the very best outcome possible.

When he'd tossed the dynamite tightly wrapped in a plastic bag toward the scalding inlet of the main pool, his hopes were to plug it forever: Goodbye hot springs - so long hippies, and geological factors aside, the charge would have been more than enough to do the job. Instead it was now wider and even more interesting in overall contour. The stream spilling over the edge of the upper pool and into the lower, in an almost perfect sheet (thank you very much) was clear of the usual boulders, rocks, and sticks, otherwise piled and daily maintained as a dam for slightly greater depth... the pool was now plenty deep.

But towering above their heads with it's unsightly tangle of dirt and gangly roots shooting out in every direction, the mammoth root-ball remained in question. Dirt clods sprinkling down on everyone's head announced Wayne's return: Appearing from over and behind the massive thing, swatting at tendrils and pushing his way through rudely shattered appendages (which had no business being above ground anyhow); he popped his head around one final clump like a jack-in-the-box; peered down at them all and said; "We, can't do it..."

Of course, then, Like-I-said-Ed described his idea again (like he'd said) and wasn't surprised when Wayne said; "Nope. Won't work."

Brown was aware that his own vision exceeded Like-I-Said's by far, but hadn't said... and had politely maneuvered his nakedness behind a wilting stand of bushes. He was the last to make eye contact with Wayne, and with his own impressive poker face, said with confidence; "Sure it will...".

The stare-down was a new development between the two. Wayne sensed something beyond the fact that Brown knew more than anyone around them about how lucky he (Wayne) was to be sliding out from under a very tight place—metaphorically and literally. But this wouldn't sufficiently explain such an authoritative stand.

Brown continued; "Here's how we can do it: That hole behind you is just waitin' for this root-ball to fall back in there. All we gotta' do is drop off the roots—cut this log at the right place and gravity will do the rest."

The loggers on the trail, expecting to feel their suspenders snapping, or at least hear thunder rolling in the background, waited; eyeing Wayne and Brown.

"Like where?" The head (still framed in dirt, woody ligaments and sinews) asked skeptically.

"Like right here," said the naked man behind the bush, waving one hand with a slow, vertical sweep upward.

"Yeah well, by god, it better work," said the very clever head.

"By god... it will," responded the man in the bush with an obvious invocation to someone other than those who were physically present.

"All right boys, you heard him... let's give this damn thang a haircut... put 'er back where she belongs. But... uh... call me for the log-cuttin' part. Understood?" The clothed men bobbled their heads up and own. "And ummhhh... you naked ones... keep clearing the pool," and the head vanished.

Shadow took notice of that trick with thoughts of trying it out himself real soon, and Jacob was astonished at Brownbro's interpretation of his own, as yet unspoken, wishes.

But Brown, instead of pulling more limbs, worked his naked butt on behind the root-ball to take another look at the hole (already examined before the loggers had even shown up), and perhaps to waylay Wayne, who, not as young as he once was, had gladly taken a seat on the edge of the crater. Brown, fatigued and weakened, sat on a nearby, severed root, poking out from the crater... looked around... catching his breath... reassessing.

Wayne slid on into the pit; "Son," he said, flipping the red suspenders off his shoulders.... "I can't sit here with no naked guy..." yanked the chambray shirt over his head... "just on principle alone..." tossed it to Myron, who, eager to be clothed, in his right mind, and principled (more so than most naked men in his situation), took the shirt, (fully aware of the gulf between principle and perfection).

He and Wayne had been friends for a long time, both relied on this to help soak up some of the tension of the last few minutes. Wayne started out with; "Where in the hell were you all this time."

"We sweated it out at the falls".

"What falls? Where?"

"Just over that hill." he said, head trapped in the neck of the still buttoned shirt... waited 'til the thing fell across his shoulders before poking a finger toward the invisible hill in a leap and a bound; skipping over the root mass... which he began to notice had an entirely different character from this vantage point.

The taproot, broken from deep down in the earth, now projected accusingly like the proboscis of some alien creature. The dirt mass, convex, led out to the periphery where mangled violence had occurred... shattered roots, from giant cochlea to tiny tendril... bare of earth except for disproportionate globs here and there; dangling... begging gravity to return them once again to their mother's heart. What went on from the periphery to the obscene proboscis was an invitation to insanity. A place where danger and delight mixed in a massed confusion of design and chaos... denying interpretation to the observer, who, without becoming part of the whole was doomed forever to contemplate whether this was the ultimate medusa, or the horror of the phalanx.

While Brown wrestled with the roots, Wayne felt around in the folds of his brain, but couldn't come up with a waterfall.

Brown interceded graciously; "Most people have never seen it. Unbelievably beautiful... the ditch's so far down you won't even see it from the road... with all the foliage n' all. Plus the culvert running to the lake is underwater in the winter."

Wayne accepted that much, but from his facial expression wanted more details about the "sweatin' it out." Brown asked to put all that on hold for a while longer... until he felt like talking about it, "In the meantime have you heard from Maggie, or mom... Flo?

Then it was Wayne's turn to squirm, trying at first to hide some of the drama playing out since the beginning, but soon opened up with less reserve and found himself becoming happier and happier from the benefits of confession and the awareness that he was actually not a murderer. He may have had lots more to say but Brown was anxious to finish the cleanup and get home to his Maggie... and said as much.

"You ain't far from home... if Maggie's it... she wuz up at the store when I left for here."

Brownie lost his root with that one... slid right on down next to Wayne, both watching the splintered root spring up and down; "Let's put the rest of this on hold Weiner, uh... Wayner... n' get this done."

Wayne ignored Brown's urgency, insisting on the telling of his own story, carefully avoiding criticism of Maggie's attitude, except to say how admirable she had been the whole danged time; "A man would want to stay on the good side of that woman... and'd be lucky to have 'er as a wife. Yep, a mighty good one..." This report was in the keeping of normal protocol in the world of real men... not to say that it was a man's world... no sir... just sayin' there's a time when there ain't nothin but men around... and then there's two general unspoken rules: no references, open criticisms, mocking (joking or otherwise), about each other's wives, n'daughters, or girlfriends and if so... never ir... irevela... irrever..ent..ly. And second: when speaking of other women, real names would never be used, known or unknown, and there would be no slanderous or descriptive specifics unless telling a joke... or really drunk; The first of which required talent, the second of which was dangerous and an open invitation for trouble. Every woman was somebody's wife or daughter... Brown read between the lines and got the message: Wayne was scared of Maggie.

When they returned from the crater conference, the cutters were poised for action: The naked man (except for chambray shirt) took a moment to "suggest" the guys trim the roots on the backside... so that the mass would drop deeper into the crater; Like I Said Ed said; "Like I said..." and Brown didn't say he didn't, but neither did he ask what Ed said about where to make the exact cut. He and Ol' Wayner, arrived at that without anybody else saying.

A portion of the trail remained. Or, to say it otherwise, most of the original trail surrounding the springs was gone, but the portion beneath the foliage of the tree and on down toward the road was intact. To drop the log onto the trail (within two inches of exact) was normally all in a day's work. But there was a problem: All the major limbs (except the one Brown wanted to save) had been removed, and would no longer support the heavy trunk once the cut was made. Sagging toward the middle as it crossed the lower end of the pool, the tension was obvious–she was locked and loaded (to use a phrase)!

When the final cut was made, where would the cutter be positioned? On top of the log, eight feet up from the trail? No. If that were the case, when the stump and root mass broke free, the cutter would be launched up the hill, smashing his skull against a boulder or a tree like a ripe tomato.

Loggers had encountered similar challenges (perhaps in this same spot) a century ago with crosscut saws, wedges and axes. They would have notched the topside and cut upward from the bottom, which would use the tension to advantage. As the upward cut progressed, the notch would begin to close, thereby reducing the tension, and also open the lower cut so that the blade would not bind up in a pinch. Before the cut was completed, the log would simply break on the cut-line. Sure, both men knew what to do in a pinch, but Myron had a different idea; "No notch... this time," he said with a shake of his head.

Wayne, couldn't break out of the box... assumed he hadn't heard correctly; "Say what?"

"No notch..."

"You're out of your gourd... this thing'll split 'fore it's half cut"

"Well, I figure about three-quarters cut..."

Wayne spat, pulled his head closer; "So. What's the difference?

"The difference will be how long the split is..."

"Of course..." Wayne answered with a touch of sarcasm. He'd always done it the safe way; never actually calculated split versus notch... nor had anyone else... ever... he was pretty sure of that.

"Well, that's what I'm after... a certain length... about twenty or thirty feet... and I want the cut... right... here." Brown said with a confident vertical sweep of his hand turned sideways like a hatchet, and well ahead of the big limb they'd saved.

Wayne lowered one brow, twisted his lips, stuck his tongue in his jaw, and backed up half a step; "I ain't doin' that."

"Nope... I am... I'm makin' the cut," said as though that had been a foregone conclusion.

Wayne rolled his head: "Too dangerous."

"Piece a' cake... "

"You're on your own, then..."

"Not anymore. But hang on a second..."

He walked away, knowing Wayne hadn't understood the veiled comment of not being alone anymore; but went on down to the changing shed, returning in just moments with an odd assortment of jaw-dropping attire: A felt drivers hat, plaid swimming shorts, and a pair of (god help us) laceless tennies. The chambray shirt was tucked inside the shorts purely as a precaution–the saw could get snagged on it (and other things) in a hurry.

When the laughter subsided, Brown looked directly at Jake and the kid... pointed his chin, jerked his head toward the shed... both got the message.

It began to dawn on everyone else that these knuckleheads could've been dressed all along. Something was not quite right with them, possibly to the exclusion of Jacob–renowned for nakedness anyway.

While Brown, now the central figure, repositioned himself at the log, the otherwise comical entrance of the two remaining "naked's" from stage right was lost on all but Ed... who for once hadn't said... and wouldn't... not ever.

Brown, strangely dressed, but a surgeon nevertheless, held out his hand; "Shotgun? Chainsaw, please...."

Wayne backed up along the trail to the group of men, still at a polite distance. Stopped midway to pass the chainsaw on; bowed and said, with a tilt of his head and extended palm up; "Have at 'er."

Brown fired up the sweetest, sharpest saw in the whole valley.

Wayne, then motioned with both hands to the group and (still sarcastic) said; "Back up fellas... show time.".

The bottom of the trunk was about shoulder height

on Brown and about five feet in diameter. The vibration of the saw was invigorating; the whizzing of the well-oiled chain over sprocket, and bearings, suspended in the raceway of a forty-two inch blade, was like music.

The blade met the wood with very little resistance. Within seconds he was cutting head-high and then seconds later, overhead. The gap of the cut widened as the cut continued. Halfway up into the cut, the gap at the bottom was a good two inches.

Three-fifths of the way through, and Brown stepped back; shut the saw off... waited... listening. The sun was at this moment about to drop over the hilltop... far more visible now, through hundreds of blackened snags silhouetted on a background of heavenly blue... clawing at the scudding clouds, which were just beginning to take on tints of gold.

Brown picked up a twig and measured the gap... waited thirty seconds and measured again. The crew, silent with open mouths, felt the breeze from the lake pick up slightly. Brown, with one pull of the rope, turned on the music... and from about two feet away made his move; held the saw overhead, aimed briefly and shimmied under the log (rotating his body one hundred eighty degrees), simultaneously slipping the blade into the gap. He, and the business-end of the saw, were now front-on with the spectators. Then, with a full-throttle rev of the engine, he shuffled backwards, but gracefully, under the log; making a continual thin and final swipe with the topside of the chain... dragging it through the cut... quite aware that a premature snap of the log would flatten him like a pancake.

All eyes were on the gap and Brown's quick and fluid movements, until all they could see were his legs and tennis shoes. Once on the other side and clear of the log, he stood, shut the engine off, allowing the blade to sag toward the ground in one motion as it whirred to a stop. The cut was three-quarters through. Stooping slightly, looking under the log at the crew... chainsaw hanging loosely from his right hand... he boldly lifted his left palm upward toward the cut; at that very moment the cracking of the log could have been heard down on the main highway, and to this day, Jacob would swear he'd heard Brown say; "Behold..." But that could have been his own embellishment for what then happened: The noise from the snap was but a prelude to the marvelous splitting asunder of countless ancient, integrated fibers... traveling at lightning speed along the trunk in a final separation twenty-five or thirty feet further along the trunk. Although the split had been sudden, instead of a thud from three feet above the ground, the log's fall on the trail had been lessened in the process... lowering to within twelve inches before final separation. Even so, the earth trembled with the enormous weight of the deceased giant embedding upon the bank of the pool, just clear of the trail... its final resting place. Thanks to the split, the topside of the log had instantly become a flat ramp, descending almost two thirds of the way across the pool; suggesting to anyone with an imagination (and a chainsaw) to flatten it the rest of the way... down to ground level... on the opposite side of the pool.

These details would be noticed later though. The root-mass and the stump eerily remained suspended in place for a moment, and then slowly began to tilt upward as predicted... the lone limb swaying like a palm... toward the hillside and the awaiting crater, increasing in speed as it passed the center of gravity, until suddenly there it was! Sitting in the crater... the stump... with it's portion of the split jutting upward twenty-five or thirty feet toward the sky, like a knife, the back of a chair... or a throne.

And, absolutely parallel with the center of the earth.

Only veteran loggers could really appreciate what had occurred. Dorman was grinning. Shotgun was thinking maybe he'd keep the name Chainsaw, after all; Like-I-said-Eddie knew he hadn't said... and really wished he had; Wayne was busy with a fresh plate of crow, and Jacob was on the throne in a flash. And of course, Shadow had disappeared.

Jacob, with stringy beard and dreadlocks, having donned numerous cast-off items from the naked brigade, looked like Neptune or Jove. Embellished with nothing less than the finery of the forest: Necklaces, armbands, headgear and a very respectable wraparound shawl from the waist down... somehow he'd grabbed his staff on the way; the perfect touch for royalty.

Wayne had no doubt that this was exactly what Brownie'd planned, and was becoming disoriented, perhaps even scared at the mystical implications all around... but definitely ready to leave.

Brown saved him the trouble; "I'm hungry... let's go home. You guys go ahead, we'll follow in the van..." and thinking of Maggie, was surprised as his eyes moistened and heart skipped a beat or two. It seemed like he hadn't seen her in a long time. Yet, he hadn't even missed supper... so far.

As Wayne began to pick up tools, orienting to the task of leaving, Brown, out of respect, added; "Is that okay with you Wayne?"

"Sure 'nough... don't get lost up here in the dark."

"Don't worry we're right behind you. Oh, and Wayne? Don't say nothin' to Maggie... okay? I wanna surprise her."

Wayne answered with a thumbs-up; shouldered his axe. Brown whistled quietly to get his attention and tossed him his shirt, noting that Wayne looked a little disappointed that he'd returned it.

Brownie took the time to shake hands with everyone in the crew (an experience some regarded on a level with shaking the Pope's hand); thanked them for coming to the rescue; then, once the crew had rounded the first curve, turned to face Jake, who was still seated on the throne; "Will that do for the Keeper of the Springs?"

Jake pointed his staff in Brown's direction; "We can share... n' when we're not here, Smokey can use it. Yuah... yuah, Brown Bear, Mon.... He's got our back!"

Brown summoned Jacob from the throne and purposely avoided thoughts regarding Shadow's hiding place. Sure enough as the two descended along the trail, with nothing but Jacob's leather bag and the clothes they wore, Shadow emerged from wherever, and stood on the trail ahead. Cool.

Brown's first sight of the van provoked mixed emotions about: The past, most of which wasn't worth considering; the future, wide as the sky above, and the present, filled with a longing for true love... starting with Maggie.

When Dorman rounded the final curve before the barricade, Wayne immediately recognized Carl's Lincoln sitting next to the patrol car. The tanker eased down slowly into a lower gear; giving the patrolman time to take down the barrier... When they passed, Dorman made as if to stop, but Wayne, noticing doors opening on the Lincoln urged him forward, "Keep going... keep going." Then, leaning over to Dorman's side he said to the deputy; "Hey, Ballard, we're going back for more equipment... tell the Lincoln to wait here... we'll be right back.",

Ballard nodded in assent, but as to why he should feel so happy–he'd have to think about that.

Safely headed up the highway, Wayne looked back to the Lincoln with satisfaction; then told the crew not to mention a word about what they'd just seen or done. Not any of it.

—◇—

The Lincoln had been at the barricade a full hour and a half. Maggie watched in frustration. Should she follow after them or hang-tight? There was something fishy about Wayne's expression.

Earlier, while still at Hepner's, she'd felt disconnected from the pulse of what was really happening; almost frazzled enough to smoke a cigarette if she'd had one. When she'd seen the tanker wheel out of the parking lot, she'd done her best in the Lincoln's lighted vanity mirror; pinching, pulling, and smoothing, and finally had given up. Then, shoulders back, went inside, rounded up Carlos and Violet; asked Joe to hang out and keep an eye on things, and practically shoved her two friends out the glass doors (Violet, intent on making a graceful exit, and Carlos intent on not rushing anything. Florence needed no shoving; groaned her way through the door and onto the backseat with a final, confirming grunt... ready... if not able.

"Back to the springs," was all Maggie had to say. The tanker was long gone, but she'd known which way. Carlos obliged, only to have been disappointed at the blockade by the well-meaning trooper who'd had no idea how close he'd come to having his weapon drawn… by Maggie. At any rate, they'd sat there an hour or more… listening to muffled calls coming and going on the trooper's radio… code this n' that… such and such in progress… or an occasional strange, unexplained noise from elsewhere in the squad car… don't ask…

Carlos nodded-out with a rumbling snore. Maggie and Violet took turns watching (though for what, not exactly sure); while one rested her eyes, the other interspersed the babble coming from the squad car with heavy sighs. Florence paced and prayed down by the riverside.

By the time the tanker pulled up and rudely sped off, Maggie, ready for an encounter… bounced from the car. The trooper listened and nodded, understanding some of her frustrations, but when she mentioned that her husband and a naked man had either died in the fire or run off together to god knows where, she had his attention. When he reached for the car-phone, she touched his arm and said… politely; "Trooper Ballard, don't put this out there… okay? The TV reporters will be down here before you can hang up the phone… please? Let's let this play out, and let them catch up on their own." That was all right with Ballard

However, at about that time, the eyes and ears of the galaxy with hearts and minds of headhunting pygmies, had cornered Ol' Joe and tricked him into revealing all… He'd done real good up to that point, but the day was wearing on him and the cold, hard floor of his house, upon which he had slept every night of his life (or any similar hard surface) beckoned his old bones.

The guys in the tanker, on their way back to the store, passed the zealous reporters who'd finally gotten Ol' Joe to give up the goods, and were headed in the opposite direction; toward the springs in tiny vans adorned with expensive, fully illustrated graphics from bumper to bumper. A blasé u-turn, (with absolutely zero chance of spinning out) began in their minds as a car-chase, but thankfully their brakes worked even if their common sense didn't. The tanker's top speed was no more than forty-five miles an hour. Since they couldn't exactly force it off the road to ask questions, the eyes and ears moseyed on up the highway in slow motion, stymied and anxious, finding themselves challenged in both instinct and intuition, as well as potential network genius... as yet not evident.

By the time they arrived back at the store, the hopefully dead, or at least critically-injured, were approaching the springs parking lot and could not even have been downgraded to walking-wounded, although they were certainly walking: Brown had no keys for the van. Felt like a fool, and even more so, slapping the ridiculous swim shorts with both hands where pockets should've been. Shadow's poetic: "Like a plucked penguin in plaid underwear..." didn't help matters.

Of course Jacob wasn't interested in riding anyway; "Mon, the house is just down the road, we can walk it."

Quite familiar with that expression, Brown judged it to be at least three miles distant. But wait, they could shove the van onto the road and coast down to the main highway! This might've worked, but the rise just past Hippie Hollow stalled them... fortunately there was room to pull over.

The colorful trio of friends, surrounded with a desolate landscape, walked side-by-side on a road bathed in a golden sheen, on a path sure to grow brighter and brighter as they disappeared over the rise. In the fading light, the normally white van, taking on tones of sepia, waited on the shoulder of the road, overlooking the blue lake in an otherwise world of black and white.

Cresting the hill, all were delighted to gaze upon a green valley as far as the eye could see... Far below, the white patrol car was almost an offensive sight, a reminder of the woes and flux of civilization. Yet, as they padded along, variously shod in tennis shoes, flip-flops, and one amazingly beautiful pair of Mexican huaraches... a flag of gratitude waved over a horizon of obligations and relationships. But nothing would ever be the same.

Brown sat on a boulder to remove a twig from his shoe. The other two marched onward... this was a good time to rest and prepare himself for... what? He missed Maggie, Julie, and little Cooper as though he'd been gone for years. Feeling quite indifferent to the Airlines job... in many ways the color of skin was nothing more than a color... heritage and nationality notwithstanding. What remained to be seen about the color of his own skin (in particular) was way down on the list: He was just glad to have it.

So... what now? He hadn't eaten since breakfast, and surprise! Food was way down on the list too.

The fire had been contained several hundred yards to the south and the smell of charred everything was dominant. Otherwise, the sun could have been setting on just another August day... even with all that had happened to him personally. He recalled the KHAPE radio announcer's cheerful voice earlier that morning: "Here's your forecast for the day: Lake City and surrounding area; temp in the mid-eighties, sunshine abundant; possible thunderstorms in the Cascades... all this perfection, and then you go to heaven... stay tuned."

—◇—

Jake marched onward while Shadow dropped back a ways; shuffled along; paused; stared down into the gorge, where occasional overflow from the reservoir sluiced over shattered rocks and fractured boulders in search of normalcy... further downstream similar obstructions from eons past have been tumbled along into smooth, round, easy going boulders and an amazing aggregate of smooth, flattened, and rounded stones, influencing happy rivulets, joyful splashes, and rolling undulations... The added bonus of tiny pebbles, and sparkling sand, reflecting gold and silver from the sun in glorious arcs and beams upward from deep pools and shallow bottoms... would be just too much for the young man to contain. For now, he eased back into the conscious world and followed after Jake, aware that something life-changing had happened, and... that some things you just can't hide from.

Brown sat on a boulder to remove a twig from his shoe. The other two marched onward... this was a good time to rest and prepare himself for... what? He missed Maggie, Julie, and little Cooper as though he'd been gone for years. Feeling quite indifferent to the Airlines job... and in many ways the color of skin was nothing more than a color... heritage and nationality notwithstanding. Whatever remained to be seen about the color of his own skin (in particular) was way down on the list: He was just glad to have it.

So... what now? He hadn't eaten since breakfast, and surprise! food was way down on the list too.

The fire had been contained several hundred yards to the south and the smell of charred everything was dominant. Otherwise, the sun could have been setting on just another August day... even with all that had happened to him personally. He recalled the KHAPE radio announcer's cheerful voice early that morning: "Here's your forecast for the day: Lake City and surrounding area; temp in the mid-eighties, sunshine abundant; possible thunderstorms in the Cascades... all this perfection, and then you go to heaven... stay tuned."

—◇—

Jake marched onward while Shadow dropped back a ways; shuffled along; paused; stared down into the gorge, where occasional overflow from the reservoir sluiced over shattered rocks and fractured boulders in search of normalcy... further downstream, similar obstructions from eons past have been tumbled along into smooth, round, easygoing boulders and an amazing aggregate of smooth, flattened, and rounded stones, influencing happy rivulets, joyful splashes, and rolling undulations... The added bonus of tiny pebbles, and sparkling sand, reflecting gold and silver from the sun in glorious arcs and beams upward from deep pools and shallow bottoms... would be just too much for the young man to contain. For now, he eased back into the conscious world and followed after Jake, aware that something life-changing had happened. And that... some things you just can't hide from.

Several hundred yards ahead, three firefighters (obviously part of the mop-up crew) emerged onto the asphalt, headed toward the blockade. Behind them was a solitary figure, walking very slowly. He saw them but did not change his pace; glad the distance between them lengthened. Glad when they passed over the shoulder of the road, slid down the embankment and trundled back into the woods... guessing that instead of climbing over, they'd apparently come out onto the road to access the next ravine. Now the focus would be the state patrol car...

white and official looking. The other car was not at all familiar. Well... whomever, whenever, and wherever... but something prevented the automatic smile; challenged the conviction of years: that everyone needed a welcome home. Now he sensed a need... to be welcomed. Strange... he could imagine it... the open arms... but no face. No smile. No words.

—◇—

A reverent hush settling in and around the patrol car and the Lincoln brought the occupants to a simultaneous respect and awe of nature as a whole. There might just as well have been no fire nearby... this was a moment of respite. All was peaceful and quiet. Each was aware that time and circumstance had a hold on them and that somehow moments like these were readily available... not so unusual and maybe even normal... though rarely did they seek them out. The light was somewhat eerie, with the setting sun penetrating the faint curls of sweet-smelling smoke. Trailing scarves of mist rising from the recent rain added a touch of fantasy, engaging the imagination. The road to the springs had taken on a yellowish glaze in between darkening patches of shade from glorious trees of green-comfort and forgiveness. Complete silence was a good thing. Yes.

Suddenly, the trooper jumped from the car with binoculars, and, once focused; "We've got a survivor!" He yelled excitedly, thinking of running up to meet the person. But then again, the survivor might appreciate a ride... He yanked the plank-and-sawhorse barrier to the side of the road, but before he could get back in his patrol car the Lincoln roared up the hill... Carl had passed him by... And it was true; there was a survivor! Jacob, opened his arms and said to the car's occupants piling out, "Welcome home, welcome home..." to whomever they might be.

Maggie jumped out, rushing toward Jacob... and then dodged on past... two other men had just rounded the bend. She would have recognized her husband a city block away. He would be the big guy, the one grinning and as happy as peach pie! Both he and the skinny youngster were certainly in strange clothing. The men quickened their pace, but she ran, closing the gap, taking it all in. The one she'd just passed had a beard and lots of hair... with gold tints... and except for a strange headdress and a shawl around his shoulders, was completely naked...

The kid wore what may have been tie-dyed leotards, so skintight that he appeared to be tattooed from the waist down, featuring boney appendages and the bulging, ever incongruous guy part. On his upper half he exhibited an all but shredded, fluffy yellow, mud-streaked blouse of some sort (with one missing sleeve). He would've appeared no less ludicrous in any other situation, but in this context couldn't have worn a more fitting Shakespearean costume. Were he to have pirouetted or simply bounded away, would've been no surprise at all.

Brown, forever tan, displayed his hairy, bare chest, wearing nothing but an outlandish plaid bathing suit, or maybe those were men's undershorts, suited for some porno film. The driver's hat however, added a certain mystique she'd never considered. His legs (had they always been this hairy?) Were firmly anchored to the sun-gilded asphalt in something she never would have imagined... tennis shoes! Now she could see why he hated them so...

She almost collided with the two, but didn't. Made as if to hug Brown, and held back for a moment. He looked older, or wiser, or more handsome or... beat up, and tired, and... and like a workingman! Handsome, damn it! She could take it no longer; grabbed him around the neck and almost split his dry, chapped lips with her deliciously wet mouth. Then hugged him again, and leaned back; her hands unable to release him; "Brown..." and for the first time in forever, seeing tears in his eyes... "Where have you been?"

"To hell and back..." and added with a grin that was no longer boyish at all; "But I'm fine now."

And then, after one quick hug from his wife, Brown heard something he'd not heard in a long, long time: She laughed aloud from deep within... filled with admiration and utter joy; "Get this man some shoes!"

Shadow sidestepped the reunion, feeling a little left out until he got the first motherly hugs he'd had in a decade: From Florence, and a big smothering one from a strange, black, African woman. He felt no need to hide (except for certain areas), and wondered if the black man, was gonna grab him next... obviously vacillating between all three with an urge to hug somebody–real soon.

Now, Violet was gushing and squishing Brownie next to her big bosoms with "Honey child" this, and "Praise the Lawd" that, until Florence caught up to everybody and took her out with one glance. Collecting her motherly dues.

By then, Carl had fulfilled Shadow's expectations, but suddenly found himself clutching thin air and wondering how any man, black or white, could just vanish like that. Then chastised his se'f for missing a turn to hug B.B. 'cause Maggie had done gone in for seconds. But he finally got his shot, and would've kept it short anyway, even if Violet hadn't grabbed them both in one big embrace. Brownie returned the hug with his one free arm and repeated,

"I'm fine, I'm fine," to the "How are you feeling? How're you feelin'? questions. And "Hanging out at the falls 'til it was safe..." to the "Where you been? Where've you been?" questions.

Jacob strolled on down to the patrol car, hugged and welcomed the embarrassed trooper home, who was certain that now he'd seen it all and excused himself, wondering if he should radio for back up...

—◇—

At the store, Wayne hadn't gone after more equipment at all, and could hardly wait to relieve Joyce with the good news. But the danged reporters held that up until he assured them Joe was a prankster from birth and had "set many a dog on the wrong scent."

Joyce turned on like a light bulb... smiling to beat the band. Acting coy, and generous with customers and reporters alike. It was so grand to know the fire was completely contained and that the mop-up was well underway.

The reporters had had about enough, feeling a little irrelevant... a little embarrassed... and perhaps unimportant.

They'd been back and forth all day, hanging out at the Volunteer Fire Department, or Hepner's; tuned-in to every squawk and squabble of communication, and by now the sizzle had fizzled... sensationalizing had become a bore. But when Joe pulled out of the parking lot, acting weird or at least a little suspicious, they followed with just a faint hope of snagging a little something (human interest or otherwise), which might trump the valley hotline; already spinning out a newer, more dramatic, distorted version than the real one and couldn't care less–"Damn the press and pass the biscuits!"

Medical assistance (EMT's from the local fire department) arrived at the barricade with fanfare and was refused. Notes were made but filing of final reports delayed; blankets accepted by all; no specific mention of the naked Jacob, who looked as though he really and truly didn't understand.

Answers to the obvious and repeated questions: where had they been? How had they survived? Were succinct and inadequate; apparently the men had made a pact of some sort to play the whole thing down, assuring everyone that they'd waited the fire out at the falls.... And boy, that rain was sure a miracle.

Oh well, no pressure. Give them some time...

No pressure from the patrolman maybe, but the press who lived and breathed pressure, arrived at the barricade as the other cars were pulling out, and merely tagged onto the tail of the caravan, adding the perfect touch of fanfare in their cheap colorful and compact vehicles... Joe's old red truck, for once actually looked cute... offering a modest ruby accent to the meandering ribbon.

Ballard, perhaps in characteristic kindness, had radioed headquarters (and anyone else with a scanner) that all was well... and that he expected to return in time for the shift change, but would leave the barrier overnight, with the Road Closed sign attached.

The patrol car was elected (by Carl) to take the unkempt, practically naked survivors to Jacob's house for clothing and general clean up. He followed with Flo, Maggie, and Violet in the Lincoln.

Ol' Joe pulled into Jake's exposed, dirt yard with his faded, red truck; the bed brimming with fruits and vegetables, which he'd had in there all along for the Hepner's, anyway (just as an example of what was really available out there). His two large watermelons didn't have a chance. They were immediately posed on upturned bolts of firewood with their fleshy, red innards exposed and disposed before the gossip pipeline knew what hit 'em!

Wesley scooted on over with a bottle of Jack Daniels... neck up... in his bib overall pocket (just in case). Wayne and Joyce arrived in what might have been record time, with washtubs of iced beer and soda pop, hot dogs, tubs of potato salad, and an endless supply of chips.

Along the perimeters of the yard, Hippies began to magically appear... all fully clothed, and soon setting up an area for music... mandolins, guitars, violins, bongos, and a digiridoo. Carl just happened to have his sax in the trunk and a tambourine or two... looked through a pouch of cables and microphones and produced three fairly good harmonicas in three of Brown's favorite keys.

Curly, Dorman, Franklin, Mark, Cal, and Jimmy showed up with their wives who were all simply flowers of the woods... in anyone's estimation... Oregon bred. Chainsaw was there too with a keen interest in every move Brown made... especially impressed when Carl fired up his sax and Brown sat in with the harmonicas. Gosh.

Carl had wrangled three rusted, truck tire-rims from the objects de arte in the back yard; had them set up with wood fires, and was soon wishing he had some meat "'cause this's some good lookin' coals goin' on here."

Brownie, who'd have been happy to keep his distance from fire of any kind, looked at Carl; Carl looked at Brownie; Brownie knew exactly what he meant: Flo's freezer was chock full of meat (courtesy of Bonnie Burger).

He looked at Flo; Flo looked at Carl; Carl shrugged, looked at Brownie; Brownie compressed his big lips and rolled his eyes; reached out and tapped 'Ol Joe on the shoulder, whispered instructions and of course, in short order, Ol' Joe and Carlos were off to see the freezer further along the double yellow line.

Thunderheads gathered in the distance, music played 'til forever... the reporters had given it up after about the hundredth, "no comment" and left peacefully... the pipeline shut it down for now and went to bed–they'd already made up their mind about what would happen next anyway...

Shadow and Jacob were heroes basking in their fame, but Brown was fading fast... anxious to go home to his bed... Carlos and Violet had stayed on beyond what would have been polite, and were very happy to oblige his request. Maggie had been so sweet; holding his hand, not leaving his side for even a minute. She was one tired but grateful gal all scrunched up tightly against her man in the spacious back seat of the Lincoln. They'd all slipped out unnoticed. Joe had taken Florence on home an hour or more earlier, and he was probably asleep on his own hardwood floor, an idiosyncrasy of a man who was tough as nails and old as dirt.

On the drive into town, Carl, looking in the rear view mirror, told Brown that A. B. Jordan had finally spoken; "We got it made B.B... Mister Jordan wants to open up a restaurant and guess what he wants to sell... mmmm hmmmm... das' right," then held his hand over the backrest for some skin... after they'd finger-fumbled for a second or two, Carlos added; "And dat ain't all... he wants t'do it in Dallas."

Brown's eyes widened to heretofore, unrealized proportions; "Dallas?"

"Mmmmm hmmmm, and I b'lieve they's a certain mister Palmie down there close by... he gon' be one jealous white man."

"So, we gotta' move to Dallas?"

"No way.... We gon' be right here, makin' our secret sauce n' supervisin' Trailmasser Towers for national locations."

Brown picked it up from there... dreamily describing the barrel shaped containers for the sauce, "...but fancy metal cans of various sizes... well done too... barrel staves and all... riveted... pictures of cattle or porkers on the top..." And for a moment (so excited he actually aroused from the comfort of Maggie's affections), sat forward with his big head hanging over into the front seat and continued; "Why, the tops of the barrels could have Carlos and Brownie faces that were..." a glance in the mirror... "Naahhhh... but then we could.... Hey! What about a whip cracking along the flanks... there somewhere? We could have a fire... nahhhhh, ditch that... but who knows? Coals maybe, with a campfire and a chicken all skewered on a spit... two cowboys... you n' me pardner... that big old moon draggin' that prairie up into the sky..."

—◇—

While Brown and Maggie cuddled like teenagers in the backseat of the Lincoln, the same wonder of life and the mysterious force behind all unions was at work at the hot springs.

The lone limb, projecting out from behind the seat of the throne, pressed against the hillside intently. Still green and now springing back to life... root happy... juices flowing. Beneath the trunk, surgical reconnection had begun, promising supple and pliant resilience greater than before. The root mass directed all resource to the lone limb, previously the oldest on the tree, now the youngest, and the only.

Destined to rise even higher than the parent trunk. Severed roots, rebounding and resounding deeper than ever, would naturally channel all energy and chemical response into paths of least resistance toward places with the greatest potential to become, in that great dynamic of give and take. The exchange of nourishment for growth and restoration; seeking nothing less than a one-to-one payback; always hoping for more, but obviously capable of coping with obstacles while capitalizing and actualizing with timing and circumstance.

There was no need for words or blueprints. That had been settled long ago. Regeneration, though easily assumed as a given, should never be taken for granted by the grateful or the dead—at any level, or at any moment. The salvaged limb... the very tip... would overnight begin to arc toward the sun, striking a balance as closely as possible to mathematical precision and perfection in an ever-changing, organic mass... with the exact center of the earth. Call it destiny, call it gravity, call it natural... or supernatural... depending. Brown and Maggie called it good.

—◇—

- Epilogue -

Later that evening, after appropriate gifts and offerings were deposited on the alter of love, Maggie pulled a very worn envelope from her purse and eased back into bed with Brown; "Who wrote this?"

Brown, with sleepy eyes and a slight smile on his lips, rolled close, sharing her pillow... the envelope glowing in candlelight could have been made of parchment from centuries past. The day had been a long one... he felt as though sleep would take him before he could explain; "How did you get that?"

"Wayne slipped it to me at the party tonight. It's lovely... Did you write it?"

Had the question been asked just yesterday, he would have felt guilty and unable to answer, but, "No, an angel named Feather, did..." he replied, snuggling tight.

She pulled the single page from the envelope and held it out in the flickering candlelight. "It sounds kind'a sappy, are you sure you didn't write it?"

Brown was silent... she nudged him gently. "Where is this angel now?" Still he remained silent... Craning her head back, she looked down on his face... his eyes were closed, the smile still playing on his lips... she nudged him with a little more force.

He seemed to rouse slightly; "What? What was that?"

"I said where... or who... is this angel?"

"I'm not really sure... can we talk about it tomorrow?"

"What do you mean? Not if you have something to tell me, Brown. When was the last time you saw her?"

"I think I saw... her for a... few minutes... at... the falls... but... you..." his voice trailed off...

"You think!?" He may have mumbled something further... Maggie wasn't sure. He still hadn't gone into details about the fire... She backed off... this was only one of the many things they had to talk about tomorrow. He was snoring peacefully. Hmmmmm... There was something different about him all right... but if he were guilty of anything, he wouldn't look like that... no matter how tired...

She held the poem back up, moving it this way and that in the light: Yes... there was no doubt... a certain someone had scribbled her name with a dull pencil across the top... and it had either faded or been hastily erased... yep:

MAGGIE.

Dearest one,

I found a small feather lying on the ground and thought of you.

For a time it may have blown over the tops of grassy fields, and perhaps it skipped across a pond.

It took but a puff of wind to send it into the air to be framed against a fluffy white cloud, or to drift along in a vast blue sky; small, fragile and delicate...

I remembered our love

And wondered why I thought it small.

An innocent thing, occasionally tainted by our thoughts and ways.

We felt it in gusts and tiny breezes...

As soft as the flutter of swallow's wings.

While I agonized over what I wanted it to be, I missed love's gentle wings, held aloft, high above our heads. We thought love had to come from us... but it was of its own.

Offering a glimpse now and then. . .

Always in hindsight.

Leaving feathers lying on the ground.

When your fingers smoothed them, were you ironing confusion from the pinions of our love? Did they remind you in your deepest heart of a song you wanted to sing?

Of a poem never written... never given?

I know I often missed the gift of loving you. A Love that was holy. But is not all love so? And doesn't it blow where it will?

When the wings of love fly over our souls. . .

Lets ruffle her feathers with songs;

Write the poems that billow and blow,

Gather the ones she drops to the ground,

Put them in jars and frames and such,

And fill our house with symbols of love. . .

Often and over much.

And it was so...

© March 2009

Kenneth M. Scott... upon my word.